Santiago Blood

Also by Lance Horner in Pan Books

The Mahound
Rogue Roman

By Lance Horner and Kyle Onstott

Child of the Sun
The Tattooed Rood
The Black Sun

The 'Falconhurst' series

Mandingo
Drum
Master of Falconhurst
Falconhurst Fancy
The Mustee
Heir to Falconhurst
The Mahound
Flight to Falconhurst
Mistress of Falconhurst
Six-Fingered Stud

Lance Horner

Santiago Blood

Pan Books London and Sydney

To my very good friend
Edward Moiselle

First published in Great Britain 1967 by Pan Books Ltd,
Cavaye Place, London SW10 9PG
12th printing 1977

ISBN 0 330 20190 5
Printed and bound in Great Britain by
Hazell Watson & Viney Ltd, Aylesbury, Bucks

A dictionary of Spanish words and phrases used in this book

Abanico	Fan
Absolutamente	Absolutely
Aficionado	Bullfight fan
Ahorita	Right away
Alpargatas	Rope soled shoes
Al punto	Exactly – as to time
Amigo	Friend
Amo	Master – signifying the master of an animal such as a slave, dog or horse
Asno	Jackass
Ay de mi!	Oh my!
Baile	Dance, ball
Bicho	Slang for penis
Caballero	Gentleman
Calle de Sol	Street of the Sun
Cantina	Cafe, saloon
Caramba!	A mild oath
Central	Sugar refinery
Chico	Small – when used as address it is an affectionate term meaning 'little fellow'
Clavel	Carnation pink
Cochero	Coachman
Cojones	Testicles
Comedor	Dining room
Con permiso	With permission
Con prisa	With haste
Dios mio!	My God!
Don	A title of respect used only with a first name, masculine
Doña	The same, feminine
Estrellita	Little Star
Estupido	Stupid

Fabrica	Factory
Finca	Plantation
Gracias a dios	Thanks to God
Guardaropa	Wardrobe for clothes
Guardias	Police
Hasta luego	Until then – 'See you later'
Hidalgo	Gentleman
Hijo de puta	Son of a whore
Ladron	Criminal
Lance	Affair
Loco	Crazy
Macho	Male, virile, masculine
Madre de dios	Mother of God
Mamacita	Little mother
Mañana	Tomorrow
Maricon	Homosexual, queer, pervert
Marquesa	Marchioness
Merda	Excrement
Mestizo	Halfbreed – originally a mixture of white and Indian blood, but in Cuba it signified white and Negro blood
Mire	Look!
Mozo	Waiter
Muchacho	Boy
Mulatto	Originally a little mule. Now a person of mixed blood. As mules are hybrids so is a person of white and Negro blood
Novia	Betrothed, sweetheart
Pan	Bread
Paseo	The hour in late afternoon or early evening when everyone came out either on foot, on horseback or in carriages to make the circle of the plaza and to see and be seen

Pantalones	Trousers
Patillas	Sideburns
Pericon	Stallion
Persianas	Venetian blinds
Primo	Cousin
Procurator del Rey	Attorney of the King, corresponding to our Attorney General
Puta	Whore
Querido, Querida	Masc. & Fem. Darling, beloved
Que grande!	How big!
Que hay!	Hello
Que lastima!	What a pity!
Que mujer!	What a woman!
Que hombre!	What a man!
Quien sabe?	Who knows?
Sala	Living room
Siesta	Afternoon nap – an established custom in all tropical Latin American countries
Tertulia	Reception, ball
Tobaco	Cigar
Todo del mundo	All the world, everybody
Toro	Bull
Torero	Bullfighter
Vamos!	Let's go!
Vamos a ver!	Let's see!
Verdad	Truly, indeed
Viejo, Viejito	Old man – an affectionate form of address
Viejo, Viejita	Same for women
Vigilante	Watchman
Volanta	A two wheeled hooded carriage, popular in Cuba

Chapter One

THE CUMBERSOME BLACK coach, with its blazon of arms in violet and silver on the door panels, rolled up to the city gates of Havana. Even in those late years of the eighteenth century, Havana was still a walled city and the gates were closed when the curfew gun of Cabañas Fortress across the bay thundered out the hour of nine.

'Open the gate, *vigilante*! Open the gate!' The voice of the black coachman echoed through the stone archway.

A soldier in the uniform of Spain appeared on the other side of the gate, yawned and waved a lazy hand. 'Go away! The gates are closed for the night. I wouldn't open them for the Governor himself nor even the King of Spain.'

'Who said anything about the Governor, or the King of Spain either. They can both roast in hell for all I care but this is the Santiago coach.'

The soldier straightened up. 'The Santiago coach? *Valgame Dios*, the Señora de Santiago?'

'If you had a brain in that stupid head of yours you'd have seen it was. Who else in Havana has a coach like this? Of course it's the señora herself, returning with her grandson Don Miguel from their plantation in the country. Make haste man, we've waited long enough. Open the gates!'

The Santiago name brought results; the sentry lost no time. He produced a huge iron key, grated it in the lock and swung the gates wide open. Goggle-eyed, he stared at it in awe as it rolled through the gate, the steel of the horses' hoofs striking sparks from the rough cobbles of the pavement. Although there was no sign of life in the coach, he genuflected as though in the presence of royalty.

Once inside the gates, the lights of the city crept dimly into the interior. Two persons occupied the coach. An elderly woman sat bolt upright in the exact centre of the rear seat, the folds of her gown of stiff taffeta arranged meticulously around her. Sprawled on the brocaded cushions of the opposite seat, his curly black head rolling with the motions of the coach, a young man snored. The señora spoke to him quietly but he did not awake and with an indulgent smile she patted his white cotton knee.

'We are almost home, Miguelito,' she said, but he continued to sleep, unmindful of her words.

The guttering candles of a corner *cantina* gilded the cobbles and burnished the doors of the coach as it turned into the Street of the Sun. The pinched narrowness of the street made it difficult for the coachman to guide the horses and the wheels grated against the curbstones, first on one side and then the other. Even though the tropical night hid much of its ugliness it could not entirely shroud its squalor, its crumbling age, nor its century-old buildings. The *Calle de Sol* hardly lived up to the magnificence of its name. Years ago, when Havana was much younger, it had been a fashionable street, now it progressed in a mean and desultory way from the city walls toward the less respectable section of the waterfront – a street of shabby shops, sagging houses and condescending *cantinas*; it was a mean and sordid street except for one small portion.

For a short distance the Street of the Sun made some pretensions to grandeur; when it passed the twin palaces of the Santiagos and what, alas, had been that of the Canadovas. The two houses stood side by side on the narrow street, their façades almost identical. Pillars of heavy masonry rose from the sidewalk, making a shady colonnade for pedestrians. Above them a long line of semicircular wrought iron balconies jutted out at regular intervals from the second floors. Above these the stuccoed stone rose for another two stories. While the two houses were identical in many respects, there was a marked difference in their appearance, for although the Casa Santiago was still the home of the Señora de Santiago, who easily superseded Her Most Catholic Majesty of Spain in importance in Havana, the once proud Casa Canadova, as the garish fresco over the door proclaimed, was now the Casa Josefina – the house of Josefina – whose music was the loudest, whose wine was the reddest and whose whores, so it was said, were the most accomplished in the world, quite ready and willing to satisfy any possible demand of their clients.

Unlike the aloof and aristocratic dignity of the Casa Santiago, the Casa Josefina sprawled out and mingled with the street itself. Tonight, as every night, its pillared colonnade covered a motley and strident crowd of flower sellers, peddlers of pornographic drawings, mincing *maricones* in tight, white *pantalones*, and sleek-haired mulatto pimps who always seemed to have a young sister to offer. It was here that the nocturnal backwash of Havana spent the night for the Casa Josefina was the one place in all Havana where there was light, music and activity every night. The illumination from the interior was as harsh and brassy as the music and from inside one could hear strident feminine voices sometimes cursing in anger, sometimes softened to muted cajolery. Drab hired vehicles drove up to the doors and disgorged their furtive occupants who hurried across the narrow sidewalk with hats tilted over their eyes or fashionable *volantas* spewed out the town's young bloods who made no secret of their distinguished patronage.

The señora's coach stopped at the dimly lit palace of the Santiagos. Tomas, the Negro coachman, climbed down from the box to pull at the dangling bell chain and by the time he had returned to open the door of the coach an aged Negro with lighted candle appeared from inside the palace to open the entrance gate.

There was a stir within the coach and the señora's voice, thin, aged and metallic, sounded above the music and bawdy songs of the house next door.

'Miguel, Miguel, wake up, we are home.' Her fragile hand rested on the window ledge – a hand that seemed to be delicately fashioned of old parchment, studded with glittering diamonds. 'Miguel,' the voice rose even higher, 'are you so lacking in manners that you cannot help your poor grandmother?' A tiny foot appeared in the doorway of the coach. 'Oh, it's no use, Andreas,' she addressed the servant on the pavement below while he bobbed his head in acquiescence, 'he's slept all the way from the *Vedado* and he'll probably keep right on sleeping in the coach house tonight.'

As she placed her foot on the carpeted steps which the coachman had unfolded, the dim form of a man emerged from the darkness of the pillars. He walked with the buoyant step of youth to the coach, bowed deeply and addressed the señora.

'Ah, but if the stupid grandson who sleeps in the coach is so lacking in manners, perhaps the other grandson who never sleeps can help his lady grandmother.'

The foot withdrew immediately into the shadows and this time when the señora spoke, her voice had the edge of fear in it.

'Miguel,' it was almost a scream now. 'Miguel, awake! Protect me from this ill-begotten whelp of a wandering street bitch.'

Another foot immediately appeared on the threshold – a strong masculine foot, encased in a polished leather boot and along with the foot the figure of another young man. Miguel de Santiago, roused at last from his slumber, jumped from the coach and landed lightly on his feet before the other. For a long moment they stared at each other, these two young men, like two fighting cocks, hackles rising. There was a certain resemblance between them. Miguel, he from the coach, was a trifle shorter but heavier muscled with a clear, dark olive complexion and hair as black as the night, while the other, he from the shadows, was an inch taller, slenderer and with a head of dark gold hair. His skin had the pasty whiteness of one who had never seen the sun in contrast to the sun bronzed darkness of the other.

It was Miguel who spoke first. 'The Señora de Santiago wishes to alight and it seems that she does not care for your company.' Anger was being restrained with difficulty and the words were evenly spaced and perfect in their formality.

The other smiled with a flash of white teeth. 'Perhaps the illustrious señora does not wish to compare her grandsons at such close range. She might discover that the one she despises is more of a man than the one she molly-coddles.'

Miguel ignored the provocative words. 'What are you doing here, anyway, Enrique?'

'Merely waiting, my cousin. The sidewalk before the Casa Santiago is public property.'

'For walking and not for loitering. Get yourself gone. Why aren't you at Josefina's. Surely there must be one of those lonely ladies whom you are paid to entertain waiting for you.'

'It's a pleasant occupation,' Enrique shrugged his shoulders and smiled, 'and it pays better than begging which is what I should have to do otherwise. Thanks to my grandmother, the Casa Josefina is the only place I have to live.'

'And a fitting place for you it is,' added the señora who had now ventured to appear in the doorway of the coach. 'It was your mother's home as well as her place of business. It was there that she forced my poor drunken son to marry her. It was there that he died and it was there that you were born, Enrique. Ah, to think that the palace of my old friends, the Canadovas, should have been sold to Josefina to become a bawdy house. To think that that rat's nest should harbour this living disgrace to the Santiagos, you, Enrique, you!'

Enrique shrugged his shoulders again but this time he did not smile. 'A bawdy house? To be sure, my honoured grandmother, and yet, as bawdy houses go, it's the best in the city and better, I've heard, than anything in Vera Cruz or Cartagena. So, being the best, it must needs have the best and that would be, of course, a Santiago. If I must work, I work for the best and I have the reputation for being the best stud in the city. Do I shock you? That's what I am and I get paid for it. I have no desire to starve nor soil my hands as a stevedore. Therefore, as I am so well equipped to do the work I am doing, I do it.'

She ignored him as she took Miguel's hands and descended the steps. He bowed low and, for a fleeting moment, she looked at him. Her eyes glittered as coldly as the diamonds on her fingers and her voice, with the commanding authority with which nearly eighty years of giving orders had endowed it spoke, not to the bowing man but to him whose arm she took.

'Miguel, if this person does not leave at once, call out our servants and have him booted next door where he belongs.' As the fellow straightened up, she stared him in the eyes, lifting her head a bit to meet his gaze. 'Enrique de Santiago, for in truth you have a right to bear the name and disgrace it, get out! I'll have none of you. I never have and I never, never intend to. For some twenty years you've been in Havana; now you live under my very nose. For all those twenty years I have known you were alive and the very thought of you has tormented me. You are my son's son, but you are also the son of that draggle-tailed Jezebel who got him to marry her. You are no grandson of mine. I shall never recognize you as such. Now, get out! and if I ever lay eyes on you again, Enrique, I'll have my servants cut you to ribbons.'

'One moment, señora, I beg of you,' Enrique's words were urgent. 'This meeting tonight was indeed of my seeking. Grant me a moment. Let me plead with you, nay, I'll even get down on my knees to you if you'll but hear me out. I'm not to blame for what my mother was, nor for my father's weakness in marrying her. But I am a Santiago. Acknowledge me as your grandson in the eyes of Havana. Just one word from you and I can take my place in the world – in that world where any grandson of yours belongs.' As the old lady started to walk away without answering him, he clutched at her sleeve, 'Señora ... grandmother,' he pleaded but she ignored him. She walked on, leaving a fragment of fragile lace torn from her sleeve in his hand.

Miguel pushed himself between Enrique and his grandmother.

'We've had enough of this, *hijo de puta*. Out of our way!'

Enrique's body blocked the way but Miguel shoved him aside. Enrique turned suddenly and there was a glint of light on the thin dagger he pulled from beneath his coat. The sliver of light made a sweeping arc in the air as his hand swept up. But the señora's scream and Miguel's hand reaching out and striking Enrique's arm sent the dagger spinning to the cobbles. With his right hand, Miguel grabbed at the buttons of Enrique's coat and his knee went behind Enrique's leg. He pushed and Enrique toppled over, stumbling backwards to fall under the wheels of the coach. Miguel dusted his hands, offered his arm to his grandmother and they entered the house. The old servant shut and locked the gates behind them. As their figures disappeared into the lighted patio of the house, Enrique crawled from the gutter and stood up. The look of polished urbanity which he had presented previously had disappeared. He was still handsome but now he was merely a handsome rogue.

'My dear grandmother,' he spat on the sidewalk, 'and my beloved cousin Miguel,' he spat again. 'Santiagos both of you with all the honour and riches and the position which that name of Santiago gives you. *Merda* for you, old woman, and a double *Merda* for you, my cousin. *Merda, maricon, Miguel!* How well the words go together. But I'm a Santiago too. Shall I rob you of all this, little *maricon*, Miguel? *Por dios*, maybe I shall, someday.' He brushed the filth of the gutter from his clothes and walked towards the house of Josefina.

Chapter Two

AS MUCH OF the sun as could find its way between the houses of its namesake street struggled to enter the jalousies of Miguel's bedroom in the Casa Santiago and lay, shattered into bright ribbons on the tiled floor. Its rays highlighted the clothing carelessly scattered on the red tiles – a waistcoat of white satin, a coat of emerald velvet and shoes with diamond buckles; then reached with narrow fingers to polish with its brilliance the gold coins which lay scattered on the floor, poured from an upturned breeches pocket.

The late afternoon heat seemed a solid thing in the room, immovable, intense. No breeze penetrated the shuttered windows. Miguel's black hair streamed out on the pillow in damp tendrils. Beads of sweat covered his naked body, channelling together into little rivulets to slither down his sides to the linen, making a moist imprint where he sprawled.

Dimly to his awakening consciousness, came the sound of voices in the gallery. During his struggle to wakefulness, he became aware of the muted remonstrances of old Andreas and the louder, younger tones of another. It sounded like Julio. *Verdad*, it was Julio and, judging from the commotion, Julio sounded angry – in fact he sounded very angry. As the voices approached, Miguel could hear Andreas forbidding Julio to disturb him, but despite the old slave's warning, the doors burst open and a young man determinedly entered the room. It was Julio. Miguel could see through his lashes without opening his eyes wide. Julio strode across the room to the windows and yanked up the jalousies, letting in the full brilliance of the sun and with it the suspicion of a breeze. Returning across the room toward the bed, he stumbled over the shoes. With a gesture of annoyance, he kicked them out of the way and came to stand over Miguel, waiting for him who seemed to be sleeping to move of his own accord. Miguel remained still and to add to the effect, shammed a slight snore. Julio grinned. The snore was not very effective. He reached over to stare down at Miguel, then took the *panatela* that he was smoking and flicked the ashes onto the bare skin. There was a smell of singed hair and with a violent contortion Miguel jacknifed into a sitting position.

'That was a dirty trick, Julito,' he yelled, both hands trying to find the spot where the hot ashes had landed. He flung his head back to shake the mass of hair from his eyes. He stared up at Julio and extended one hand; the middle finger was rigid, the fingers on each side of it curled. 'That for you!' he shook his hand before Julio but his laugh took the sting from the insult.

'And the same for you, Miguelito,' Julio answered. 'A shame on you, lazy one, for sleeping at this hour of the day. The time of the *siesta* has passed and all Havana is out on the streets.'

Miguel sat up, cross-legged on the bed, pushing the damp curls away from his eyes again. He yawned slowly, then stretched his body out in luxurious relaxation. He smiled sleepily at Julio, turned his back to the bright afternoon sun, punched the pillow into shape and prepared to go back to sleep.

'You are my best friend, Julito, and I like you very much but please go away.' Miguel closed his eyes contentedly, sighed fondly and buried his head in the pillow. A second later he opened one eye and looked up at Julio. 'What – you still here?'

'Yes, still here and here I intend to stay. Have you forgotten your appointment with me, *amigo mio?* Seven o'clock, if you remember, at the Cantina "El Chico". Probably you have even forgotten why you were to meet me.'

Miguel struggled to remember, then suddenly exclaimed. '*Valgame dios!* La Clavelita, the inaccessible one! We are going to meet her. Then what are we waiting for, Julito? The greatest dancer in Spain and you let me dawdle in bed. This is my one opportunity to accomplish what every other fellow in Havana wants – meet the fair Clavelita and lay her, eh, Julito?'

'La Clavelita is no prostitute, Miguel.'

'Bah, all dancers use their legs for dancing and spread them to make a living. She's no different: she only uses a little different approach. But she'll no longer play hard to get when I see her or rather, when she sees me. Ring, Julio! Ring three times. That will bring Juan. I don't want Andreas; he's too old and fussy.'

Miguel jumped from the bed and ran into the adjoining room. 'When Juan comes, tell him to bring hot water. I'll bathe and shave myself while he's laying out my clothes. And Julito, did I tell you about the little mulatto girl at the *finca?* A virgin, Julio! An honest-to-god-virgin! Her mama'd been saving it for me and believe me, the little wench enjoyed losing it, especially to her master.'

'You've already told me twice and here's Juan.'

A young Negro came in, carrying a big metal pitcher of hot water in one hand and a covered tray in the other. Julio waved the slave toward the bathroom and sat down in a chair. Presently he called to Miguel, 'Did you see your cousin Enrique last night?'

'I had a glimpse of him,' the voice came from the other room, 'why?'

'Oh, I heard that you met him.'

'I saw him for a moment in the doorway of Josefina's but he disappeared almost immediately. Guess he didn't want to see me after I pushed him into the gutter a few nights ago. You know, Julio, he's not a bad looking chap. I suppose he got his blonde hair from his mother. I wish grandmother would do something for him, really I do. He's not to blame that his mother was a whore and his father a drunkard. With half a chance he might amount to something more than a stud at Josefina's. Somehow I don't blame him for hating me. If the tables were turned I'd probably hate him too.'

'Better watch your step around him, Miguel. He's not one to be trusted . . .'

'But why, in the name of god, should I fear him?'

Julio did not answer but stood up and paced nervously around the room. He looked down at his own watch and compared it with Miguel's which was lying in a tangle of gold fobs on the table.

'What are you doing now?' Julio was impatient. 'If we are going to meet La Clavelita, we'll have to hurry. *Vamos!*'

Miguel stuck his head out the door. His face was covered with lather and he had added fanciful tufts to his chin and ears. He grimaced like a clown. 'What am I doing? I'm shaving, *amigito.*' He looked at Julio as if seeing him for the first time. 'What are you wearing tonight? Black? To meet this resplendent creature? Ah, I see you wear black to enhance the convent-like atmosphere which surrounds the fair charmer. Wear black if you wish, but not for me. White for me tonight, Julito. I intend to appear as virginal as she pretends to be. Imagine, Miguel de Santiago appearing virginal!'

His head disappeared from the doorway. 'Go, Juan, I'll shave myself. You lay out my clothes. Let's see. The new white satin coat – the one embroidered in silver, the rose waistcoat and the new Alencon ruffles.'

A few moments later, Miguel appeared – black hair curled

and glossily wet from his bath; smooth skin the colour of antique ivory, glowing pink under the olive; flashing brown eyes, sparkling under long lashes. His nose was a trifle too short, his lips too redly full, his chest and arms more heavily muscled than one would have expected from a young *don* of the town, but there was a certain devil-may-care about him – an effervescence of spirits – that made him even handsomer than he actually was.

'Don't look so grim, Julio. See, I hurry. Could anyone move faster? Powder? No, my hair is too wet.' He clambered into the clothes that Juan held for him. 'Now, boy, my watch, my rings, the snuff box. No, *estupido*, the white enamelled one with the picture of Venus. It brings me good luck. My hat! See, I'm ready, Julio, so smile.'

Julio grinned: Miguel's mood was infectious.

'How do I look?' Miguel spun around. 'Will I cause the famous La Clavelita to swoon?'

'*Amigo mio*,' Julio regarded him, 'you are indeed an admirable example of a young *picaron* who squanders his nights and sleeps away his days. By rights you should have a generally dissipated appearance, black circles under your eyes that would warn young ladies to beware of you but you haven't. However, despite the wild oats you sow you look like one of those innocent young angels that Murillo paints – sickeningly angelic.'

'What a horrible comparison. You could at least be complimentary and say that I look like a menace to any young girl's chastity, which I do believe I am.'

'No, let's pretend you are an angel and here is your reward,' he poured some gold pieces into Miguel's hand.

'And what are these?'

'Yours! I picked them up from the floor. You would never have missed them but think for but a moment, Miguel. In your hand you hold enough money to buy a slave. Yes, you hold a man's life in your hand. If he had those,' he pointed to the boy who was hanging up Miguel's clothes, 'he could be free. It's time money came to mean something to you.'

'It does,' Miguel flipped one of the coins in the direction of Juan who caught it with a grin, 'it means something to spend. Here in my hand I hold wine, music, even love that can be bought for a night. A man's life, you say, Julio? *Verdad*, I never thought of that,' his face grew sober for a moment as he looked at Juan who was staring at the gold piece in his hand. 'Wake up, Juan, tell Tomas to bring a carriage around, not the coach, a *volanta*. No, never mind, we'll walk. It's cooler now and the air will do me good. But first, Julio, I must pay my respects to my grandmother whom I have not seen all day. *Un momento*, Julio, and you know she always likes to see you. She feels I am in respectable company when I am with you.'

They passed out onto the gallery which ran around the patio, then down the stairs to the second floor. Miguel rapped softly on the tall mahogany doors to his grandmother's salon.'

'Who is it?' came a voice from the other side.

'It is Miguel, grandmother, and Julio de Castenaro is with me. May we come in?'

The señora was sitting by the opened window when they entered. She sat in a high-backed chair, her thin fingers engaged in a piece of frivolous needlework. As she looked up at Miguel, her face lighted up. She smiled at him and held out her hands. He kissed her gently on the forehead and then with a quick, furtive movement, he loosened the heavy jewelled comb which supported her *mantilla*. It fell in her lap. It was an old trick in which he had always indulged since a child.

She retrieved the comb, affecting anger and slapped his face ever so gently. Then she pushed him away from her and held out her hand to Julio. 'Greetings to you, don Julio, and how is your dear mother?' she asked.

He kissed her hand. 'Thank you, señora, my mother enjoys the best of health as I trust you do. I am stealing Miguel away from you tonight.'

'Tonight, Julio? Bah! Someone steals him away from me every night and yet I do not think the thief has too difficult a time to spirit away his stolen goods. I do not see my Miguel at all. He is out all night, he sleeps all day or else he is at the *finca*. And that reminds me, Miguel. If you must sleep all day I insist that you close and bolt your door. Old Andreas tells me that the girls in the house invent errands that will take them to the third floor and several times he has caught them peeking into your room. Shame on you! I'll not enter into competition with that Josefina.'

She reached out her hand, heavy with its glittering diamonds and drew Miguel close to her. He knelt beside her chair and she ran her fingers through his hair. 'Oh, how I am blessed, Julito, with this wonderful grandson. It is not every woman at my age who is fortunate to have so fine a grandson who is also so much one's own son. May Miguel's mother in heaven forgive me for forgetting sometimes that he is not wholly mine. But then, you see, his mother and father both died when he was born so he has been mine from the very day he came to this earth.'

She let her hands wander to the nape of his neck. Her rings glittered in the blackness of his hair as her frail fingers stealthily untied the black taffeta ribbon. The mass of hair fell over his face as he grabbed at her fan but she was too quick for him and rapped him over the knuckles with it. Having paid him back for disarranging her mantilla, she clubbed his hair and retied the ribbon.

'Off with you, both of you! Why should you wish to stay here with an old woman like myself. You'd bore me as much as I'd bore you. My old friend, the Marquesa de Villaroja, is coming to call on me this evening. She's the biggest gossip in Havana and how I love her. We'll sit and cackle over our cups of chocolate like two old hens, raking up every scandal that ever happened in Havana and not a few in Spain as well. Nobody will have a decent reputation when we get through with them.' She stood up and waved to the door. 'Run along and have a good time. Enjoy yourselves! You are young and the blood runs hot in your veins.' She halted them with a gesture of one hand. 'Only remember! You are *caballeros* – gentlemen. There is much you might do which really should not be done but a gentleman always finds a way to do such things in a manner which makes them appear that they should be done. *Buenas noches, hijos mios, buenas noches.*'

Chapter Three

MIGUEL AND JULIO were forced to walk single file, owing to the narrowness of the sidewalk in the *Calle de Sol.* A passing cart, loaded with green stalks of sugarcane, forced them to seek refuge in a doorway and they had to wait there until it passed. It brushed by, leaving a fresh green smell in its wake which caused a momentary nostalgia in Miguel's thoughts for the big plantation – the Santiago *finca* – out in the country. As much as he loved the life and gaiety of the city, he really felt that the *finca* was his home. It had been the basis of the Santiago fortunes and now that he was managing the estate, he was proud of the ways he had managed to increase its production. But the nostalgia passed with the farm cart and they continued on. Conversation was impossible, owing to Julio's rapid pace and the numerous greetings Miguel had to bestow. For every child he had a pat on the head and a copper centavo in his palm; a bow for the older men and a happy *'Que hay'* for the others. They all knew him, this Santiago of the Casa de Santiago and of La Estrellita, the big *finca* with its thousands of acres and hundreds of slaves.

As the street broadened and they could walk abreast, Miguel put his hand on Julio's arm. 'Must I remind you, *chico*, that one gains little by running in Havana. Another hundred feet at this pace and I shall have to return home, take another bath and dress again. I've no desire to present myself to your young lady, out of breath and stinking like a black buck that's been cutting cane all day. Even now my shirt is damp and my crotch itches from sweat. Let's take a carriage.'

'It was your own brilliant idea that we walk – fresh air and all that, you said.'

'Walk then but stop running.'

'All right! If it will keep your crotch from itching, we'll find a carriage at the *cantina* at the corner.'

Miguel moistened his lips with the tip of his tongue. He glanced at his watch and then at Julio. 'Ah, the *cantina* on the corner! I've been thinking about it with all the beautiful Spanish hams hanging from the rafters and the delicious smells of food. That's it, Julio, food! See, I have it all figured out. We had enough time to walk to the lady's house. *Bueno!* If we hire a carriage we shall arrive too early and we'll have to wait in her stuffy *sala* while she paints her face. So then, we shall have to waste a few moments because we do not want her to think we are over-anxious to arrive. It's always better to be too late than too early; it causes a woman to wonder if one is really coming and when you do arrive they are happier to see you. So I have been thinking....'

'Something new for you?' Julio grinned.

'No, really, I often think. It's an amusing pastime and this time I was thinking that I am hungry. Thus if we stop at the *cantina* for *un momentito* I can have a cup of coffee. Don't you think we shall have time for one small cup of coffee?'

Julio bit his lips with exasperation. Miguel always got his own way. 'But we are to have dinner at her house – an early dinner to be sure, as she goes to the theatre.'

'And you know what it will be. She won't be able to eat anything because she is going to dance. The wing of a chicken, perhaps with a salad of lettuce. Bah, I'm starving and I'm not going to dance at least not until the theatre lets out and then I'll have her dancing to a different tune but I can't do *my* dancing on a chicken wing and a lettuce leaf.'

They walked a few more steps in silence. Julio sighed. 'You always get what you want, don't you, Miguel?'

Miguel clapped Julio on the back. 'True, I'm a spoiled brat. So far my record is unbroken.'

'Far be it from me to break your record. I agree. Coffee for you and a glass of rum for me.'

They stepped off the narrow sidewalk into the dim interior of the little shop. It was situated on a corner, two sides open to the street. Candles guttered in the breeze and were reflected in the damply scrubbed surfaces of the small marble-topped tables. The rough wooden chairs were occupied by neighbourhood masculinity. From the shadows of the high ceiling, the festoons of Spanish sausages and hams shone warmly brown. A waiter in a soiled apron quickly dismissed a group from a table and wiped it with a corner of his voluminous garment. His bow was low and obsequious as he pulled out the chairs.

'You said rum, Julio?' Miguel asked.

'Yes, rum.'

'Then I too will have rum; it is far more nourishing than coffee.'

'Rum? Ah no, *chico*. This breaks your record of always getting what you want. I forbid it! You have not eaten all day. No rum for you.'

Miguel smiled up at the waiter who had been listening to the conversation. He shrugged his shoulders and waved toward Julio. '*Mi dueña*,' he laughed.

While they were waiting for their coffee, a girl stood up from a table where she had been sitting with two men and came over to Miguel. She looked not more than sixteen under her heavy paint. Her black hair was smooth against her head and it was adorned with many small coloured combs. With a provocative wiggle of her hips and a bounce of her breasts, she stood beside Miguel, her thigh pressed close against his arm. Miguel recognized her as one of the little whores who plied their business in the cantina and entertained their clients in the rooms upstairs. He pulled her to him and patted her round buttocks, feeling the warmth of her flesh under the thin cotton. 'Rosita, Florita, Carmen?' He shook his head. 'Ah yes, Perlita! Now I remember.'

'No, Anita! You have a short memory don Miguel but perhaps you remember that night two weeks ago?'

'Of course, how could I forget it.' His hand was under her skirt now and her bare flesh felt hot under his hands. A flush crept up over her face and he could see the sudden thrusting of her copper tipped breasts through the sweat-dampened cotton of her dress. She spraddled her legs a little wider to accommodate his hands.

'Then come, don Miguel! There will be no charge tonight. I'll show you such a good time you will stagger home and not from wine.'

'I believe you but not tonight little one.' He reached in his pocket and took out a gold piece and dropped it down the low 'V' of her dress, then dismissed her with a little slap on her rear. 'Go, *chica!* Quickly! If you stand beside me another minute it will be fatal. Ay de mi! There is a conspiracy against me tonight that I must needs go home and change my clothes one way or another.'

She smiled knowingly. 'Then if I have that power over you, don Miguel, I think it will be soon that I shall see you again.'

'Soon, Anita. It will be my pleasure. I promise you.'

'No, mine, don Miguel.' She brushed a kiss on his hair and returned to her table.

'Is there one woman in Havana you haven't had?' Julio followed the little *puta* with his eyes.

'Thousands, Julito! Thousands! But I'm doing all I can to diminish the figure. That's why I never try the same one twice because I think of all those lovely ones I have not yet had. Ah, here's our waiter.'

The man set the coffee and rum on the table and looked questioningly at Miguel, awaiting further orders but Julio waved him away. He gulped his rum in one swallow and sat back in his chair waiting for Miguel to finish his coffee. The beverage was hot and black. Miguel sipped it leisurely, added more sugar, stirred it slowly and nodded his head wisely.

'It seems to me, *amigo mio*, that you place altogether too much importance on our meeting with this La Clavelita. To be sure, there has been much talk about her but after all she is only a dancer and as such she is little better than the little Anita which just left us. Dancers are a penny a dozen and they are all whores. I've known some and so have you. I seem to remember a little blonde who was here with the ballet from Paris last year that you raved about for several days. But all dancers have ugly legs – great bunches of muscles in the wrong places that grip one like a vice. Dancers! Bah!'

'But not La Clavelita, Miguel. You have not seen her. You were in the country the first time she danced. Perhaps after you have seen her you will understand why I am so very anxious. Do you realize that the lady has been here two weeks and that outside of the one appearance she made at the theatre no one has seen her? No one! Not even a glimpse in the *paseo!* All Havana is talking about her.'

'Of course,' Miguel shrugged his shoulders and sipped his coffee. 'How wise of her. Sometimes it pays to be mysterious. But, if she is so damned aloof and exclusive why are you so favoured and why am I?'

'Believe me, I was as much surprised as you. Yesterday morning a note arrived. But why should I tell you all this again? I told you last night. Were you too drunk to remember?'

Miguel made a sharp hissing noise – the peculiar way of attracting attention to which Cubans are extremely prone. As the waiter came running, he pointed to his empty cup. Despite Julio's protestations, he sat still until the second cup was brought. 'Perhaps I was a trifle drunk but come, be a good *muchacho*, Julito, and tell me all over again. You got a note from La Clavelita and then what?'

'Yes, I got the note and in it she said that she had known my sister, Maria de la Luz, while they were attending the same convent in Spain and that they had always been very good friends and that...'

'A dancer in a convent?'

'Don't interrupt, stupid! She wasn't a dancer then; she was only a girl going to school. She had always heard Maria speak much of me and much of you also. Maria was always very fond of you. Remember, she even took a miniature of you with her when she went to Spain – the little one in the gold frame that you gave her; the one that was painted when you were at the sickening age of fifteen. You looked so damned angelic, even though at that age you had laid every wench at the *finca*.'

Miguel laughed. 'You are fond of that word. That is the second time you have used it today. I was an angel at fifteen, I am an angel today. Well, after all, Miguel is one of the archangels.'

'And so was Satan before he fell from heaven. But you interrupt me.'

'Only to insist that I am still an angel and that I always rather admired Satan. Probably he was bored in heaven.'

Julio made a quick sign of the cross to avert any evil effects of Miguel's blasphemy. 'And now that we have settled the affairs of the angels, may I proceed or do you wish to hear any more? La Clavelita who, by the way, signs herself as Margerita Lopez del Valle, tells me that she is quite alone in Havana; that she has no friends here and that she would much appreciate the honour of my acquaintance. She feels that she already knows me from having known my sister so well; also that she has heard much of a certain Miguel de Santiago ...'

'You see, Julito, your sister thinks I'm an angel too.'

'That, Miguel, is your greatest problem. Too many people think that about you, even I. But to continue, La Clavelita wishes, if possible, that she might have the pleasure of meeting me and this certain Miguel de Santiago. Why she should desire such a thing is more than I can imagine but women have strange ideas. Then she says further that being alone in Havana, she feels she might call on me as a brother.'

Miguel leaned back in his chair and laughed. His hand slapped the table so smartly that the cup danced in its saucer. 'A brother! *Dios mio*!' He broke into another fit of laughter. 'How nice for you. To be her brother! Now you can protect this frail rose of the theatre who springs from the dust of the stage. But am I getting mixed up – she is a carnation, *verdad?* And me? Am I to be her brother too?'

'Probably.'

Miguel struggled to control his paroxysms of laughter. He became thoughtful, bit his lip and nodded his head. 'Ay, she's a wise one. She has a little game, this Clavelita and she is playing it nicely. She has put the bait on the hook. Is it for me, Julito, or for you? Seeing as how we represent two of the richest families in Cuba perhaps it doesn't matter. Well, *vamos a ver!* I, for one, can play her little game. Can you? No, of course you can't. You are one of those trusting souls who think women always mean what they say and always speak the truth. Bah! Women are all the same. One night they whimper and pant and clutch you while they say "I love you, I adore you, I worship you" and the next day they are ogling some other man over their fan. But it's a charming game and I love to play it. So, I shall play it with this one who is the same as all the rest only perhaps a little deeper. But perhaps it would be better if I played it a different way. Perhaps I shall stay here with the little Anita and let you go and tell her that the Archangel Miquel de Santiago y del Monte regrets that he is unable to be a big brother to La Clavelita. That he, in fact, shudders to think what it would mean to be a brother to any woman. He has quite different ideas on the subject and brotherly affection is not one of them.

Julio stood up from the table and motioned to the waiter. 'Do as you damn please, I am going,' he said. 'Maria *was* in a convent in Spain as you well know and I have no reason to doubt this young lady's word that she was a friend of my sister's. At least let us remember our manners and extend La Clavelita a sample of Cuban hospitality.'

Miguel threw some coins on the table, rose and put his arm around Julio's shoulders. 'By all means, let us be hospitable. I must not forget the role you have inflicted on me for the evening. So I shall be Miguel and not Satan. Let us call on this poor defenceless damsel who so desires our protection in this barbarous city. We shall conduct her frail presence to the theatre. *Ay de mi*, we shall be her brothers. We shall guard her virtue with our very lives. Let us hope she can see my halo. *Mozo*, call a carriage. My friend and I go forth to defend the honour of the sacred womanhood of Spain. But tell the little Anita that I may be back within the hour and for her to put clean sheets on her bed and wash under her arms. The last time, if I remember rightly, they stank. *Vamos, Julito!*'

Chapter Four

THE HIRED CARRIAGE wearily came to a stop before a small house in the Street of the Lieutenant of the King – the *Calle de Teniente Rey* – a quietly fashionable little street, not far from the Church of San Francisco. It was a modest house, scarcely distinguishable from its neighbours. It gave the appearance of a house where one's maiden aunt might live with propriety. There was little about it to connect it with the glamour of La Clavelita's name.

Somewhere inside the house a bell rang softly as Julio pulled the cord. He and Miguel waited on the sidewalk while the house came to life. Behind the door, they could hear a muffled running of feet; voices called; lights appeared in the lower *sala* and half of the tall mahogany door opened to admit them.

Inside the small but brilliantly lighted hall, they were met by an aged man, clad in a decent livery of black. He bowed as he closed the door behind them. 'The Señor don Julio de Castenaro and the Señor don Miguel de Santiago, I believe?' His voice was full of awed respect as he looked at the two men. Julio nodded assent while Miguel took a quick glance around the hall, noting the rich furnishings.

The old man seemed to be trying to make up his mind which was which. He scrutinized them carefully as he continued, 'Doña Margerita is awaiting you. She has taken the liberty, owing to the inconvenience of the early hour that she has asked you to call, of presuming that you would care to dine with her.'

'Please present our compliments to doña Margerita and inform her that the Señor de Santiago and I shall be honoured to dine with her.'

The old man, now that Miguel had been identified, inventoried him carefully, then tiptoed away.

Julio turned to Miguel and whispered, 'That one will

know you the next time he sees you, that's sure. Come, let's sit down.'

They entered the *sala* and sat down. It was a small room but furnished with elegance, even with taste. Miguel took a quick glance at the room. The girandoles, the damask, the tapestries! He closed one eye and nodded his head suggestively with an 'I-told-you-so' expression. 'The young lady seems to have done very well for herself so far, without protection. Of course it is always possible that she has already received protection in Madrid or Paris. Probably she has brothers all over Europe. I imagine that when she gets to Mexico or Peru or wherever she goes next, she figures on having an even more elaborate place, thanks to you ... or me.'

'Quiet, I hear her coming,' warned Julio.

The doors to the *sala* opened and La Clavelita entered. She advanced toward Julio without hesitation. 'You, señor, are don Julio, I am sure. The resemblance to your dear sister is unmistakable. I would have recognized you anywhere.' She turned to Miguel with the easy assurance of a woman of the world but for one tiny second her poise seemed to vanish. In that second, there was a frightened look in her eyes. It vanished and she addressed him easily and with composure. 'And you, señor, you are don Miguel. I must admit, however, that I have always pictured you as a young lad, perhaps fifteen.'

She stood, poised expectantly, awaiting their answers. Eyes, like the blackness of a tropic night, seemed to glow in the whiteness of her skin – a skin so smooth and white that it was difficult to distinguish between it and the creamy petals of the carnations which cascaded from her shoulder. Her hair was like polished jet. She was tall and slender of waist but her swelling breasts were round and full. Her satin dress was the same creamy white as the flowers which caught up her white lace mantilla. Her throat and arms shone with the fire of rubies and there were diamond buckles on her tiny scarlet satin shoes.

She extended her hand to Julio and he brushed it with his lips. 'The señorita is too kind,' he murmured.

For the sake of convention, Miguel realized that he must speak but he knew that any words he uttered would be inane and meaningless. He could not think; his mind had suddenly become an immense vacuum which seemed to be filling with flood after flood of hot blood which raced from his head down to his thighs. Just looking at this woman produced the same sensations as when the little tavern whore had brushed up against him and he feared that he might soon make a spectacle of himself. As he leaned over to kiss her hand he closed his eyes, felt his lips touch warm flesh and then raised his head, opening his eyes. He realized that he was still loutishly holding her hand and dropped it. Gone was the faint trace of sarcasm which he had so glibly rehearsed before he saw her.

'How amiable of the señorita to remember the picture of a young lad.' He mumbled the words, feeling as he did so that any Negro slave on his plantation could have voiced them more fluently.

Apparently she did not notice his confusion. 'One does not always remember the likeness of a young lad,' she replied opening her fan. Her eyes were dancing now and she hid them for a moment behind the cobweb of lace and ivory, 'but, *ay de mi*, when the lad is as beautiful as a Murillo angel....'

The remark served to establish Miguel's aplomb. He turned to Julio, 'Ay, Julito! You see, you see! I am Miguel and not Satan,' then turning to Margerita he apologized for his exuberance. 'My enthusiasm ... please excuse it señorita but it was your remark about Murillo. It was indeed apropos. All this evening I have been trying to persuade my friend, and likewise myself, of just what you have said. We were talking of angels which may seem most unusual to you and discussing the comparative merits of two of them – the Archangel Michael and the fallen angel Satan. I do not know whether to categorize myself with my namesake or the other but now you have convinced me, and I hope you can convince him, that I am Miguel for certainly he cannot doubt the word of so charming a person as yourself.'

'It would seem, señor, that you bother yourself unnecessarily. For me the ideal combination would be a man that has a little of both in him.'

'Then let me assure you, Señorita, my friend Miguel *does* combine both.'

She laughed. She had a curious laugh. It sounded like a breeze tinkling the crystal pendants of the chandelier; it bubbled like champagne being poured into a fragile glass which broke and fell in pieces on the floor – all tinkly glass and effervescent wine.

'Ah, señores, I see that you are the best of friends. But I must not keep you standing while we discuss angels, fallen or otherwise. Now may I offer you a bit of supper? The hour at which I invited you is most inconvenient I know. But it is necessary that I be at the theatre at ten and so, if you please, I shall allow you to escort me into the dining room.'

They both offered their arms.

'And what shall I do with two arms, except this?' she asked, placing a hand on each. 'You will both escort me. I am charmed that you deigned to call on me. I know my conduct must appear most shocking and not at all befitting a Spanish lady, particularly one who is not married. Yet, as La Clavelita I do have certain privileges which I would never have as doña Margerita. As the Señorita del Valle, I could not have invited you to come here – as La Clavelita it is my privilege. Yet, I do not dispense with all the formalities. I have a dueña who will be the fourth at our dinner. The Señora de Quesada is quite capable of guarding all the proprieties.'

Miguel felt the pressure of her hand on his arm. Did it rest a little more intimately than he had expected? He flexed the muscles of his arm and they hardened under the smooth satin of his sleeve. Was there an answering response – just the slightest pressure of fingers? He was not sure but at least the hand was not withdrawn. The contact of her flesh continued to excite him and he longed to take his seat at the table to hide his burgeoning excitement. But with his elation he sensed a feeling of depression as though he might stand a chance of losing something very wonderful. He glanced under his lashes without turning his head and he could see the curve of her throat half hidden by the lace of her mantilla. Suddenly he knew that he had never wanted anything in his life so much as to press his lips against that cool whiteness and slowly move his lips up to hers. *Por dios!* Let him get to that table soon and get seated!

As they entered the dining room and he mentally made a note of the number of steps it would take him to gain the table, they halted. A tall gaunt woman, dressed in rusty black, rose to greet them and Miguel realized by the quick shifting of her glance to his face that she had discovered his secret. Margerita presented her and she bowed stiffly first to Julio and them to himself. Her brief nod in his direction conveyed her utter disapproval of him and he could willingly have cut the old hag's throat. She plumped into her chair, and while Julio held Margerita's chair, Miguel dropped to his own, grateful for the enveloping lace of the tablecloth.

The small room was bright with candles and gleaming silver, its only discordant note the disapproving face of the señora who, without addressing a word to either of them, proceeded to pick at her food. It was plain that the Quesada did not count for much, but her decayed gentility lent an air of sober respectability to the dinner. It was almost, Miguel thought, as if they were being entertained by a lady, rather than a dancer. The same old man who had met them in the hall served them with a quick deftness. Miguel had no idea what he was eating, it was probably a slice of cold chicken as he had prophesied but all food would have tasted the same to him.

Margerita lifted her glass of wine and smiled at them. 'Again, señores, I must tell you how happy I am that you accepted my invitation. I feel that I am dining with old friends rather than strangers. I feel that I have known you both for years.'

Miguel and Julio nodded in approval as she continued. 'Maria and I were inseparable, you know, and I vow, she spoke of nothing but her brother and her brother's friend Miguel. Ah, I know so many things – so very many things –

about you both. About the time you tried to be a bullfighter, don Julio, and decided to run away from home; how once you got sick from eating green mangoes and swore if you got well you would go to mass every morning the rest of your life – a resolution which lasted exactly two days.'

'I shudder to think of what you may know about me,' Miguel leaned toward her.

She touched his hand lightly with her fan. 'La, don Miguel, I know *so* many things about you. Maria spoke more about you than her brother. Now let me see. There was the time you stole the bottle of cognac and got both don Julio and the poor Maria most awfully drunk and the time....'

Julio held up a warning hand. 'It would seem that you already know much about us. We tremble at the extent of your knowledge.'

'And there are some which Maria might have told you about that would cause us to blush,' Miguel added.

Margerita tapped him again with her fan. 'Now, don Miguel, that is something I would like to see. Nothing would give me greater pleasure than to see you blush. But alas, don Miguel, you must remember that we were girls in a convent, Maria and I, and of course there was much that Maria did not know about, so you will have no opportunity to blush.' She turned to Julio. 'But let us speak of your sister. I have been a miserable correspondent. Since her marriage we have drifted apart.'

'Maria?' Julio shrugged his shoulders. 'She is worse than a miserable correspondent, señorita. They are living in Madrid and there are two children. She would like to come to Cuba but her husband is required at court and cannot leave.'

'It would be delightful for her to return. I know she loves Cuba more than Spain. Her fondest memories centre around the Santiago plantation, La Estrellita is it not?'

Miguel nodded.

'She told me so much about it. Do you go there often?'

'Yes, I spend much of my time there,' Miguel replied. 'It is very large you know. We support some six hundred slaves.'

'Slaves, señor? I must confess I do not like the idea of slaves – of one man owning another.'

'Yet it is necessary. How else could we keep those many acres under cultivation and the two big sugar *centrals* grinding cane? The Negroes are important to our economy, señorita. I know. I am not merely a dilettante; I am a working farmer. I spend much of my time at the *finca* – fortunately it is not far from Havana.'

'Maria told me how beautiful it is; the gardens; the house; the vast rooms.'

'Some eighty, I believe, señorita. I suppose there are some I have never entered. The original house, you know, was destroyed by a hurricane the very day I was born. It was there my mother and father met their death. My grandmother had the ruins levelled off and planted a rose garden there. Only a single marble pillar remains.'

'I know,' Margerita sympathized. 'Maria told me of the terrible tragedy. But how fortunate that you did not perish too. Am I right? Didn't your nurse put you in a heavy old chest and after the storm had passed, searchers in the ruins heard your cries. Or was there something about a dog finding you? Anyway, it was a miracle that you were saved, *gracias a dios*.'

'Most fortunate for me,' Miguel grinned.

Julio brought the palm of his hand down sharply on the table. 'For once, señorita, I agree with him. I do not always agree but this time I do. Miguel is a good friend and I'll say it before his face that he is a wonderful person. He has many faults,' he looked at Miguel who made a wry face, 'oh yes, he is selfish and spoiled by his grandmother and all of Havana including myself, but after all, he is *The* Santiago and so we forgive him much. Really, señorita, I am most sincere. Believe me, there is no one in all Havana, no not in *todo del mundo*, for whom I have a higher regard or deeper affection than for this Miguel de Santiago.'

Miguel lost his flippant attitude for a brief moment and the sincerity of Julio's words caused him to pale under his olive tan. There was a strained silence. Had it been in the theatre, applause would have filled the emotional void.

Margerita hastened to fill the awkward pause. 'You must deserve those words, don Miguel, because don Julio knows you very well.'

Miguel did not answer but raised his eyes and thanked Julio with a glance of appreciation and a smile which seemed oddly humble on his lips.

Margerita continued. 'How I wish someone might say the same of me. How strange it is that love, which is supposed to be far more precious than friendship, is so much more easily obtained. Gentlemen, I shall not bore you by telling you how often I have had love of a sort offered to me. There was a little Parmesan princeling and a Russian Grand Duke and an English Milord. I do not say it to boast. Please do not misunderstand me. But this matter of love has become a trifle tiresome. Since I attained some prominence in my art, I have been forced to stumble over men of all ages who offer me their hearts for a night, or a month or forever, so they say. They storm my dressing room; they besiege my house; all of them presenting their palpitating hearts on a silver platter. But never, no never, have I had an offer of friendship. So, from you both I have but one thing to ask, provided you will be generous and give it to me.'

'And what is that?' Miguel asked automatically.

'Friendship, don Miguel. A friendship which does not need to prove itself with cartloads of flowers or be bolstered up with little pieces of coloured stones set in gold. These things I do not need and should I need them I can afford to buy them myself. I'd like something that would last longer than flowers which wilt and jewels that become lost. I do not seek a love that dies in the cold grey dawn of morning. No, I would treasure your friendship. True, I have little to offer you in return. My profession makes me a marked woman – the prey of drooling creatures who think to buy me with a few gold coins or a string of baubles. The fact that I am willing to exhibit myself on the stage makes people believe I am for sale – as much for sale as the tickets they buy to see me. But I am not for sale – not to Russian Grand Dukes or Parmesan Princes. When love does enter my life, I shall accept it and glory in it because I know that

I am a woman capable of love. But until that time, may I have your friendship? I do not mean the friendship of La Clavelita, that creature of the theatre, that castanet-clicking strumpet who stomps the floor boards in time to flamenco music. No, I mean the friendship of Margerita del Valle who has, in her own strange way, tried to make something of herself that she can be proud of, even though she has had to risk her reputation in doing so.' The two men arose from the table almost simultaneously. Each held a glass of wine in his hand. The light of the candles struck through the wine glasses, making them glow like topazes. As though it were an act, rehearsed many times, yet spontaneous in its enthusiasm, they bowed and lifted their glasses.

Miguel saw the woman before him in a different light. She was no longer the famous dancer who had been sought after over all Europe. This was no trollop, no whore of the theatre who used her beauty to hang another string of diamonds around her neck. This was a lone woman, fighting against great odds, and any woman as beautiful as she was must certainly have great odds to fight against. Suddenly he felt ashamed for the suspicions he had entertained about her. He saw that Julio was waiting for him to speak. He heard his own voice as curiously strained.

'To the Señorita del Valle – to doña Margerita – yes to La Clavelita, we pledge our friendship tonight. It is but a poor offering, I am sure, but such as it is, we give it to her.'

They drank their wine slowly, their eyes on Margerita, then sent their glasses crashing to the tiled floor. She sat for a long moment in the silence that followed then she too stood and raised her glass. 'I thank you and I return your pledge.' She flung her own glass to the floor where its sparkle of diamond crystals glinted in the spilled wine.

'Señorita del Valle . . .' Miguel began.

'Since when do friends use all the tiresome words like señorita and señor. To me you are Miguel and you are Julio. It is as such I have always known you and thought of you. But I interrupted you.'

'I merely wanted to offer you my apology,' Miguel dropped his eyes.

'Apologize to me? Why?'

'Since we are friends, I can be frank and you will forgive me. I misunderstood your purpose in inviting us here tonight. I thought it some new game – shall we say a new approach. The glamorous dancer, the inaccessible one, the mysterious woman who allowed nobody to see her. Well – it could be that she was playing for high stakes. How terribly wrong I was. So, I apologize and I crave your forgiveness for having misjudged you.'

She did not answer him at once nor did she look at him. Her fingers picked at the lace of the tablecloth and her eyes remained intent upon her plate. When she looked up there was the suspicion of a tear but she did not wipe it away. 'I am sorry that my innocent invitation was misunderstood but I understand how it might have been. You thought I was playing for high stakes. I suppose you mean money. I do not blame you. Women of my profession are doing it every day. No, my friends, I am not interested in your fortunes.' She rose from the table.

They followed her action. The old señora remained behind at Margerita's bidding. She had been so busy cramming food into her mouth that she had paid no attention to their conversation. Again the young men offered Margerita their arms.

As they started to leave the room, Miguel turned to her.

'One question, Margerita?'

She looked up at him, smiling now.

'Friendship is a wonderful thing,' he smiled back. 'But I have never had a woman for a friend. With women I have only known – well, call it love for want of a better word. And I admit, I have known it many times for I have known many women. I agree, it is not love but at the time it seems like love yet when it dies I have no regrets.' He turned his head to address Julio. 'Now, my friendship with Julio is a real friendship – it has never changed. But – and this is my question – suppose my friendship for you should change to something else, an emotion perhaps baser or perhaps higher but an emotion which we shall call love. What then?'

'Must we anticipate the future? Tonight we are friends,

verdad? Tomorrow is not yet here. So why worry about it? And now would you both care to accompany me to the theatre? I am told the house is sold out but I have reserved seats for you.'

'Alas,' Julio's regrets were apparent in his voice, 'tonight I escort my *novia* and sit with her parents in their box. We are to be married next year, you know. But I could, just for tonight, sit with Miguel.'

'How happy I am for you. And you, Miguel, does your *novia* await you too?'

'There is none, Margerita.'

'Then...?'

'I shall be happy to escort you.'

'And bring me home after the performance?'

'I shall be honoured.'

This time there was no mistaking the pressure on his arm. He drew it closer to his side, imprisoning the hand on his arm against his chest. He could feel his heart pounding and he knew that the fingers on his arm could feel it too but – *caramba!* – not only his heart was pounding and there was no table to hide him now. He released the pressure on her hand and took a long breath. He made up his mind to visit Josefina's after he had escorted Margerita home.

Chapter Five

NEVER BEFORE HAD the shabby old theatre been more crowded than it was on the night of La Clavelita's second appearance in Havana. Those who had seen her the first time had added their words of enthusiasm to the fame which she had won in Madrid, Seville, Paris, even in London; a fame which had long ago preceded her arrival in Cuba. Everybody from the Governor down who had been able to beg, borrow or steal the price of admission; or to cajole, bribe or flatter the management, had been anxiously awaiting her second appearance.

The candles in the big chandeliers of the theatre guttered in the cool breeze that came through the open shutters, sometimes spilling hot wax on the satin gowns below; gowns which rivalled the elaborate appearance of the men in the brilliance of their colours. Wigs and powder had gone out of fashion in Europe but were still in vogue in Cuba where the new styles would not be adopted for another few years. Paris more than Madrid influenced the styles of Cuba and although Paris was fast assuming the more severe modes of the Revolution, Cuba was loath to give up the fanciful styles of the monarchy.

There was a constant flow of movement in the audience – it was like a restless sea, stirred by a breeze. The old theatre – for this was before Tacon arrived in Cuba and built the sumptuous Teatro Nacional – lost some of its shabbiness with the brilliance of the scene. Never, since the great Rosa Blanco had sung there, had such homage been paid to one woman. But never had there been such a dancer as La Clavelita and surely she warranted such homage. Such a dancer! Never before had anyone been able to infuse into the dance so much of the romance of Andalusia, the grace of Castile, the high-nosed aristocracy of Aragon or to flavour their steps so well with the reckless abandon of the *gitanas* of the Sacramonte. La Clavelita was more than a dancer. She was the heart and soul of Spain and although the Cubans were not *simpatico* towards Spain, their roots were deep in the mother country.

The chandeliers were lowered, the unoiled pulleys squeaking as the ropes ran through them and the candles were snuffed out one by one. There was the usual hush of expectancy but when the curtains parted there was a sigh of disappointment. The stage was empty – black, bare, unadorned and almost devoid of light. Gradually as the audience became accustomed to the gloom, they could make out the white linen collars of the musicians and then their faces, pallid in the obscurity, lighted only by a few candles left burning. There was a glint of splintery reflections on guitar strings, nothing more. The quietness was broken now and then by the click of nervous fans in the audience. Then a faint whisper of music was heard – the mere brushing of a hand across strings, soon echoed by another and then another chord.

Suddenly the white limelight burned a small circle on the stage and with this spot of blinding light, the music burst into a terrifying mad crescendo, bringing with it, as if she had been cast forth from the stage's dark womb, La Clavelita herself. She stood tall and slender in the blinding light. The blackness of her hair and the shining blackness of her simple dress melted into the velvety blackness of the stage while the whiteness of her skin seemed to absorb all the brilliance of the light. The single red carnation she wore in her hair burned like a bright coal but when she lifted her head to stare imperiously at the unseen audience, the carnation was no redder than her lips which were a red wound on her white face. The music whispered and died away, until it was only an echo of music – a ghost of something that had been played many years ago.

She raised her arms slowly over her head and, through the faint murmur of music, one became aware of the low chattering of her castanets. It sounded like a chattering of many voices but far away in another world. Although her hands barely moved, the noise became louder, as though an angry mob were now approaching. It ceased to be a chattering and became frenzied – a horde of bickering people who engulfed one. Still she stood motionless and only her talking fingers moved. The clamour stopped. For a fraction of a second a deep silence stretched tautly over the theatre. Then followed a crash of guitar strings, strident and forceful and she started to dance. The music was one of many moods. It became soft and seductive while the clicking of the castanets paced the movements of her body which now, wholly feminine and seductive, accommodated itself to the towering masculinity of her lover. Her body met his and they embraced while the castanets whimpered and moaned of love and desire. She yielded but only for a second and then burst forth with vituperations of bitter hatred. He had been unfaithful to her. He thought he could take from her and give nothing in return. But no? It was a mistake? Then she would forgive him. And she would love him as he had never been loved before.

One forgot there was only a lone woman dancing. The whole drama of love and life was taking place on the stage. Around and around she danced in an ecstasy of motion, her skirts making midnight billows about her while her heels tapped out a tattoo that answered the chattering of the castanets. The music stopped on a high note suddenly and without warning. The light flickered and disappeared. Where there had been life and light there was nothing but darkness. La Clavelita had disappeared.

The house rose to its feet and called her name. Candles appeared on the stage, lighting the huge bouquets that were tossed there. The applause died down grudgingly, was revived and died again but she did not return.

Not until the house was quiet did she reappear. This time the stage was lighted and she was elaborately gowned. Her dress of red satin was heavy with gold embroidery. The tall ivory comb in her hair was massed with red carnations. Her shawl was embroidered with the flowers and she carried sheaves of them in her arms. It was the famous dance of the *claveles*, the dance from which she had taken her name – the dance that had made her famous. Slowly she circled to almost inaudible music. The flowers in her arms became a part of her. They too became living things and as she danced they appeared to dance with her. The sharp spicy odour of the carnations drifted out over the audience and it seemed as though La Clavelita herself became a flower, growing in the sunshine and dancing in the wind. Suddenly her feet stopped and only her arms continued the motion of the dance. It was the moment they all awaited. To whom would she throw her flowers.

The Governor learned forward in his box. Everyone present from a doddering old *hidalgo* sucking his toothless gums to a ragged mulatto who had crawled halfway through an open window hoped that one of her flowers would come his way. The moment she spent in apparent indecision seemed like hours. *Ay de mi!* To be favoured with just one flower from La Clavelita! It would be something to talk about tomorrow; to display in the *cantina*; to sleep beside on one's pillow and dream that it was La Clavelita herself.

Finally she turned to the box in which Miguel and Julio were sitting. Taking one flower, she brushed it with her lips and threw it toward their box. Miguel stood up and plucked it from the air. She smiled at him as he too touched it to his lips. A cheer arose from the house as she chose another flower and tossed it to Julio but she did not kiss the second flower. A sea of hands reached up; there were cries of '*aqui, aqui*' and as the music increased in volume, she danced from side to side of the stage throwing the flowers to the audience. Eager hands grabbed for them. To each the flower seemed like a personal message from her – a veritable part of her.

She danced several times again either alone or with a partner, an adder slim, swarthy young gypsy with black *patillos* stencilled against his cheeks, and pouting red lips. His heels pounded the boards like small triphammers, raising ancient dust from them and his arm encircled her waist with a possessiveness that made Miguel grind his teeth. They danced the fiery *flamenco* dances of Andalusia with their underlying strain of sadness; they danced the stately measures of the old Court of Castile and the ingenuous rural dances of the peasants. But the gypsy lad was only a prop – a nonentity for her convenience – in the eyes of all but Miguel whose fierce jealousy surprised even himself. Encore followed encore after her finale and then nothing would bring her back.

As the candles were lighted and the audience started to move toward the door, Julio leaned over and spoke to Miguel. 'My *novia* consented to my sitting with you tonight but she will never forgive me, if I do not join her now, so you too will forgive me if I leave?'

Miguel's eyes were dancing. 'Forgive you, Julito? If you don't make yourself scarce in five seconds, I'll never forgive you. Go, Julito, and tonight I thank god for the little Sara who takes you. How fortunate that you have a *novia*. Perhaps I should have one too. *Adios!*'

The stream of people parted their handshake. Miguel

made his way through the crush of satin and velvet to the street and then through a dark little alley to the stage door. He had been deaf to the many greetings and blind to the lash-veiled glances that had accompanied his leaving.

His mind was a maelstrom of thoughts. What girl in Cuba, *ay de mi*, what girl in all the world possessed the fire and beauty that belonged to Margerita! Who could compare with her? Beside her all the little fillies of Havana seemed inane and vacuous. And . . . he was a friend of hers. To be sure their friendship had existed for only a few hours but it seemed that he had known her forever. A friend! Bah! He was no longer a friend of hers nor she of him. The kiss on the carnation had told him otherwise. Surely she had intended it to. He remembered the warmth of her hand on his arm. Her flower was in his hand and he crushed it to his lips. Its fragrance was overpowering. His teeth tore at the petals and their bitter taste stung his mouth. Was this an omen – a moment of pungent sweetness and then an aftermath of bitterness? Of course not, no bitterness could ever touch him. He was Miguel de Santiago.

A candle, shining dimly through the dirty glass of a tin lantern, revealed a crowd of people around the stage door. Instinctively they made way for Miguel.

'*Que tal*, Miguel? Have you come to claim another *clavelita*? Just because you were lucky enough to catch one tonight is no reason why you may catch another. You happened to be nearest, that's all.'

Miguel recognized one of his friends, Juan Bobadilla. '*Que tal*, Juanito,' he called, 'what are you doing here tonight?' He frowned, shook his head and shrugged his shoulders. 'After all this is no place for a boy like you. You are too young, Juanito, all of three months younger than I – a mere babe. And besides,' his voice became a whisper, 'your waiting will avail you nothing. Take my word for it, La Clavelita is interested only in a man – *un hombre muy macho, como yo*.' Miguel noticed another acquaintance, Arturo Garay. 'Come, come, *muchachos*, I'll save you time and trouble. Your waiting here is time wasted. Of course La Clavelita and I both appreciate the honour you boys do her, but we regret she is engaged for the rest of the evening. So, run along, boys, the lady is coming and I see no reason why I should present her to you. She is not interested in the riff-raff of Havana,' he grinned at them.

'Hear him, Arturo,' Juan exclaimed. 'We – the riff-raff of Havana! And who is he?'

'Some *rustico* from a *finca* called La Estrellita. 'Tis easy to see this is the first time he has ever worn shoes.' Arturo slapped Miguel on his back. 'How did you get the cow dung out from between your toes, fellow? Are you trying to get rid of us because you fear competition?'

'Competition? From you two? I'll bet ten gold pieces that I can take any girl away from either of you in ten minutes. Why, all they have to do is look at me and pf-f-t.'

Juan nodded wisely to Arturo. 'He doesn't know that La Clavelita is an old friend of ours and that as soon as she sees us, she'll turn her back on him.' He turned to Miguel. 'She is almost here. Prepare to be snubbed, Miguelito.'

Juan rushed up to La Clavelita as she opened the door. He swept the ground with his hat. 'Juan Bobadilla, señorita. At your service. My carriage is waiting. May I have the honour of escorting you through this rather alarming crowd of peasants which has gathered at your door?'

She looked at him and smiled. 'I regret, Señor Bobadilla, that I do not have the pleasure of knowing you. Nevertheless, *muchas gracias* for your offer. But as to an alarming crowd, I do not agree with you. These young men look very civilized and not at all frightening. However, I have my own carriage and here is Señor de Santiago waiting to escort me, so I cannot avail myself of the pleasure of your company. Miguel,' she sidled up close to him, 'your arm, if you please.'

Miguel offered her his arm, glad once more to feel the warmth of her hand. 'As long as they are here, Margerita, let me introduce these young lads. This fellow is my very good friend, Juan Bobadilla and we have high hopes that when he grows up he will be quite a man. And this here is Arturo Garay who is also a nice boy but he hasn't been around much and is rather lacking in the graces of a *caballero.*'

She silenced him with a wave of her hand. 'I do not believe a word that he is saying, señores. If you are friends of Miguel's, I am most happy to know you.' She opened her fan and held the bit of lace between herself and Miguel, whispering, '*Ay de mi*, but he is a jealous one, this Miguel, but as long as you are friends of his, you must be friends of mine and lest you feel I am too selfish in seeming to prefer his company, allow me to present each of you with one of La Clavelita's *clavelitos.*'

She handed a carnation to each of them and, placing her hand more securely on Miguel's arm, walked down the alley with him and entered the waiting carriage.

'I'll be damned!' Juan looked at their retreating figures and shook his head.

'And double-damned,' Arturo added, 'he did know her after all. Leave it to Miguel to succeed where others fail.'

Chapter Six

MARGERITA LEANED BACK against the cushions of the carriage and allowed a little wave of fatigue to claim her for a moment. It was a relief to relax, away from the staring Argus of the audience. She glanced covertly at Miguel. Neither of them had spoken since the carriage left the theatre. In the quiet darkness of the streets, his face took on the colour of night. The shadow of his hat completely obscured his eyes. She could see only the full red lips, the whiteness of his teeth, the strong line of his chin and the corner of his ear where it joined the sturdy column of his neck. His hand lay near hers on the cushion. Slowly, almost imperceptibly she moved hers toward it as if it were drawn by a magnet. Their two hands were almost touching; she could feel the heat from his. Looking down, she stole a glance from the corner of her eye to see if their hands were actually touching.

With an involuntary start, she pulled her hand away. Was

it the shadow of the night; was it her imagination; or was it true that the hand beside hers seemed so dark in colour. She had heard about the influx of coloured blood in Cubans but no! It could not possibly be in this case. It was only because her own hand was so white that his seemed so dark. What a silly trick her imagination had played on her. Naturally his hand would be darker than hers for he lived in the sunshine. And, of course, the light was poor and his hand was in a shadow. Stealthily she replaced her hand to its close proximity.

A lurch of the carriage brought their hands together. At first only their fingers touched – a mere brushing together. A strange thrill ran through her and she could see him bite his under lip. He did not move his hand but an obliging cobble in the street swung the frail *volanta* on its springs and their hands came in closer contact. Slowly one of his fingers moved and touched hers. It stroked the length of her little finger then, emboldened because her hand was not removed, it journeyed up onto her hand and finding itself not repulsed it was followed by other fingers. Neither spoke. It was a moment of electric silence. Then his hand closed over hers and she felt her fingers crushed in the warmth of his palm. His hand was moist and yet it was a strangely comforting dampness. Although she gloried in the firm pressure of his hand, she made a slight effort to withdraw her own but it was held too urgently.

For the first time since leaving the theatre, Miguel turned toward her. His eyes sought hers and although he burned to pour forth his desire for her in a torrent of words, he chose the most commonplace that came to his mind. He hoped she would not notice his hoarseness. 'Julio was very sorry not to come with us. He had to attend to his *novia* – she is a prim little thing and insists on his dancing attention.'

'I am sorry too.' She found as much difficulty speaking the banal words as he had. 'No, Miguel, I am not sorry,' her words came quickly. 'Why should I lie? I am glad he is not here with us. I prefer to be here alone with you this little time.'

'Little time?'

'Yes, for we shall soon be at my home.' It was a statement but her inflection almost made it into a question.

'And then?' he asked hopefully.

'And then, Miguel, I shall bid you good night and thank you a thousand times for having come to see me.'

'Nothing more?'

'Nothing more! Margerita del Valle could hardly invite a gentleman to call on her at this hour of the night, could she?'

'But how about La Clavelita. Surely the world would not take it amiss if *she* invited a friend to partake of a glass of wine.'

'Ah, that one! What a reputation she has, that Clavelita. But even she must be careful. Could she trust that friend?'

Miguel lifted her hand to his lips. He was loath to relinquish it and when he did, he whispered, 'It would be difficult to vouch for that friend because perhaps he could not trust himself.'

'But at least he could try and of course there is always the Quesada.'

'Damn the Quesada!'

'Then let us see if this friend of La Clavelita's can be trusted. So, if Miguel would have a glass of wine with the dancer, he is welcome.'

'But what will become of Margerita?'

'She will be waiting for the Señor de Santiago to call tomorrow formally, with a big bunch of roses and mouthing compliments.'

'*Bien!* But let us stop acting. We are not the stage. I have much to say to you that cannot wait until tomorrow. I must say it now, tonight.'

She withdrew her hand and placed it on his arm, leaned her head back against the cushion and closed her eyes. 'Oh, Miguel, you have no idea how much I want to hear it, every word of it.'

The carriage drew up in front of her house and the coachman lifted the heavy knocker of the door. Miguel helped her down, and together they passed into the house. Once inside, he turned to look at her. And she, removing the high comb, the mantilla and the mass of flowers from her hair, returned his look steadily. For a second she studied him carefully. *Gracias a dios!* How utterly foolish she had been even to think of such a thing. To imagine for even a moment that this Miguel de Santiago might be cursed with that touch of colour which so many Cubans were credited with. The clear olive of his skin, his fine cut features, his smiling lips! All brushed away that momentary fright she had had in the carriage. Of course, the days on the *finca*! The sun bronze made him even handsomer.

Side by side they walked into the *sala*. Fortunately the Quesada was nowhere to be seen. Margerita herself pulled the curtains together, rang for a servant and seated herself on a low stool, spreading her skirts in a wide circle. The servant came and then returned in a few moments with the wine. 'The Señora de Quesada is sleeping?' she asked.

'Si, si, señorita.'

'Then do not wake her. See that I am not disturbed.'

He left and she waited for him to close the door. 'And now, Miguel, we are alone. You said you have much to say to me. I too have much to say to you.'

'*Quizas*, it is better that you start.'

'But there is so much to say – so very much. I hardly know where to begin. First you should know something about me as I already know so much about you. My father was General del Valle. Perhaps you have heard of him?'

Miguel nodded assent as she continued.

'As a young girl I received the usual sheltered upbringing which is accorded every young girl of my position in Spain. I went to a covent. That is where, as you know, I met Maria de la Luz. Life proceeded as usual until one day word came to me that my father had committed suicide. The loss of his position, his money and his prestige took away his desire to live. My mother had died many years before. She was English and I presume I had relatives in England but they were strangers to me. I was entirely alone in the world without a penny.'

Miguel's eyes were sympathetic. He started to speak but she waved him aside.

'The good sisters were willing to keep me there but the life of a nun did not appeal to me. I left the convent and took refuge with an old servant of my father's – he who opened the door for you tonight. Poor as he was he made a place for me in his home. His sister was the famous Encarnacion, the greatest dancer Spain has ever had.'

'I thought Spain's greatest dancer was named La Clavelita,' Miguel interrupted.

'I wish that were true,' she replied, 'but if I have any right to that title, it is only because Encarnacion has been forgotten. I can never hope to excel her. She was living with her brother. She was a fat little person, always smiling but always sad. In her youth, all Europe had been at her feet but when she was no longer able to dance she had nothing. Everything was gone except the supreme artistry which lived on in her head.

'She taught me to dance. It was not easy because she demanded perfection. Many times she despaired of me. Day after day, from early morning until late at night, over and over again we practised. At times I dropped from sheer exhaustion but we kept on. Finally one day she told me that I was beginning to learn. But there were many more months of practice. The hand must be just so; the back must be arched in one certain curve; the chin, the fingers, the arms! *Ay de mi!* To her one single click of a castanet was an art in itself. Then after all those months, she grudgingly consented to let me appear in public. Oh, it was a mean little cantina on a poor little street in Seville but the gypsy audience was a critical one. When they applauded it meant something. So, her teaching had been successful because, soon after, I received another offer and then a better one and a still better one. So it has always been, climbing up and up until today I am La Clavelita. But it has not been an easy road, Miguel. No, not easy.'

'Why has life been so difficult for you and so easy for me?'

She did not answer his question except to thank him with her eyes. 'Encarnacion taught me to dance but she also taught me to live. She taught me to avoid the mistakes she had made: to beware of love – even the words of love; to distrust men; to refuse everything; to trust only myself; to work hard, and once having become a success to avoid following the way of so many in my profession. I have no desire to flash across the capitals of Europe like a brilliant comet, burning myself out with a thousand admirers and then after I had pawned the jewels and sold the dresses and the carriages, enter an oblivion of poverty. I have seen Encarnacion; I have seen the once great Trigueñita and the famous La Palomita. Once they were all famous but today they are broken old women, living on their memories. No, Miguel, that is not what I want.'

'Then what do you want, Margerita?' he asked. 'Surely there must be something more in life than work and success. They are cold words, my dear. Cold and impersonal. Even if you despise the word *love*, it is a warmer word – a happier word.'

She was quiet for a moment and seemed at a loss for an answer. She sipped her wine thoughtfully. 'Perhaps you are right. Love is a happier word. And maybe, if it is meant for me, it will someday come to me. But for the present, I can only go on as I have been going. It is not always pleasant. Many doors are closed to me which would have been open had my father lived. My old friends – those who knew me when I was young and my friends of the convent, even Maria de la Luz – have all found it convenient to forget me. When I meet them on the street in Madrid, they find some excuse for looking the other way. I am an *artista*; therefore I am no better than a street walker. How strange that we Spanish who put art itself on a pedestal so debase our artists. But then, perhaps we are to blame for it ourselves. Most of the women of the theatre in Spain are. . . .'

'Yes, it is taken for granted,' Miguel nodded in assent, 'one always feels that an actress is fair game. Oh, poor Margerita. . . .'

'No pity, Miguel,' she interrupted him. 'Above all, no pity. I do not need it. Only the weak need pity and I am not weak. I am sorry to have taken up so much of your time with my story but I wanted you to know something about me.'

Miguel rose from his chair and stood above her. She raised her head slowly, her eyes sweeping up his body to his face. It was strangely flushed and his tongue made the circle of his lips, wetting them so that they shone in the candlelight.

'We are being frank tonight. I too shall be frank. You asked for my friendship and I cannot give it to you.'

She stood up quickly, turned her back on him and walked toward the window. Without looking around to see if he had followed her, she pulled the cord and the curtains parted. For a long moment she looked out into the darkness then turned. Her voice was cold – the words deliberately spoken and evenly spaced. 'Thank you for your frankness, señor. I can well understand how *The* Santiago might find it impossible to be friends with a dancer, especially one with such a shabby background.'

'*Dios mio*, Margerita! You did not hear me out.'

'No? Then speak! Manufacture what pretty excuses you can to soften the blow. And when you have finished, get out.' She turned again, facing the open window.

'Words cannot express my thoughts,' he spun her around and enveloped her in his arms. His lips crushed against hers and although she struggled just a little, his arms held her to him. Without releasing her, he lifted his lips from hers. 'Friendship, Margerita? Bah! What does a man in love have to do with friendship? It is a pallid word when his heart is on fire. We are in Cuba, *querida*, and here we love quickly. The blood of Cuban men boils under the tropic sun. And, we love intensely. It is only necessary for two carriages to stop in the *paseo*; two eyes meet; love is born. A veil is raised in church and a man sees a woman's face while the priest mumbles his prayers. Love! It is quick, sudden, overpowering like my love for you.'

'But I do not want that kind of love. I do not want such love as you offer me.'

'How do you know what kind of love I offer you? Did not my kiss tell you something of it?'

'It is the first time a man has kissed me so. How do I

know but what that is the same kind of love I have had offered to me so many times.'

'But my love is different.' He released her and stepped back from her.

She looked at him. She saw his tall clean limbs, his strong arms, the way his black hair curled at the temples. She looked at his hands, broad and strong, and the width of his shoulders. She gazed into his eyes, brown pools in the pink-flushed olive of his face. She even saw the dark stain of sweat under the arms of his coat and a corded artery that throbbed on the bronze column of his throat.

'Different? Of course it would be different. You are a splendid young animal, and any woman would enjoy the little time your love lasted. What a choice morsel the Havana gossips would have. The Santiago has taken up with the dancer. Your friends would slap you on the back and say "How is she, Miguel?" And, of course, it would be pleasant for me. You'd show me off before all Havana in the *Paseo*. I'd have new jewels and I'd treasure them in memory of the nights with you. Yes, it would be almost worth it until that certain day when I would notice a coolness in your manner. There would be an appointment with me you would forget; an excuse for your absence. But, I suppose for the little time it lasted it would be worth it.'

'Little time? You are unjust. Who said anything about a little time. As my wife you would always have me.'

She lifted her head to stare at him. 'Are you offering me marriage, Miguel?'

'What else except my love to go with that marriage?'

She was silent. Tears came to her eyes and she made a quick gesture to wipe them away but one eluded her and traced its way down her cheek. 'I have been offered love many times but never marriage. Men do not offer that to a woman in my position. Yet, if you love me and you love me sufficiently to offer me marriage I shall accept it, although I shall not hold you to it. But let me add just one thing, one very important thing. You do not have to seek my love: you have always had it. You say that you love me. How old is your love? A few hours? A few minutes? But mine! I have loved you for years.'

He looked incredulous.

'You do not believe me? But it is true. Convent girls get silly ideas. They fall madly in love with each other or else idolize some nun. Some even fall in love with the picture of a saint but always a young and handsome one like St Sebastian. But I did not. From the moment I saw the little miniature of you which Maria had I fell in love with you. I worshipped that picture. You see my dear you have always been loved. You have always been very close to my heart. See!'

She pulled at the fine gold chain which encircled her neck. From under the lace of her dress, there appeared a small frame and in it the portrait of a boy.

Miguel took it, feeling the warmth of her body on the gold.

'Myself.'

'Yes, you. It has never left me from the moment I begged it from Maria when she left to be married. You have always been with me and I have never been lonely. Every man I met I measured against this little picture and every one of them was found wanting.'

He reached out his arms for her and she stepped back.

'Oh how right you were when you thought I was playing for high stakes, but it was not the Santiago fortune that tempted me, it was you. I had to meet you but it could not be at the stage door along with other drooling men. So I invited you here just that I might see you and hope ... Oh, Miguel ...'

His arms were still extended; his hands invited her; his eyes beckoned to her; his lips desired her. She came toward him shyly. Softly she touched his face, his hair, his mouth and his throat. His arms encircled her for the second time and this time she did not try to escape. Her long lashes swept his cheek. His lips sought hers and he could feel the weight of her body as she clung to him. Gently he disengaged one hand and picked up the picture of himself. Pulling down the lace of her dress, he inserted the bit of gold and ivory back in its nesting place, kissing it and the flesh beneath it.

A stray breeze came into the room from the open window – a breeze coming up from the sea with the dawn. At first it was soft and gentle. It hardly stirred in the room. Then it grew fresh and strong. It pulsated with life and vigour. It swept through the room, forcing the damask draperies apart. One by one it extinguished the candles.

'No, Margerita, no!' he pushed her gently from him. 'This is a new experience for me. I must not. I love you too much. There are some things we shall have to save for our wedding night.'

'Now I know that you really love me, Miguel.' She kissed him lightly on the lips and pushed him around. 'Go, my love. You've proved your love to me. Until tomorrow.'

'Until tomorrow.'

He found the door in the darkness and stumbled through the hall. The heavy door opened to the street and he stepped out into the night. He had walked only a few steps towards the Church of San Francisco when a passing carriage stopped. The old *cochero* leaned out, scenting a fare.

'Where to, *hombre*?'

Miguel got in the decrepit *volanta* and sank back on the mended cushions. 'The Street of the Sun.'

'Ah, the house of Josefina. Always when a young man calls on his *novia*, I take him to the house of Josefina afterwards. So he can sleep, heh?'

'Yes,' Miguel nodded, 'the house of Josefina, so I can sleep. Afterwards.'

Chapter Seven

EXCEPT FOR THE clear songs of the caged birds and the metronomic splash of the fountain falling into the blue-tiled basin, the patio of the Casa Santiago was quiet. Miguel lolled indolently under the shade of a red and white striped awning watching Juan, who had now been promoted to being his personal slave, serve his breakfast. He sniffed the warm, crusty aroma of the *pan de flauta*, fresh from the oven, with fragments of banana leaves still clinging to it. The fragrance of the bread and the steaming coffee mingled with the strong perfume of orange blossoms, verbena and the white mariposa lilies which grew in luxurious abundance around the fountain.

He stretched luxuriously, extending one foot from the shelter of the striped shadow, and kicked off the *alpargata* from his foot to curl his bare brown toes with sensual gratification in the mid-morning sunshine. The air of the patio danced in heat waves – shimmering, glittering, pulsating. It inspired one to dream but not to act.

While Miguel watched Juan pour his coffee and hot milk, he stretched again, rippling his muscles like a jungle cat, and loosened the neck of his white linen shirt. 'Ay, Juanito, let's hope the coffee wakes me up.' He sipped at it, then straightened up in his chair, 'Chico, it's wonderful to be alive this morning; to be a part of all this light and heat – this Cuba. Yes, chico, it's good to be *The* Santiago and one of my many blessings is to have you to wait on me. You're a good boy, Juanito, and you take good care of me.'

'Gracias, mi amo,' Juan accepted the compliment with a smile that showed his teeth white against the plum-darkness of his lips.

Miguel continued to stare at the lad as if seeing him for the first time. Really not a bad looking boy, even if he was black. Tall and well formed with good features. But of course all the Santiago slaves were good looking. They had been chosen with care, mostly Mandingos, Hausas, Jaloffs and Krus. They cost more but they were worth it. Fine thoroughbreds cost more than ordinary animals. But no! Slaves were not animals. Herein Miguel differed from the opinion of most Cubans. Slaves were human even if their skin was black. Of course they were!

'Juanito, how old are you?' Miguel asked, noticing the slight fuzz on the brown velvet of the boy's upper lip.

'Seventeen, *mi amo*. I'll be eighteen soon.'

'And what do you do for fun, boy?'

'I live but to serve those in the house of Santiago, *mi amo*.'

'Sure! And you do it well. But tell me, what about the girls? Isn't there some special one that you like?'

Juan hung his head. His big foot swung in a lazy circle on the tiles. He swallowed hard, then looked up at Miguel. 'You will not beat me, *amo*?'

'Beat you, why?'

'Because of Edita? Oh, it was not my fault, *amo*. I did not mean to do it but the passageway was narrow and we brushed up against each other and then she reached down her hand and...'

'*Caramba!* Why did you wait for her to reach down *her* hand? Haven't you got a hand of your own? Time you got started, boy. We'd like to get some pups out of you but if you're going to wait for the girls to reach down their hands at you, we'll never get them. The next time you meet Edita in a narrow passageway, show her who's master.'

'With your permission, *mi amo*. You see I love her.'

Miguel looked at the boy, grinning now. This lad, who had hitherto served him with a straight face and the utmost decorum was in love. In love? Could he, under his black skin, feel the same way about this Edita that Miguel felt about Margerita? What a miracle this thing called love was. His thoughts wandered back to the night before, skipping the final episode at Josefina's and dwelling only on Margerita. *Ay*, how she had entered into his heart. How she dominated his life now. What did any plans he had made for the future amount to unless she shared them? Everything was changed. Today there was a new purpose in living. His future held something more than planting sugar-cane, tumbling wenches in the fields or in the soiled sheets of Josefina's beds. Now there was Margerita, *ay*, Margerita.

'When you finish, Juanito, run up to my room. On my table you will find some gold pieces. Take one, mind you only one, and go to the *mercado* and buy something for your Edita. Girls like little presents, lad.' He looked up, startled to see Juan turn away from him and point upwards.

'*Amo, mire!* There on the roof!' Juan shouted, still pointing.

Miguel's eyes followed the sweep of his arm. There on

the roof of Josefina's house, silhouetted against the strong light was the figure of a man. He was dressed in white. Miguel leaped up from the table and walked to the centre of the courtyard so he could see better. It was his cousin, Enrique. Miguel stared, shading his eyes with his hand but Enrique did not move or speak. Miguel could see hatred and contempt in his glance, even at that distance. Suddenly it seemed that the peace and quietude of the patio had been shattered. He had been enjoying the shade but now this new shadow had chilled him. What was it Julio had said to him? 'Better watch your step around Enrique ... he is not one to be trusted.' Miguel could sense the spirit of hate and distrust that had insinuated itself among the birds and flowers. Even the water in the fountain fell with a different cadence.

He watched Enrique turn slowly with an obscene gesture of his fingers and walk away from the edge of the roof, passing out of his sight. Miguel returned to his breakfast but found he was no longer hungry. He rang for Andreas. In a few moments the old man appeared, his black face smiling, his feeble hands trembling.

Miguel's voice was hoarse with anger. 'Our fine neighbour has quite forgotten the law of the *azotea*. Since when has it been the custom for whores and pimps from her house to wander over the roof and look down in our patio without our "*con permiso*"? Depraved as she is, she has no right to violate the law. It is one of the oldest in Havana. No one has the right to intrude on the privacy of another's home. As much as my grandmother detests the old bitch, she would first send a slave to ask Josefina's permission if it were necessary for one of our household to go on the roof.'

'That too has always been the custom of doña Josefina, don Miguel. If there is a loose tile on the roof or something needs to be repaired, she always asks permission which has always been granted. I have never known her to fail.'

'But just now there was a man on the roof, looking down into this patio. Had permission been granted?'

'No, none had been granted and none had been asked. I wonder who it was.'

'My precious cousin, Enrique. He had no right there any more than anyone else. He is a member of Josefina's household, not mine. Go to Josefina's. Tell her I shall have no more of this spying. The streets are big enough for Enrique's pandering. Tell her if this happens again, I'll take matters into my own hands. Now go!'

The old man started to shuffle away then turned and retraced his steps. 'I had almost forgotten, don Miguel. I seem to forget so easily these days. The señora wishes to see you in her *sala* as soon as possible.'

'But first I shall finish my breakfast,' Miguel jumped up as he saw the old man totter for an instant, then regain his balance. '*Que pase, viejito?* Are you sick? Come, sit down.'

Andreas remained standing, ignoring the chair that Miguel pushed behind him. 'No, don Miguel, I am not sick. Old age, I guess. I do not know how old I am, but I have been with your lady grandmother for sixty years.'

'And you would like your freedom. Well, you deserve it.'

'My freedom, don Miguel? Oh, no,' the tired old voice replied. 'I am too old for that. Many years ago I desired it when the memory of Africa was fresh in my mind; when my thoughts were always travelling back to the woman and the sons I had left behind. But I forgot them long ago. This is my life now. I do not want my freedom. But there is one thing that I might desire yet I hesitate to ask for it. I do not do my work as well as I should. There is no strength in my old hands and no power in my old head. I have trouble keeping the household accounts; I have difficulty in disciplining the household slaves. My poor legs do not carry me as well as they did and my old eyes are nearly blind. Someone should take over my work while I am yet here to teach him.'

'Of course, of course, Andreas. How stupid of me not to have thought of it before. You've always been here and we just took it for granted you always would be. The house could not run without you but you shall have help. How about Juanito here?'

'He is too young to discipline the others and he cannot read nor write. Besides his thoughts are in his pants not in his head. May I suggest you get someone from outside. Why not visit don Solano, the slave merchant? He always has likely men, sometimes even those who can read and write.'

'Don Solano's,' Miguel shuddered and spat. 'I hate that place. It makes my skin crawl just to step inside. Buying servants is the one thing I dislike. At least I've never sold one and I suppose any slave the Santiagos buy is lucky. I'll attend to it. And now my grandmother! Holy Saints! She's probably in a temper by now, waiting for me.' Miguel skipped up the stairs at the side of the patio. Without waiting for her to answer his knock, he opened the door and forestalled any chiding on her part by kissing her on the mouth. A quick movement of his hand sent her comb tumbling into her lap.

She pushed him away impatiently. 'Stop your foolishness, Miguel. You sleep till noon. You come up here dressed like a cane cutter. You were out all night. You are absolutely irresponsible and I love you, but now we become serious. I have matters to discuss that will make you angry but they must be discussed and don't you dare raise your voice to me.'

'My, my, my, how serious the little grandmother is! What now? Which of my black sins am I to be chastened for? What is so important?'

The señora rose and walked slowly to a nearby table. She picked up a pierced silver ball and applied it to her nose. The scent of the pomander seemed to give her courage. Wheeling about suddenly, she announced sharply, 'You are going to get married!'

His face turned pale under his tan. 'How did you know about that?'

'How did I know about that?' she mocked him. 'Because I am going to arrange it. That's how I know about it, my young cockerel. And I am going to arrange it soon. There'll be no repetition of last night.'

'Last night?' he asked in astonishment.

'Yes, last night. Don't think because I'm an old lady and so senile I have to spend all my time in the house I do not know what is going on in Havana. Already three old hens have been to call on me this morning, cackling for all they're worth about how some strumpet threw flowers to you at the theatre and how you fell all over yourself trying to catch them and then,' she pointed her finger at him, 'before all Havana you kissed one of those stupid flowers. Bah! And then you waited at the stage door like a love-sick puppy. And you drove her home. And as far as I know you bedded yourself with her because you didn't return here until morning. Enough's enough! You've already sowed enough wild oats to last you a lifetime. You are young and I expect you to have some sordid experiences but must you flaunt them before all Havana? It's high time you married. Mayhap it will settle you down a bit. A wife should be able to cool off that hot blood of yours.'

Miguel's voice had an edge of temper which he did not attempt to conceal. 'Your spies have kept you well informed. Now, whom do you suggest that I marry?'

'Whom? Whom? I don't care whom as long as she is a girl of good family with a substantial dowry. I suppose you can have any little goggle-eyed filly in Havana, but I've settled on one and I've made up my mind.'

'And who is the lucky girl?'

The moment that she delayed in answering him was long enough for him to die in.

'Inocencia Gonzalez!'

Had she struck him in the face he would not have been more startled.

'Are you stark, raving mad? That fat pig? I thought you said any girl of good family. Since when have you considered the Gonzalez family in that respect? Inocencia? I'd rather cut my throat.'

'You won't cut your throat, you love life too much and to answer your questions: I am not mad; I have seen her; I do know her family. I'll admit she's no beauty.'

'*Merda!* She's fat...'

'Like a mattress tied in the middle with a cord.'

'She's ugly...'

'With a face that would frighten the devil himself.'

'And she has a moustache.'

'*Merda* yourself! She can have a full beard for all I care; she can be wall-eyed and hare-lipped and bow-legged. But who cares? Least of all not I.'

'But you're not marrying her.'

'And neither are you. You're marrying the Gonzalez fortune which is the largest in Cuba. It's one of the largest in the world. It makes no difference how it was obtained – it's there.'

'But, Grandmother, I couldn't even bear to look at her.'

'Then don't. Just marry her that's all. Calm down and let's talk this matter over. The idea would never have entered my head if old Gonzalez himself had not sent his fawning lawyer to me. Seems he wants his grandsons to be Santiagos. A million pesetas for a dowry, a castle in Spain and a town house in Madrid. All yours, Miguel, for letting the Bishop mumble a few words over you. But, alas, I suppose you are thinking about love...'

Miguel picked up a fragile vase of Murano glass. Sea green and gold. How like Margerita it was! Fragile, cool and beautiful. He placed it carefully back on the table. 'Yesterday, Grandmother, I might have said *yes*. Today I cannot. I have discovered the meaning of the word love. I have never experienced it before. It is much grander and more wonderful than I had ever imagined.'

'But Miguel, youth always thinks of marriage as synonymous with love. After one has lived one's life one finds there never was such a thing as love. There is passion – that wonderful passion of youth and then there is companionship which comes when passion has burned itself out and, of course, there is habit which weaves a strong halter around us when companionship slackens. But love? Bah? Love, Miguelito, is a lie! It is something we hope exists but which never does.'

She walked to a small gilded cabinet at the end of the room and brought back a miniature set in a frame of gold and pearls. Her fingers caressed it lovingly as she placed it in Miguel's hand.

'Your grandfather. Look at him! He was handsome, strong and young. He was rich too. But do you think I loved him? Do you think he was the man of my choice. Do you think I wanted to marry him?'

The painted eyes in the picture looked back at Miguel. 'I suppose you did. I can't imagine you doing anything you didn't want to do.'

'You are wrong.' She took the picture from him, gazing down at it. 'I cried for weeks before I married him. You see I was in love or so I imagined. He was a young lieutenant and oh so handsome. Handsomer than your poor grandfather. *Dios mio*, but was he handsome? Such black curly hair, such white teeth, such red lips, and such a figure. Oh, I can assure you I was in love with him and he with me. But I didn't marry him. I married your grandfather and he cured my broken heart. Then years later in Spain I met my Prince Charming again. He was fat and he was bald and he was still a Lieutenant. Do you think for one moment that curly hair and handsome face could have ever made me as happy as I have been as the Señora de Santiago? Oh, there would have been a few months of what you call love and then I would have had to sit back and watch him grow fat and bald on a lieutenant's pay. As it was,' she leaned toward him, the picture in her hand, 'I learned to care for your grandfather very much. I worshipped him, adored him, idolized him.'

She fumbled for the bit of lace that was her handkerchief and wiped away a tear that was making a damp path through the rice powder on her face. 'Think me avaricious if you wish. Possibly I am. But I am an old lady and I know the power of money. Power and money, Miguel! We've got money, Miguel, and we've got power here in Havana. You'll be a rich man – a rich Cuban. But I want more than that for you. The Gonzalez fortune is not merely Cuban; it reaches into every country in Europe. There is nobody to inherit it but that misshapen lump of a girl. Her fortune, combined with yours will make you one of the wealthiest men in the world.'

'And will that make me happy? Is that all I need to live for? Money and Power?'

'Are you entirely stupid? Because you marry the Gonzalez fortune, you don't have to devote the rest of your life to the Gonzalez wench. You can have your pick of women. I never thought I'd be advising my grandson to take a mistress but I know you will anyway, regardless of whom you marry. All men do. Even your grandfather did and I didn't mind. Marry the Gonzalez and take the gypsy dancer for a mistress. I suppose she is the one you've fallen head-over-heels in love with.'

She rose from her chair, turned her back on him and walked to the window. The light, coming through the coloured glass panes above the jalousy, stained her white hair with its colours. Miguel followed her and put his arm around her shoulders.

'Dear little grandmother, you've spoken your piece and done your duty and I'm sure you don't mean a word of it. Must the next generation of Santiagos look like Inocencia Gonzalez?'

'They might look like you.'

'But if they didn't, you'd come back and haunt them.' He leaned down and kissed her. He saw that she was smiling, and he continued. 'I've got all the money I shall ever need, haven't I?'

She nodded her head.

'Then just one question. The name del Valle? Are you familiar with it?'

She thought for a moment. 'Of course. There are two families. The Salamanca one doesn't amount to much but the Toledo branch is the important one. That's the famous General del Valle, he whom Godoy was so jealous of that he managed to start a cabal against him, lied about the poor general, stripped him of all his honours and banished him from court. That Godoy is a devil even if Maria Louisa has made him Prince of the Peace. But why do you ask me about the del Valles?'

'Because Margerita del Valle is the girl I want to marry.'

'But I don't know her. Is she in Cuba?'

'Yes, in Cuba and I have asked her to marry me.'

'In the name of God when did you do that?'

'Last night.'

'But last night, so the gossips tell me, you were with that gypsy – that La Rosa or La Azucena or whatever her name is. La Clavelita, that's it. I knew it was some kind of a flower.'

'And, little grandmother, Margerita del Valle and La Clavelita are the same. She's the daughter of General del Valle. Now, don't say it. Don't condemn her. You've never refused me anything in my life. Bear with me now. Grant me this one favour. Meet her, talk with her and reserve your decision until then.'

She pushed him away from her but as she did, a quick move of his hands loosened the comb from her hair. It fell to the floor and the brittle tortoiseshell snapped. She stamped her foot angrily, took a step and trampled on the comb. Her heels ground it to pieces, beating a shrill tattoo on the tiles. Suddenly her fit of temper passed and she started to laugh.

'How do you do it, Miguel? I say to myself, "this time I will command and he shall obey." I will be the master. And then you manage to twist me around your little finger. Now get out before I lay down an ultimatum that you must marry the Gonzalez wench. I just might do it you know to show you that for once I can gain my end. But what you said about your children looking like Inocencia set me to thinking. Imagine a generation of Santiagos with pigs' snouts! But I'll keep old Gonzalez dangling for a while longer in case we change our mind. We won't close that door for any dancing trollop. I'll not have her in my house. There'll be no castanet clicking, heel pounding here. . . .'

'There you go. I asked you not to judge. . . .'

She waved him aside. 'This time I will have my own way. I've spoken and I mean it. No dancer!' She reached up and pulled his face down to hers, kissing him, 'but, of course, if the daughter of the illustrious General del Valle should wish to call on me, I should be honoured. Now out! And if you dare to come back without the most beautiful comb in all Havana, I'll marry you off to Josefina. That I will.'

By the time he reached the door they were both laughing.

Chapter Eight

MIGUEL HAD FOUND it easy to procrastinate in the matter of purchasing a slave to take the place of old Andreas. Buying slaves was a pastime he did not share with the other young bloods of Havana, half of whom hung around the slave sales and the slave market almost daily. It was a pleasure to finger the wenches, particularly the beautiful mulatto ones, and to have the strong bucks strip before them while they cupped their testicles in their hands and marvelled at the superior development of these black bucks from Africa. Whether they purchased a slave or not, it was quite the thing to do and Don Solano's, the principal slave market, was a fashionable gathering place, late in the afternoon when the siesta was over and there was nothing much to do until nightfall. But Miguel had never shared this enthusiasm for pawing over other human beings. Although he found it necessary from time to time to add to his slave stock for La Estrellita, he did it from necessity only and not for pleasure. The purchase of another human being seemed almost as degrading to himself as it did to that one purchased. His was one of the few voices in all Cuba that was raised against slavery. The plantation records had proved that it was uneconomical. He could quote statistics to show that hired labour was cheaper than slave labour but nobody would believe him. Slaves were the thing! Of course! Who ever heard of running a plantation without slaves?

But it was not so. La Estrellita supported some six hundred slaves the year around. During certain periods of the year, all six hundred were necessary in the fields and in the *central* but at other times of the year some two-thirds of them were idle but they had to be supported just the same. No, it was a wasteful practice but it was the custom. Who was he to go against the established custom of generations?

So, if he wanted a servant to take the place of old Andreas he would have to buy one and if he was to buy one, Solano's Mercado de San Martin was the place to go. Solano had the best slaves in all Cuba, not only field hands but *especialidades* – fancies, such as beautiful quadroon and octoroon girls, handsome young boys, extra virile young men or any particular speciality that some perverted taste would want. If Solano didn't have the particular *especialidad* on hand, he was sure to get it. One only had to leave an order with the exact specifications and sooner or later it would be filled. A house servant who could read, write and keep accounts was certainly a fancy. No matter how much he disliked it, Miguel went to Solano's Mercado de San Martin, but he chose to go early in the morning when the place would be empty of buyers.

The Mercado de San Martin was the end of a long journey. Its wares originated in the green jungles of Africa and came down the rivers in canoes to the coast; then the narrow hulls of the slavers' sleek black boats took up the burden and brought it across the Atlantic. After many days – days of heat and suffering, sickness and pain – they sailed between the beacons of Morro and La Punta. There they disgorged their cargo of black humanity on the red earth of Cuba – to make that earth redder by their blood and more productive by their toil. One more step remained – a short one this time – and the cargo of slaves, marching in single file to the monotonous clank of the heavy iron chain, made its tortuous way from the docks to the Mercado.

The market faced on a mean little street by the waterfront – a street which has been lost to memory for it disappeared many years ago and with it has gone even its name. The Mercado was a long bare building, one storey high in front with a crazy superstructure facing an alley in the rear. At one time, many years ago, it had received a coat of grey stucco but this had long since disintegrated, leaving a blistered, scabrous appearance, further heightened by the pockmarked coral rock of which it had been built. From it arose the evil stench of death and decay, the putrid odour of unwashed sweaty bodies and the sharp smell of burned and branded human flesh. Passing by one might hear cries and moans or occasionally a rich African voice, lifted in a mournful lament. Nor was it unusual to hear on occasion the staccato cries of pain, following the dull thud of the whip as its whirling tongue bit into flesh.

A double set of iron gates, effective and strong despite their sagging appearance, barred the entrance. The whole place appeared abandoned but when Miguel's *volanța* threaded the narrow street and stopped before the gates, a Negro porter in dirty white pantaloons appeared from inside to open them. Miguel entered and as he did an involuntary shudder passed over him as the gates closed behind him. Inside, in the semi-darkness of the passage way, he picked his way over the uneven flagging, slippery from the polish of countless bare feet, then out into the dazzling brilliance of the patio. Here, ranged round the four sides of the courtyard were iron cages – some empty, some filled with humanity varying in shades from nearly white to black – the shiny ebon black of Africa.

When he stepped into the patio, a loud murmur arose from the cages for experience had taught the hapless occupants that here was a prospective purchaser. Regardless of who he was or what he wanted them for, each longed for liberation from his present surroundings. Some had been there a long time; others only a few days. Until the cages were full, it was customary for Solano, the proprietor, to wait. The more slaves he could gather together for an auction, the larger the crowd he would attract. Each day that they remained with him, he was paid for their food and small as the amount might be, the actual victuals they received allowed him an agreeable profit.

Don Solano himself was seated in a corner of the patio, under a ragged strip of sailcloth, which made a pool of dark shadow in the brilliant whiteness of the sun. Don Solano was eating. Food had become more than a habit with him – it had grown to be an obsession, a fetish which he worshipped. A chair, especially built of heavy timbers, massive squared logs of mahogany, supported his colossal obesity. From its depths there mounted pile on pile of greasy white flesh, barely discernible as human until one caught the glint of small, red-rimmed eyes embedded in the thick lardy folds of a face. Every vestige of hair had long since disappeared from his head, leaving a dome of soiled ivory. Circles of dirty diamonds hung from his pendulous ears. Folds of dead-looking white flesh like suet protruded from rents in the linen of his shirt down the front of which a succession of drippings testified to the rich brown sauces and the rare red wines with which he surfeited himself.

Miguel advanced with a peculiar loathing and stood facing Solano across the table. Instead of rising to welcome him, Solano struggled to wave one grimy bejewelled paw towards the empty chair across from him. A reedy falsetto issued from the wet red lips. 'Indeed I am honoured, don Miguel, by your presence here. It is not often that The Santiago visits poor don Solano. For many years I have had the pleasure of serving your family, and well, eh?'

Miguel nodded curtly as Solano continued.

'But sit down, my dear boy, sit down. *Valgame dios*, but you grow handsomer every year! You are a true Cuban, don Miguel, not like those pasty faced Spaniards. Pardon me for not rising to greet you. It is such an effort, dear don Miguel, but do not let it rob my welcome of its warmth. I'm always happy to see you. May I offer you food, wine, some sort of refreshment? These shrimps,' he smacked his lips, 'cooked in white wine? They are delectable and this chicken stewed with a bit of *oregano* and tiny oysters is worth tasting. Can't I tempt you?' Saliva drooled down his chins as his fat fingers explored the gravy in a bowl, discovered a succulent bit of meat and transferred it to his mouth. He sucked his fingers clean, curling his tongue around a large ruby on one finger to lap the gravy that adhered to it.

Miguel backed away from the table, feeling the vomit rise in his throat but he swallowed fast. 'No thank you, don Solano, I have but just had my breakfast. I came on business. I want to buy a slave.'

'Ah, a slave,' the thin voice became unctious. 'Had you asked for a dozen slaves or fifty slaves, I would have known it was a matter of business. But just one slave, just one? Ah, that is different,' his voice became intimate in its caress. '*Solamenta una?* That is not business, don Miguel, that is pleasure. How well I know you young blades. No matter how many cherries you pluck on the outside it is always nice to have one waiting for you when you get home, *verdad*? Well, you've come to the right place. I have just what you want. Only fourteen years of age, as white as snow, and a virgin. Yes, don Miguel, a guaranteed virgin just waiting to be split open by a strong healthy young fellow like yourself. Virgins are scarce these days, don Miguel, and. . . .'

Miguel held up a warning finger. 'You take too much for granted, Solano. I did not say I was interested in a female slave. I have something far different in mind.'

'A lad, don Miguel? I didn't think you'd be interested but you've come to the right place.'

'Perhaps you'll allow me to finish, Solano. I am looking for a man, an educated man; one who is able to read and write and keep accounts. I need somebody to take the place of our major domo who is very old. It is a responsible position. The man will handle large sums of money and will be responsible for discipline among the other slaves. He will manage the Havana house. Therefore I want an exceptional slave. Perhaps you do not have such a man today and if not, I will leave an order with you.'

Solano was silent as he made a mental inventory of his stock. He seemed to be counting on his fat fingers. '*Ay de mi!* nothing is impossible with Solano. I have just the man for you. It is one of my services – always being able to supply every demand. But frankly, I hesitate to offer this slave even to The Santiago. I know you do not haggle over money but I warn you, he is expensive.'

'I do not haggle, señor, and yet I am not an idiot. I buy and expect to pay for value received but before we discuss price, tell me about this man or better still let me see him. If I am not interested, we need not even discuss prices.'

'Such a hurry, don Miguel,' Solano waggled an admonitory finger at him.

'I am always in a hurry when I come here,' Miguel replied. 'Frankly your place offends my nostrils and you,

Solano, offend me but I am forced to do business with you.'

Solano's lips curled at the insult but his voice still dripped honey. 'Of course I shall overlook your words, don Miguel. One is never insulted by a prospective client, even though one is prone to remember the insult. So, I shall tell you about the particular slave I have in mind. Despite your unwillingness to remain here overlong, I shall have to go back a few years to begin my story; some twenty years. You will not remember but at that time this island was honoured by a visit from the young Duke of Ramar. He came here to represent His Majesty.'

Miguel nodded impatiently. 'Go on, Solano. I cannot connect the duke's visit with my purchase of a slave but proceed.'

'In order to make the young duke, shall we say, more comfortable, the deAragons sent one of their young serving maids to wait on him while he was here. She was very beautiful, an octoroon with just enough coloured blood to make her ravishing. I recall her well for I sold her to young deAragon only a few weeks before the duke's visit. That she succeeded in pleasing the young duke was proven quite conclusively several months later by the birth of a child. The deAragons felt somewhat embarrassed at having a slave of ducal blood and as a young lad he was sold to the Etchegaray family who, knowing of his background, educated him thinking to use him as a tutor for future generations of grandchildren. When Señor Etchegaray died a few months ago, all of his slaves were brought here and Antonio, for that is his name, remains with me. No one has yet appeared who is willing to pay the asking price for him. But for you, don Miguel, I consider him a rare find.'

'An interesting history. Possibly he would meet my requirements. May I see him?'

Solano reached across the stained cloth, upsetting a decanter of wine as he did so and forced his huge hand to clutch at a small silver bell. It tinkled throughout the patio, bringing the gatekeeper.

'Babu, conduct don Miguel to the upper floor. He wishes to see the slave Antonio. Don Miguel, if you will follow

Babu and forgive me for not accompanying you myself, he will take you to see the man.'

The black beckoned Miguel to follow him. They crossed the patio, picking their way over the accumulation of filth which encrusted it; the excrement of fowls, various odds and ends of offal and the bleached and broken bones of furniture. Finally they came to a flight of rickety steps which led to the jerrybuilt second storey in the rear. When they reached the second floor, Miguel could see that conditions here were somewhat better. The cells although narrow and cramped were each ventilated by a single barred window. There was some attempt by the occupants to keep them clean. Even here, however, despite the fresh air, the slave odour persisted. Miguel followed Babu down a narrow corridor to a cell at the corner. Inside were two young men, sleeping on the single narrow cot that the cell possessed. The cries of entreaty and the voluble pleadings for purchase that had followed Miguel down the hall had not awakened the two. They were sleeping soundly.

Babu unlocked the heavy iron grille and entered the cell. With a light flick of his whip which was always with him, he roused the sleepers. They stared up at him with sullen eyes and then, noticing Miguel in the background they disengaged their arms and legs and arose sleepily to stand by the side of the cot.

'Which one of you is Antonio?' Miguel felt embarrassed, as though he had intruded on a bedroom intimacy which he should not have seen.

The elder advanced a step. 'I am he, señor, and this, my companion in misery, is Fidel.'

This Antonio was a tall fellow. The only garment he possessed was a pair of soiled white pantaloons, one leg of which was ripped off at the knee. The whiteness of his skin was brought into contrast by the dingy grey of the trousers. Long waves of black hair swept down over his shoulders which were broad and well muscled. His chest was a mat of curling black hair which proved the extreme dilution of his coloured blood. The features of the face were finely cut, even classical with only the slightest thickening of lips to hint that somewhere in his background there might have been an African ancestor. Blue eyes looked directly at Miguel. Had Miguel ever seen the Duke of Ramar, he would have been struck by the resemblance between father and son.

He glanced from Antonio to the other whom he had called Fidel who was younger, smaller and adolescent. He was more negroid as to lips and nostrils, but of a strange honey colour, which seemed to be the same as his crinkly blond hair and the tawny gold of his eyes. Again Miguel felt the same wave of embarrassment or, was it pity? What crime had these two youths committed that they should be imprisoned here in the filth of Solano's barracoons? What did they possess besides a few drops of Negro blood that made them different from himself? Why should he be able to walk the streets at will, live in comfort, sleep in his own bed at night, when these two youths, both well formed and handsome and apparently intelligent, were condemned to be bought and sold as cattle, to have no will, no life of their own? Always before, he had felt a certain repugnance about buying a slave, but on former occasions he had been interested only in field hands whose worth was ascertained by their muscles and not their intelligence. That was bad enough, but now! He could not get over the fact that he, himself, was standing in Antonio's place . . . for sale. To reassure himself, he stared at Antonio whose eyes met his. There was an utter hopelessness in them. He glanced at the boy called Fidel but Fidel was looking only at Antonio.

Miguel turned angrily to Babu. Anger, he felt, might save him from sympathizing with the other two. 'Go back to your master! Leave the door unlocked. I'll be responsible.'

'But these men! There are two of them. They might overpower you and try to escape.'

'Don't be ridiculous. How could they? Now, back to your master. Tell don Solano I'll return presently.' He waited for the slave's footsteps to recede and heard him descend the stairs. Seating himself on the edge of the cot which was surprisingly clean, he looked up at Antonio and Fidel.

'We are lacking a major domo at our house in Havana.

The position requires education, tact and diplomacy. I understand that you, Antonio, have some learning. You read and write?'

'Si, señor. May I ask a question?'

Miguel nodded assent.

'Would that be the casa de Santiago. I recognize you as Miguel de Santiago.'

Again Miguel nodded. 'Your *pantalones* don't conceal much, but take them off. I just want to be sure you haven't got the French pox. I wouldn't want that spreading through the house.'

Antonio unbuttoned the single button that held up his trousers and dropped them. Miguel allowed only a cursory glance as Antonio demonstrated his freedom from disease but the thought ran through Miguel's mind that there must be a preponderance of white blood in the fellow. The enormity of Negro genitalia was lacking in him; in fact, for such a big fellow he was rather puny. But Miguel was not buying him for breeding purposes and it made little difference. He wondered, however, if he were in Antonio's place what the remarks of a prospective buyer would be. With his own capabilities, he'd probably be put out at stud.

'You're clean,' he said to Antonio. 'And now for another question. Would you like to come with me? I'd prefer that you wanted to come. A servant who comes against his will is sullen and hard to manage. You'll be taking the place of an old man who has been with us many years. I would hope that in time you would be as devoted to the Santiagos as he is. Speak up, man, I give you permission to state your mind.'

Antonio hesitated in his answer. He looked at Fidel and the conflict in his mind showed in his eyes. Fidel started to speak but Antonio silenced him. 'I have a desire to serve you, don Miguel. I have an even greater desire to leave this prison. I have been here for over three months. Here I have sat through my days and here I have tried to sleep at night. Then, two months ago Fidel was brought here. Since his coming I have been able to forget my own misery in trying to watch over him. Solano has a little minion, more girl than boy, by the name of Pajarito. He's had his eyes on Fidel to replace Pajarito but so far I've been able to prevent it. Watching over Fidel has made life a little happier for me but now it makes it more difficult. I know that if you purchase me I shall have to go. I have no voice in the matter. I am not like you,' he added bitterly.

'Yet the Casa de Santiago would be far more comfortable than here.'

'That I know and I know the fine reputation your family has for its treatment of slaves. But, don Miguel, you asked me if I wanted to go with you and you gave me permission to speak. I cannot dissemble. My answer is that I do not want to go with you and leave this boy here,' he pointed to Fidel, 'to the unspeakable obscenities of that monster below. If it could be arranged for him to go with me, then yes, I would be happy to serve you faithfully and well but if I go alone, my thoughts will be back here with him.'

There was a degree of pride in the fellow's voice and a ring of sincerity that Miguel admired. He didn't speak like a slave and he had stood up to Solano, although how he had been able to do that Miguel could not fathom. He liked the fellow.

'While you were talking,' Miguel smiled for the first time since he had entered the room, 'I almost forgot that I came here to purchase you as I would a horse. You speak like a man, Antonio, not a fawning slave. I like you for it, but you, boy,' he turned to Fidel, 'have you anything to say?'

Fidel threw himself at Miguel's feet. He was crying and his words choked on his sobs. 'Señor, señor, do not separate Tonio and me. He's all I've got. If he leaves I'll have to share Solano's bed and I'll kill myself before that. I know I cost money but buy me and I'll repay you by working hard. Yes, I will, señor. I'll work day and night if I can be bought with Antonio.'

Antonio lifted Fidel from the floor. 'Stand up. Stop acting. Don Miguel has said that I spoke like a man, therefore let him think of you as a man and not a snivelling boy. I am a slave and so are you. We have no right to think – after all, we are animals and animals cannot think. If you have to sleep with that fat *maricon* below, do it. You have no choice in the matter.' He pulled up his ragged *pantalones* and buttoned them. 'I am ready, señor. If you wish to purchase me I shall be happy to serve you. Your giving me permission to speak was a mistake, señor. Never allow a slave to think. It is dangerous because, for a moment, I almost felt like a man.'

Miguel stood up and walked the length of the narrow cell to stare through the barred window. He had made up his mind that he would buy Antonio. It would be hard to find another slave to fill the requirements. The room was hot and his face was sweaty. He removed his hat and wiped his forehead with a lace-bordered handkerchief. In returning it to his pocket, he dropped it. Fidel retrieved it and handed it to him. The fluttering of the handkerchief showed how the boy's hand was trembling.

'Are you buying Antonio?' he asked.

Miguel nodded, not daring to look at the boy.

'You would have no place for me?'

The harshness of his voice was merely to cloak his emotions.

'Damn it all, boy, I've been trying to think of a place where I could use you. There's no place at the Havana house or at the *finca* where you'd fit in. We're overrun with house servants now. But I'll tell you what I'll do. I'll speak to my friends about you and no doubt, on my recommendation, one of them will have a place for you.'

Fidel threw himself face down on the narrow cot, burying his face in the thin mattress. At a sign from Miguel, Antonio walked over to the boy. He sat down on the cot and placed his hand on Fidel's shoulder, stroking the honey coloured flesh. '*Pobrecito*, it's finally come. We've been dreading it and it's here. I go and you stay. We may never see each other again but I shall never forget you and I hope you get a kind and decent master. What more can I say? We've anticipated this a thousand times and we knew it was coming. We've already said all the words that can be said. Now, no words can tell you how I feel. You know what is in my heart, Fidel, so it's *adios*.'

Miguel led the way out of the room. Antonio turned back as Miguel closed the grating but Fidel's face was still buried in the mattress. Slowly they descended the stairs to the patio below. Solano's bulk was still seated under the ragged awning but he was no longer alone. A willow-slim adolescent with the face of a ravaged virgin and long hair that reached to his elbows was standing beside Solano's chair. He was dressed in one of Solano's discarded shirts which hung around him like a tent but reached only to his thighs. Solano removed his hand from under the boy's garment when he saw Miguel approaching and wiped it on the boy's ragged shirtail.

'Ah, don Miguel! I see you have made up your mind.'

'How much are you asking for this man?'

Solano indicated by a wave of his hand that he wanted the boy to pour him a glass of wine. He watched the topaz liquid fill the glass, lifted it and sipped. Only then did he answer.

'Still in a hurry, don Miguel? Still anxious to quit yourself of Solano's hospitality?'

'As much as before.'

'But you wish to make a purchase.'

'Yes.'

'Quite an important purchase,' he handed the glass to the boy who drained the few drops left in it. 'And when one makes important purchases, don Miguel, one expects to pay for them.'

'Only what they are worth. Come, what is the price?'

Solano's voice lost its cloying sweetness and his words were sharp and decisive. 'I prefer to do business like a gentleman, don Miguel, over a glass of wine and with a certain amount of leisure. You may have forgotten it, but I happen to be as much of a *caballero* as yourself.' His eyes burned deep within the folds of flesh. 'But I shall overlook your insults. One is supposed to overlook the actions of The Santiago as one would the King of Spain himself. But since you wish to treat me as nothing more than a tradesman, we'll talk business. Three thousand pesos for this man. Take it or leave it.'

'I suppose the amount is double because I refused to drink a glass of wine with you.'

'No, that is my asking price.'

'Ridiculous.'

'Ridiculous? Bah! Josefina would pay that much. This Antonio is handsome enough to be an assistant to your pimping cousin Enrique. Think of the veiled ladies who'd come to Josefina's for Antonio's services. Look at him! He's not hung very heavy but what does that matter with his profile. Besides, all of Josefina's customers don't demand stallions. If Josefina buys him that poor hard-working cousin of yours will have a little time to rest.'

'Leave my cousin out of this. Sell him to Josefina! Why hasn't she bought him before if he's such a bargain? Two thousand pesos and that's my offer. Do you accept?'

Solano saw that Miguel was in no mood for the usual bargaining that the slave dealer enjoyed. 'But, don Miguel, it would leave me no profit. I'm a businessman, I've got to make something on him.'

Miguel laughed. 'A moment ago you were a gentleman, now you're a slave trader. Make up your mind. You have my offer. Think about it. Call your gatekeeper and have him let me out of here.' He started to walk across the courtyard, delaying his steps a bit, feeling certain that the last word had not been spoken but he reached the passageway to the gates before Solano called.

'Wait, don Miguel. *Un momento!* Do me the favour of returning. I'll consider the matter. Yes, I will.'

Miguel turned and his eyes locked with those of Antonio's. Was it misery or pleasure he saw there? He could not tell which. Was Antonio sorry not to go or happy to return to his Fidel? He crossed the patio. 'You have my offer. Two thousand pesos?'

Solano picked up the tail of the lad's shirt and wiped his mouth. 'Very well, two thousand pesos but I tell you, don Miguel, I'm not making a penny on the deal. In fact, I'm....'

'Enough, Solano,' Miguel cried. He called to Babu, 'Bring pen and ink.'

The man rushed up with a battered quill and inkwell. Miguel scratched a few words on a piece of paper and handed it to Solano. 'Here is an order on my bankers, the Castaneros, for the amount. And now, Solano, I hope this ends our business dealings for ever. Rather than buy any more slaves from you, I'll hire free men to work on the *finca*. Something has happened to me within the last hour – a firm conviction that I shall never buy another slave. Come, Antonio.'

They started for the door together.

As they reached the centre of the patio, Solano called softly to Miguel. 'One word, *por favor*, don Miguel.'

Miguel stopped and turned.

Solano's lips curled in a sneer. 'Now that the papers are signed and that bastard is your property, let me tell you something, you high and mighty little cockerel. Nobody gets the best of Solano in a slave deal. Nobody! Not even The Santiago! Not by a damn sight! Two thousand pesos! Bah! I would have sold the bastard for a thousand. I came near having him flogged to death and I swear that had he remained another week I'd have killed him. He defied me – me, Solano. Just because I wanted that puling little *mulatto* to serve me. And what did this bastard do? He told me that rather than have that snivelling Fidel leave him, he would strangle the lad. And he'd have done it too. So I've had to deny myself of the boy and I'm sick to death of this little *maricon*, this Pajarito. But now ...' He shifted his ponderous weight and called, 'Babu, where are you?'

The slave appeared from behind one of the pillars.

'Go to the second floor and bring that yellow-headed bastard down – that Fidel. I want to show this Antonio something and his new master too.'

Antonio made a move as if to start towards Solano but Miguel restrained him. The fellow's hands were clenched tightly. He bit his lips so that a tiny stream of blood ran down his chin.

'Quiet, Antonio,' Miguel whispered.

'But Fidel?'

'Hush!'

Miguel walked slowly back towards the table. He stood facing Solano and with a quick movement he drew his sword and placed it against the slave merchant's chest. It pricked the lardlike skin and a blotch of blood stained the dirty linen. 'Don't move, Solano,' he commanded. 'If you have a heart, I would judge it to be located somewhere near the point of my sword and if you as much as speak, I'll run you through. If you want to live, listen to me. No filthy *maricon* of a slave dealer ever got the best of me. So, you think you got the best of the bargain? So, you overcharged me a thousand pesos for Antonio? Oh no, you didn't. I've just paid two thousand pesos for *two* slaves. Take up that quill and write, Solano! A bill of sale for the slave Antonio and the slave Fidel. Write it out and receipt it as paid in full. Write, you son of a whore, write!'

With the sharp steel pinking him, Solano pawed with shaking hands for the quill and scratched the words on a piece of paper. Miguel reached for it and read it, slipping it into his pocket. He gave the sword a tiny jab and the spot of blood widened on Solano's shirt. When he withdrew the blade, Solano slumped forward on the table. He gasped for wine and the frightened Pajarito poured a glass from the decanter and held it to his lips. Antonio and Miguel ran for the stairs, Antonio two steps ahead of Miguel.

'Hurry, don Miguel, the door has not been locked yet.'

They pushed open the grating. Fidel was still face down on the cot. His sobbing had quieted and his breath was coming in hysterical gasps. He did not look up as the door opened. Antonio rushed into the cell. 'Fidel,' he cried, 'Fidel it is Antonio. I have come back.'

Fidel sat up, rubbing his eyes.

'Tonio? Back? But why?'

'To get you. Don Miguel has bought you too. You are going with us.'

'You mean....?'

'Our prayers have been answered. We have the best master in all Cuba and we'll be together, *tu y yo como siempre*.'

Fidel looked up, first at Antonio and then at Miguel. He

rubbed his eyes, reddened from his tears. 'Is it true? *Verdad?*'

'Yes, it's true,' Miguel answered stepping into the room. 'Come, let's get to hell out of here. This room oppresses me. I never want to see it again. Hurry.'

They ran down the stairs. Solano still sat at the table with Pajarita holding a glass of wine and Babu fanning him. Babu dropped the fan and ran to open the outside gates. He was grinning and slapped Antonio on the back as they passed out to where Miguel's *volanta* was waiting.

'You both stink like goats,' Miguel said, 'but you, Fidel, climb up beside the coachman, and you, Antonio, sit behind with me. I can't have you running almost bare-assed naked through the streets of Havana. Let's get home *con prisa! Rapidamente!*'

Chapter Nine

LIFE AT THE Casa Josefina did not start officially until late afternoon. The mornings were quiet with little or no break in the drowsy monotony except perhaps the stealthy departure of a client who had remained all night. There was a sense of disillusion which was heightened by the strong morning sun and a guilty conscience did not always make the excesses of the night before seem pleasant in retrospect. Many a man made excellent resolutions as he quitted Josefina's in the glare of the day – resolutions only to be broken again under the spell of the moon.

Amistad, the old Negress, was always the first in the house to arise. She had become so accustomed to noctural revels that nothing disturbed her rest. Actually she was the only person in the whole establishment who led a blameless life and that she did so now was solely because of her age. All the rest, even the maids and the mulatto houseboys, yes, even the coachman, were pressed into duty at times. Josefina boasted that she could supply any desire, no matter how perverted, that her customers requested, and she was always prepared. Josefina was a woman of business.

One of the first sounds in the morning would be the

shuffling of Amistad's bare feet on the tiles as she gathered up bundles of soiled linen and vigorously soaped them in a corner of the patio. This done, she would scrub the tiles of the gallery floors and occasionally wander into the *salas* at the front of the house to dust their gaudy gimcracks. As the morning stretched into noon and she made certain that there were no longer any paying patrons in the house, she was wont to stand in the middle of the patio and pound lustily on a copper pan, shouting in her guttural African voice to awake the girls. One by one the doors around the gallery would open.

The girls would come out, drowsy from their short sleep, their hair hastily pinned back, the make-up of the night before streaked and uneven, their feet thrust into comfortably run-down slippers. They would clutch their soiled wrappers around their tired flesh and lean over the gallery railing reviling Amistad for rousing them and for her delay in bringing their coffee. As they managed to unglue their eyelids, they would call back and forth to each other across the patio and as they became more awake, they would display a morbid curiosity in each other's experiences of the night before. It was a time of boasting and bantering; a time of flattering and reviling; an opportunity to release their pent-up emotions.

'*Ay*, Chiquita,' one full-blown beauty would shout across the courtyard, 'you were busy last night. How many did I count? Fourteen?'

'Eighteen, you missed four, busybody. How did you have time to keep track of me? Didn't anyone ask for you? *Ay*, you're getting old Elvira.'

'And you, Negrita, I saw you had Christobal last night. You're a lucky girl. What a man he is! *Que grande! Que macho!* I spent one night with him and I swear I had no desire to get up the next day.'

'It's the only night you'll ever spend with him.'

'You dirty bitch. He's mine, I had him first.'

'Then why didn't he ask for you last night. I'll tell you why. He said you were like a log of wood. Watch your step. Men like fire in a woman. That's why they like me.'

'Slut!'

'Last night I had that gypsy that dances with La Clavelita.'

'What's he coming here for? Can't he get it from her?'

'He says she's a virgin.'

'A virgin? Ho! A dancer a virgin? If she is, then so's an alley cat.'

'That's what he said. I asked him.'

'She uses her legs for dancing but she makes her money between them; all dancers do.'

'Who had that bastard Villanova last night?'

'I did. Look!' One of the girls let her robe fall to the waist to display the red welts on her back. 'But I gave it right back to him. That's what he wants.'

'And you, Carlotta ... and Mimi ... and Olga....?'

So it went, the bragging banter of whores who love to discuss their business more than members of any other profession. Hard rolls were soaked in cups of coffee and the bantering conversation went on. It was their time for relaxation; the only time of day when they could be natural. Gone were the airy gentilities, the studied affectations and the forced air of romance with which they surrounded themselves in the evening. Now they could afford to be the bawds they really were. They discussed all their experiences in the most intimate and lurid details. They compared the physical merits of their companions of the night before minutely. In truth, they enjoyed their work and talking shop was not only natural but the only thing they had to talk about. Usually in the midst of the conversation, Josefina would appear, fresh from her trip to the market or the bank. Then one by one, the girls would desert the galleries and go back to clean their rooms and start their elaborate toilettes.

Josefina was an arresting personality; a powerful woman probably later in her fifties than the artistry of her *maquillage* would lead one to believe. She had a strong, broad, red face, above which rose a mass of hair, dyed a metallic black and piled in tight, steely curls. Her bulging figure was always stiffly corseted, the heavy stays showing through the rich black silk of her gown. Josefina possessed none of the airs and graces of her girls. She was a woman of business and she ruled her little world with an iron hand. She never indulged in sentiment.

The prosperity of her establishment attested to her excellent management. Charming as she was to her clients – especially the wealthy ones – she was unrelenting and without mercy where her household was concerned. Her finger was in the tiniest detail. She was everywhere at once with a knowledge of everything that was happening. She was as quick to detect a torn bit of lace or an unwashed neck as she was to complain about too much pepper in the *ensalada*. Let one of her customers complain about a girl – some unwillingness on the girl's part or a disinclination to do something demanded – and the luckless girl would feel the whole weight of Josefina's hand against her cheek.

She never unbent. She had no intimates among the girls and played no favourites. Yet, she treated them fairly, gave them the best of food to eat and a percentage of their earnings – a small one to be sure – but an honest one. She governed them with an impersonal impartiality. As soon as their usefulness to her was over, they departed, starting on their always downward path to smaller, less pretentious houses. If, however, as sometimes happened, they prevailed upon some man to set them up in an establishment of their own, Josefina never demurred against their leaving but was always the first to wish them good fortune. Josefina did not fear competition. She was secure; hers was the best and the biggest establishment of its kind in Havana. It was the first place distinguished visitors wished to see and they were never disappointed.

But, like most dictators, there was a tiny chink in her armour: Enrique de Santiago. She had raised him from the time his father had died, drunkenly gasping his last on one of her beds; from the time his mother had disappeared, the transient love of some Spanish soldier. When he had grown older, her business acumen, always to the fore, caused her to recognize in the perfection of his physique and the beauty of his features, a distinct and most unusual asset to her establishment. As a young lad, he had been greatly in demand by certain of her male clients. After he was eighteen, he started pimping for her on the streets in addition to becoming a star attraction of the house itself.

So Enrique had made his home at Josefina's. Although his coming of age had presented a new angle to her business, the very novelty of it had made it a most successful one. She had advertised his availability – most subtly of course, among those young wives of decrepit Spanish dons; or those languishing females whose husbands were in Spain or Mexico, or better still, those who had never had any husbands and were anxious to know what the word meant. News of Enrique de Santiago – 'the cousin of The Santiago, my dear, and as handsome as all get-out' – his vigour and his peculiar talents had crept in the back doors of *palacios*, been carried up the back stairs and whispered to frustrated and petulant señoras by their maids. 'Such an excellent cure for the vapors, señora, and it can all be handled most discreetly.' Soon hired carriages began to arrive at the back door of Josefina's house, which led directly from the narrow alley into Enrique's room. Heavily veiled ladies hastily alighted, knocked at the door and peered up and down the alley to see if they were being observed. Then the door would open and they would slip inside. Enrique was a busy man; he had learned his trade well. He had learned how to breathe heavily, to pant, to utter strangulated cries and put on a wonderful performance without expending himself. Of course he had to in his public exhibitions; there was no faking those, but in private he quite satisfied ten clients a day without draining himself. Josefina charged ten times as much for his services as she did for her girls. He was her biggest profit maker.

Unwilling to admit, even to herself, that she was starved for affection, Josefina grudgingly bestowed on Enrique the things she would like to have given him openly. It was Enrique for whom the choicest cuts of meat, the most succulent oysters, the finest wines were purchased. His clothes were new and of good materials. He was permitted to sleep long after the rest of the household had awakened and woe betide the luckless girl who disturbed him. These indulgences Josefina excused to herself as being merely good business: to feed him well, dress him decently, and let him recuperate as much as possible in sleep. For him the rigid discipline that ruled the girls was missing. The front gates opened both ways at his demand. Josefina had even decided in her own mind that when she was no longer on earth to manage it, the Casa Josefina would be her legacy to him. He was the son she had never had; the male stallion she had always wanted; and the little boy she ached to pillow on her capacious bosom.

The sleepy morning would pass, luncheon would be served, and then the shadows would start to lengthen in the patio. Occasionally visitors came during the siesta hours, stealing an hour from their businesses or their complaining wives, to sidle up to Josefina's door; brave men to wait there in the broad publicity of the sunny street for an answer to the bell. The afternoon trade was desultory; it was in the evening that Josefina's house came to life. Then business really began.

The huge reception rooms, carefully shuttered from the street, would then be ablaze with wax candles which sprouted from crystal chandeliers, their flames reflected in the gilt-framed mirrors which lined the walls. These mirrors gave a regal touch to the room unless one examined them closely and found that the silver was peeling from their backs. Josefina had bought well at bankrupt sales and auctions: cheap rugs covered mellow old Spanish tiles; a Goya portrait nudged a fly-blown nude in a brassy frame. The rooms reeked of sandlewood, patchouli, musk and the cloying heavy scent of fresh tuberoses. The girls wore their most brilliant toilettes. They were sumptuously gowned for Josefina – as many a lady's maid was well aware – was always in the market for worn ball gowns.

There was always a blaze of jewels at Josefina's and if the diamonds, rubies and emeralds were only bits of glass, they shone bravely in the candlelight. Evenings at Josefina's were an ambassador's ball in opera bouffe; a court reception by the king of Spain; an opening night at the opera. It was all tinsel and dross. Nothing was real but the burning lust in the eyes of the men and the calculating gleam in Josefina's eyes. Here the clink of gold could buy anything a man might desire – a glabrous boy whose cheeks had never felt a razor; a girl who had never lain with a man before; a Negro stallion; a woman trained in rare perversities. Expensive? Yes, but what was money compared with the gratification of one's secret desires?

It was a hot night. Even a late afternoon shower had failed to cool the air and the heavily shuttered windows allowed no breeze to enter. There had been dancing and the girls stood talking with their partners in the middle of the floor as Josefina pushed her way through the press to where Enrique was standing alone by the buffet. He was pouring a glass of wine from the decanter.

'I can't compliment you on your sherry, *Viejita*,' he smiled at her.

'A bottle of fine Amontillado awaits you in your room. Why should I waste good wine on these pigs? If they want good wine, they can pay for it.' She came closer and whispered, 'Besides the Amontillado there is something else in your room.'

'*Valgame dios*, not the Señora Guttierez again?'

'And what's the matter with the señora? She's filthy with money.'

'Not only money, *Viejita*,' he wrinkled his nose.

She made a gesture of impatience. 'Follow me,' she urged, 'it's not the señora,' she stepped even closer and whispered in his ear, 'it's Inocencia.'

'What, again?' he curled his lips.

'Yes, again, and why not?'

'There's a limit to my ability to act. Have you any idea how difficult it is to profess undying love to that face. Have you any conception of what it is to pretend a fiery passion for that fat body, that bristly face, those stumpy legs? I heave and pant and thrust and sometimes I think I shall vomit in her face.'

'But if her fortune were not the largest in Cuba it would be even more difficult, wouldn't it?'

'Ah, without the fortune, I could not even get it up for her. As it is, I think of all those golden *reals* and it stands at attention. How she loves it. She's even named it. She calls is "Cabo Pronto" – Corporal Pronto – but I insist he should be made a general. Corporal doesn't befit his rank.'

'Be serious, Enrique,' she pleaded. 'This is your chance. It's the greatest chance you ever had or ever will have. She's not coming here night after night without a good reason.'

'Corporal Pronto,' he grinned, 'he's the reason, *Viejita.*'

'And what better reason could a woman have? Play your cards well, my boy, and you'll have your hands on the Gonzalez fortune thanks to Corporal Pronto. The old man is dying. He's been dying for months and then she'll marry you. After all, you've got the Santiago name. Play your cards right. Marry Inocencia and to hell with her fat hips and bristly face. You'll be more powerful than your fine cousin. You'll be The Santiago then. Marry her and when you do, don't forget Josefina, eh?'

'*Vamos, Viejita!* Corporal Pronto's already standing at attention. The Santiago, huh? He's ready and willing to work for that, aren't you, lad?'

She started to laugh with him as she pushed him across the crowded room. Josefina's set smile greeted everyone alike; Enrique stalking beside her, saw nobody. Money and power and the Gonzalez fortune almost in his hand. The old man dying. The daughter bound to him by iron chains of desire. Corporal Pronto to the rescue. He would be The Santiago. How he would lord it over that whelp of a cousin. Just as soon as old Gonzalez died. Let the old bastard die tonight.

They came out into the dimly lit patio, walked past all the eloquently closed doors and stopped at a door in the far corner of the patio. Josefina knocked softly and the door opened. A heavy figure, entirely swathed in grey veils rose to meet them.

'A guest for you, don Enrique,' Josefina ushered him into the room, then turning to the woman, said, 'Don Enrique is honoured by your visit. I regret I cannot address you by name but no names are ever mentioned here.'

The woman advanced toward Josefina with clumsy, heavy steps and without speaking or raising her heavy veil, handed her a small purse. Josefina took it, listened to the pleasant clink it made as it touched her hand and left the room.

'Is it you, Inocencia?' Enrique whispered.

'Yes,' she answered. 'Quickly, *mi querido*, bolt the door and blow out the candle. No, wait a moment. I must look at you. I am hungry for the sight of you. It seems ages ago that I was here yet it was only last night. Just one moment, my heart, one moment,' she laid her hand on his arm as he took up the candlestick, 'stand still so that I may see the light on your face. You are so handsome, Enrique, so much a man. Ah, you have on the new blue suit that I ordered for you. How well it suits you with your pale complexion. Now, bolt the door and blow out the candle. Tell me, do you like the suit?'

'I have it on, Inocencia,' he puffed at the candle and the room was in darkness except the pale square of the window which led onto the back alley.

'Did you find the purse in the pocket?'

'Yes, *muchas gracias.*' He reached for her hand in the darkness and lifted it to his lips.

'Not now, Enrique. No matter how important it is to me, there is something more important. Something dreadful has happened.'

'What is it,' he was anxious now. 'Has your coming here been discovered?'

'Far worse than that.'

'Then out with it. Take off those damn veils; it's hot in here. Sit down and let's be comfortable. Without the light I can open the shutters and it will be cooler. I can even open the door onto the street.' He got up and walked across the room and flung open the door. At least with the door open he would not be forced to make love to her. 'Now, Inocencia, tell me all about it.'

'It's this,' she said, groping for his hand in the darkness, 'my father is dying.'

'And that distresses you? You've been waiting for the old bastard to die – praying for it.'

'Yes, I've lighted candles to every saint in the cathedral. I've always hated him but since I've known you I've hated him even more. I always felt that when he died there might be some future for us.'

'Meaning what?'

'Meaning that after his death, there would be no one to tell me what to do and I would be free to marry you.'

'You would marry me, Inocencia?'

'Gladly, and why not? If I've paid for your love here in Josefina's house, I'll gladly pay for it further. But I believe you love me a little,' her voice was soft and pleading but it changed to a stronger note as she added, 'I could make the name of Enrique de Santiago much honoured in Havana.'

He sighed, catching his voice in his throat as though overcome by emotion. 'How can you doubt I love you, Inocencia.' It really sounded sincere the way he said it. 'How can such a feeling as I have for you be feigned? If I didn't love you, would Corporal Pronto be standing at attention? See!' He guided her hand in the darkness. 'That proves it doesn't it. If you were not such an innocent one, you would know that that is something a man cannot feign. Corporal Pronto doesn't stand at attention for everyone, *querida mia*. Sometimes the rogue has to be coaxed and coaxed. Now,' he stretched his legs out straight before him, 'don't you realize how sincerely I am in love with you?'

'Perhaps I do not dare to doubt you. The Gonzalez fortune is large and the Gonzalez heiress is by no means a beauty. No, Enrique, do not protest. My mirror does not lie. But I want you. I'll take you under any circumstances, even to coming to a place like this to have you.'

He groaned just enough to make the result of her ministrations effective and then removed her hand. 'But there is another proof, *querida*. The first time you came here, even the second or the third, I did not know your name so it was not the Gonzalez fortune that made Corporal Pronto perform the way he did.' His voice was reassuring.

She stood up and went to the window. He did not follow

her as she had hoped so she went back to his side. 'That was a pretty speech my love and I shall do my best to believe it. But Josefina knows everything and she could have told you who I was. But enough! These matters can be discussed some other time. The important thing is that I want you and you say you want me. Don't underrate my intelligence, Enrique. I am not stupid. My father's fortune is large. I have little to offer you except that. Now listen! I have reason to believe that we shall both be losers, Enrique.'

'*Dios mio*, what has happened?' He stood up from the bed and looked down at her.

'Just this. My father thinks that money is not enough. He wants to add to his prestige. We lack a name. What is the name of Gonzalez? Any tradesman can have that name. No, he wants to know that his grandsons will be Santiagos.'

'And so they will if you marry me. Tell him so.'

'Tell him that I want to marry Enrique de Santiago, the stud at Josefina's? Tell him that? You know what he would say. No, it's your cousin Miguel. Even now he is negotiating with that old witch, your grandmother. It seems that both she and Miguel are interested in the proposition.'

'Good God, Miguel?' Enrique gasped.

'Yes and how I have always hated him. Ever since he refused to dance with me once when we were children. It was his turn to dance with me at dancing class and he left me standing in the middle of the floor while he shouted, 'I won't dance with the fat pig.' And, unless I marry him, my father will pack me off to some convent in Spain and leave all his money to some church to have masses said for his miserable soul. His heart is set on this marriage. Oh, Enrique, what shall I do? I'm going to lose you.' She flung her arms around his waist and pressed her face against him, seeking consolation from the warmth and strength of his body.

He tried mechanically to soothe her. In the quiet darkness he could see his brilliant future vanishing. For a long time he stood here, suffering her embrace, listening to her sobs. At length, when they had subsided, he spoke and his voice was cold and calculating. Each word was ominous.

'Have no fear, Inocencia. Trust me and believe me when I say there is nothing to fear. For the first time in my life I have the upper hand over Miguel.'

'What do you mean? Can I believe you?'

'You can. I see it is time for me to act. For a time I thought it would not be necessary for me to do so. We both felt that as soon as your old man started on his journey to hell, we could get married. But now I have a plan and I'll not fail. I promise you – you shall never marry my cousin. Believe in me.'

'I will.'

'I'll not fail, Inocencia, because I love you so much.'

'Sh-h-h! Protest not your love over much and I'll believe you more. But, if the time ever comes when we can marry, you'll find me an indulgent wife. With the dowry that I can bring you, you will be happy and with you I can be happy. The poor Santiago who is rich in beauty but has no fortune and the poor Gonzalez who is rich in gold but has no beauty! It's a good combination, Enrique. Each of us has what the other lacks. And now, as much as I hate to leave you and my dear Corporal Pronto, I am going. Tonight I shall not see the first streaks of dawn creeping through the window and lighting your face on the pillow. But I'll be back soon.'

'Something tells me you may not be coming here much more, Inocencia. We shall be meeting in a better place than this.'

'Not here? Then I'll not ask you where it shall be. I trust you and if any plan you have might bring us together I'll pray for its success. Good night,' she pressed her face against his, 'just one kiss and I'll pass out through that door, that dear little door which has led me to the only happiness I have ever known.'

He embraced her for a moment and stood at the door as he watched her enter the hired carriage which had been waiting down the street. He closed the door and lighted the candle. Then he pulled the bellcord to summon Josefina. As he waited, a smile of satisfaction crept over his face. To have planned for years and now to find success nearly in his grasp. He stroked the blue satin of his thigh. Damn! When he had finished with Josefina he'd go out and get himself a woman of his own choosing tonight. That little bitch in the corner *cantina*. He'd feel more like a man to mount a woman that he'd paid for rather than one that had paid for him. There was a scratch on the door.

'Josefina?' he called out.

'Yes.'

'Come in!'

She entered and stared in astonishment to see Enrique alone.

'Where is she? Gone already? Why did you call me? Your high and mighty cousin Miguel has just arrived with ten friends, his pockets loaded with gold. They're probably all in bed by now and I'll sell them no wine, get no tips for the maids or presents for the girls. Don't detain me. I've got work to do even if you haven't. If those boys aren't in bed, I'll try to sell them on a circus with you as the principal actor.'

He shook his head. 'Not tonight, old girl, not before Miguel anyway. As a matter of fact, never again.'

'I pay you well for it.' Her anger was rising.

'Chicken shit, old girl. Why concern yourself with a few miserable pesos when I want to talk about millions? Listen to me! I need your help and I'll see to it that you'll be richly rewarded.'

'And how will you pay me?' she taunted, 'with Corporal Pronto? Bah! I'm too old for that.'

'But not too old to be interested in the Gonzalez *and* the Santiago fortunes, eh? Both of them together.'

'Did you say the Gonzalez *and* the Santiago fortunes? What deviltry are you up to now? Are you going to kill Miguel and old Gonzalez too?'

'Gonzalez is dying and killing is too good for Miguel. Listen! Old Gonzalez wants Inocencia to marry Miguel, of all people in this world. If he does, I'll lose everything. I can't let it happen. I've got to stop it and I can. But I want to talk it over with you, old girl. I can trust you. You're the only friend I ever had and whether you know it or not, you care a hell of a lot about me.'

'I'll not deny it.'

'Then help me. Look, I've gone over this thing in my mind a thousand times but there may be a loophole in it that I've overlooked; something I have forgotten; something I haven't figured on. I need your advice. The stakes are big, *viejita*, the two biggest fortunes in Cuba.'

She stared down at him, her lips pressed tightly together. 'The Santiago *and* the Gonzalez fortunes. *Dios mio!* That's something to think about.' She turned on her heel and went over to the door and bolted it. Sitting down on the bed, she lifted up her skirt and from a pocket in her petticoat she took out a cigar and lighted it. 'I'm listening. That cousin of yours and his pretty companions can be guests of the house tonight for all I care. Now let's see. The Santiago *and* the Gonzalez fortunes together, eh?'

Chapter Ten

MIGUEL STOOD WITH his back to the marble railing of the balcony, his eyes fastened on the heavy mahogany door of his grandmother's room. Would it never open? It was impossible for him to wait patiently. Don Geronimo might be the best physician in Havana but must he take up an hour to make up his mind as to what was ailing his little grandmother? While he nervously paced back and forth, coming to rest and to stare at the door again, he felt floods of remorse overwhelming him. Why hadn't he spent more time with her? Why didn't he stay home once in a while and devote his whole evening to her? She would have enjoyed it and now his conscience would not hurt him for the nights he had spent romping in strange beds. Good God! Was the stupid idiot going to stay in there all day? There was nothing the matter with his grandmother; there couldn't be. Despite her frailty she was as strong as a mule.

At last! The bronze latch of the door moved. Miguel waited expectantly. It stopped. It moved again and stopped.

Unable to contain himself any longer, he sprang across the gallery, grasped the handle and pulled the door open.

He collided with don Geronimo who was taking his sedate and formal goodbyes. The poor doctor was nearly bowled over but he managed to recover his balance, readjusted his cumbersome black wig and bowed in the direction of the bed, then with an almost imperceptible wiggling of his finger, he beckoned Miguel out onto the gallery again.

His lips pursed together and he made a sympathetic clucking noise. 'Don Miguel, I have just attended the illustrious señora, your grandmother.'

'Yes, yes, I know,' Miguel interrupted. 'What did you find? Answer me, don Geronimo. What is wrong? She had this sudden attack. It must be serious. Is it?'

Don Geronimo clucked several times like a mother hen trying to collect her brood around her. 'It's her heart, don Miguel, her heart. The heart is a very remarkable organ, my boy. It works day and night, throughout the entire lifetime, never stopping, always pumping the blood of life through the body. Is it any wonder that with age it tires and sometimes tries to shirk its work. Ah, no, don Miguel, the heart is ...'

'Then it's my grandmother's heart?'

'Quite so. The señora has been a most active lady. Now she is no longer young and the poor heart is tired. Another of these attacks might be fatal. She must have rest.'

'Fatal? Did you say fatal?' Miguel wondered how the doctor could retain his composure in the face of such dire words. 'But, don Geronimo, the señora cannot die. Why, why, is there no medicine?'

The old doctor held up the bag he was carrying. 'I have excellent medicines. Pearls dissolved in spirits of wine build blood, you know, and the stronger the blood, the stronger the heart. But medicine is not enough. Medicine cannot rebuild a worn-out machine. I've prescribed medicines but mostly it is in the hands of God. She needs rest but above all she needs calmness. No excitement, nothing to worry about! Just calm and rest and perhaps some of the excellent wine of Oporto with a raw egg in it.'

'Must she stay in bed?'

'Mercy, no! Not at all, not at all. Knowing the señora, I can well imagine that she had rather be dead than stay abed. Oh, for a day or two perhaps. Then she may be up and about, but not as usual.' He shook his head with ponderous gravity. 'Only once a day over the stairs. No exertion and above all, no shock. Tranquillity! No temper tantrums. Not of course that the señora would ever give way to temper...'

'You know damn well she does.'

'Perhaps, on occasions, but those occasions must be avoided,' Don Geronimo shifted his wig from over his right eye to over his left. With as dignified a bow as he could muster, he started toward the stairs. Antonio came rushing up to take the doctor's bag and escort him to the gate.

Miguel delayed a moment before entering his grandmother's room. He wanted time to erase the worried look the doctor's words had caused. Having done that he opened the door and smiled. The señora looked up as Miguel's heels struck the tiles. She appeared very frail and tiny – a little island of life – in the huge whiteness of the old Spanish bed with its soaring draperies of Chinese silk. Only the sparkle in her eyes attested to the vitality with which she clung to life. She smiled up expectantly at Miguel. He ran over to the bed and reached for her frail little hand. As he kissed it, she turned her hand in his until her fingers could caress his cheek. They glided over his face with tenderness but her voice, when she spoke, lacked much of its wilful imperiousness.

'Has that mewling idiot left?' she asked.

'You mean the great don Geronimo?'

'That charlatan! That quack! That dolt! That knave! Doctor? Bah! What veterinary college did he attend? He's not fit to prescribe a purge for a sick slave. A little blood letting; a sniff of a vinaigrette! That's all I needed. Why did you call him?'

'Because you had fainted away.'

'Then why didn't you burn a few feathers under my nose? It was just an attack of the vapors. I was too tightly laced.

Now call one of my maids. I must be up and dressed. Tell her to lay out my pink organza with the black Chantilly lace and I'll wear my amethysts with it. You certainly didn't inherit your desire to dawdle in bed from me. You must have got it from your mother's family – the del Montes were notoriously lazy; why your mother's uncle Pedro ....'

Miguel held up his hand. '*Abuela mia*,' he mimicked her voice, 'you are not the only Santiago who can give orders. No, now I give them. I, the little Miguel, give orders to the great Señora de Santiago. Do you hear me?'

'I do,' she had become very meek.

'Then I order you to stay in bed all day today, all night tonight and all day tomorrow. The Santiago has spoken.'

The señora's moment of meekness passed. She raised herself and sat upright in bed but the strain of the exertion showed in her face although she did not allow herself to flinch. 'You young idiot! Do you think you can give orders here? Me, in bed? I've never missed having dinner served to me in the *comedor* and I'll not miss it tonight. I'll not, I'll not!' Her face went suddenly white and her hand grasped for his. The spasm of pain passed and she looked up at Miguel with the ghost of a smile.

'However, if I had company,' she added, 'such as a handsome grandson, I just might consider dining in bed for this one night. *Tu y yo*, Miguelito,' she patted the white counterpane. 'With you sitting here and helping your poor old grandmother, I might consent. Are you going to feed the poor old lady gruel with a silver spoon?'

'What poor old lady are you talking about? Yourself? No, grandmother, you're not suited to the role of sweet senility. It doesn't become you. Admit it – you're a she-devil with the heart of an angel and I wouldn't want you otherwise.'

She laughed and for the first time her laugh sounded natural. There was a knock at the door and with Miguel's *venga* the door opened and Antonio entered.

'About dinner tonight, don Miguel?'

'My grandmother and I shall dine here beside her bed. What are we having for dinner tonight?'

Antonio produced a folded sheet from his pocket and passed it to Miguel who looked at the various entries in fine copperplate script. It showed the menus for the day for the family and for the slaves and against each item the cost was carefully noted.

'Some of the breast of chicken, Antonio, for the señora – the very tenderest – and a cup of soup, very hot. Then have Andreas decant a bottle of the best Oporto. As for me, well, bring it all, I'm starved.'

As Antonio turned to go, the señora called to him. '*Un momento, Antonio.*' Then turning to Miguel, she said, 'Observe, my boy, the excellently turned calf of our major domo. *Dios mio!* Ill I may be and confined to this damned bed but I'm still interested in a well turned leg. I do believe it's better than your own, my Miguelito. But those cotton stockings! They spoil it. Go, Antonio, to my grandson's room and there find yourself a pair of silk stockings and put them on and never appear before me again with those beautiful legs covered with cotton.'

Antonio thanked her and left. After he had gone, the señora motioned to Miguel to sit down on her bed. She suddenly became serious. 'This, my son, is not the first of these attacks I've had. I've had others too and to be thoroughly honest, they are not from tight lacing. The pain is like a knife but I did not want to tell anyone. I know don Geronimo is telling the truth and I shall not be too unhappy to die. My only regret will be in leaving you.'

'Don't! Don't you dare to mention death. I won't listen to it.'

'Only fools ignore death; the wise prepare for it. It is well to prepare one's soul for God and one's material things for distribution to those one loves. It is about the latter I wish to speak. You have seen my will. Everything I own with the exception of a few bequests to old friends and a little something to keep the Bishop happy will go to you. That Enrique must have nothing – not one *centavo*. I cannot allow the spawn of that woman who brought so much sorrow into my life to have anything that belongs to me. But, Miguel, there is one thing that worries me; one thing I would like to do but I cannot do it without your consent because I have no right to rob you of your inheritance.'

'You do anything you want, my dear, as long as you do not insist I marry Inocencia.'

'Mayhap you'll want her money when you find out how much my little whim will cost you. But it is this. Our slaves. The Santiago family has always held the ownership of its slaves as a sacred trust. The last words your grandfather said to me before he died were, "The slaves, Elena, don't ever sell the slaves." I never have.'

'And of course I never shall, Grandmother.'

'I know but remember when my old friend Maria Estremadura died? Remember how only a few days afterwards, her son Ramon was thrown from his horse and killed? God forbid that such a thing should ever happen to you! But you know the results of Ramon's accident. Ramon's wife wanted to return to Spain and every one of the Estremadura slaves was sold at an auction at don Solano's. It was a crime, Miguel. Some of them had been in family service for over half a century. Yet they were all sold at Solano's.'

A look of understanding came to Miguel. 'I think I understand. You mean that if anything should happen to me, Enrique might get a clever lawyer or bribe some public official on the strength of what he stood to gain. Then he would have everything, including the slaves?'

'Outside of you he is my only heir. It is only logical that he might get his hands on everything. I'd shudder to think of what he'd do to our servants. I'd not want him for a master.'

'But they represent a vast fortune, Grandmother.'

She nodded.

'A lot of money.'

'Yes, a lot of money. But what good is that money to us except to appear in the inventory of the Santiago slaves? When one buries gold in the ground and leaves it there, it has no value. The slaves are of no value to us unless we sell them and we have never sold a slave. Think for a moment, Miguel. Think of Andreas, Maria, Tomas, Juan. Just picture them stepping onto the auction block and being sold. It worries me, Miguel.'

He sat quietly, his forehead wrinkled in thought. A resurgence of the feelings he had had at the Mercado de San Martin when he had purchased Antonio and Fidel came over him. What was it he had said to Solano? He would never buy another slave! A picture of Solano, sitting like some fat spider battening on the bodies of his victims became real in his mind. He remembered the look in Antonio's eyes when he had quit the place; Fidel's joy to be purchased; and above all the strong feeling that it was he himself who was being bought and sold.

'You're right, Grandmother. You are always right. We'll free every Santiago slave. I see now that I have always hated owning *people*. It's not only brutal but it's costly and inefficient. One pays a high price for a slave. One feeds him, clothes him, nurses him and eventually the slave dies. The investment is gone. And besides, when a man has to work without any reward, he never really works. There's no incentive. Consequently it takes three slaves to do the work of one man hired by the hour. If our slaves were free men and working for us, they would be earning money and self-supporting. They would work harder and be happier, each man with his little *bohio*, his wife and family, his plot of ground, his pig and mule. When I invest five hundred pesos in a field hand, I have the burden of his existence on my hands until he dies. Sick or well, I must support him. Actually, Grandmother, I believe we would make more money if we freed every slave. I'm not much good at figures, but I'll get Antonio to help me. We'll work out the costs. Who knows, maybe we have discovered the key to a new economy for Cuba...'

Chapter Eleven

THE TRIP FROM Havana to the vast Santiago *finca*, La Estrellita, usually took the most of a day, if one went by coach in a leisurely fashion. Miguel always rode on horseback and made the trip in a few hours but he realized it would be impossible for Margerita to go on that way. He was anxious for her to see La Estrellita but, as convention forbade their spending the night there, he had decided to make the trip by coach and return the same day. He had assured her that they would return in time for her performance at the theatre, provided they could make a sufficiently early start. The first flushes of dawn were beginning to light the city as the Santiago coach came to a stop in front of Margerita's door.

At this hour, Havana – a city which never sleeps but sometimes dozes – was at its quietest. Even the cries of the milk vendors, driving their goats through the narrow streets, were strangely hushed. The goats themselves, their heavy udders swinging between their legs, marched sedately, putting their small hooves down daintily on the uneven cobbles. Boys with armfuls of fresh loaves waited patiently at kitchen doors, fearing to awaken the sleeping cooks too quickly. Workmen made their way to the docks, occasionally making way for those returning from the all-night *cantinas.* What movement there was, was slow and peaceful as if the city, awakened for a moment by the dawn, had turned over on its other side and gone to sleep again.

Miguel slept soundly in the coach. His head rolled sideways against the stiff brocade which upholstered the interior. The ruffle of his lace jabot rose and fell with his measured breathing. His strong hands, brown against the whiteness of his linen suit, were strangely quiet for they were never quiet when he was awake. The uneven paving stones and the resiliency of the springs had caused his hat to tumble down over his face.

Fidel sat facing him. From time to time, the young slave softly caressed the gold satin of his suit and let his fingers move with sensuous satisfaction over the soft velvet of the cuffs. It was an old suit of Miguel's – one he had long since discarded. The peculiar gold of Fidel's hair and eyes had inspired a hunt for it and, when it was found, a few alterations adapted it to the adolescent figure.

Fidel leaned over and broke the silence. 'Your pardon,

my lord master, we have arrived at the señorita's. The coach has stopped.'

'What? Are we here already?' Miguel muttered, awakening with a start. Then with a look of annoyance, he added, 'You stupid fellow! Letting me sleep! Now I shall present myself looking like an idiot, my eyes half-closed, my clothes all awry. Come, attend me before I descend. Tell me, my hair, my ruffles – do I look presentable?'

Fidel reached over, brushed an imaginary fleck of dust from Miguel's collar, flicked the ruffles of his shirt into position and rescued the tricorne which had fallen to the floor. As the coachman opened the door, Miguel bounded to the pavement.

His arrival was anticipated for the door of the house slowly opened from within. The Quesada met him in the hall as austere and as disapproving as ever. She welcomed him with an abrupt curtsey, sweeping the floor with her rusty black skirts, her back rigid, her head unbowed. With a curt nod, Miguel rushed past her into the *sala*. Here, despite the open windows, the air was heavy with the scent of carnations; the room was steeped with their clove-like pungency.

Margerita was waiting for him, seated on a little gilt chair near the door. Her suit of dark green silk clasped her tightly around the waist but the rest of her body was lost in the billowing folds of her skirt. From the top of her small velvet hat a cascade of golden plumes – the incomparable feathers of the Paradise – fell over her shoulders mingling with the black of her hair. She rose and smiled at Miguel as he entered the room. For a moment each stood still. His eyes filled with the beauty of her face, the swelling curves of the green silk bodice and the lustre of the pearls at her neck. He appeared to her as a Goya etching, all black and white; white starched linen, white teeth, black hair, black shoes, black hat. The splash of red that was his lips was the only colour.

He kissed her at first lightly on the cheeks and then his lips sought hers. The tip of his tongue, like a darting adder, parted her teeth and for a moment she responded then evaded his clutching arms. 'We both play with fire, Miguel. Let us not start a blaze for fear we cannot stop it. Come, let us go.'

Reluctantly he released her. 'But a fire is such a pretty thing....'

She put her fingers on his lips and gave him a gentle push toward the door. The Quesada followed them, which Miguel had known would be the case. Convention unfortunately demanded her presence. She was a lady and could not be put out on the coachman's seat so she must therefore sit and stare at him and Margerita throughout their journey. Aware of this and feeling that two pairs of eyes would be kinder than the steely glare of the lone señora, he had brought Fidel along to sit beside her and warm the chill of her austerity.

Margerita settled herself in the coach and, noticing Fidel on the opposite seat, questioned Miguel with a gay little smile in the lad's direction. 'And who might this golden boy be, Miguelito? Perhaps it's the odd light of this early morning sun but I would swear him to be made of gold – his skin, his hair, even his eyes look to be of bright burnished gold...'

Miguel laughed. 'The señorita enquires about you, Fidel. You, with your sixteen years, have accomplished something which none of the young *caballeros* of Havana have been able to do. Do you know how many there are in this city who would give anything to have the señorita notice them? Come, greet her, boy, for she is not in the habit of doing such things.'

'You embarrass me, Miguel,' she fluttered her fan, 'and I am sure you equally embarrass your friend. How can he greet me before he is introduced to me. You are lacking in manners not to have presented him?'

'Present Fidel? Margerita, are you serious?'

'And why not?'

Miguel shook his head. '*Ay de mi!* I can see you are not a Cuban. Had you been Cuban, you would have taken one look at Fidel – that would have been enough – and had I presented him to you you would have been shocked.'

'Stop talking in riddles, or I shall become angry with you. I see a handsome young lad who accompanies you in your coach. I take him for a friend of yours and I would naturally suppose you would introduce us.'

Miguel winked at Fidel but spoke to Margerita. 'Fidel may be a friend of mine and yet he is not a friend. It just happens that I bought him a few days ago. Look closely, my dear, can't you see he is not white? He is a slave. Therefore I could not possibly introduce you to him or him to you for, according to our custom here in Cuba, it would be like introducing you to one of the horses that pull our coach.'

'I can't believe it. The boy is not black. I always thought all slaves were black.'

Miguel motioned to Fidel to move nearer and the boy dropped on one knee on the bottom of the coach. Miguel loosened the neckband of his shirt and pulled coat and shirt down, revealing the boy's bare shoulder. 'Look! Now will you believe?'

Her face whitened. 'I see a scar. No, it is not a scar. *Valgame dios!* He's been branded.'

'Of course, all slaves are.'

'But why did you do this to him?'

'Look more closely, my dear. The Santiago arms are two falcons; this is a lion rampant. The brand is not of my doing. He was branded when I bought him.'

'Is that true, Fidel?' Margerita's unbelief almost made her doubt Miguel.

'*Por supuesto*, señorita. I was branded before don Miguel bought me.'

'Yes, Margerita, he's a slave and he belongs to me. I bought him only a few days ago in the Mercado. As a matter of fact, I bought two slaves and Fidel is one of them.'

'What sort of a country is this where one buys a human being with money?'

'Just like one buys a dog or a horse or a cow. Exactly. You see, although I am an exception, Cubans do not consider a boy like Fidel human. In the eyes of all the world he's an animal – a little higher in breeding than a horse or a dog because he has the ability to reason and to express himself but an animal nevertheless. This I do not subscribe to. Yet, despite my feelings in the matter, the other day I entered Solano's market as casually as I might go to my tailors to buy a new suit or to the jewellers to buy a snuff box. I went there to make a purchase of a man. It was not the first time, of course, because previously I have bought field hands – blacks often straight from Africa whom I purchased as I would an animal by looking at their teeth and the sleekness of their skins.

'But this time it was different. I went to buy a servant to replace our aging major domo and I ended up by buying two – the fellow Antonio and this Fidel here. Fidel looks up to Antonio as though he were a god. I must confess I myself was impressed with the fellow – he's good looking, intelligent and well educated and I would defy anybody to detect the slightest taint of Negro blood in the man. In fact,' Miguel was almost apologetic, 'having been in prison, his skin was even whiter than mine which had been exposed to the sun. Do you know, as I considered his purchase, something strange happened to me.'

'What?' Margerita asked.

'For one fleeting moment, I felt that I was for sale and he was buying me. I do not know what came over me but it was such a revulsion that I was tempted to free every slave I owned. Then my grandmother and I decided to do exactly that and from now on the Santiago family will employ only free labour.'

Margerita placed her hand over Miguel's. Her fingers closed tightly around his. She glanced across at Fidel but his cheerful grin denoted nothing but happiness. She was near to tears but they seemed wasted.

'How pitiful!' She had been deeply moved by Miguel's words. 'I shall be proud of you if you do free your slaves.'

'But all Cuba will hate me,' he shrugged his shoulders. 'Well, let them. We Santiagos are a law unto ourselves.'

The mask that formed the Quesada's face showed signs of coming to life. It started to move, like plaster cracking, and the thin line of her lips parted sufficiently to allow the words to come out. Her eyes, steely blue, were fastened on Miguel.

'Am I right in believing, señor, that these unfortunates are all of them persons of colour?'

Miguel nodded. 'Yes, everyone held in slavery or sold in slavery has coloured blood. Even a single drop of Negro blood damns a man to servitude. All issue of female slaves in turn become slaves. Now this boy here,' he pointed to Fidel, 'I would judge to be a quadroon. That is, he has three-quarters white blood and from his looks I would imagine that some of it came from some Scandinavian, a sailor perhaps, whose blond hair has shown up in this lad. Negro blood is always on the distaff side, you know. Although the gentlemen of Cuba have been strict at drawing the line between white and coloured in public, they have always had a fondness for crossing the colour line behind the closed shutters of their bedrooms. Therefore we have many here in Cuba which you might not easily recognize as coloured. Some of them can boast noble blood in their veins. This Antonio that I bought – his mother was an octoroon girl and his father the Duke of Ramar. So, you see he is just one-sixteenth or possibly one-thirty-second coloured.'

'The Duke of Ramar?' The señora was impressed. 'You mean . . .?'

'I mean that my slave is the natural son of the Duke. Through his father he is related to half the kings of Europe but according to Cuban law, he is as black as any black *bruto* newly arrived from Africa with a stick in his nose.'

The señora sniffed. It was apparent that she did not credit the mingling of blue blood with black. In recomposing her mask, she narrowed her lips and then retreated behind the façade of what she fondly imagined to be aristocratic snobbishness.

Margerita leaned over and patted Fidel's hand. 'Stop talking about slaves. You embarrass the boy and in truth you embarrass me.'

But Fidel was not embarrassed. He was far too happy. That his feelings should even be considered was a new experience to him. Previously nobody had ever noticed his existence as a person. Now he was dressed in silk and velvet, riding in the Santiago coach alongside the master whom he worshipped as a god and the most beautiful woman he had ever seen who had patted him on his hand.

'The señorita must not distress herself over me. Truly, I had rather be a slave to don Miguel than be Governor of Cuba. You see, señorita, Antonio and I are together and we belong to don Miguel and we are happy and we love him.' He reached over for Miguel's hand and carried it to his lips.

Miguel drew his hand away quickly and gave Fidel a slap. 'The boy's an actor, Margerita, a born actor. He loves to dramatize himself. You should have seen the show he put on at Solano's to get me to buy him. He knows how to play on one's sympathies. See how he has affected you. I think I'll send the beggar to Spain and put him on the stage. All his swooning and posturing. But in spite of it all, he's a good boy.'

Margerita settled back in the corner of the coach and Miguel found her hand hidden under the folds of her skirt. Fidel, who had never been out of the city before, stared out the window and the señora looked blankly at the passing landscape, so different from the pinched grey-greenness of Spain. The coach had left the city far behind and was now well on its way to Marianao, beyond which lay the *finca*. The cobblestones had disappeared. The road was thick with dust, which rose in a cloud around the horses' hooves, turning into golden motes as it filtered through the windows of the coach. The burning heat of the tropics was replacing the cool paleness of the early morning sun. Cuba spread its wealth before them – a lavish opulence of tropical verdure. The coach rolled on, under poinciana trees which showered them with a rain of flower-coloured petals, under royal palms which reared their feathery fronds high in the air, past rich fields of whispering cane and lush meadows of grazing cattle.

Miguel, thinking of the day ahead of them, went over in his mind the arrangements he had made and the special courier he had sent to the *finca* to see that they were carried out. It was to be a perfect day: the luncheon, the gift he intended for Margerita, and the talk he was to give to the assembled slaves. Suddenly an idea came to him. He turned his eyes toward Margerita and then toward Fidel. Margerita alone in Cuba! No one to protect her when he was not with her except a feeble old man and this useless sprig of dried up Spanish blue-blood who sat opposite him. Margerita, alone in a city inflamed by her beauty and her dancing! What was to stop some young libertine, drunk with rum and inflamed with desire, from scaling the walls of her house and entering her bedroom? He might have been tempted to do it himself, had he not known her. It had been done before in Havana. Suddenly he snapped his fingers and his words broke the heat filled somnolence of the coach.

'*Caramba*! Such an idea as I have just had. Sometimes we Santiagos actually surprise ourselves by thinking. *Ay de mi*, we are a clever family. So . . . I have an idea.'

'Congratulations,' Margerita laughed and squeezed his hand a little tighter. 'Do you have one every day?'

'Ah, no. That would tax my brain too much and keep me from thinking about you. But wait! When you have heard my idea you will realize how truly clever I am. Really, *querida*, I'm quite the cleverest person in the world.'

'You're quite sure of that?'

'*Absolutamente*! And one proof of my cleverness is that I picked the most beautiful woman in the world to be my *novia*. But now to my idea.'

'I cannot wait but I doubt if it will make me love you any more.'

'Then here is where I can prove it to you. But wait – *un momento*. Strange as it may seem, this stupendous idea of mine must be approved by my slave. Never tell anyone that Miguel de Santiago felt it necessary to ask his slave's approval. They will all think I am *loco*, but they are going to think so anyway pretty soon. Listen! We must be in one accord. At present, *querida mia*, there is nobody in your house to protect you but one old man and he would be no use against some hot-blooded Suban youth. So, you must have someone to protect you and that someone must be devoted to you. It must be a man, although in this case it is a youth, but he has the strength of a man. So if he, of his own free will, were willing to serve you, you would have a slave to protect you.'

She shook her head. 'I shall never own a slave.'

'You need not. If I give you a slave you can free him and employ him as a free man. Now Fidel, you speak because you are the one I intend to give to the señorita.'

'Me, don Miguel? Ay, it would be an honour to belong to the señorita, but that would mean I had to leave Antonio.'

'Perforce yes,' Miguel spoke to Fidel but he looked at Margerita, 'but that would only be for a little while because very soon you would be back in the Casa Santiago again with your mistress. Did you nod, Margerita?'

'Did I,' she laughed.

'I'm sure you did.'

'Well, perhaps,' she admitted.

'And so you see, Fidel, you would not really be separated from your Antonio. That obstacle being removed, would you promise to serve the señorita well – guard and protect her and never leave her?'

Fidel, ever mindful of an occasion for histrionics, rose from the seat as much as the roof of the coach would permit and bowed to Margerita. A lurch of the vehicle sent him sprawling into the old lady's lap. She clucked unpleasantly and pushed him back into his own corner, brushing off her skirts and rearranging them. Undaunted Fidel resumed his obeisance and turned to Miguel.'

'I would be happy to serve so gracious a mistress as the señorita.'

'Well spoken, *muchacho*, even if the effect of your words was spoiled by a rut in the road. So here, Margerita, is my first present to you, live flesh and blood, not flowers that fade or jewels which are no more than bits of coloured glass. Here's devotion which money cannot buy.'

Margerita leaned back against the cushions. She tried to control her emotions, reaching into her bag for the silver ball of pomander and applied it to her nose. Turning, she faced them.

'I cannot thank you in words, either one of you. Fidel, I shall accept you on one condition. If you belong to me you are free. You shall belong only to yourself, Fidel . . . what is your name?'

'A slave has but one name, señorita.'

'But free men have two and you are no longer a slave. I like your name *Fidel* which means faithful, but, for your other name? Ah, I have it! When I first saw you with your yellow hair, your bright skin and your amber suit, I said you looked golden. So, it will be Fidel Dorado – Fidel the golden. How's that?'

'Better than the rascal deserves,' Miguel made a feint to slap him.

She pushed Miguel's hand aside. 'He's mine now, don't you dare strike him. Look, Fidel, don Miguel has said that you are an actor and in truth I think you are. So am I because a good dancer must be an actress too. So we have something in common and let us make something really dramatic of it and, if don Miguel does not like it, he need not look. Stop the coach, Miguel, and hand me that sword which I see on the wall behind the seat.'

The coach stopped and the three of them alighted. Margerita led the way to a spot of shade beneath a group of palms. She motioned to Miguel to stand by her side and to Fidel to stand in front of her. Miguel looked on with a quizzical smile. Fidel's eyes were dancing. Suddenly Miguel started to laugh.

'*Dios mio*, are you going to run the beggar through, Margerita?'

'Hush!' she held up a warning finger. 'We're actors on a stage. Once when I was a little girl I went to the theatre in Madrid. I do not remember the name of the play but in it an English king touched a man's back with his sword and made him a knight. Surely if a king can make a knight out of a man, I can make a man out of a slave. Kneel, Fidel!'

Fidel dropped to one knee before her and she took the sword from Miguel. It caught the brightness of the sun and the polished steel touched Fidel's shoulder like a ray of light.

'I name you Fidel Dorado,' she said. 'Arise Señor Dorado. You are now a free man with a name.'

Miguel started clapping his hands together. 'I'm the audience,' he laughed. 'Somebody's got to applaud you too for such a pretty scene.' His laugh died away and he became serious. 'Just because you're free, young fellow, doesn't mean you can do as you please. You mind your mistress because free or slave, she's still your mistress and if I hear any complaint from her about you, I'll take your britches down and use the flat of my hand where it will do the most good.'

'You'll never have to, don Miguel,' Fidel brushed the dust from his knee, 'because, you see, I love the señorita too.'

Chapter Twelve

THE NOON CHIMES were ringing from the stone chapel beside the gates of Estrellita when the coach and the nearly exhausted horses arrived at the *finca*. As Miguel and Margerita drove up, willing hands pushed open the heavy wrought iron gates. The door of the coach opened and Miguel appeared in the doorway. A lusty shout welcomed him.

One very old slave, his face deeply lined and his hair little more than two white cotton tufts on a shiny black poll, advanced to the front of the crowd. 'Welcome to La Estrellita, don Miguel,' he piped, 'the *little star* shines only when you are here. We, your people, welcome you back.' A chorus of *vivas* echoed his words and, as the tumult died down, the shout was picked up and revived by a large body of slaves who were coming down the road from the fields. Hearing the cries of welcome and knowing of the anticipated visit, they broke into a run, arriving almost too breathlessly to add their voices to the general acclaim. Miguel held up his hand for silence and beckoned the old man to him.

'Thank you, Mtambo, and thank you all. It wouldn't be La Estrellita without you to open the gates, *viejo*. Now I have an errand for you to do. Go at once to don Jose and tell him that I want all the Santiago people to stop work at one o'clock. No matter what they are doing, all work must cease because at three o'clock they are to assemble here in the chapel. Every slave, male and female, old and young must be here. Afterwards they need not return to work. It will be a *fiesta*. And, another question; has the new priest arrived who was to take Father Eliseo's place?'

'*Si*, señor. He arrived but a day ago.'

'Then present my compliments to him and bid him come to the chapel also. I have an announcement to make and it is well that a man of God is here to witness it. So hurry, *viejo*, for we leave at four and I do not wish to be delayed.'

The carriage rolled on with the horses refreshed by their brief rest. Gravel flew from the wheels. Margerita leaned forward in the coach to look out of the window in the door. Fidel leaned from the other window. The señora still sat bolt upright; she had no curiosity about a Cuban farmhouse – she who, at least so she claimed, had been a frequent visitor at the royal palace in Madrid.

A mile-long avenue led straight from the gates to the house. Bordering it on both sides was an uninterrupted procession of royal palms, their smooth trunks making a living colonnade of stone-grey pillars. The close-cropped grass extended under them on either side to a wall of coral, covered in places by purple bougainvillea and red hibiscus. Here and there thick branches of trees – tamarind, almond, mamey and mango – threw a dense shade from the other side of the walls. As the avenue approached the house, it widened into a circle and swept around a fountain – a bronze goddess eternally bathed in tall jets of water, the spray, dashing high into the air, hanging rainbows of colour around her shoulders.

From the circle of the fountain the entire front of the house was visible. To a European travelling in Cuba, the first sight of La Estrellita always came as a surprise. This was no colonial farmhouse – no white-stuccoed, red-tiled building – such as one might anticipate. This was France, not Spain. The long façade of pinkish marble, the white Ionic pillars, the sculptured friezes belonged more properly in Versailles or St Cloud than in an isolated spot in rural Cuba. In truth, the house was but an echo of France. The great LeBlanc, fresh from the architectural triumphs he had designed for the Court of France, chanced to be passing through Havana on his way to New Orleans. It was soon after the destruction of the original house and Miguel's grandfather had prevailed on him to design a new house for the *finca*. LeBlanc, with unlimited funds at his disposal, had done so with consummate artistry. The lush green of the tropical landscape; the metallic green of the palm fronds which framed the building; and the eternally blue sky brought out the faint rose of the marble which had been so laboriously transported from Italy by boat and creaking ox cart. Instead of being straight, the façade curved in a bow, a long arc broken only by the tall windows and the pilasters of white marble which flanked them. It was a building of only one storey but statues and urns filled with flowering plants alternating along the edge of the roof gave an illusion of height and the horseshoe staircase which swept up to the main entrance in the centre subtly joined its reverse curve to the sweeping arc of the mansion.

As the carriage came to a stop at the foot of the steps, a procession of slaves in the violet and silver livery of the Santiagos came and stood at attention, lining the stairs. Two others came to open the doors of the coach, another to stand at the horses' heads and still another to place a low stool before the door. White teeth gleamed in black, brown and *café-au-lait* faces as the door of the coach opened.

Miguel leaped to the ground and assisted Margerita and the señora to alight. He motioned Fidel to remain inside and the weary horses started the short drive to the stables. The two women stood in silence at the foot of the steps, acknowledging with nods the deep obeisances of the footmen.

For once, with the broad curve of Estrellita in front of her, the liveried slaves, the curving sweep of the marble stairs, the impassive señora lost her composure. She actually smiled at Miguel – a vapid, toothy smile. 'My dear don Miguel, this is really lovely. I had no idea. Utterly charming. Quite as lovely as the palace in Madrid and I'm sure the dear queen would forgive me for making such a comparison. But I should know, don Miguel, I've been a guest at the palace so many times. But it's lovely. Quite lovely even if it is Cuban.'

Miguel bowed. 'You are most kind to compliment my little house, Señora, little as it may deserve your praise.'

Miguel and Margerita ascended the stairs together, the señora following. Once inside, away from the incandescent glare of the sun, there was a dim coolness. The patio, which formed the centre, was a courtyard where thick vines, strung between towering palms, kept out the brilliant sun. Margerita saw broad corridors, paved with black and white marble, stretching away on either side of the entrance, walls covered with painted tiles, chandeliers of dripping crystal looking like snowstorms eternally suspended in mid-air. It was a mingling of the beauty of France, the artistry of Spain and over it all the sensuous, almost overpowering, charm of the tropics. A smiling Negress advanced to meet them. Her stiffly starched skirts chattered against the tiles and her brilliant turban of red and gold made a bright spot in the semi-darkness.

'Hortensia,' Miguel grinned at her, proud in her appraisal of Margerita's beauty, 'show the ladies to their rooms. Attend them there.' Then turning to Margerita, he said, 'She will care for all your wants. You have only to ask for whatever you desire. I'll let you leave me, *querida*, for this little while but I shall count the moments until we meet for luncheon. *Hasta luego.*'

'*Vaya con dios,*' she answered as she and the señora followed Hortensia, but she had gone only a few steps when she turned and blew him a kiss.

Miguel clapped his hands and soon heard the soft padding of bare feet on the tiles. A Negro lad appeared – this one not clad in formal livery.

'You, Francisco,' Miguel said, 'go to the coach house and fetch Señor Dorado who came with us. Serve him his luncheon in the small breakfast room and see to it that he is served as is befitting a gentleman. Then run out to see if old Mtambo has delivered my message to don Jose. After that tell every one of the house servants to assemble with the other slaves at the chapel at three o'clock, *al punto*.'

The boy trotted away and Miguel walked down the broad corridor to his own apartments. The tall double doors of carved mahogany opened at his touch. The room was large with a high-domed ceiling covered in gold leaf. It was supported on pillars of green marble. The furniture of gilded wood was massive in construction from the bed with its towering posts and draperies of dark green damask to the enormous armoires which stood against the wall. An elderly slave was standing by the door of one of these. Miguel entered unnoticed, softly tiptoed over to him and flung his arms around the old man.

'Pepito, good old Pepito,' he exclaimed. 'How good it is to see you once more. I miss you in Havana, *viejo*. Oh yes, Juan does very well. You trained him excellently but the lad's mind is more on what the wenches hide under their skirts than it is on his work.'

'A little taste of the whip would cure that, don Miguel. Not too heavy, just a taste.'

'Bah! I wouldn't have him otherwise; he's young and full of sap and most of the time he's busting out of his britches just thinking about the wenches. But I was the same at his age. And how are you, Pepito?'

'Well, don Miguel, well enough.'

'It's always good to see you. After all my father and mother never existed for me except in gold frames in the *sala*, so it was old Pepito who was really father and mother to me. It was Pepito who brushed away the tears and . . .'

'Got you out of a good many scrapes and told a great many lies about you to your lady grandmother. *Ay de mi!* You were worse than Juan. By the time you were eighteen you'd had every wench on the *finca*. You should see all the little *mestizos* we have running around here. And they all look like you. But you've settled down now. Tell me how is Pilar?'

'Pilar? Oh yes, Pilar. You know, Pepito,' Miguel winked, 'I discovered that she had just the slightest cast in one eye and the little Pilar is already forgotten.'

'Forgotten? Why just a week or so ago you told me that your sun rose and set in her. Nobody, but nobody, had ever kissed so divinely unless it was Teresa or perhaps it was Manuela or Luisa.'

'Enough, Pepito, enough! Once those names were delightful to my ear but please don't ever mention them again. From now on, I swear, there will be only one name – Margerita. This time, Pepito, I am in love.'

'Perhaps I'll believe you if the next time you come out the name has not changed.'

'It won't, I assure you, and now that we have disposed of my heart, how about my body? My bath? Is it ready? I'm hot and dusty and my clothes are sweaty. A bath will make a new man of me.'

'It is waiting for you,' was the ready answer, 'and your clothes are all ready too. I laid out the rose satin – the one with the black braid in the *torero* style that just arrived from Spain.'

Miguel stepped into the bathing room and shed his clothes onto the floor, stepping out of the circle of soiled linen into his bath. When he stepped out, dripping on the tiles, he rubbed his skin until it glowed pinkly under the tan.

'Pepito!' he called, 'in these few minutes while I am dressing and we are alone, tell me all the gossip of the *finca* – all that has happened since I left.'

Miguel started to dress, having some difficulty with the skin-tight trousers until Pepito, borrowing a trick from the *toreros* of Spain, inched them up his legs with a rolled up towel in the crotch until they shone on Miguel's legs like a skin of pink satin. As he worked, he recited the various domestic problems of the slaves; the births, deaths, loves and quarrels of the little community. From time to time, Miguel would interrupt with concise orders – a new *bohio* to be built for a couple recently paired up; a silver peso for a new baby; a visit to the hospital to console an ailing slave; or a cross to be erected over a new grave. It was the same familiar story; he had heard it all many times before – the little everyday happenings of that small group of people that he owned. They were simple people and the news about them was of simple things.

Suddenly he stopped Pepito. 'What did you say? Did I understand you to say that my cousin Enrique was here?'

'Yes, I said he was here only recently.'

'That son of a bitch! He's been altogether too much interested in me lately. He's been spying on me in Havana and now what is he looking for out here? Did he come here to the house?'

'No, not to the house. He came in the afternoon – evidently he rode out from Havana on horseback – and went directly to the chapel. I just happened to be going to the priest's house to see that all was in readiness for the young Padre who was to arrive the next day. I'd never seen Enrique but once before on the streets of Havana but I recognized him. I would have asked him what he was doing here but he leaped up onto his horse and rode away before I could get the words out.'

Miguel walked slowly across the room. 'Was that the first time he ever came here?'

'I don't know, don Miguel. A couple of months ago, Mtambo said a young fellow rode up, went into the chapel and spent some time. When he came out he gave Mtambo a peso and said he went in there to pray. I didn't think anything about it at the time, but now I wonder if it wasn't this Enrique.'

'Well, there's no harm in anyone going into the chapel to pray. That's what it's there for but with all the churches in Havana, I don't see why he comes out here to say his prayers. He never struck me as the praying kind. I've never seen him perform at the Casa Josefina but I understand he puts on quite a show there when somebody pays him. Someday I may be able to do something for him; after all it isn't fitting for a Santiago to be a paid stud in Josefina's circuses. Still I can't see why he came out here.'

'I think he was also in the priest's house, although I didn't see him there, but things had been disturbed in there. I was a little suspicious and I sent a man to follow him. He soon caught up with him and reported that after leaving here, he went to the house of Roberto Garcia in Marianao.'

Miguel took hold of the old man's shoulders. Their eyes met. Miguel's lips hardly moved as he spoke. 'Something's wrong, Pepito. Those two rats belong together. Roberto's always carried a grudge against me since I fired him as overseer here. I didn't even know that Enrique knew him. Well, to hell with them! Come, Pepito, button me up.'

The old man finished dressing Miguel, then got down on his knees to give his shoes an extra polish. He rose slowly, looked Miguel over carefully, turning him around as he would a mannequin. '*Dios mio*, Miguelito, but you are a handsome lad. No *torero* of Spain could fill that suit better than yourself. I'm proud of you, my boy.' He adjusted the full length mirror so that Miguel could see himself.

The short coat fitted tightly across his broad shoulders and the bold design of black braid on the satin accentuated their breadth. The shirt of fine white lawn, with ruffles down the front, was crisp and delicate. The high waisted trousers, were like the skin of a sausage around his slender hips and down his thighs, widening as they reached his shoes, and the slits on each side parted to reveal white lace under them. He smiled and winked at his reflection in the glass. 'Not bad, eh, Pepito? Spanish clothes look better on me than French but that's the style in Havana now.' He walked toward the door.

'Look, *viejo*, I want you to see what your little Miguel has found for himself. While we are eating, slip into the dining room and hide behind one of the pillars. You'll see such beauty as you've never seen before and she's mine, Pepito, and let's hope that someday you'll be taking orders from her here at Estrellita.'

Pepito, with the familiarity of an old servant, slapped Miguel on his back. 'You know, my boy, I think you mean it and it's about time for you to settle down after having tried out all the little fillies in Havana.'

'That's how I know that I'm getting the right one, old man, because I've tried out all the rest.' He walked out into the hall.

Chapter Thirteen

'HOW DIFFERENT YOU look!' exclaimed Margerita as she advanced down the hall to meet Miguel. 'You're a naughty one to have changed your clothes. Now you are no longer my country gentleman in white linen but an Andalusian dandy from Seville while I remain but a simple girl who came to the country for the day. It's unfair to shame me by your magnificence,' but under her breath she added, 'I'm proud of you.'

'It's only to honour you, my dear,' he looked behind her, shading his eyes as he scanned the hall. 'But the dear señora, where is that old crow?'

'Unfortunately – yes unfortunately – the extreme heat of the sun, the distance of the journey, the rocking of the coach, the odour of the horses and the long hours of confinement, all these forced her to stay in her room, none of which is true because I told her she'd have to stay. As a matter of fact she was quite willing because she can stuff herself there without having to be so nastily genteel every moment before you.'

They both started to laugh.

'Let's hope she chokes on a chicken bone,' Miguel said. 'The old buzzard doesn't like me because I'm Cuban, I suppose.'

'Naturally, she's Spanish. Did you ever hear of a Spaniard liking a Cuban?'

'Only one,' he nodded his head.

'Who?'

'You,' and he pointed to her and then to himself.

'Oh, but there you are wrong,' she laughed. 'Whatever

made you think I liked you? I don't. I love you, love you, love you.'

'Then prove it to me.'

She came to his arms and their lips met. Now it was impossible for him to relinquish her, but she finally managed to free herself. 'Remember what we said about playing with fire?'

'But I like to play with fire. Watch!' He dragged a heavy old chair from its position near the wall and pushed it under the crystal chandelier, balancing himself precariously on the arms as he struck a light from his flint. The tiny flame flared in the tinder and he applied it to one of the candles, watched it catch on the wick, then leaped lightly to the floor and pushed the chair across the tiles.

He clasped her in his arms again. His hand sought the thin gold chain around her neck and slowly followed its length where it disappeared down under her bodice. Once there his hand did not seek the gold locket but something infinitely softer and more precious. He whispered so softly his words were scarcely audible. 'My love, as long as Estrellita shall stand, a candle shall burn here day and night as a pledge of our love. Now, I claim a kiss or rather, dear one, I give you a kiss.' His fingers released the tiny buttons of her bodice and his head was buried in the lace, his lips touching the softness of her flesh. When he lifted his head, he whispered again. 'In the years to come, Margerita mia, each time we meet here under this burning candle I shall claim a kiss from you.'

'And you may have it,' she whispered back.

'Can you possibly be as happy as I am?' he asked.

Her body flattened against him. 'Can you doubt it? I've dreamed about you even though I never thought you would be flesh and blood. Now I am here and it is no longer a dream and you are flesh and blood.'

'No, it is no dream. It's just the two of us – *tu y yo*. And this enormous thing which is our love. But as much as I love you, I must jump down from the clouds because our lunch is waiting and we have only a little time. Besides,' he pushed her gently away, 'I'm starving.'

'How romantic! My Andalusian dandy thinks of food while he makes love. But lest I accuse you of not being able to exist on love alone, let me tell you that I'm ravenous.'

With her head on his shoulder and his arm around her waist they walked down the long corridor into the dining room. Their entrance caused a stir of excitement. Footmen took their places behind the tall chairs and the meal commenced. Servants arrived with silver platters heaped with delicacies; wine flowed into tall goblets of Venetian glass with twisted stems; and to crown it all an ample Negress appeared, carrying a massive tray piled high with saffron coloured rice, dotted with red pimientos, from which arose a most tantalizing odour. She carried it to Miguel. He looked at it searchingly, took a long breath and closed his eyes. He motioned her to show it to Margerita. The white teeth of the Negress shone as she lowered the platter.

Margerita sniffed. 'It's divine: what is it?'

'Something to prove to you that Cuba is better than Spain because this is a Cuban dish and nobody can prepare it like our Rosa. It's *arroz con pollo*, my dear. The perfect wedding! Chicken and rice!'

Margerita eyed it as Rosa placed it on the buffet. 'Oh, Miguel, I'm glad it's such a large platter.'

They sat at either end of a long table – a table made from a single mahogany log – separated by its vast length and a multitude of flowers, a profusion of silver and the lace of the tablecloth. Miguel, jealous of the distance that separated them, signalled to one of the footmen to move his chair nearer to Margerita.

'This big room was never designed for two, my dear, but I thought the old buzzard would be eating with us and it would be safer, under her eyes, for me to be at one end of the table and you at the other. But had I known you intended to confine her to her room, we would have eaten *tu y yo* in the patio. There's a corner there, all surrounded by a thick screen of vines and in that corner there is a tiny fountain which trickles over ferns as delicate as maiden's hair, keeping them all embroidered with crystal drops which are not half as brilliant as your eyes. There are flowers there too – mariposa lilies nearly as white as your skin and roses almost as red as your lips; yes, even carnations, the beautiful *claveles* which would honour you.'

'My flowers, Miguel?'

'Your flowers, my dear.'

They ate slowly, scarcely keeping their eyes away from each other until the last tray of sweets was taken away by the servants. Miguel rose and walked to the windows, pulling up the jalousies so that the light of the sun shot through the cool dimness of the room. It shone full on the opposite wall, lighting with its brilliance the two portraits which hung there.

'My father and mother, Margerita,' he said. 'I want you to meet them. I never knew them for they died soon after I was born. Grandmother has been all I ever had except Rodana my nurse and Pepito. Rodano died a few years ago but I still have Pepito.' He repeated the name. 'Good old Pepito.'

There was a faint rustling behind one of the pillars in the far corner of the room and a door closed quietly. All the servants had left.

Margerita studied the pictures in silence. One showed a handsome young man, as dark as Miguel, with the bright jewel of the Golden Fleece pinned to his coat. The other was a young woman with jet black hair and large dark brown eyes. 'I like them,' she said slowly, 'and they must have been wonderful people to have a son like you. I wish they might know how sad I feel for them that they have never seen their wonderful son.'

Miguel did not answer her. He allowed the sun to flood them with light for another moment, they closed the jalousies. The room resumed its twilight coolness. She sat down and he sat on the arm of her chair. 'I would like to tell you something,' he began 'some of which you may already have heard. There are several versions which are told in Havana but it is only right that you should know the correct one.'

'How fortunate that I do know the *correct* one.' She pressed his hand.

'I was born here,' he continued. 'Not in this house for

there was another house here at the time. It was an old house, one of the oldest in Cuba – some parts of it wood, some of it stone. My father and mother lived here and he wished me to be born here rather than in the city. He said Havana was Spanish but that this was Cuba and he wanted me to be a Cuban. My mother was very ill after I was born; the midwife stayed with her constantly and my father never left her side. When I was but three days old there was a bad hurricane – probably the worst that ever hit the island. The slaves left off their work and took shelter in their houses which were made of stone, small, snug and secure. My father dispatched Roberto Garcia, who was our head overseer, to see that all the slaves were properly taken care of and to return to the house and fasten all the doors and windows.

'No sooner had Garcia left the house than the winds struck, along with a torrential rain. Never before had a hurricane struck so quickly and with such force. The wind blew in through the open windows, blew the roof off and dropped it back on the house. The walls bulged outward and the house was crushed like an eggshell. With the first gust of wind, however, the midwife grabbed me from my mother's side, lifted the lid of a huge chest – the one you see against the wall under the portraits and placed me inside. It was partly filled with baby clothes which my mother had ordered from the Santa Clara Convent. As you can see it is an old Spanish *cajon* made of solid oak and almost covered with wrought iron. No sooner had she placed me in it and closed the lid than the walls collapsed. My father and mother were killed as was the midwife.

'Most of the slaves survived the storm. After the wind died down, father's dog, which in some way had survived, was noticed sitting near a pile of heavy timbers. He would not leave and kept barking and whining. Pepito noticed the dog and called for help, thinking perhaps that my father was still alive in the rubble. After the slaves had cleared away the timbers and the broken tiles, they opened the chest and found...'

'You, my dear, sleeping peacefully on a bed of soft linen. What a miracle that you did not smother.'

'I believe I was yelling at the top of my lungs but I had not smothered because the chest is large. They immediately summoned a young mulatto slave whose child, born a day or so after I was, had died at birth. She was an octoroon girl whom my father had purchased from a cousin who had a jealous wife. Her breasts were full and she nursed me. My grandmother arrived only moments after they found me. She had been on the road from Havana when the storm broke – having been summoned to the *finca* by the critical condition of my mother – but Tomas, the coachman, had saved her by placing her behind a stone wall and shielding her with his body. Well, my grandmother took me back to Havana along with my wet nurse, Rodana, and that is my story.'

Margerita released his hand and walked slowly across the room to where the chest stood. Her hands caressed the iron bossings, and dropping to her knees she laid her cheek on the cover. Miguel lifted her to her feet and together they walked out the door into the patio.

The afternoon sun, creeping between the thick leaves of the vines, cast mottled shadows on the tiles. The faint music of the fountains mingled with the singing of the birds in cages. As they passed along, their faces were alternately in shadow and sunshine. Miguel led her to a small door, heavy with steel nailheads, which he unlocked with an enormous iron key. They entered a small room, its walls lined with wooden shelves. Boxes of all sizes were piled on them – large boxes of native woods, smaller ones covered with cowhide, chests of brass and strong boxes of steel.

'The family dungeon?' Margerita laughed.

'It might be, from its appearance, *querida*.'

'Or it might be Bluebeard's chamber.'

'Or just the room where the silver and other valuables are kept.' Miguel found a wooden stool and climbed up on it, examining the different boxes one by one until he came to a certain inlaid box with silver corners. Taking it down from the shelf and motioning for her to follow, he carried it to a bench in the patio. As he fitted a small key in the lock, he said, 'I promised you a gift today – not the slave Fidel, nor even the kiss I gave you under the candle, but this. It once belonged to my mother and it has never been used since she died. I remembered it and it seemed made for you. Carnations for La Clavelita!'

He opened the box. There against the yellowed satin, each in its separate compartment, were the various pieces of a toilet set. Mirrors, combs, brushes, boxes for unguents – all were fashioned of gold and each in the shape of a carnation, with the edges of the petals outlined with tiny rubies. 'Carnations were my mother's favourite flower too and my father had this fashioned for her in Paris for a wedding present.' He picked up one of the pieces and handed it to her.

She lifted the various pieces one by one and admired them. The little boxes were perfect blooms; the backs of the mirrors were bouquets of flowers, their stems interwoven to form the handles. Even the candlesticks were growing plants.

'How stupid of me!' Miguel exclaimed. 'The monograms! I had forgotten they were marked. Each piece has my mother's monogram on it.'

'Oh they are lovely, Miguel! All my life I have loved these flowers but I never expected to see them in gold. But the monograms do not harm them.'

'No, they must be changed because from now on they are yours and they must be entirely yours. We can remedy it at once if you are willing to wait for them a few days. I know of a place. We shall pass it on our way back to Havana and we can leave them there.'

Reluctantly she put the pieces back but after they were all arranged and he was ready to close the chest, she put her hand on his arm. She touched the various pieces thoughtfully and then finally chose one of the smallest boxes which she removed. 'This tiny one I wish to keep, Miguel, exactly as it is. The monogram on this must not be changed. Do you mind?'

'It's all yours, darling, to do with as you please.'

'How can I ever thank you. You have overwhelmed we with gifts today – gifts which I adore but not as much as I do the one who gave them to me. I can only say that whenever I look at these things I shall see you as you are now – so strong, so tall, so handsome, with the shadows and the sunshine on your face and the light of love in your eyes.'

'What more can a man ask? But isn't it a coincidence that my mother's favourite flowers are yours too? It must mean something. Tell me, why do you love these flowers so?'

She waited a long moment before answering him. A rush of memories came over her: memories of work and struggles, of mean theatres and shabby dressing rooms, of poverty that was in such a contrast to this opulence.

'Yes, Miguel, there is a reason why I love these flowers. They have been my talisman, my bringer of good luck, my protector. The first time I danced in public – a young girl quite alone with all the world against me – Encarnacion, my old teacher, plucked a flower from her only plant and placed it behind my ear. "'Twill bring you luck," she said. It was a carnation, red and spicy-smelling. All through the dance when my heart was in my mouth and I did not know how my feet were behaving, the perfume of that brave little flower came to me. Since then I have never danced without one. That is why they call me La Clavelita.'

Surely no carnation could be redder than her lips. He pressed his own against hers.

'The fire is lit again,' he murmured, 'but, alas, there is no time to play with fire.'

'The fire will die down if it is not kindled,' she drew him closer.

'But that is not the way to quench it,' his lips nuzzled her cheek.

'And this is,' she laughed, forcibly removing his seeking hands. 'The day will come when there will be time and then, my love, what a glorious fire we shall both light.'

'A fire that will never be put out. Come, darling.'

Chapter Fourteen

FOR OVER AN HOUR there had been a constant stream of Negroes passing up and down the gravelled drive of La Estrellita. Slaves were returning from the fields, their garments clinging wetly to their skins, their faces blue-black in the shadow of their big straw hats. They would disappear into their neat little cabins behind the big house and through the constant stream of high-pitched conversation which issued from the open doors and windows of the slave quarters came the sound of water splashing. Children made innumerable trips to the big fountain in the rear of the house and occasionally one, tired of waiting in line, would run around the house to the front and brave the spray of the bronze goddess to dip his gourd into the basin.

No sooner had the last stragglers come in from the distant fields than the earlier arrivals began to reappear. Gone were the sweaty rags, the bedraggled garments, the torn pantaloons. The Santiago slaves were a credit to their master. Stiffly starched skirts brushed the gravel of the drive and swept it into swirling patterns; turbans and bandanas in stark, crude colours – reds and purples and golds – made a shifting kaleidoscope of colour. *Caramba!* It was a time of *fiesta!* Laugh and be merry because don Miguel, their lord and master, had said there would be no more work today. And tonight there would be a *baile. Hurra! Viva don Miguel!*

Down the long avenue they promenaded – men and women and children; old men tottering along on canes; toothless old women; stout buxom matrons, ample of breast; young women, some bulging with child; straight, clean-limbed young bucks, their bodies outlined under the thin cotton shirts and pantaloons, walking with the lithe grace of the jungle; children walking sedately beside their parents or running around them in circles; babies, their heads rolling back and forth as their wide eyes surveyed an unknown world. Down the long avenue they came, the shadows of the palms passing over their faces in rhythmical regularity.

The line swelled and grew until, from the house to the distant gates, the drive was alive with people – a mass of white and black and gaudy colour. They sang as they walked – sometimes a Spanish song but more often a weird nameless chant with a strange one-two-THREE-four beat – the African conga.

Generations before their ancestors had developed the rhythm as they walked along, stumbling over the heavy chain that bound them together in single file. They had timed their steps to this chant and only by keeping time to it could they prevent stumbling over the chain, stumbling and tripping and falling on the dark earth of Africa, that land they were so soon to leave; stumbling and falling and being dragged on because the line could not stop. The line must go on. It must reach the sea and then cross the sea and take up its heavy burden again. One-two-*three*-four! The beat of the conga!

Then it had been a sad plaint of their homeland. It had told of their wives and children left behind, of husbands they would never see again, of babies torn from mothers' breasts; it had wailed of young men who had been torn away from the palm-oiled bodies of their sweethearts; of women who longed for the throbbing strength of their men at night; it had spoken of huts in the forests, of remote little villages, of hunting and fishing and primitive love under the tamarisks. But now the old words had been forgotten and new words had been invented – foolish words, simple words, funny words – and the conga was a song of joy not of sorrow yet through its rhythm, the mystic drums of Africa still sounded.

As they neared the chapel, the singing stopped and they walked reverently, for here was the house of God. It was not the god their fathers had known – that pot-bellied, black, Priapic god whose horribly swollen manhood had hidden all else. his was a strange white God who lived on a cross and wore a crown of thorns. He looked down at them with anguished eyes but he taught all men to love one another. His mother was the lovely lady in a robe of blue with silver stars who stretched out her hands to them. She loved them too and they had only to ask for whatever they wanted and she would grant it, or at least that is what the *padre* said but of course she was white and she did not always hear what the black people said. But she had loved her son and through Him all the world. Yes, they could understand her, these slave women. They had sons and they loved them. But the cross they could not understand for the cross meant pain and suffering and why must a god suffer? It was enough for men and women like themselves to suffer.

When they entered the doors of the chapel, they made the sign of the cross and genuflected before the gaunt white figure on the crucifix. They took their seats on the narrow wooden benches, looking straight ahead except for the young bucks whose eyes sought those of the wenches whose drooping eyelids and almost imperceptible nods assured them they would be welcome partners at the dance later. When the chapel had been filled, men and boys stood in the back of the church, in the aisles, in the doorway and even out on the steps.

Miguel, still in his rose and black, and Margerita, followed by the Quesada and Fidel, entered through a side door and seated themselves in a large carved pew in the front of the church. It was cushioned in red damask and fat pillows of the same red damask offered comfortable places for prayer. They all knelt for a brief moment. When they arose, Miguel turned to Margerita and whispered, 'I must leave you for a little while, my dear. I must introduce myself to the new priest for I have never seen him. Father Eliseo was always here, long before I was born. He died only a few weeks ago.' He crossed himself and left her, disappearing through a small door beside the altar.

In a few moments a young priest whose round, peasant face betokened no particular asceticism, came out and held up his hands, blessing the congregation in thickly-accented Latin. Then Miguel appeared. The priest made room for him.

Miguel faced him. 'Father Manuel,' he began, 'I welcome you to La Estrellita. These are my people; make them yours. Take good care of them. They are simple people, Father, and there is no wrong in their hearts. You will have only sins of the flesh to combat and to these people those are not really sins.'

The priest inclined his head. Miguel turned to the congregation.

'My friends,' he began, to the hundreds of upturned faces which confronted him from the benches – faces in all shades and degrees of black and brown and beige; faces ivory and cream and even white, 'I call you my friends because I know that you are. Here at Estrellita we are all friends and I am sure there is not one of you who is not a friend of mine...'

Smiles became broader, white teeth gleamed and heads were nodded in agreement. He continued: 'There is not one of you I would not be proud to call my friend for you are all loyal and faithful to me and one can ask for nothing more from a friend.

'For many years we have lived here together – here on this *finca* – each of us trying to make it a better place. It is as much home to you as it is to me.

'During the time you have been here and during the time I have had authority over you, I have tried to treat you well. If I have failed it is because I am human and, being human, I have made mistakes and I have allowed those under me to make mistakes. But all in all I feel that your lot has been a bearable one compared to that on some of the other *fincas*. Here there has seldom been any need for a whip, no call for chains, no indulgence in cruelty. In all the years that my family has owned this *finca* no slave has ever run away and none has ever been sold.

'But recently I have begun to think more seriously about you. I do not wish to own you any longer. I have decided that there will be no slaves at Estrellita.'

A loud murmur arose from the front benches and gained in volume as it swept back over the church. There were sobs and moans, loud cries and entreaties. Women stood up in the seats with arms outstretched, others stumbled down the aisles sobbing, to throw themselves in front of the altar, while from all sides there arose the cry:

'Do not sell us, don Miguel. Do not sell us. Let us stay here. Oh, for the love of God, let us stay here.'

He held up his hand for quiet, but Pepito, emboldened by years of intimate service, made his way up to the altar and stood in front of the steps. Tears were streaming down his face. He grasped the rail. 'Miguelito,' he cried, 'are you mad? What are you saying?' His eyes searched Miguel's face.

Miguel reached down and guided the old man up the steps. They stood beside each other and he grasped Pepito's hand. 'You misjudge me, *viejo*. You do not give me time to finish. Hear me out and you, my people, attend my words. I have no intention of selling you. Rest assured, you will never be sold because nobody will ever be able to buy you. Every slave on this plantation is to be free; free to stay or free to go; free to live and free to love, to marry and to beget free children. Free! Yes, each one of you will be free because you will no longer be bondsmen and women.'

As the full import of his words slowly dawned on them, they started to rise but with a motion of his hand he restrained them. 'Quiet, my children, I have more to say. I told you that I had been thinking seriously about you. I have been thinking how your happiness, your future, your very lives depend on a slender thread – the lives of an aged lady and myself. Think for a moment. If anything should happen to the two of us, you would be driven from your homes and sold on the block. Families would be separated; wives sold from husbands, sons and daughters sold from each other. This I cannot allow for you are my people. I have known you since I was a child. I have lived among you.

'You, Pedro,' he pointed to a massive Negro in the front, 'you taught me how to ride. Even now I can feel the tenderness of your hands, lifting me onto the horse and their strength as they steadied me. And you, Domingo,' he singled out a youth his own age, 'you taught me how to swim when we used to steal away to the river together, and you, Santo,' he pointed to a slender mulatto, 'I used to sneak out of my bed at night and run down to your cabin to crawl in beside you and we'd stay awake half the night telling each other fantastic stories. Do you remember, Rosita, how

I always ran to the kitchen when anything went wrong and how, after you had dried my tears on the corner of your apron, you would let me sit at the end of your big table and feed me little cakes that you had baked for me? Oh, my people, I could go on and on and on. I could single you out one by one and tell you what you have done for me. Each of you has been kind and good to me all my life.

'Most of my life has been spent with you yet never did I realize that I possessed this terrible power over you. Lest this power fall into another's hand, I intend to set you all free. Tonight I return to Havana and I shall start tomorrow to secure that freedom for you. It will take some time for there are many of you. But the next time I come back to Estrellita I promise you – and you, Father Manuel, witness my words – that each of you will hold in your hands a slip of paper with magic words on it that will make you free.'

A mighty shout arose from the assembly – cries of joy, songs and tears of happiness mingled together – then with one mighty surge they came towards the altar, a pulsating tide of faces. Frantic hands clutched at him. They wanted to touch him, to feel his hands, his clothes, even his shoes. Miguel stepped back and motioned to the young priest to step forward. As the young Father raised his hands in benediction, there was a hush, broken only by Margerita's weeping. Miguel looked at her over the sea of hands surrounding him. She smiled at him through her tears and pointed to something behind him. He turned and stared in amazement. By some strange coincidence there was one lighted candle on the altar. Who had lighted it, he did not know but as Margerita's fingers made the Sign of the Cross, he felt, as he knew she did, that it was kindled by the same flame that burned in the hallway at La Estrellita.

Chapter Fifteen

THE FOUR OCCUPANTS of the coach sat quietly in the dusky interior. It had been a long day and they were tired – too exhausted to talk. Margerita slept lightly with her head against Miguel's shoulder. Her hand, suspended by the brocaded strap, swung gently with the motion of the coach. On the opposite seat, the señora sat as stiffly erect and uncompromising as when she had left in the morning. Her black-mitted hands were tightly clasped in her lap. Even the dust of Cuba seemed afraid to settle on her. She was as stiff as a gothic statue carved from old wormeaten wood.

Fidel lolled back in his corner. His hair was powdered with the dust of the road and his amber eyes stared sleepily at Miguel from under lowered eyelids. The lad was at peace. True, he felt he still belonged to Antonio by reason of their mutual attachment but although he was willing to concede his heart to Antonio, he gloried in the fact that his body belonged to himself. He shifted the weight of the rosewood box on his knees and leaned forward to touch Miguel's knee.

'We have arrived in Marianao, don Miguel. You said you wished to stop at the Academia de Diana.'

'Ah, yes, the house of Rodriguez,' Miguel stirred himself. He put his hand under Margerita's chin and raised her face to his.

She awakened at his kiss. 'Darling, I've been asleep and I do hope I did not sleep with my mouth open.'

'Open or closed it will always be a charming mouth but now you must wake up. We are nearly there and I wish you to come with me.'

She opened her eyes and looked up at him. 'Nearly where, *querido*?'

'Nearly to the house of Rodriguez. You must help me plan the design for the new monogram.'

'Are you quite sure this man is competent to do it? The pieces are far too precious to be spoiled by some amateur.'

'Oh, absolutely! You've probably never heard of him but he has quite a reputation here in Havana. He arrived here some years ago from Spain, accompanied by rumours of some sort of scandal – something which caused him to leave and seek a certain amount of anonymity here. When he arrived he set himself up as a public letter-writer and sat at a folding table day after day in a shady corner of the Plaza. The man was extraordinarily gifted in penmanship. His script was so lovely that even people who could write hired him and he did engraving too on silver and gold. His work attracted so much attention that he was prevailed upon to open a school, which he did, calling it the Academia de Diana. Most every afternoon, you can see all our señoritas, big and little, assembled there to accomplish the beautifully shaded scrolls in which he is so proficient. He has succeeded quite well for most of the letters our young ladies write are quite legible...'

'Especially those addressed to don Miguel de Santiago! I can well imagine that there is a great amount of pains taken with the shading and scrolls on those particular letters and I can well believe that this dashing don Miguel has received hundreds of them.'

He laughed and started counting on his fingers. 'Far too many to count, my dear, but I refuse to commit myself further. I was talking about Rodriguez when your jealous....'

'I'm not jealous, Miguel, I'm not, I'm not, I'm not!'

'But I want you to be. Say that you are. I hope you will scratch the eyes out of any minx who writes me another letter.'

'Of course I'm jealous and I shall do just that. But there! I've interrupted again and you will say "just like a woman" so do, please, tell me more about this Rodriguez.'

'Well, as I told you he is not only a clever penman but an engraver on gold and silver. He marks all my grandmother's silver and if he satisfies her you can rest assured that he is competent. So that is the reason why we are stopping to see him. In fact, we are already here because Tomas is stopping the coach.'

Miguel opened the door and jumped out. 'Señora, you and Fidel please to remain inside. We shall be but a moment, just long enough to leave the box and decide on a new monogram. No, Fidel, I can carry it. Come, Margerita.'

The little house was curiously crooked as if the houses on

either side of it were exerting too heavy a pressure against it. Its tall barred windows looked out suspiciously onto the street. Miguel pulled the bellcord which stirred faint echoes inside and soon a shuffling servant came to the door, opened it a crack and looked at them stupidly. 'The school is closed for the day,' he muttered.

'We have come to see Señor Rodriguez,' Miguel kicked the door open and entered. 'Is he here?'

The servant, a young mulatto buck with long oily hair to his shoulders and a hoop of gold in one ear, grudgingly stood aside for them to enter. He wore only a pair of white cotton drawers and reeked of some sickly sweet perfume which mingled with the musk of his body. 'He is here, señor.'

'Tell him The Santiago would see him.'

The slave scanned Miguel's face. 'Are you the Señor Santiago?' he asked incredulously.

'Of course! Run now and tell your master.'

They stepped into a narrow hall onto a floor of cracked and broken tiles and turned right into a room whose windows faced the street. The walls were of smooth plaster, painted black to a part of their height and embellished with chalky scrolls and flourishes. Small tables, equipped with ink bottles and quills, filled the room.

'This must be the classroom,' Miguel said as they entered. Almost immediately a door in the rear of the room opened and a tiny man entered. In the grey light he too seemed grey. He appeared ill at ease; his fingers were fumbling with an inky quill. With a frightened glance, he looked up at Miguel. His voice trembled as he spoke. 'You are the Señor de Santiago?' His words betrayed the fact that he did not believe it possible.

'Of course, I am Miguel de Santiago.'

'Oh!' the man advanced a step into the room, closing the door through which he had entered carefully behind him. He made a visible effort to control himself. 'Of course! Don Miguel! The grandson of the señora! To be sure! The light is so uncertain. Permit me to light a candle.' He struck a flint and applied the flame to the wick and by its light scanned Miguel's face.

Miguel was shocked to see that the man's face was rouged and painted with even a tiny star of black court plaster stuck on one cheek.

'Why do you visit my poor house, don Miguel?' he asked.

'Because I have business with you. Is that so unusual? Come, man, you are most inhospitable and rude. It almost appears that I am unwelcome here.'

Rodriguez made an effort to smile without cracking the enamel on his cheeks. 'Not at all, not at all, don Miguel. You are most welcome and the señorita too but the lateness of your visit.... you see the school is closed....' his voice brightened, 'ah, perhaps you have a pupil for me. The señorita desires lessons in penmanship. Of course, that is the reason you are here. Yes, I shall be most happy to instruct her. Will you return tomorrow, señorita?'

'What's got into you, Rodriguez?' Miguel's voice showed his annoyance. 'The señorita is not interested in penmanship. I've come on business of my own and I do not intend to return tomorrow.'

The man flinched. 'Important business?'

Miguel was really annoyed and showed it. 'Look! I want you to do some engraving for me and it's most important that it be done well. You're the best in Havana. Now, will you please stop looking at me like a frightened mouse and let me explain to you.'

The man relinquished his position in front of the door and minced across the room. His tenseness had disappeared and he was now all smiles and cordiality. 'Engraving, don Miguel? But, of course. You will excuse me. The name of Santiago upset me – it is of such importance in Havana you know. I could not imagine why you were favouring my humble abode. I seem to be nervous lately,' he made a dainty gesture to brush a strand of hair from his forehead. 'You said engraving? Oh, I shall be most happy to serve you.'

Miguel's annoyance disappeared. This Rodriguez was some sort of an eccentric – a queer character now that Miguel remembered some of the gossip he had heard about him. He moved the candlestick on the table and placed the box near it. When he had opened the cover, he pointed to the pieces inside.

'Now this is what I have in mind. These pieces already have a monogram on them and I believe you can do it. Instead of *"J de S"* I want you to change it to *"M de V"*. Can you do that?'

The man's twittering had almost subsided. He picked up one of the mirrors and examined it closely under the candle. While his hands caressed the gold lovingly, his fingertips lingered on the sharp facets of the rubies.

''Twill be difficult, don Miguel. Painstaking and difficult. The old monograms will have to be obliterated which is a deal of work in itself. Rubbing them out will be a long and tedious process but it is possible. Then the new monogram can be engraved. Have you something in mind – any particular style?'

'What would you suggest?' Miguel turned to Margerita.

She seated herself at one of the little tables and picked up a pen, drawing a piece of paper in front of her. For a few moments she tapped the pen on the table, then with sudden inspiration started to speak. 'I can only make a rough sketch but it will be sufficient to show Señor Rodriguez my idea. Let him draw my initials so – the "M" and the "V" intertwined with a tiny "del" inside them.' She turned toward Miguel, 'Oh, how clumsy they look when I draw them!' Her pen traced a laborious line on the paper. 'Then, around the "M" and the "V", I desire another "M" – a large bold one which must entwine around them, supporting them, enclosing them, protecting them. The small "M" and the "V" will stand for Margerita but the strong, bold "M" is for my Miguel who holds the little feminine letters in his grasp.'

She passed the sketch to Rodriguez, who examined it closely, holding it beside the candle. He laid it on the table, went to a desk in the rear of the room and returned with a magnifying glass.

'I left my spectacles in the other room,' he explained, 'but this will suffice. A clever idea, señorita, and a most artistic one.' He passed the paper to Miguel.

Miguel nodded approval. Margerita stood up and sought the shelter of his arm. Rodriguez seated himself and peered through the glass. Miguel placed the sketch on the table beside him, 'Copy this, señor, as only you can do it. Draw it out on a piece of paper. I want to keep this one,' he added.

There was no noise in the room but the scratching of the quill as the old man traced the letters. Slowly they took shape under his hand, flowing from the pen onto the paper; the "M" and the "V" with the little "del" between them and all around them, weaving through them, touching them, embracing them and intertwining among them was another "M" – big, bold and protecting. He handed the paper to Miguel and Margerita for their comments.

'Excellent, señor,' Miguel held the paper so Margerita might see, 'do you approve, my dear?' She nodded. 'Then, señor, start in on the work at once. It must be done quickly. How long will it take – two days, three days, four days?'

'Instead of days you must say weeks,' Rodriguez answered. 'The work is very difficult and I have other work which must be finished before I can start this. A previous commitment, you know, and very important.'

'Put it off! I'll pay you double.'

'Oh, I should like to, don Miguel, but I've promised and it's a legal matter which cannot be delayed. I must finish it, my dear don Miguel, I really must.'

'Oh well, but it is a shame to keep the lady waiting. However send it to the Casa de Santiago when you have finished and the money will be waiting for you. Do it as quickly as possible. Now, señor, we must be going and please, should I come again do not stare at me as if a ghost had walked into your house. I thought I had frightened you but, as you said, the hour was late, the light was dim and you did not have your spectacles. *Buenas noches, señor.*'

'*Buenas noches* to you both. I am always at your service.' He tripped along before them to open the outside door and watched them enter the carriage and drive away. Only then did he allow himself the luxury of a long breath. Closing the outside door and bolting it, he almost ran through the lighted schoolroom, extinguishing the candle and opening the door into the backroom.

'Oh, my dear,' he said, stopping for a moment on the threshold, his face illuminated by a fatuous smile of adoration, 'there's no comparison, absolutely no comparison. There are those who say that Miguel de Santiago is the handsomest fellow in Havana, nay in all Cuba, but they are wrong. Oh, he's good looking enough in a dark, Latin manner but he can't compare with you, my dear. He's not half the man that you are, not half.'

'It's a good thing you didn't let him come out here. Come on now, get back to work. We've had enough interruptions.'

'And after I finish? You know you promised?'

'So I did. Close the door.'

Chapter Sixteen

THE AFTERNOON SUN slanted through the jalousies of the Casa Santiago as Miguel wearily pushed his chair back from the desk and leaned his head against the high back. Through the door which opened onto the gallery, he could see Juan's shadow as the boy swept the tiles. He waited for the shadow to materialize into Juan himself, then called to him, 'Juan, fetch Antonio.'

There was a clutter of dusty papers on his desk. He listlessly thumbed through them with a sigh of disgust, seeking a sufficiently heavy piece of parchment to use for a fan. The gold threads in the tapestry of the chair scratched his neck and he stood up impatiently, sweeping all the papers to the floor, and flung himself into another chair whose smooth gilded leather would not offend his nape.

'*Caramba!* I was never cut out to dawdle with papers. I'd much rather be out at the *finca*. There I can accomplish something but these goddamned papers will drive me crazy.'

The business of freeing the Santiago slaves was proving far more complicated than he had imagined. It was one thing to promise them their freedom and quite another thing to obtain it. True, his actions were unpopular and he knew that more than ordinary legal red tape was being wound around every action. The legal technicalities had attracted a throng of Spanish lawyers and Cuban advocates who collected and buzzed around like fat green flies on carrion flesh. All the time, reams of paper and parchment, written in fine and delicate script must be prepared and these decorated with blobs of red wax and submitted to this Excellency and that Excellency for approval and then buried in files where they were lost forever. Hurry the bastards he could not for the longer they delayed and the more involved the process became, the larger the fees they would be able to collect and the more they could say to prospective clients, 'If it hadn't been for us, señores, that young Santiago fool would have freed all his slaves and what a precedent *that* would have set.'

This afternoon, after a long and tortuous session which had ended by getting nowhere, Miguel had returned home in desperation, sickened by the unctuous voices and the scrawny fingers pointing out special clauses in yellowed law books. His one source of satisfaction was the fact that he had secured papers of freedom for both Antonio and Fidel. This he had been able to do because their very recent purchase had engendered a minimum of discussions as to ownership, birth, title and other ramifications of the sale trade. The bill of sale was not disputed although Miguel had suspected that Solano's rancour might have caused it to be questioned. Miguel's title to the slaves was clear and he was able to get their papers of manumission without any difficulty. But that was all he had accomplished except to bog down deeper and deeper into the legal morass.

His revolutionary move had hit Havana exactly as he had expected. It was causing heavy repercussions and the result was growing ever more menacing as it travelled through the tortuous grapevine of Havana gossip. All the great planters were hearing about his efforts to free his slaves.

'Arrogant little pup!'

'Spoiled by his grandmother!'

'Thinks because he's a Santiago he can do anything he wants!'

'Somebody ought to put a stop to it!'

'He should be sent to prison.'

For the first time in his life, Miguel was unpopular. People at whose home he had always been welcomed most effusively were cool towards him. Elderly men who were in the habit of complimenting him on his management of the *finca* began to speak of him as that 'rattle-brained young Santiago'. It was dangerous to fool around with such matters. The blacks had always been slaves. Why, who would do the work? Slaves were nothing but animals, unable to care for themselves. Who would free horses or cows and let them fend for themselves? Besides, they profited from slavery – or so they thought – so god damn it anyway, let Elena de Santiago's brat keep his mouth closed.

The name of Santiago resounded from city wall to city wall – from *finca* to *finca*. It was discussed over cups of coffee and smooth Havana cigars with a thumping of tables and a waving of hands. It was argued about in the bodegas and the plazas and even found its way into the boudoirs and, of all places, bedrooms. When a matter of business penetrates a Cuban bedroom it is serious indeed. Fists were shaken, fans were snapped open and shut, satin coats were buttonholed by aristocratic fingers and rough cotton coats by work-stained thumbs. The result of all the arguments, all the lifted voices, all the whispered conferences was always the same. Someone ought to do something about it and do it soon – *ahorita!* And there the matter rested for there was always *mañana*.

Miguel reached for the bell cord and was about to ring it when Antonio came through the doorway.

'Your pardon, *mi amo*,' he apologized, 'I was about to answer Juan's summons when I was interrupted by an urgent request from your grandmother, which I thought I had better answer at once.'

Miguel's voice was petulant, like a little boy's. The failure of his plans for the slaves and the fact that he had been forced to wait for Antonio showed in his face.

'All right, all right! I want that damned chair by my desk taken away and re-upholstered. Have somebody rip that tapestry off and put on something that will not scratch me.'

Antonio started toward the chair but Miguel halted him.

'Not now! Not now! Later! Get somebody else to do it. There's no reason for you to do such a thing when the house is overrun with servants. I wanted to see you – oh yes – about my grandmother. You are quite right to attend to her first.' His voice lost the edge of annoyance and became softer. 'I am glad, Toñito, that she likes you. She is always most complimentary in regard to you and she says you have such fine legs,' Miguel grinned, his petulance gone, 'even the Marquesa noticed them.'

'Thank you, don Miguel. It's a pleasure to serve the señora and I am glad that my legs please the marquesa.'

Miguel looked up at Antonio, inventorying him with a searching glance that took in everything from his head to the soles of his shoes. How different he was from the half nude wretch he had purchased in Solano's. Antonio's hair was sleekly brushed in an attempt to smooth out the wide-channelled waves and was clubbed behind with a narrow taffeta ribbon. His well cut coat of sleek black mohair fitted him faultlessly as did the breeches of white merino. The black silk stockings added the correct sheen to the muscled calves and the silver buckles on his shoes shone as brilliantly as the silver buttons on his coat. But it was not the clothes which had made the change in him. His eyes which had been so devoid of hope were now full of life. He held his head at a proud angle, his shoulders were squared and he had an air of confidence in himself.

'Sit down, Toñito,' Miguel pointed to the offending chair, 'I have something to discuss with you.'

Without moving toward the chair to which Miguel had pointed, Antonio answered, 'You forget, don Miguel, a slave does not sit with his *amo*.'

'Quite true, Toñito, quite true. If some slaves did it with some masters it would merit ten lashes at the public whipping post. True, "a slave does not sit with his master" but there is another equally good expression "a slave does not disobey his master" and if I say *sit*, I mean *sit*.'

'Very well, don Miguel.'

'Then, goddamn it, sit down!'

'I had no desire to disobey you, don Miguel. I shall do as you bid,' Antonio sat gingerly on the very edge of the chair, his back bolt upright.

'Come, come, let's put an end to this,' Miguel jumped up and took Antonio by the shoulders and pushed him back into the chair. 'I didn't say to sit on the edge like a rooster perched on a pole. Sit back, relax! Here have a *tobaco*, they come from don Pedro's *fabrica*. No? Then let us talk, you and I. Let us talk as though we were friends – as though you were Julio Castanero come to see me. Surely we have something in common besides the fact that I purchased you from Solano.'

Antonio thought for a moment. 'Well, I can tell you about the state of the finances here at the Casa; how much we have spent for wine this past month; how much we have been overcharged by the *carnicero* and about the accident to your grandmother's Murano vases. I can show you the samples of the new upholstery for the chairs in the blue salon. I can . . .'

'*Merda!* Do you think Julio and I would talk about butcher's bills and the chairs in the blue salon. Hell no! We'd talk about the girls we had last night, or at least that is what we would have talked about before I met Margerita. *Caramba*, Toñito, the little *putas* of Havana must be missing me. But I forgot,' he looked at Antonio quizzically, 'you're not much interested in women are you?' He held up his hand as Antonio started to speak. 'Not that I hold it against you. Not at all. Myself, I've never been tempted by pretty boys but a lot of my friends are and they are not ashamed of it. After all, the King and Queen of Spain share their Manuel Godoy together so if you prefer Fidel to any of the girls in the Casa, you have as much right to your preference as the King of Spain.'

'May I speak, don Miguel?'

'Well, damn it, man, that's what I've been wanting you to do.'

'As a slave, if I take a woman I cannot be married to her. My children will be slaves, more fodder for the auction block. I have no desire to bring children into the world who will be bought and sold. Why create a life of misery. Oh, I realize that you would benefit by it. The slaves I sired would be light of skin and command good prices. But so far, don Miguel, I have never lain with a woman and that is why. I shall not beget a brood of little animals for the vendue table, not if I can help it. Of course, I must needs do it if you command me.'

'That I will not do. I've no desire to have you act as stud merely to add a few pesos to the Santiago fortune. At least we've found something to talk about besides butchers' bills and blue upholstery.'

'Those, don Miguel, are my interests.'

'Well then, it's high time you got other interests.'

Antonio sat forward in his chair. For a second the old worried look came into his eyes.

'I don't understand you, don Miguel,' he said with an obvious effort. 'I have tried to make these things my interest thinking that that was what you wanted.'

'Perhaps it was but it just happens that I don't want it any longer. Do you understand?' Miguel spoke sharply but he seemed to be hiding a desire not to smile.

Antonio started to rise but Miguel barked at him. 'Sit down, god damn it. I haven't said for you to stand up.'

'You ask me if I understand you, don Miguel, and I must confess I do not. I've tried in every way to serve you well and now you appear angry because I have. What have I done to offend you? Really, I don't understand.'

'A slave is not supposed to understand. And what right have you to question me? Don't forget, just because I asked you to sit here and carry on some sort of an interesting conversation with me, I still own you. Remember that!'

Antonio stared straight ahead; only a slight quiver of his nostrils betrayed his resentment.

Miguel opened a drawer of the desk and took out a folded

parchment. 'Perhaps now you'll understand. I find you unsatisfactory as a major domo. You are no longer to work around the house and get involved with butchers' bills and blue satin upholstery.'

Antonio was baffled. He could only stare at Miguel and comprehend the increasing sternness in his master's face. The silence of the room became tense, broken only by Miguel's fit of coughing. He coughed so hard he had to hold a handkerchief in front of his face. 'I find don Pedro's cigars too strong,' he threw the stub on the floor and crushed it with his shoe.

Antonio still stared at him. 'May I say I'm sorry, don Miguel. I have tried hard to please you.'

Miguel tapped the folded parchment with his finger.

'This is a bill of sale. Why don't you ask me to whom I am selling you?'

'It doesn't matter. I am happy that Fidel is in good hands. If I leave your service nothing much matters to me.'

Miguel unfolded the parchment slowly. It crackled in his hands and the blob of red wax in the corner weighted the page down.

'But I insist that you know. Here,' he passed the paper to Antonio, 'read this. That's an order and if you disobey me I'll send you to the whips.'

Antonio took it but he seemed unable to look at it. The parchment trembled in his hands.

'If I were a free man, I'd kill you, don Miguel.'

'For a slave to threaten his master warrants a hundred lashes and no slave has ever lived through that number. Read that bill of sale! Read it!'

Antonio looked at the parchment. He quickly grasped the portent of the words. The lines in his face relaxed and he started to smile. 'A slave,' he began, 'always obeys his master. That is a lesson I have spent a lifetime to learn but tell me, don Miguel, what does a free man do when another man gives him an order?'

'That's a question I cannot answer because no man ever dared give me an order. If he did I'd tell him to go to hell.'

'Then go to hell. If you want it read, read it yourself.'

For a long moment they sat looking at each other until Miguel could no longer control his laughter. It was infectious and Antonio too started to laugh. They roared at each other, slapping each other's knees, until the tears rolled down their cheeks. When Miguel finally managed to control himself, he managed to speak.

'Well spoken, *hombre*. You paid me back with my own coin. You threatened to kill me and you consigned me to hell. Ho, ho! I'll read it. *Por dios*, I'll do just that. But first pass me the paper, if you will be so kind, *don* Antonio.'

Miguel took the paper and read:

> Be it known to all men that I don Miguel de Santiago y del Monte, the lawful and rightful owner of the slave Antonio, age 22 years, five feet, eleven and one-half inches tall, black hair, blue eyes, fair skin, branded on the right shoulder with the arms of the Etchegaray family and formerly owned by the late Señor don Manuel Etchegaray and purchased by me from his estate through the agency of don Solano Moreno, do hereby confer on the slave Antonio, born in slavery, his freedom and with the manumission all the rights and privileges of a free man. Signed by me, this fifth day of August in the year of our Precious Lord, one thousand, seven hundred and ninety-two in the presence of witnesses.
>
> Miguel de Santiago
>
> Witnesses
> Domingo Garay
> Jose Antonio Estevez

'There, *hombre*, now does it make any difference to you who your new master is? I hope this new master, this don Antonio, treats you well.'

'How can I put into words what I feel, don Miguel?'

'There are no words, Toñito. I don't ask for words. I need your help to manage the complicated affairs of this house and the plantation. I've no head for figures, for bargaining tradesmen and haggling merchants. I'll raise the cane and make the sugar and then you handle all the other details. I need somebody I can trust. That's why I can't waste you on butchers' bills and upholstering chairs. From now on you will be my secretary, my manager, or whatever you want to call it. There will be a salary and it will be ample – enough to support a wife on if you wish, or you can buy yourself a pretty yellow-haired boy like Fidel if you prefer. I'll not bother with your private life. All I want to know is if you will continue to serve me as a free man as you did as a slave. With loyalty!'

Antonio walked to the big mahogany desk which sprawled along one side of the room. He reached up and took down the ivory crucifix which hung over it. Advancing toward Miguel, he placed one hand on Miguel's shoulder, lifting the crucifix.

'Before God, our Eternal Father; before Christ, his Holy son; before the Blessed Virgin and all the Saints, I take an oath to be faithful and loyal to you, don Miguel.'

'And I believe you. Thank you, Antonio. But here, take my handkerchief. You must have a speck of dust in your eye or else you laughed too hard. Surely you are not crying, Antonio.'

'A man can weep from joy, Miguel, as well as sorrow.'

'Then go ahead and blubber, Antonio. *Por dios*, you've got me doing it too but then, we are Latins and our emotions are always near the surface. We love to dramatize our lives, don't we, Antonio, and it's too goddamned bad that Fidel wasn't here. How he would have revelled in it. I'm sorry I frightened you, Antonio, but I goaded you on just to see if there was a man hidden under the slave. By God, there was! You even threatened to kill me.'

'Forgive me, Miguel.'

'Forgive you? Hell, I glory in it. You've got spirit, Antonio. That's what I like. And some day, *hombre*, I'm going to take you to Josefina's for a special occasion. I'm going to put you in a room with her prettiest little whore and her cutest boy and you can take your choice. Then you can compare them and, *hombre*,' Miguel waggled a finger at him, 'after Josefina's girl gets through with you, you'll tell the lad to go to hell just like you did me.'

'It's worth trying,' Antonio grinned back.

Chapter Seventeen

ANTONIO and Miguel sat back in their chairs awaiting Fidel's arrival. He was late, much to Miguel's annoyance for he had wished Fidel to be present when Antonio received his freedom. It had been Fidel's idea at first to frighten Antonio. His love for the dramatic always prompted such scenes and he had made Miguel promise to keep Antonio a little in suspense. But, although Fidel had missed the drama, nevertheless the parchment with its words of freedom, had made a different person of Antonio. In the few moments that had passed since he had received it, he had lost his tenseness and his air of subservience. He realized he would never in his life have to call another man '*amo*' again. There was something particularly demeaning about the word. A man was *amo* to a dog, a horse or a slave. It was degrading and purposely so. Now, in his new status, he could talk with Miguel almost like an old friend. He could even question him if he desired without first having to ask permission.

'We had quite a performance over christening Fidel the other day,' the remembrance of the occasion caused Miguel to think of Margerita – everything caused him to think of her these days, 'that lad should be on the stage. Actually it was his idea that I scare you and make you believe I was selling you. He had planned to stand by and beg, with tears in his eyes probably, that I change my mind. Then, through his entreaties I was to offer you your freedom and Fidel would knight you as Margerita did him. Which reminds me, you've got to have a name too.'

'A name? I had forgotten that. I've never had one, have I?'

'Well, there's a certain advantage to that. Now you can choose any name you like. You can be a Bourbon like the King of Spain, or a Borgia like that Spanish Pope, or even a Santiago. Listen, *hombre*! Your father is the Duke of Ramar. You certainly have a right to the name although you'll never be able to claim the title your half-brother has. So how about Antonio de Ramar? Sound good to you?'

Before Antonio had a chance to answer, Fidel burst into the room. The suit of amber satin shone in the sunlight. The boy had evidently begged some stage jewellery from Margerita for his hands sparkled with enormous gems. When he saw Antonio seated in Miguel's presence, he realized that he had missed the important scene.

'He knows, don Miguel?'

Miguel nodded.

'And did you scare him to death before you told him?'

'He even offered to kill me and then he told me to go to hell. Sorry you missed it. One word led to another and before I knew it, I'd handed him the paper. By the way, *hombrecito,* I don't believe you've ever been introduced to this fellow. Señor Dorado, may I present my new manager and man of confidence, Señor Antonio de Ramar?'

Fidel rushed up to Antonio and embraced him. For a moment all was quiet – even the voices in the street were hushed. Fidel broke the silence. 'You too, Antonio? *Tu y yo!* You and I! Remember how many times you used those words when we were at Solano's. You and I. Now we are both free.'

'It's a wonderful feeling,' Antonio laughed. 'A little too new for me to be used to but I'm beginning to understand. We owe it to don Miguel. And now you swear to him as I did that even though he has freed our bodies, he cannot free our souls because they will always belong to him.'

'Do you take me for an idiot, Antonio?' Fidel exclaimed. 'That was what made me late. I stopped at the cathedral and burned a candle at every shrine so that every saint would be a witness to my vow. And I put a *peseta* in the box too – the first one I ever had – that I would never forget that my first *peseta* came through the kindness of don Miguel.'

'I suppose you considered it a good investment,' Miguel could not help laughing at the boy's posturing, 'but now how about some wine? The occasion seems to demand it.'

Antonio, at Miguel's request, rang for Juan. When the boy arrived, he gazed in astonishment at the three of them sitting there. Miguel dispatched him for some wine, cautioning him to bring only the very best Jerez and reminding him that don Antonio was a judge of good wine. Fidel surreptitiously polished the glassy jewels in his rings, hoping that Antonio would notice them. When Antonio did, Fidel was loath to admit that there might be some possible doubt as to their authenticity, a fact altogether too well corroborated by the black marks the brass had left on his fingers.

Juan reappeared in a few moments, his eyes round with questioning wonderment, and placed the decanter and glasses on the table. Miguel poured the wine and Juan, still in open-mouthed astonishment to see his master not only sitting with two slaves but actually drinking with them, passed the glasses to Antonio and Fidel. They lifted their glasses and drank, but each drank a different toast: Miguel to Margerita and their life ahead of them; Antonio to freedom and the chance to be a man; and Fidel – well – Fidel drank to Antonio and he drank to himself also.

'I realize,' Miguel began, placing his glass back on the tray, 'that you may feel embarrassed as time goes on and you come in contact with people who may look at you askance. You, Antonio, will probably have little trouble. As far as I can see you haven't a trace of Negro blood that shows. But you, Fidel, you are not as white as Antonio and, as a matter of fact, I don't seem to be either.' He placed his sunburned hand beside Antonio's whiter one, 'but always remember this, you can't help being a *mestizo*, but you can make men respect you even if you are one. As a matter of fact, Antonio, I suppose you are related to half the royalty in Europe but it will avail you nothing. You've got to make your life yourself. At least you can put the past behind you and you have the future ahead of you.'

'*Gracias a Dios*, we have a future now, thanks to you.'

Fidel nodded in approval while he eyed the bottle of wine.

Miguel caught his glance. 'But we are forgetting our hospitality, Antonio. We have a guest. Señor Dorado has come to call on us so let us sit here and enjoy ourselves. Tell me about Margerita, Fidel. I have not seen her since last night.'

'She does nothing but talk about you.'

'*Ay de mi!* Could she find a better subject?'

'Why, even this morning that old bitch – pardon me, I

mean the Señora de Quesada – was talking to Luis and I overheard them. She said, "It's Miguel this and Miguel that! Oh, how handsome he is! What marvellous hands he has! How his hair curls away from his temples! Why, when he smiles one corner of his mouth is higher than the other! Bah! I'm so tired of this Cuban puppy I could retch."' Fidel minced across the room, aping the straight-laced señora with her acid smile so perfectly that Miguel roared.

'How like the old hag. You've never met this old turkey who is forever casting her shadow on my Margerita. *Que mujer!* I think she is a witch and that she leaves at night, riding through the sky on a broomstick. Are there any broomsticks in Margerita's house, Fidel? No, never mind! But tell me more. What does Margerita herself say?'

'Well, she says she is only happy when you are with her and that her only joy is in looking at you and being with you.'

'Yes, yes, go on.' Fidel's words were like music to Miguel.

'And that she loves to watch you do things, even ordinary little things like eating mangoes. She loves to see you bite into them with your white teeth and . . .'

'I gather the impression that the lady loves you,' Antonio interrupted.

'Loves him, Antonio?' Fidel poured himself another glass of wine. '*Dios mio!* I think she loves him almost as much as we do.'

There was a rap at the door and Juan entered. The three young men were sitting at their ease – Miguel in white, Antonio in black and Fidel in gold – and chatting as amicably as three old friends, quite oblivious to the fact that a few hours ago there was no common ground on which they could meet.'

'A caller for you, *amo*,' Juan announced. 'It is don Lorenzo de Riojas.'

'Don Lorenzo? Show him up, Juan. Have him come here. No, Antonio,' he held out a restraining hand as the boys rose to go. 'Remain here. He probably comes on business. His *finca* adjoins mine and you, as my man of confidence, must be here. You stay also, Fidel. I shall want to hear more about Margerita when you leave. Open the jalousies, Fidel. No, leave them closed, the sun is too hot.'

Long before don Lorenzo came into the room, he could be heard puffing and snorting on the stairs. The heavy tap of his cane on the tiles shattered the quiet of the afternoon like a series of pistol shots. Without waiting for Juan to announce him, he burst through the doors, his face purple from exertion and his cane shaking in his hands.

'See here, Miguel, see here. What's all this nonsense I hear about you freeing the slaves at Estrellita? Has Elena gone mad? Are you *absolutamente loco* yourself? I've come today as a representative of some twenty plantation owners to reason with you. I volunteered because I know you so well. You are ruining us, Miguel, and not only us but Cuba.'

Miguel sprang up to take don Lorenzo's arm and guided him to a chair. The word '*abanico*' sent Fidel hurrying for a fan and Antonio brought a low footstool on which don Lorenzo rested one leg with difficulty.

'Sit down, don Lorenzo, you are quite out of breath,' Miguel said, 'and then, one question at a time. A glass of wine? Antonio, please pass me the decanter. Oh, a thousand pardons, Antonio, and yours too, Fidel. You do not know my good neighbour. Don Lorenzo, may I present my friends, Antonio de Ramar and Fidel Dorado. Señores, my illustrious neighbour and good friend, don Lorenzo de Riojas.'

Don Lorenzo steered the wine to his lips. 'Hrrumph,' he muttered. 'An honour to be sure. Ramar? Ramar? I know of nobody by that name in Cuba. There's a Duke of Ramar in Spain.'

'A relative, señor,' Antonio replied.

'I'm happy to know you. I met the Duke when he was here in Havana many years ago. Come to my house some day with Miguelito, and you too, señor,' he nodded at Fidel.

Fidel had retreated to the far corner of the room and sat in the shadow. He stood up and bowed.

Don Lorenzo promptly forgot them as he turned to Miguel.

'I want to talk to you privately.'

'Do, don Lorenzo. Señor de Ramar is my man of confidence, my manager, my agent, and Señor Dorado works with him. Whatever you have to say to me concerns them also.'

'By God, Miguelito, do you know what you are doing?' Don Lorenzo chewed at his under lip.

'Quite.'

'Do you know what Havana is saying about you?'

'I can imagine.'

'And don't you care?'

'I've never thought about it, don Lorenzo. Now that you mention it, however, I don't believe I give a good goddamn.'

'I still cannot believe it until I have heard it from your own lips. It's common rumour in Havana and not only in Havana; it's being talked about from Oriente to Santiago and from Pinar del Rio to Cienfuegos that you are freeing all the slaves at Estrellita.'

'For once Havana gossip is right, don Lorenzo. All the slaves at the *finca* and the house servants here in the city.'

'But people are talking . . .'

'So you said before. Allow me to remind you, however, that the Santiagos have rarely paid much attention to what people say.'

'And Elena?'

'Approves of what I am doing. As a matter of fact it was her idea. Probably I would never have thought of it.'

'I'll see her. I'll try to talk some sense into her head.'

Miguel laughed. 'You do that, don Lorenzo. I think my grandmother would appreciate your telling her what to do. You know her as well as I do.'

'No, I'll not tackle her but I'll try to put some sense into your head. Don't you realize that as soon as all the slaves at Estrellita are freed, my slaves will want to be freed? Don't you realize we are all sitting on a powder keg and you are applying a lighted match. The niggers will revolt. There's unrest among the slaves in St Domingue already. It will be the end of the world. They'll murder us in our beds. We'll be hacked to death with machetes.'

Miguel tried hard to curb his temper although the quickness of the Santiago temper was difficult to control.

'They will not hack me to pieces, don Lorenzo, and if you free your slaves they will bless you instead of murdering you.'

'Free my slaves? I'll see the stupid black beasts in hell first. Free my slaves? Who will do the work? Who will cut the cane? Who will work in the house. Free those black *brutos*? No!'

'And why not; they are men.'

'They are not men, they are slaves, brutes, animals, beasts.'

'I disagree. Despite the colour of their skins they are human beings.'

Don Lorenzo could find no place to put the wine glass. In desperation he flung it to the floor. 'I'll not allow such a thing. I'll stop it. I'll get the governor to see you. I'll go to him today. I'll . . .'

'Don Lorenzo, I beg of you. Desist! You'll have a stroke. Really there is nothing you can do. I've examined the matter quite thoroughly. Manumission is provided for by law. Why, even you, don Lorenzo, freed Pablo, your *mestizo* boy I used to play with and gave him a plot of land for his own.'

'That's different. He is my own son and he is only one slave.'

'And what is the difference between one slave and five hundred? There's a dozen or more bright-skinned children at Estrellita that I've sired myself. Would you offer any objections if I freed them?'

'Of course not.'

'Then why is all Cuba so upset? It didn't set heads to wagging from Oriente to Santiago when you freed your bastard Pablo. The heavens wouldn't fall if I freed my own little yellow bastards. My grandmother desires this, don Lorenzo. It is very important to her peace of mind that every Santiago slave be freed while she still lives. I would honour my grandmother whether I believed in it or not but now I agree with her.'

Don Lorenzo hitched his chair across the tiles to where Miguel was sitting. His voice lost its peremptory tone and became sincerely kind. He laid a hand on Miguel's arm.

'My boy, I'm an old man. I knew your grandfather, may

he rest in peace, and I knew your father and mother. Even though Elena and I could never agree on anything, we have always been the best of friends. I remember holding you on my knee when you came to my home and as you grew older, you and Pablo were like brothers. I was always proud when you came to me for advice about running your plantation. Now, my dear boy, for the last time, I beg of you. Will you prevail on your grandmother to abandon the whole idea?'

Miguel grasped the old man's hand. 'Thank you, don Lorenzo, I do believe you came here with my own best interests at heart, but truly neither my grandmother nor I can be swerved. Please believe me, it will not be the radical change you anticipate. The Santiago slaves will continue to work at La Estrellita, but they will work as free men and at wages. They will no longer be bought and sold, that is all. I do not believe in the barter of humans. Do you, don Lorenzo, in your own heart believe it right? If you do, you would not have freed Pablo. Look, here are my friends. Here am I. Would you think of buying them? Would you buy me? Would you put us on the auction block and bid on us as if we were something other than human? Would you, don Lorenzo?'

'It's an unfair question, Miguel,' the old man answered. 'You and your friends are not to be compared with slaves – brute niggers. You are gentlemen, men of culture, breeding and education. There is no comparison.'

'Oh yes there is, señor.' Miguel stared straight at don Lorenzo. 'Consider my question again. Here is Antonio. Please stand up, Antonio. There, señor, look at him. Would you bid on him if he were on the auction block?'

'Don't be ridiculous, Miguelito. But, to answer your question. Of course not. It is beyond the realm of human thought to place your friend in such a position. Did you not say that he is related to the Duke of Ramar? Well, then, it is a situation which could never exist.'

Miguel stood up. He could no longer control himself. His words tumbled out, his voice rising, his finger pointing at don Lorenzo.

'It is you who are ridiculous, don Lorenzo. Up until an

hour ago this man was a slave, and that boy too,' he pointed to Fidel. 'I bought them from Solano. I bought them as I would buy a horse. I stripped them of their clothes, felt of their teeth, weighed their genitals in my hand. I paid money for them and brought them home. But, they were no different when I bought them than they are today except that then they were in rags and today they are well dressed. Even you cannot tell the difference between a man and a slave. In the face of that do you uphold a law which allows me to sell them to anyone who has the money to pay for them. Did you consider your own son, Pablo, an animal? No, you freed him so that in case something happened to you, your own blood would not be sold on the vendue table.' He strode across the room and flung open the doors.

'Now go, don Lorenzo! Tell all of Havana, yes all of Cuba from Oriente to Santiago and from Pinar del Rio to Cienfuegos that I, Miguel de Santiago, am freeing my slaves as I have these two and as you did your yellow-skinned bastard Pablo. And then, don Lorenzo, tell them why. Tell them that not even you could tell the difference between a slave and a gentleman. Tell them that! Tell them that you sat here this afternoon and that you drank wine with two slaves who a short time ago were stinking wretches in Solano's barracoon, with only a filthy rag to cover their naked balls. Tell them, don Lorenzo. Tell them and let them laugh in your face.'

The old man slumped back in his chair. His hands shook so with rage that the cane he held in them made a tapping sound on the tiles like the ticking of a clock.

'You've done this to me? You, Miguel? Foisted a couple of impostors on me. You've lost your mind. Have you no honour left to trick an old man like me who has always been your friend. Never come to my house again. Never! Go to hell in your own way. You Santiagos! Bah! Who are you to be so high and mighty? I should challenge you to a duel but I will not dishonour my sword by running it through your guts. I leave this house forever. Tell your grandmother she has only my pity for her senility and the fact that she has a fool for a grandson. Tell her she made a mistake. The other one, Jorge's boy, would have had more brains. She'd better send you to stud for Josefina and take Enrique in. To hell with you, you nigger loving, worthless little *maricon*. I don't believe you've got it in you to sire the dozen *mestizo* pups you brag about. Probably you freed these two *maricons* here with you because you sleep with them.' He heaved himself up from the chair and stamped to the opened door. On the threshold he turned and glared, shaking his cane. 'Go to hell, Miguel de Santiago.'

Miguel bowed.

'You are the second person to send me to hell today. Your age has protected you, don Lorenzo. I would not take such words from anybody else. And as for going to hell, hear me out. I do not fear the devil himself and even less than I fear him do I fear you and your twenty illustrious planters. I am *The* Santiago and I shall continue to do in the future as I have done in the past – exactly as I damn please.'

He waited until the sound of don Lorenzo's cane was lost in the patio below. Turning to Antonio and Fidel, he spread his hands wide and although he was still shaking with rage, he began to laugh.

'*Maricon!* I've covered more wenches in my short life than don Lorenzo has in all of his and all he ever had to show for it was Pablo. While I,' he grabbed the carafe and let the wine spurt down his throat, 'can prove that I'm more a man than he is. *Maricon*, indeed!'

Chapter Eighteen

LIGHTS WERE BEGINNING to show in the houses as Miguel and Julio turned into the Alameda de Paula and, as they entered the Plaza de Armas, they could see workmen stringing lights across the façade of the Governor's palace. The huge stone building with its massive arches spanned one side of the Plaza.

'I suppose you are going to the *tertulia* tomorrow night at the Palace,' Julio asked, yawning.

'I suppose so,' Miguel yawned in return. 'These balls bore me. But my grandmother wishes to go and she has no other escort. I'd rather spend the evening alone with Margerita but she will be at the reception,' Miguel's boredom vanished at the mention of her name. 'She will be through at the theatre at ten as she is cutting short her performance because of the ball. I shall go to the theatre to fetch her. Then, for the first time, Grandmother and Margerita will meet. Grandmother has promised to receive her without prejudice and, better still, she has promised she'll hold off the matter of Inocencia Gonzalez until she meets Margerita.'

'What do you think will happen?' Julio asked, anticipating the drama that might ensue when the señora met Margerita.

'I do not know and I wish I did.' A trace of worry crept into Miguel's voice. 'She wants me to marry Inocencia; the Gonzalez fortune tempts her but she just can't swallow the idea of the old man. However, hard as it may be for her to admit that she might be wrong for once, I don't think she'll insist on it. I found out one thing – it was old Gonzalez who started things, not Grandmother.'

Julio had tried hard to picture Miguel with Inocencia even with her gold plating. Although he himself was not much in love with his *novia*, he realized that there was a certain happiness in store for him. But Miguel and Inocencia! Never! Miguel and Margerita! Ah, there was the ideal combination.

'Your grandmother and Margerita . . .' he began.

'Oh, once they have met, I think everything will be all right. Grandmother objects to her being a dancer but she admits that she is far better born than Inocencia. I wanted Grandmother to call on her but she thought a meeting, as though by chance, at the Governor's ball, would be easier. So, Julio, tomorrow decides my future. In the meantime, it's far too early to have dinner. Let us sit a while in a cafe.'

'Which one?'

'We're not far from the Tres Hermanos. Perhaps Oswaldo will be there.'

'Oswaldo? But since the affair of the slaves he is rather cool towards you.'

'Bah! Oswaldo is merely following the fashion. You seem, Julito, to be one of the few to whom it makes no difference whether I own them or set them free.'

'Why should it? The Castenaros are bankers and not planters. Come on, *chico*, we're not far from the Tres Hermanos.'

They stepped from the narrow sidewalk into the open cafe. Here at scores of small tables, the men of Havana were having their cups of coffee or glasses of wine. The cafes of Havana were a favourite stopping place for men on their way home from offices and work. They were the birthplace of Cuban democracy for in them, rich planters and dock workers could sit at adjoining tables. Frantic wives, however, struggling to keep a dinner warm on charcoal fires, would curse the Tres Hermanos and others of its kind. Yet, even while they cursed the cafes and cantinas, they prayed that their husbands were there and not at Josefina's or other like establishments.

A steady hum of conversation greeted Miguel and Julio as they entered the cafe. The sharp staccato of Spanish consonants rising above the torrent of liquid vowels engulfed them. They made their way between crowded tables and, as they went, a wave of silence followed their progress, only to surge up again into conversation as they passed. Some of the men stared at Miguel without seeing him; others turned away; while others mumbled words under their breath that Miguel did not hear. Julio discovered a vacant table near the inner wall and seated himself with his back to the wall, pushing the other chair forward for his friend.

Miguel, realizing the generous gesture on Julio's part to keep him from facing the crowded room, smiled wanly and shrugged his shoulders. 'The Santiago is not very popular tonight.'

'Like the poor *toro* who does not see a friendly face as he enters the bull ring.'

'Ah, there you are wrong, Julito, because I see yours, *amigo mio*. But, like the poor *toro*, I hear the hisses of the *aficionados*. Like the poor *toro*, I don't want to kill anybody, only return to my green fields and blue skies in peace.'

'*Ay de mi!* It's always the poor *toro* who suffers.'

'How right you are,' Miguel spread his hands wide, 'but really, Julio, I never thought I would cause such a storm. When my grandmother brought it up I agreed. Now, having started it I can see that it is the right thing to do and do it I shall. It's a matter of principle now and, god damn it, I'll do it if every door in Havana is shut to me. Even if you forsake me, even you.'

Julio reached across the table and laid a reassuring hand on Miguel's arm. 'There's not much danger of that. I think I know how you feel and I, for one, admire you for it. We've never owned any but house slaves but I feel almost as much affection for Mama Francisca as I do for my own mother and Cleon still sleeps in my room at nights as he has done every night since I can remember. I'd never think of selling either of them and I suggested to my father that he free them. I think he will after all this fuss blows over. So stick to your guns, Miguelito, and some day all these people who revile you will praise you. The main trouble is this: people always love the comfortable little ruts that they fit themselves into, the manner of living to which they have become accustomed. They resent new things, new ideas and new ways of life. New ideas mean new things to think about and you know, thinking for most Cubans is the hardest kind of work they can do. Therefore they want things to stay as they are because it takes less energy. But things are bound to change and those who come after us will look back not on those who were interested in standing still but the few who wanted to try something new. Some day there will be no slavery in the world. People, reading the history of this Cuba, will find on some page these words: "Among the first to broach the idea of freeing the slaves was one Miguel de Santiago."'

'Now you insist on making a martyr out of me. No, Julito, I'm no martyr who is willing to die for a principle. I love life too much, but I'm willing to fight for what I think and I'm damned well going to.'

'You'll never be a martyr, Miguelito. Oh, no. Martyrs are made of sterner stuff than you. But you are a humanitarian. You suffer when others suffer and you feel if you can relieve their suffering you will suffer less. I am convinced that every lofty ambition we have is primarily a selfish one.'

They sat in silence for a while. The cafe was becoming crowded. A *mozo* poured black coffee into their cups and Julio was about to raise his cup to his lips when he suddenly stopped, his hand poised in mid-air.

Miguel noticed the look of surprise on his face. 'What is it, *chico*?' he asked.

Julio leaned across the table and whispered, scarcely moving his lips. 'Do not turn around, I beg of you, Miguel. There is someone immediately behind you, seated at the next table. His shoulders are almost touching yours. Don't make a move. I'll touch your foot under the table when I think his attention is the other way and you can turn and get a look at him.'

Miguel sat rigidly in his chair, his eyes staring at the blank wall before him. 'Don't keep me in suspense! Who is it? Oswaldo?'

'No, it is not Oswaldo. It is your cousin Enrique.'

Without moving, Miguel's eyes sought Julio's. '*Amigo mio*, I am about to do something very foolish. A selfish thing, you will say, something to keep myself from suffering, but such things seem to be in my mind these days. Perhaps this will be the most foolish and the most selfish of all.'

Sliding from his chair without moving it, Miguel stood up and walked quietly around Enrique's table, drew out the other chair and sat down. It was a second before Enrique realized what had happened. He glanced up from his coffee and a startled look came into his eyes as he recognized Miguel. By a strange coincidence, both men were dressed in white, so similarly dressed that it was almost as though each were looking into a mirror and seeing himself reflected there. For one long, tense moment they regarded each other as if they had never laid eyes on each other before. The tenseness crept to the other tables and there was a gradual lull in the conversation as one by one the patrons stopped talking, realizing the dramatic importance of the situation. Finally there was silence, broken only by the scraping of chairs as their occupants turned around to face them. Every eye in the cafe was on the two cousins.

Miguel broke the silence and his words, although quietly spoken, resounded through the cafe. 'At last, *primo mio*, we meet each other face to face. May we talk?'

Enrique nodded his head slightly, never taking his eyes from Miguel.

'You may not believe me but I have been wanting to talk to you for a long time. I have not sought the opportunity and that is my fault but now that it has come, I would talk with you. Shall we stay here or go elsewhere?'

'What have you to say to me that cannot be said before all Havana. The whole city knows about us; they might as well know more. So, what have you to say to me? Say it and get it over with.'

'There is much to say. There is bad blood between us. That is not my fault nor is it yours. I'd like to make amends. It seems stupid for us to go on hating each other.'

'And why not, cousin? It pleases me to hate you.'

Miguel shrugged his shoulders. 'But why?'

Enrique's voice trembled as he answered – trembled with anger and the pent-up jealousy of a lifetime. His face became white, so drained of colour that Miguel could see the blue veins at his temples. 'I'll tell you why,' he began, 'because my hatred for you has been the only thing in life I have had to live for. Take that away and I would no longer care to live. What can you do to make amends? Charity? Half of what you have belongs to me rightfully so where would there be any charity? Shit on you! Yes, I shit on you.'

'I had no idea of offering you money, Enrique.'

'Well then, if I don't want your money I sure as hell don't want your words. It's too late for words.' Enrique looked around the cafe. 'Señores,' he bowed slightly, 'my cousin and I have been discussing family matters. That they are of interest to you I can see by the expression on your faces yet I regret that you will have so little to entertain you. In case you have not heard every word I have said to my cousin, I'll repeat. I shit on you, Miguel.' He stood up quickly and his hand moved across the table until it encountered the coffee cup. His fingers closed around it and suddenly he flung its contents into Miguel's face. Then, without waiting to observe the effects, looking neither to the right nor left, he started to leave the cafe.

Miguel, blinded by the coffee in his eyes, started to rise, his hands groping for a napkin. Julio jumped up and rushed to him, putting his handkerchief in Miguel's hand. Fortunately the coffee had cooled so Miguel had not been burned. He wiped the drops from his face and saw Enrique making his way through the cafe. A few of the men arose as he passed, grabbed his hand and shook it or slapped him on the back. Miguel started after him and as Enrique saw him coming, he started to walk faster, almost running.

'Coward,' yelled Miguel, 'you dirty yellow bastard! Wait for me!'

With another apprehensive glance over his shoulder, Enrique made a dive for the street but someone – and Miguel never did discover the person who was still friendly to him – tripped Enrique. He sprawled out on the tiles.

Miguel reached down and grabbed him by the coat and lifted him to his feet. 'Are you still a man,' Miguel spat the words at him, 'or have you so drained yourself at Josefina's that you have forgotten that a man does not run away?'

Enrique did not move. He turned his head away.

'I offered you kindness and some attempt at understanding,' Miguel's words were like a whiplash, 'but you paid me as you did. So you enjoy hating me, my cousin, well then, I'll give you something to hate me for. I'd challenge you to a duel but I don't fight a stud from Josefina's. Not with a sword, at least, but with this ...'

Miguel struck him so hard across the face that Enrique reeled under the blow and the red mark of Miguel's hand stained the whiteness of his cheek. Enrique staggered and as he recovered his balance, his hand crept up under his coat. Suddenly it reappeared and there was a flash of steel.

'A knife, Miguel, a knife,' Julio cried.

Miguel had seen the motion and he cut down through the

air, his hand chopping at Enrique's wrist, and the blade fell to the floor. A fist, solid as stone, hit Enrique's chin. He clawed at Miguel's shirt, ripping the lace from the neck. Again Miguel hit him but this time Enrique struck back – a savage unaimed blow which struck Miguel on the temple and sent him reeling among the tables, one of which collapsed under him to send him sprawling on the floor. Enrique jumped on him, kneeling over him, one hand clutching at Miguel's hair, the other seeking his throat. Enrique was powerfully built but Miguel was the stronger, toughened by hard work on the *finca*. Arching his body, Enrique toppled off. They scrambled to their feet. Their fists hit each other with the dull thud of flesh on flesh.

Tables were quickly pushed out of the way until there was a cleared space in the centre of the cafe. Still the struggle continued. What Enrique lacked in strength he made up in craftiness. He was aiming his blows better now and they beat on Miguel's chest with a hollow sound. Once again Miguel felt Enrique's hands clawing at his hair and the thumb of his right hand was aimed at Miguel's eye but a blow from Miguel deflected the menace. Enrique staggered back a few steps and, crouching, he rushed at Miguel. His head struck Miguel in the belly and sent him reeling. As he landed on the tiles, he felt the force of Enrique's boots in his face. He reached up, caught his fingers in Enrique's belt and felt the waistband of Enrique's pantaloons give way. Again he fell back on the floor but with his trousers down around his ankles, Enrique was impeded and as he stumbled toward Miguel, Miguel caught him by the knees and Enrique tumbled down on him but Miguel's arms straightened and he somersaulted over him. Miguel rolled onto him, pinning him to the floor. In rolling, he felt a sharp prick in his back and when he sat up, Enrique's body between his knees, he saw the knife. Automatically he reached for it, holding the point of it to Enrique's throat.

Miguel gulped for breath, trying to find enough to form the words he wanted to speak.

'One move and I'll slit your worthless gullet. Now listen to me. You started this fight, I didn't. But I'm going to end it. You're going to lose your *cojones* because I'm going to cut them off. Even Josefina won't want you without your balls.' His left hand crept to Enrique's throat and he half turned, the knife in his right hand. At that moment he fully intended to castrate his cousin.

'Not that, Miguel!' Julio rushed up. 'Anything but that! Here, give me the knife. You are no *ladrone* to be fighting with a knife. There'll be no murder or mutilation and you'll thank me for it tomorrow.'

Miguel handed the knife to Julio. He clambered to his feet and as Enrique struggled to stand up, Miguel grabbed him and lifted the struggling man bodily. The crowd parted and Miguel toted the clawing, scratching, screaming Enrique to the street and with one mighty effort flung him into the road. Miguel stood in the doorway, feet wide apart, his hands on his hips. His clothes were in rags, the skin of his back torn by Enrique's fingernails and blood oozing from Enrique's teethmarks on his arm. He stood there as he watched Enrique crawl naked in the gutter.

He made an effort to rise, slumped back, then managed to get up onto his knees. Slowly he raised himself erect and staggered to the wall of the house for support. Miguel remained standing erect and triumphant in the doorway, his chest heaving as he gulped in huge quantities of fresh air. He saw the tatters of Enrique's trousers on the floor and kicked them toward him.

'Cover yourself! You'll lose customers for Josefina if you walk through the streets naked.' He watched Enrique stumble down the street, holding the rags of his trousers in front of him. When he turned the corner, Miguel turned to face the crowd. From behind the bar, Julio appeared with a bowl of water and a towel. Someone wiped the blood and sweat from Miguel's face and body. Somebody else proferred a jacket which Miguel put on. As he and Julio started to leave, Miguel held up his hand for silence.

'We fought, my cousin and I. He is not a coward. No Santiago is a coward and he is still a man.'

'And so are you, don Miguel,' a voice from the crowd answered. 'Twice the man your pimping cousin is.'

'Thank you,' Miguel recognized the man whose jacket he was wearing. 'If you will call at the Casa Santiago tomorrow, I will return your jacket and thank you again.' His hand made an all-encompassing gesture. *'Hasta luego, señores.'*

They strode on, he and Julio, through the darkness to the Casa Santiago. The streets of Havana were not lighted at night and the cobbles were hazardous but they walked, arm in arm, until the lights of the Casa Santiago welcomed them. From the Casa Josefina next door came the sound of music and the high pitch of feminine laughter. They continued past up to the Casa Santiago.

'You are late, Miguel,' Antonio remarked as he closed the gates.

'Yes, I made a fool of myself tonight, but not quite a fool, thanks to Julio.'

They entered the patio. For a moment, silhouetted against the darkling brightness of the sky, they saw the shadow of a man on the roof. Then suddenly it disappeared, leaving them bewildered, wondering if they had really seen it.

'Thank you again, Julio. I nearly killed him.'

'Better to have killed him than what you threatened.'

'But I didn't do it, thanks to you.'

Chapter Nineteen

THE NIGHT OF the Governor's *tertulia* had followed an excessively hot day, even for Havana. The light breeze that had sprung up after sundown failed completely to cool the second floor ballroom of the palace, despite the fact that the *persianas* had been raised. The women sweated under their elaborate toilettes and around the armholes of the men's suits damp stains appeared. The heat of the candles mingled with the heat of bodies and the oppressive heat of the evening to dampen somewhat the spirit of festivity. It was really too hot to dance and people stood about fanning themselves listlessly and wishing they were back home where stays could be loosened, coats removed and some attempt made to combat the heat. As usual the company was divided – Spaniards on one side of the ballroom and Cubans on the other. It was only the young men who crossed from one side to the other, asking for dances for it mattered little to the young Cubans or the young Spaniards if a pretty face belonged to the other side.

Suddenly everybody in the ballroom came to life. Miguel entered with La Clavelita on his arm. Even those who disapproved of Miguel's recent stand and those who disapproved of Margerita because she was an artist were forced to admit that they made a handsome couple. Miguel was all concern for her as they walked straight across the now deserted ballroom floor – for even the orchestra had ceased playing. Never had she looked lovelier. Her dress of cerise taffeta exactly matched the mass of carnations banked against the high tortoise-shell comb holding the black cobweb of her *mantilla* which enveloped her like a cloud of smoke. Miguel wore a coat of white moiré, breeches of white satin and white silk stockings. His shoes, gleaming with diamond buckles, complimented the black of his hair which shone with as many highlights as the gems. All eyes were rivetted on them as they walked slowly across the polished tiles straight to the alcove where the Señora de Santiago was seated. It seemed an interminable distance to Margerita. Fortunately the training she had given her body carried her proudly through the ordeal. As they approached the señora, Margerita sank to the floor in a curtsy, then rose as Miguel extended his hand to her.

'Grandmother,' his eyes twinkled as he surveyed the imperious old lady, sensing more than seeing the look of approbation on her face, 'may I present the Señorita Margerita del Valle who has but recently arrived from Spain? Margerita, my grandmother.'

For one long instant they inventoried each other. There was a challenge in their glances. The fragile *grande dame* eyed the girl, but the girl returned her glance. Each realized that the other had a claim on Miguel.

The señora, mindful of the fact that they were the centre of attraction, extended her bejewelled hand to Margerita.

'Del Valle, you said, Miguel?' and then to Margerita, 'which family – the Salamanca branch or the del Valles from Toledo?'

'My grandmother is a walking *almanaque de Gotha*, Margerita,' Miguel laughed, 'she can tell the name of everyone's grandfather, whom he married and how many children he had.'

Margerita realized that the señora's casual words were intended as a mask for her emotions. They had served their purpose, however, for Margerita no longer felt ill at ease. 'My father came from Toledo, señora,' she said as she bowed over the señora's hand.

'Ah yes, the illustrious general. I remember him.'

'And your mother?' the señora continued.

'She was English. She died when I was very young. I cannot remember her.'

'Ah, but I do,' the señora smiled. 'She was a lovely creature – her father was connected with the English embassy. I was in Madrid the year she was presented at court and her name was on everyone's lips. It was . . .' she hesitated a moment, 'Lady Mary Rockingham, if I have the barbarous English name correct.'

'You knew my parents?' Margerita asked in amazement.

'I knew your father well. All Spain honoured him. And I had the pleasure of meeting your mother. Miguel, your arm! The heat is oppressive here and everyone in Havana is staring at us to see what I shall say or do next. Let us go downstairs into the patio where it is cooler and cheat all of Havana. Every man and woman here is hanging on my every word. See all the gaping mouths. They will never dare to follow us below, at least not *en masse*.'

The lull that accompanied their exit was, they knew, only the prelude to the babble of whispering that would soon start. Every word, every expression of the señora's would be analyzed and discussed. As she reached the doorway, she turned, raised her fan and glanced over her shoulder. She nodded impishly as much as to say: 'Well, in a moment we shall be gone. Then you can start your vicious buzzing.'

They descended the stairs to the patio. Miguel found a

secluded spot in one corner, well screened by vines and palms. The señora sat on a marble bench and beckoned to Margerita to sit beside her. It was an inviting gesture and the señora's smile made it even more so. Miguel took up a position behind them, the tips of his fingers resting lightly on the shoulders of each.

The señora reached over and clasped Margerita's hand.

'One look at you, my dear, and I understand why Miguel is so entirely enamoured of you. Frankly, I cannot blame him. I am sure, if I were a man, I would tear down the gates of hell to claim you.' The old lady studied Margerita carefully but Margerita withstood the scrutiny without flinching. Reassuringly the señora patted her hand. 'Forgive me, Margerita. I am a rude old woman. I'll tell you the truth. I had other plans for Miguel. Now, he has upset them. He is in love with you. It is not what I had planned.'

'Can you plan love, señora?' Margerita asked.

'Unfortunately no!'

'But you object to his being in love with me?'

'My dear, how can he help it?' She held up her hand to ward off an answer to her question. For a long moment, during which Miguel died, was resuscitated and nearly died again, the señora held her silence. She turned the rings on her fingers, smoothed the mantilla over her comb, pleated the satin of her skirt and opened and closed her fan. Finally she looked up at Miguel. He was not looking at her but at Margerita.

Miguel broke the silence. 'Grandmother . . .'

'Hush, let me think,' she turned to Margerita. 'You are so lovely I am not able to convince myself of something which I feel I must. Oh, my dear, how can I think sensible thoughts when I consider your loveliness and see my Miguel look at you with his heart in his eyes? Let me say this: I can think of nobody whom I would be prouder to see bear the name of Santiago than yourself. But first, I must ask you a question. You love my Miguelito?'

Margerita bent her head and kissed the señora. 'Oh, very much, so very very much. But just how much I cannot tell because I have never loved anyone else, so I have no way of making a comparison. All I can say is that he is my life, my beginning and my end, my everything and my all. Nothing in the world matters but my love for him.'

'And you, Miguel?' the señora tilted her head back to look up at him.

'Need I tell you, little grandmother? Oh, need I tell you?'

'No, my boy, it's written all over your face,' the old lady started to stand, sank back for a second and then managed to stand. Had Miguel been looking at her, he would have seen the lines of pain in her face. Without speaking, she motioned to Miguel to take her place on the bench beside Margerita. She placed Margerita's hand in his and, as they embraced, she quietly tiptoed away from the corner, pushing back the frond of a palm to pass through the screen of foliage. She took a long breath and steadied herself. '*Ay de mi!* Imagine an old fool like myself trying to play Cupid. But he'll appreciate her all the more for having had a little difficulty in getting her. And I would have married him off to that Gonzalez bitch. I must be getting senile.'

She reached the centre of the patio, turned and looked back at them still in each other's arms. As she neared the stairs to the ballroom above, she caught the sound of voices near the door – rough voices raised in anger. For a moment she hesitated, dreading the stairs, her hand on the cool marble of the balustrade. A word rang out above the others. The name Santiago! Sensing that in some way the voices concerned her, she turned and ran to the corner where Miguel and Margerita were sitting. Running, she stumbled and fell, striking her head sharply on the tiles. For a moment she was stunned but she raised herself with difficulty and tottered to the bench.

'Miguel!' she panted, her words hoarse with the strain she required to speak them, 'something is happening! What, I do not know. Soldiers. They come across the patio . . .' She sank down on the bench, gasping for breath. The heavy steps of the soldiers cut through the thin music of the violins coming from an upper balcony. Suddenly the music stopped and the railing surrounding the patio began to fill with people. The steps came nearer.

Margerita drew the señora closer to her, pillowing her head on her breast. 'She's ill, Miguel,' she whispered.

'Keep her quiet for a moment,' he cautioned, 'whoever it is they are coming towards us. In a few seconds they will be here.' He advanced a few steps to meet them, then turned quickly and came back. 'Grandmother!'

The señora did not raise her head.

'Margerita!' his voice betrayed his astonishment, 'my cousin Enrique! He is with them.'

The soldiers burst through the screen of vines and confronted the little group in the corner. They stood at attention as a young lieutenant stepped up beside Enrique. The young officer's voice trembled and he looked to Enrique first for confirmation when he addressed Miguel. 'Are you don Miguel de Santiago and is she,' he pointed to the señora, 'doña Elena de Santiago?'

'What a stupid question,' Miguel's temper was rising. 'Every person in Havana knows us.'

'A formality, señor,' the young lieutenant's voice cracked like that of an adolescent. 'I have orders for your arrest.'

'Now that's even more stupid.'

'Yours and the Señora de Santiago's.'

'Good God! Why should you arrest my grandmother . . . and me? What are the charges and what is that man doing here?' he pointed to Enrique.

'That is the gentleman who is preferring charges against you, señor.'

Miguel took a few steps to stand directly in front of Enrique. The whole situation seemed so preposterous that he started to laugh. 'Well, out with it, Enrique! What sort of an insane joke are you playing. Out with it quickly! As you can see my grandmother – rather *our* grandmother – is ill. I wish to take her home.'

By this time a crowd had gathered behind the soldiers. Those who had been peering over the balconies had come downstairs so that they might eavesdrop more easily. The Governor himself pushed his way through the press of ball gowns and uniforms and made his way to Miguel and in answer to his questioning look, Miguel could only shrug his shoulders and point to the lieutenant.

'What is the meaning of this, sir?' the Governor's tone made the young officer quake.

'I am only obeying orders, Your Excellency. We have orders to arrest this lady and this gentleman.'

'Arrest whom?' The Governor stuttered in his amazement. 'The Señora de Santiago? *Madre de Dios!* Why, the señora is the most respected lady in Havana. She is . . .'

'A criminal, Your Excellency,' Enrique interrupted.

The Governor turned around, noticing Enrique for the first time. 'And who are you?' The Governor was not a client of Josefina's.

'Enrique de Santiago. The lady in question is my grandmother.'

The Governor turned to the señora whose face was nearly hidden in the folds of Margerita's mantilla. 'Is this true, Elena? Is this fellow your grandson?'

She nodded her head and a barely audible 'yes' escaped her lips.

'Then why – why in the name of God do you wish to arrest your grandmother and your cousin?' the Governor asked Enrique.

It was the moment for which Enrique had been waiting. He was now in full command of the situation. 'My cousin?' he asked with a sneer. 'I have no cousin. The old lady is my grandmother as she has just admitted but this man is no relative of mine. He is – one moment – let me say this so all can hear.' He turned and faced the crowd. 'Señores and señoras, I desire to say something. This fellow whom you all know as Miguel de Santiago is not Miguel de Santiago at all. He never has been! He is an impostor – a rank impostor – foisted on you by a bitter and jealous old woman, my grandmother. This fellow,' he pointed to Miguel and waited for a dramatic moment.

There was no sound in the patio, not even the rustle of silk.

'This fellow, señores and señoras, is nothing but a mulatto slave. Yes, a nigger! A nigger whom my grandmother has allowed to mingle with you as a social equal, to dance with your daughters, to be a friend of your sons. Believe me, I do not make this statement without proof. That is why I am arresting the woman who has perpetrated this crime and the Negro slave she has masqueraded before you I am taking into custody.'

There was a gasp from the crowd. It was as though hundreds of people sucked in their breath at one time. Miguel turned pale under his tan. Margerita did not move.

The words came dimly to the old señora. She made an effort to sit up, clutched at Miguel's elbow and slowly raised herself to her feet. 'What are you saying?' she pointed a quavering finger at Enrique. 'This is my grandson, my Miguel.' One side of the poor woman's face had a curiously sagged appearance and her words came thickly. Her left arm hung limply at her side.

There was no pity in Enrique's face as he looked at her and his words were harsh. 'You might as well confess, señora. I have the proof. You know I speak the truth and you have known it much longer than I have. He is no relation to you or to me. He is only a slave, no better than the *brutos* who cut cane on your plantation,' he turned, smiling grimly at the crowd. 'No wonder the old lady and her so-called grandson wanted to free all their slaves. In doing so, she would have achieved legal manumission for this one.'

The señora tottered but Margerita rose and supported her on the other side. The señora gasped for breath. 'You say that he is a slave?'

Enrique nodded curtly, his thin lips pressed together.

'Then why do you come to arrest him if he is a slave? Since when, you stupid dolt, have the Santiagos asked others to interfere in matters between master and slave. A slave you say? You lie! But even if he were a slave, he would be my property and not yours. Nothing I have belongs to you or ever shall. And if he should perchance be a slave then I have the right to free him. A paper, a pen, ink! Let me write it out at once.'

'What does he mean, grandmother? What is he talking about? Me, a slave?'

'Utter and absolute nonsense,' the señora had seemed to pull herself together. 'It's some diabolical scheme he's hatched up. The whoreson! But clever as he is I can spoil his scheme. I'll sign a paper this minute, freeing every slave I possess. Then I'll have him arrested. Let him produce whatever proof he's manufactured.'

The effort of talking had weakened her. She clutched frantically at Miguel's arm, her voice only a thick whisper. 'Paper, pen! Quickly, before it is too late . . .'

Someone pushed through the crowd with paper and a quill. The señora reached for them but as she did so, Enrique interrupted. 'There is also the charge of conspiracy.'

The señora reached for the quill, closed her fingers around it with difficulty and dipped it into the ink well. She wavered for a moment, then freed her arm from Miguel's so she could write. But before she could place the pen to the paper that the Governor himself was holding it slipped from her fingers and she fell in a heap of satin and laces on the floor. Miguel bent over her and Margerita knelt beside her and raised her head.

She struggled to speak. 'Not true,' she gasped, 'not true . . .' She tried to sit up, using all the strength left in her frail body. Then, the struggle too much for her, she collapsed.

Margerita tried to revive her. Water was brought; vinaigrettes were passed but Margerita waved them away. Sitting on the tiles with the señora's head in her lap, she looked up at Miguel. Her eyes were misty with tears.

'She is dead.'

Miguel buried his face in her hands. 'Grandmother!' he cried, 'don't leave me, don't.' Then wheeling about to face Enrique he shouted, 'You, you have killed her! Is this the revenge you wanted? If so, isn't it complete? You've killed her. What more can you want?'

Enrique stepped forward. 'You,' he said, 'you are what I want and now, by God, I've got you. Just where I want you! You'll wish, as time goes on, that you could trade places with the old lady. Don't waste any sniffles on her. She wasn't your grandmother anyway. She couldn't be. She's white and you're nothing but a goddamn nigger.' He turned to the officer. 'Lieutenant, have you forgotten what you are here for. Arrest that man. Take him to the office of the *procurador del rey*, who issued the warrant.'

Now it was the Governor's turn to step forward.

'Surely you cannot mean to arrest this man! Not now, in the face of this sorrow he is suffering. His grandmother is dead.'

Enrique laughed. 'His grandmother? Mine, you mean. I'll shed the family tears. I insist that this slave be apprehended and taken before the Minister of Justice. If you prevent it, you will be obstructing justice. A great crime has been committed – far greater than you realize. Any leniency towards this slave will come to the King's attention. Perhaps you have overlooked one fact, Your Excellency,' his voice lowered and his smile was almost patronizing. 'Since the unfortunate death of my beloved grandmother, I am now the sole heir to the Santiago estates and all the Santiago property and he,' he pointed to Miguel, 'is mine because he is part of the Santiago property. I am his sole owner and as such I have the right to say what shall be done with him. Take him to the office of the Minister of Justice, Lieutenant, and let's waste no more time arguing about it.'

Miguel had not moved. He stood where he was, numbed by the suddenness of everything that had happened. The lieutenant took him by the arm and led him away. Miguel followed as though in a daze. Suddenly he lifted his head, shook off the officer's arm and ran back to where Margerita was sitting, still supporting the señora's head in her lap. He knelt on the tiles, took his grandmother's lifeless hand in his and carried it to his lips. Gently he laid it back in her lap.

'I don't know what has happened, my love. I don't understand any of this. Maybe this is only a dream but if it isn't take care of her,' he said, pointing to his grandmother, 'and trust me, dearest, trust me and wait for me.'

He put his arms around her and kissed her then stood up and without turning again in her direction, walked to the lieutenant who placed his hand on Miguel's arm. Miguel shook it off but the lieutenant at a word from Enrique, forced both Miguel's arms behind him and fastened them with a pair of heavy iron manacles. Then stooping, he clasped leg-irons on both his ankles. When he had finished, Enrique nodded with satisfaction but, as the soldiers formed a guard around Miguel, he waved them away. Stooping quickly he ripped the diamond buckles from Miguel's shoes.

The soldiers surrounded Miguel with Enrique and the lieutenant leading them. The crowd, open-mouthed with astonishment and awed at the sight, opened up to make a pathway for them. No one spoke as they passed.

Margerita followed the little procession with her eyes until they had passed from the patio. Gentle hands lifted the señora's slight body from her arms. Then those same gentle hands assisted her to rise. Somehow she made her way to her carriage and only then, beneath the enveloping hood of the *volanta*, did she indulge in tears but once they had started she felt she would never be able to stop them.

Chapter Twenty

ENRIQUE HAD LAID his plans well and, in truth, it seemed that Providence was on his side because the sudden death of doña Elena de Santiago was something which he could not have counted on but had been of inestimable help to him. To be sure, the glamorous, colourful *tertulia* had been relegated to second place by the far greater drama that had been substituted. But what was a stiff Governor's ball in comparison to this debacle which would supply a choice titbit of gossip in Havana for years to come. Miguel de Santiago! *The* Santiago! A common nigger buck nothing more nor less! *Caramba*, what a sensation!

Few even bothered to take leave of the Governor in their haste to get from the Palace over to the Ministry of Justice. The streets leading to the Ministry were blocked with *volantas* and coaches so that progress was impossible. Many, at the risk of spoiling satin shoes, abandoned their carriages and hurried over the cobbles just to get there and see the final act of this drama. It would be something to tell their children about. Miguel de Santiago! A nigger! How he had lorded it over everyone else! And what a handsome fellow that Enrique de Santiago was! Far better looking than Miguel had ever been.

It was well known in Havana that Spanish justice moved swiftly and that Enrique could not have held a warrant for Miguel's arrest if lengthy investigations had not preceded the arrest. But once convinced that an accusation was justified, once a warrant had been issued for arrest, it meant that an action would be swift and unrelenting. The Minister moved cautiously in his investigations but once satisfied of a wrong, his dictatorial powers were absolute. Arrest, trial and sentence seldom took more than two hours. Of course, and here heads were wagged and nodded, lips were pursed and ears cupped to listen to whispered words, Enrique, with the promise of all the Santiago pesetas, could have in turn promised some of them to even a personage as high as the Minister of Justice. It was wonderful how pesetas could grease the wheels of Justice to make them run more smoothly and rapidly. So, although arrest was tantamount to guilt and sentencing, it was pretty certain that this case was already sentenced. After all, if the Minister had not felt Enrique to have a substantial claim he could probably have collected more from the señora and Miguel.

But if it was true, then there must be proof and that would be the most interesting part of all.

Although the distance between the Governor's Palace and the Ministry of Justice was short, it seemed an eternity to Miguel. He was unable to sort out his thoughts or realize what had happened but he was certain of one thing. His whole world had collapsed about him. Margerita, his grandmother, his home, his name, yes even his freedom. He trudged along, shortening his steps to the length of chain that fastened his shackles, praying that a righteous God might strike him dead but even prayers failed him and he found that the journey was over. They had arrived at the Ministry.

Just as Miguel passed through the door, a coach, the horses panting from their wild dash through circuitous streets to avoid the stalled coaches, slowed down and a man jumped out. It was Julio. Following him on horseback came Oswaldo, his suit of grey satin flecked with foamy spittle from his horse's mouth. They rushed to Miguel's side. Julio grabbed his hand and Oswaldo put a protecting arm around his shoulders. Miguel welcomed their arrival; he felt less alone, but he shrank from their touch. He was, if Enrique was right, black and they were white, slave and they were free. An enormous gulf separated them.

Another carriage stopped with a grating of iron on the cobbles and the Governor jumped out, reaching up a hand to help Margerita whom he had rescued from her *volanta* which had been halted several blocks away. He gave her his arm and escorted her into the building but the lieutenant, after a whispered conference with Enrique, bowed most deferentially before the Governor. 'I regret, Your Excellency, this is a private hearing. You, of course, may be admitted but these two gentlemen here' – he indicated Julio and Oswaldo, 'and the young lady may not come in.'

'On whose orders?' the Governor demanded.

'Those of the Minister of Justice.'

'Then I shall countermand them,' he brushed him aside and beckoned to Margerita, Julio and Oswaldo to follow. They proceeded up the wide marble staircase; Margerita on the arm of the Governor, Julio and Oswaldo forming a guard for Miguel, and Enrique and the lieutenant in the rear. Don Francisco Sovero, the Minister of Justice, was standing at the head of the stairs. The appearance of the Governor startled him momentarily but he welcomed him with a bow and waved him on in the direction of his chambers. They all entered. A chair was placed for the Governor and another for Margerita. Sufficient chairs were lacking so don Francisco called for more so that all the company were seated except Miguel who was left standing in front of the long table behind which don Francisco took his seat.

Miguel looked around the room. He recognized the smiling face of Roberto Garcia who had formerly been the overseer at Estrellita, and the ashen face of old Pepito. What were they doing here? His knees felt weak and the iron fetters chafed his wrists. His ankles with the heavy shackles felt curiously weighted down and unnatural. Strange words kept chasing each other through his head – slave, mulatto, Negro. If he was a *mestizo*, he wondered if he was an octoroon or a quadroon. Such ridiculous thoughts! He was Miguel de Santiago nothing more, nothing less.

Don Francisco Sovero seated himself behind his desk. He spent several moments in fussily rearranging his papers, examining the point of his quill and adjusting the position of his inkwell. This done, he again bowed to the Governor, then again turned his attention to the desk. Searching through one of the drawers, he found a keyring, fitted it to the door of a cabinet behind him and from it took out a metal box which, in turn, he unlocked and removed an ancient, leather-bound book which he centred carefully on the desk before him, aligning it precisely with his long, bony fingers. Then, and only then, did he recognize Miguel's presence.

'Are you the man who has been known as Miguel de Santiago?'

Miguel stood without answering him. Only the expression in his eyes indicated that he had heard the question.

Don Francisco stared at him, awaiting an answer. When none was forthcoming, he rapped on the desk. 'Answer me! When I ask you a question, and you answer me do it respectfully.'

'Yes, don Francisco.'

'I am not *don Francisco* to you any longer, I am *my lord the Minister*.' He pointed an accusing finger at Miguel. 'Now, answer my question.'

'I am Miguel de Santiago.'

'My lord Minister, remember that.'

'My lord Minister.'

'Now,' don Francisco swept the assemblage with squinting eyes, 'where is doña Elena de Santiago?'

The Governor leaned forward and whispered.

Margerita, unable to bear the suspense any longer, stood up and came toward the desk. She halted at Miguel's side and asked, 'May we know the charges against Señor de Santiago? What is this all about? One tragedy has already occurred tonight: the Señora de Santiago has died – been murdered you might say. For the love of God, spare us another.'

The Minister smiled but the sarcasm in his voice disproved the character of his smile. 'You are the dancer, La Clavelita, I believe?' His words made Margerita feel as if she were a two-peseta whore. 'May I inquire why you are interested in this case?'

'I intend to marry don Miguel.'

The Minister shrugged his shoulders and permitted himself a dry, humourless laugh. 'But that's impossible. The fellow's a slave. Enough now! Please take your seat and if you interrupt me again I shall have you ejected from the room. I constitute His Majesty's law in Cuba. Even the Governor must recognize my rights. If you wish to remain, restrain your emotions and keep silent. If you are needed as a witness I'll permit you to answer questions. Please be seated and,' he glowered, 'no more interruptions.'

Don Francisco patiently waited for her to take her seat and then resumed his questioning of Miguel.

'You admit that you have been known as Miguel de Santiago?'

'Yes, my lord Minister,' Miguel was learning fast.

'And whom did you suppose your father to be?'

'Eugenio de Santiago.'

'And your mother?'

'Juana del Monte.'

'Quite so! And your grandmother,' don Francisco nodded his head knowingly, 'was supposed to be doña Elena de Santiago.'

It was a statement and not a question so Miguel did not answer.

The Minister sat forward in his chair, 'And now,' he snapped, 'have you any reason to believe that you are other than Miguel de Santiago? Answer me!'

Miguel looked around the room in bewilderment. Julio, Oswaldo, Margerita, even old Pepito! But how did one go about proving such a thing! He felt helpless but suddenly a wave of his old assurance came over him.

'Why of course not. Everybody knows me as Miguel de Santiago. Tell him, Julio, tell him who I am. And you, Oswaldo, you have known me all my life. Tell him that I am myself and nobody else.' He turned to Enrique. 'Even you, yes, even you Enrique, know who I am. And, as far as that goes, don Francisco, so do you. Why, only a couple of months ago, I entertained you and your daughter at Estrellita.'

Don Francisco held up his hand for silence. 'It all proves nothing. For all we know you were nothing but a masquerader. The fact remains that I have proof that you are *not* Miguel de Santiago. Therefore I, together with these gentlemen, will have to admit that we were wrong. This gentleman here,' he smiled and nodded at Enrique, 'has brought me indisputable proof that you are not what you claim to be.'

'Then who am I?' Miguel asked.

'That in good time,' answered the Minister, 'and let me remind you that it is I who ask the questions here. To continue. What are the facts of your birth?'

Miguel answered him at length. He told of the hurricane that had destroyed the house at La Estrellita three days after he was born; of the death of his father and mother and of his own miraculous escape in the chest. As he progressed with his story the minister continued to nod with satisfaction and approbation.

After Miguel finished speaking the room was unbearably quiet. Margerita half rose as though to speak but don Francisco glared at her and she sat down.

'And so you see, Your Excellency, señores and señoras this young man admits that the circumstances shortly following his birth were unusual to say the least. There is no witness alive who can testify that the child found in the chest was actually the son of Eugenio de Santiago and his wife Juana. The father and mother perished in the hurricane as did the midwife. No one survived. But, if the identity of the child in the chest cannot be proved, it does not follow that it cannot be disproved. That I am able to do. I shall now tell you what happened and how the machinations of an evil woman. . . .'

Miguel started toward the desk, his shackles clanking but one of the soldiers restrained him.

Don Francisco ignored the interruption and continued.

'. . . the Señora de Santiago, spurred on by hatred of her younger son's wife, determined that his son, Enrique, who was then a child of two years, would never inherit her property. Remember, the child Enrique would have been sole heir had her son Eugenio died childless. As a matter of fact he did not have a child and the child Enrique *was* the rightful heir. Yet, the Señora de Santiago was so obsessed with the idea that Enrique's mother should never profit that she engineered a cruel and diabolical scheme to defraud a man of his patrimony and give it to another who had no right to it, neither by birth because he was not a Santiago nor by colour because he was not white. Shall I proceed, Your Excellency?'

The Governor was becoming more interested. Don Francisco's words seemed plausible. He had a convincing way when he spoke. The Governor nodded assent.

'Then I shall continue,' don Francisco said. 'Astounding as the story may seem, I am able to offer proof of every statement. I have the proof here,' he placed a hand on the leather-covered book, 'and here,' he pointed to a small wooden box on the desk.

'The child of Eugenio de Santiago and Juana his wife was stillborn,' he paused, waiting for the portent of his words to sink in. 'The young Señora de Santiago suffered an extremely hard labour and the child never breathed. It was hastily wrapped in a blanket, put in a wooden box, furnished by Roberto Garcia, the overseer of the plantation at that time, then given to Pepito, a Negro servant who buried it. Consequently there was never a Santiago son. Never!' He stopped to take a drink of water, then called, 'Roberto Garcia.'

A well-built man, past middle age, came to the centre of the floor. A quick look passed between him and Enrique. He took his position not far from Miguel.

Don Francisco leaned forward in his chair. 'Do you remember a night shortly before the hurricane when the Santiago *finca* was destroyed? Did not a woman, employed as a midwife by the Santiago family, come to you and ask you to supply a heavy wooden box, similar in size to this?' he pointed to the box on the table.

'*Si, señor.*'

'What was the purpose of this box?'

'For the burial of a stillborn child.'

'*Gracias, señor.* That is all.'

As Garcia made his way back to his chair, the Minister called for Pepito. The old Negro came forward. Tears were streaming down his cheeks.

'Was a box containing the body of a stillborn child given to you on the night we have been discussing? And were you asked to bury the same?'

'But it was not the Señora de Santiago's child. It was . . .'

'Enough! Answer my question. Did you bury a newborn infant?'

'I did but it was Rodana's child.'

Don Francisco turned to the assemblage. 'Do not let that statement influence you. The testimony of a slave is not legal anyway, but we have called this man merely to corroborate other testimony. Remember one thing! As Negroes do not possess souls, they cannot bear true testimony in a court of law. Evidently the old fellow merely believed what was told him.' He waved to one of the soldiers, 'Take him from the room.' He waited until they led Pepito away and then continued.

'The old man is not the only one who believed it to be the body of an offspring of the octoroon slave, Rodana. The paternity of this child is in question but we can reasonably suppose it was sired by the son of a cousin of Eugenio de Santiago as he purchased the slave from his cousin. Then again,' the Minister shrugged his shoulders, 'it can well be that Eugenio de Santiago himself was the father. Whoever sired it is immaterial. Rodana and the Señora de Santiago were both pregnant and the same midwife attended both mistress and slave. Later it was feared that Rodana might disturb her mistress, so she was moved to one of the slave cabins. These cabins, being small and constructed of stone, survived the hurricane. Am I right, Señor Garcia?'

The man stood up and nodded his head and the Minister droned on.

'Several of the slaves on the plantation recall the birth of this child to Rodana but,' he paused to make his words more impressive, 'not one of them remembers the *death* of this child and the mother herself is dead. However, there was one person on the *finca* whose word cannot be doubted and whose reputation for truthfulness is well known. I speak of the priest, Father Eliseo, who, despite the fact that Negroes are not human beings possessed of a soul, nevertheless kept records of their birth and death. These records have only just now come to light. It is evident that the Señora de Santiago,' the Minister interrupted himself to make a hasty Sign of the Cross, 'either did not know of their existence or failed to destroy them.'

What few looks of sympathy there had been for Miguel were lost in the strained interest of everyone in the room with the exception of Margerita and Julio. Don Francisco polished his spectacles, reached for the bound volume and held it up for all to see.

'This is the register of births and deaths on the Santiago *finca*. I shall read from it.' He opened the book, turned a few pages, found the right place and commenced to read.

> 'October 4th. On this night there was born to our illustrious doña Juana de Santiago y del Monte, a male child, stillborn, which was later buried the same night. On the same night there was born to Rodana, the slave of doña Juana, a male child.'

'Lieutenant, will you kindly pass the book to the Governor so that he may read this passage. This book was the personal property of Padre Eliseo. Did you know about the existence of this book?' He pointed his finger at Miguel.

'I had heard of it but had never examined it. In fact I had completely forgotten about it. Had I remembered, it would have been helpful in the process of freeing the Santiago slaves.'

'More about that later,' don Francisco cut Miguel off. 'To return to the facts of my investigation which I can assure you have been arrived at after much study. Doña Elena, the so-called grandmother of this man, was on her way to the *finca* from Havana, probably summoned by the death of the Santiago heir because she must have been aware of this. A messenger had been dispatched from the *finca* to her, presumably with the news. She was on the road when the storm broke. Her carriage was overturned and demolished. With the help of her coachman, who had to be put to the torture to elicit the information and who is now in no condition to testify, we learned that she managed to reach the slave cabin where Rodana and her child were. Here she learned of the destruction of the house and the death of her son and his wife.

'We were all well acquainted with the late lamented doña Elena. We knew her for a proud, imperious woman who was determined to have her own way in everything. She was clever and she was quick-witted. Her resentment against the marriage that her other son had made impelled her to go to any lengths so that his son, the present Enrique de Santiago, could not inherit her estate. So, she took Rodana's baby and carried it to the ruins of the house. She had doubtless observed that, to all appearances, the child was quite white. Remember, its mother was only an octoroon and its father white. She noticed the chest in the ruins, opened the cover and placed the child – Rodana's child – therein. Then, she reappeared from another direction to give the impression that she had just arrived on the scene. The chest was opened and the child discovered. The señora immediately accepted it as her grandson and this child, born of the slave mother Rodana and itself born a slave for life, is no other than he who stands before you.' The Minister arose and pointed to Miguel. 'He who has been foisted on all Havana as Miguel de Santiago.'

All eyes were upon Miguel. The scene of doña Elena's collapse was still so fresh in their minds and the fact that Enrique's accusations had stimulated the collapse seemed, momentarily, to undo a lifetime of that distinguished lady's deeds and actions. Miguel himself re-created in his own mind the scene of his birth and he froze at the realization that he could – indeed he could – visualize his grandmother taking such action. Was it, then, all true? Was he, could he be . . .'

The Minister of Justice was speaking, his words coiling the bonds of slavery ever more tightly about Miguel's shoulders.

'The Señora de Santiago left at once for Havana, accompanied by the slave Rodana who nursed her own child. Through all these years we and in fact all Havana have been maliciously led to believe that this slave, this *mestizo*, this man of polluted blood, was white and the legitimate Miguel de Santiago. It has not only been a foul crime, directed to all of us, but it nearly succeeded in doing what doña Elena intended it to do. Rob Enrique de Santiago of his birthright. Now, there is one further bit of evidence, circumstantial it is true, which I would like to add. I believe that doña Elena feared that after her death, the truth might leak out. This explains her insane desire to free all her slaves, an act unprecedented in the history of Cuba. By so doing, she would have automatically freed this man who then, being a free man, could have inherited her property.'

There was a hush in the room as don Francisco finished. The Governor had carefully examined the entry in the book, holding it under his nose and gazing at it intently through his eyeglass. He had passed it on to Margerita who studied it for a moment and in turn passed it on to Julio and Oswaldo. Each had believed that it might have been a forgery but it was palpably not.

Miguel wilted under the accusation and the all too evident proof. Gone was his debonair look, his proud bearing. He did not lift his head to refute the charges.

It was Margerita who broke the silence. 'You have proof beyond this book, señor?' she asked.

'Ample proof,' don Francisco answered. 'At first when this matter was called to my attention I was only too willing to disbelieve it. But I examined the case thoroughly before I ordered the arrest of the señora and her so-called grandson. I visited the *finca* myself and saw the grave opened. I had the small casket opened and observed the tiny skeleton inside which is here in case anyone disputes my words. I have kept the slave Pepito in custody so that no word could leak out. I waited till the Santiago coachman drove the señora to the Governor's Palace before I took him into custody and applied the torture to make him confess. I maintained the most absolute secrecy so that if there were no truth in the matter the Santiagos would not suffer embarrassment. But the more I studied the case, the more certain I was that a great injustice had been done. Knowing Elena de Santiago as I did, I knew she would not stop at anything to keep her other grandson from inheriting her estate, even to foisting a nigger slave on her friends. And you, señorita, can thank God that the truth has come out before you married this fellow and raised children which in turn could be sold as slaves.'

The Governor walked over to the small box in front of the Minister, opened the cover and stared briefly at the tiny skeleton inside. Nodding his head, he closed the lid, and motioned to the Minister. They left the room together, only to return in a few moments. This time the Governor sat in the minister's chair.

'Señorita del Valle, will you please leave the room and,' he swept the room with an all-encompassing gesture, 'all other ladies who are present.'

'But why . . .?' Margerita stretched out her arms to Miguel. 'I cannot believe all this, it is not true, there must be some mistake. Let me stay here with him.'

'No, Margerita,' Miguel roused himself to speak. 'Go! It will be easier for me if you are not here and when you pass out that door try to forget me. If what they say about me is true, it is better that you never think of me again.'

'I shall never forget you, never! And, as God is my witness, I shall never love nor marry another. I go, Miguel, but my heart remains here. Adios.'

'*Vaya con Dios*,' he watched as Julio and Oswaldo helped

her to her feet and he watched as she followed the other ladies from the room. As she neared the door, she turned suddenly, ran back, kissed him quickly and then ran out the door sobbing.

There was a scraping of chairs along the floor as the men drew a closer circle around Miguel. They all looked at the Governor, wondering what might happen next. The Governor's face was serious. He addressed Enrique and now there was a marked deference in his manner which had not been present before.

'Will you, don Enrique, do me the favour to stand beside the man we have known and believed to be your cousin?'

Enrique walked to the centre of the room to stand beside Miguel. Despite the similarity of their appearance there was one fact glaringly apparent in the brilliantly lighted room. Enrique's skin was white – a transparent, unhealthy white – which seemed even whiter in contrast to the deep olive of Miguel's.

The Governor scrutinized them carefully then nodded his head as much as to say 'just as I thought'. He addressed himself to the Minister but included all in his remarks. 'While listening to your story, my dear don Francisco, I found myself mentally comparing the two men. There is, to be sure, a certain facial resemblance between them which may be accounted for by the doubtful paternity of the slave Miguel. I was, however, certain that I detected a difference in colour. Now you can see how right I was.'

Everyone stared at Miguel and Enrique, nodding their heads in approval of the Governor's perspicacity and not a few murmured that they had always been aware of it.

The statement did, however, cause Miguel to rouse himself in his own defence. 'It is a difference brought on by the sun, Your Excellency. I have lived much in the country whereas my cousin lives in the city.'

'That being the case,' the minister was now anxious to be again in the limelight, 'certain parts of your body will be lighter in colour than your hands and face. Take off your clothes!'

'Here? Before all these people?' Miguel was aghast. 'But

it will prove nothing. My whole body is the same colour. We swim much in the river at Estrellita. Julio will vouch for it. The place where we swim is secluded and we wear no clothing and lie for long hours in the sun so that my body is all the same colour.'

'Enough! Do as I say! A slave can have no false modesty in displaying his body. 'Tis a common thing. And besides, I have a feeling I shall be able to add one more proof to a theory I have long had. Off with your clothes, boy, or I shall have one of the soldiers strip you.'

So, he was to suffer this final indignity before all these men whom he had known and who had known him. He, who had been *The* Santiago was to stand before them, naked and ashamed, no longer a man. Slowly he removed his finery and when he took off the coat, Enrique grabbed it from him along with the lace trimmed shirt. He kicked off his pumps from which Enrique had ripped the diamond buckles, rolled down his white silk stockings and hesitated a moment before he unbuttoned the waistband of his breeches. Realizing that there was no alternative, he slipped the buttons out of the holes and let the breeches and his small clothes drop to the floor. Slowly he stepped out of them.

The Minister nudged the Governor. 'How right I was, Your Excellency! How very right!' He stepped out onto the floor and came to where Miguel was standing. With a bow to Enrique, he said, 'Pray be seated, don Enrique, there is no longer any cause for you to stand.' With his hands on Miguel's shoulders he slowly turned him around so that everyone could get a full view of him.

'Señores,' the Minister was smiling smugly. 'I mentioned to you that I had a certain theory. Although I was not sure what I might see, I can tell you that my theory has already been proved. Oh, most substantially! During my tenure of office I have had the necessity of examining many men both slave and free, both white and coloured. I have seen them stripped of their clothes to exchange them for prison garb. I have seen them naked on the rack when we extracted confessions from them and, señores, I have always noticed one very particular thing in which I think you will concur with me. The African and those of African blood are always much more impressively endowed by nature in their private parts. It is the one respect in which no white man can compete with them. It is, of course, a sign of their bestiality, their lack of souls which places them in the category of animals and not humans. For surely, señores, no human being would possess a member like that. It would be a source of shame to any white man and would most certainly prevent him from mating with a white woman. Look, señores! Regard carefully that abnormality which is more befitting a stallion than a man. I ask you, do you need any more proof? Do you have the slightest doubt in your minds now that this creature is not human? Come, señores, come over and see for yourselves.'

As the minister stepped back, the others pressed forward, closing in around Miguel. He felt strange hands pawing at him, lifting, testing, and it must be admitted marvelling, but each had the same verdict as the Minister. It was, they exclaimed, proof positive. Absolutely! Nothing but a nigger could be hung like that.

The Governor returned to his seat and rapped on the table. 'Señores, if either don Francisco or I passed sentence on this quondam Miguel de Santiago, malicious gossip might say that we had been bribed. I can assure you that I have not and I know that a man of don Francisco's sterling character would not stoop to such a thing. Therefore both don Francisco and I will refrain from condemning this man until I have heard from all of you. Will all of you who have heard the evidence tonight be the judges. I call for a show of hands. Everyone who believes the fellow standing there to be a Negro slave, the property of don Enrique de Santiago, please raise their right hand.'

Every hand in the assemblage with the exception of Julio's and Oswaldo's was raised.

'And do you also believe that Enrique de Santiago is the lawful heir to the Santiago estates?'

Again the same hands fluttered.

'Then I concur in your judgment. The fellow before you

is a slave. He is the lawful property of don Enrique. Do you agree with me, don Francisco?'

'My mind was made up long ago, Your Excellency. He is.'

'Then, don Enrique, dispose of your property as you see fit.'

'One moment,' Julio raised his voice. 'Do you know who I am, Enrique de Santiago?'

'*Por supuesto*,' Enrique inclined his head. 'You are don Julio de Castanaro.'

'And as such do you believe I am able to pay any debts I might incur?'

'Oh, most certainly, señor.'

'Then, name your price for Miguel and I will pay it.'

Enrique started to laugh but it was a half-frenzied, half-hysterical laughter. 'You'll have an opportunity, don Julio, I can promise you that but it will be at a time and place that I shall decide and most certainly not now. Right at this moment there is not enough money in the Castanaro banks to buy my slave.' He strode over towards Miguel and kicked the white satin breeches along the floor.

'Dress yourself, you nigger bastard! And you, Lieutenant, if His Excellency and don Francisco will indulge me with your services a little longer, take this slave to don Solano's barracoons. Tell don Solano he is to be treated like any other nigger slave, no better and no worse. And also tell don Solano, with my compliments, that I will call on him in the morning.'

Chapter Twenty-one

THE PALE, WATERY light of a new day filtered through the iron grating of a little window set high in the pock-marked coral wall. The grey light struggled down into the cage, high-lighting the ebon skins of the men sleeping on the floor, making a purple iridescence on the sweaty curves of arms and legs. One of them woke, nudged his nearest companion and he in turn his until they were all awake, scratching their naked bodies and staring in amazement at the newcomer who had been thrust into their cage in the darkness of the night. Waking only briefly they had grunted and made room for him on the floor, too sleepy to observe what he was by the brief light of the smoking torch. Having cleared a small place for him on the floor they went back to sleep but now they were awake and he was sleeping, stretched out flat on the floor, his head pillowed on the thigh of one of them who did not move for fear of waking him.

He was a white man and what few clothes he had on had the glitter of richness; his hair was long and straight and his body had the clean look of many washings. Their stares in turn engendered words and they chattered back and forth in their strange thick words, pointing to him and shaking their heads excitedly. The noise awakened him and he sat up, frightened at his strange surroundings and at the naked black men around him.

For a few brief hours he had forgotten. Now in the first moments of wakefulness, he tried to orient himself and force back the fear that overwhelmed him. He struggled to his feet, not heeding the fact that a strong black arm helped him arise and walked to the front of the cage, absent-mindedly brushing the dirt from his breeches which were his only article of clothing. Now it began to come back to him. In a frenzy of rage, the night before, he had turned on the soldiers in the street. Somewhere in the back of his mind had been the thought that if he provoked them enough they would kill him and that was what he wanted. He had pounded them with his fists, kicked, bitten and torn at their uniforms and they in turn had clubbed him with their muskets until he had fallen on the cobbles unconscious. Would that they had killed him but apparently they had carried him here and dumped him in this cage and here he was. *Madre de Dios!* Here he was! Just another stinking nigger slave with other stinking nigger slaves.

He felt of his head gingerly for the lump was large. One eye seemed glued together and when his fingers touched it, he felt it caked with dried blood which had congealed from a wound on his forehead. And how he ached! Every muscle, every bone seemed to have been stretched and pounded. With a painful effort, he managed to grasp the bars which fronted the cage and looked out into the same dirty patio from which he had walked so haughtily with head so high in the air that day when he had purchased Antonio and Fidel. Better that he had awakened in hell than here at Solano's.

The chattering continued but by its tone he realized it was not unfriendly and there was a timbre of pity in it. A black hand reached up and stroked the silken smoothness of his breeches and when he looked down at the half-recumbent form at his feet, he was rewarded by the flash of white teeth in a friendly grin. The grin broadened as he stared down at the man and there was a certain protecting fellowship in it. He reached down and patted the fellow's wiry pate. The man waved his arms, muttered something unintelligible to Miguel but it sounded kindly so Miguel smiled back at him.

Gradually the events of the night before came back to him. The ball at the Governor's palace; his grandmother's acceptance of Margerita and her death. Would they bury her today? Who would attend her funeral? Margerita perhaps if Enrique would allow her. He wondered if Enrique was sleeping in the Casa de Santiago. Would Juan be surprised when he came into his room and found Enrique instead of himself? And Antonio? What would become of him? At least *he* was free. Miguel felt he had accomplished one thing. Fidel? Fidel was free too and Fidel was with Margerita. What was Margerita thinking? Good God! He had one thing to be thankful for; this had happened before he and Margerita were married.

The more he thought about the case the more logical it began to seem. Yes, his grandmother had hated Enrique's mother with a deep, unrelenting hatred. She had always vowed that nothing belonging to her would ever go to that woman's son. His grandmother could have taken him, a mewling slave baby, from Rodana's arms and put him in the chest. She could have and yes, *por dios*, she would have done it to gratify her own ends. But then – and this was the only flaw in his reasoning – could she have loved him so much, lavished so much affection on him, knowing all the time that he was not her own grandson and the nigger whelp of a slave mother?

But the books! The books of Padre Eliseo! He tried to remember them and recalled having seen them, standing on a shelf in the good father's white walled bedroom. All these years the priest had kept the secret and that was another flaw because Padre Eliseo was a good man and he had stood up to his grandmother many times. Would he have countenanced such a deceit? But, Padre Eliseo had always maintained that Negroes were humans and perhaps he took a certain satisfaction in knowing that at least one of them, Miguel himself, was being accorded that distinction. As for Garcia, he was a man whom his grandfather had sent to prison so his testimony could be discounted. Yet Pepe had testified and Pepe loved him. And, of course, there was the evidence in black and white, although Miguel had not seen it himself but Margerita had and so had Julio and the Governor. They had all agreed. Julio must have believed it or he would not have tried to purchase him. Purchase him! Yes, he, Miguel de Santiago was for sale. He was a slave! A nigger!

He clutched the bars of the cage and screamed – a piercing maniacal scream that echoed back and forth between the rotting balconies of the patio. Once he had started he could not stop and he continued to yell while he beat his fists against the bars of the cage. Then, in a wild frenzy, he turned from the bars and beat his hands against the stone wall at the back until he lacerated the skin and the blood trickled down his arms. Quite beyond himself, he started to strike the slaves, kicking at those on the floor and still screaming until his voice finally gave out and came only in hoarse racking sobs. At first the Negroes had smiled indulgently at him. Then, resenting his blows, two of them stood up, pinioned his arms and tried to quiet him. But his feet still kicked at them and his arms slipped from their grasp until in the end, overpowered by numbers, he was thrown to the floor, his hands and feet pinioned. Slowly, as he gasped for breath, his hysteria left him and some degree of sanity returned.

Awakened by the turmoil, Babu came running across the patio. He peered into the cage and then ran back to knock loudly on the door of Solano's apartment. In a few moments, Solano appeared fully dressed – he never removed his clothes. Supporting him was the lad Pajarito, whom Miguel had seen on his last visit. He was entirely nude, except for a ragged towel which he held in front of himself. Solano shaded his eyes with his hands and looked across the patio, then turned, cuffed the boy on the head and spoke to him. He ducked back into the room while Solano supported himself at the door, only to return wearing one of Solano's shirts – a grotesque garment which fell below his knees.

With Babu on one side and the lad on the other, Solano progressed across the courtyard. It was as though a mountain moved, so slow his progress and so awkward. Step by step he lumbered across, until he arrived at the door of Miguel's cage. Leaning heavily on the boy, he waited until Babu ran back for the massive chair. Babu placed it for him and, with a sigh of exhaustion, Solano sank heavily into it. A gesture from him sent Babu to the cage and he spoke to the men. They released Miguel and huddled together in the back of the cage, jibbering like apes.

'Don Miguel,' Solano's voice dripped oil and honey, 'Oh, don Miguel, for I shall still call you that this morning, do you realize how you have been honoured? Your devoted friend Solano has awakened at this unearthly hour of the morning just to pay you a call. Come, don Miguel, you must not lie on the floor when I am already up. Babu,' he called, 'go in and get my dear don Miguel up off the floor. He seems to have forgotten his manners. Bring him out here so that I may talk to him.'

Babu fumbled in the folds of Solano's garments and produced a key which unlocked the cage. He entered, picked Miguel up in his arms and dumped him unceremoniously at Solano's feet.

'Dear, dear, not awake yet,' Solano clucked. 'Babu, the poor don Miguel has his eyes closed and how shall we rouse him? Let us think. Now in his own home how was he awakened? A servant would come tiptoeing into his room, softly open the *persianas* and have water ready for his bath. That's it, Babu! Water, of course! Get a bucket of water. Ah, one so handy. Then throw it over the nigger bastard.'

Babu reached into the cage and took out the bucket of water and sloshed it over Miguel. The shock brought him to his senses. He stirred on the dirty tiles, made a move as if to brush something away from his eyes, sat up slowly and stared at Solano.

'My, my, how lacking in respect you are. Is it quite proper for you to loll on the floor while I honour you with a visit? Get up you nigger son-of-a-bitch. Stand on your feet! Consider what you are and who I am. Get up or I'll have you flogged. I'll have the meat stripped off your back. Come! Learn that when I speak to you, you jump!'

Miguel managed to get to his knees and then slowly to his feet. The balconies of the patio reeled before his eyes and he would have fallen had he not clutched the arm of Solano's chair. Regaining his balance, he stood facing Solano, whose little eyes gloated at the sight of so much misery. Again Solano spoke to him and this time his voice had regained its feminine sweetness.

'So, here is *The* Santiago. Before me is the one that all the ladies in Cuba have smiled at and all the little whores have squirmed under. Now what do you suppose they saw in you that gave them that awful itch? Oh yes, you're pretty! As much as I've disliked you, I had to admit that, don Miguel. *Ay*, how careless I am don Esclavo, don Negro, don Bastardo! But it takes more than a pretty face to make the señoritas spread their legs. Now what do you suppose it was? What did you have, don Negro, answer me!'

Miguel remained silent but Solano intended to press the matter. 'Answer me!'

'I suppose it is what all men have that women want; mine no more or no less than any other man's.'

'Ah, but I am curious. I must see for myself. Come, don Negro, shuck down your britches. And get over being coy and bashful – you'll be shucking them down for every prospective customer who wants to buy you.'

Miguel realized the truth of Solano's words; he had

bought slaves himself. There was nothing he could do but obey Solano's command. His breeches dropped to the floor and Solano beckoned for him to come nearer. Solano's inspection was far more than cursory and Miguel felt himself responding even against his will. He stood there, wishing he had a knife to plunge into the back of Solano's fat neck but he was powerless. Solano pushed him away, wiped his hands on the towel around Pajarito's waist and motioned to the breeches, new only last night, but now soiled and crumpled. Miguel put them on.

'A fancy! A goddamned fancy if I ever saw one! I'll let it be known around Havana and there'll be no dearth of buyers for you, don Negro. They'll come flocking, yes flocking to buy you. Why, you're a fortune in itself for your *amo*. Don Enrique will make more on you than he'll clear in sugar for a year. The old Señora Gutherez would love to have you for a footman; the Conde de Caradonga has had an order in for someone like you for over six months and, oh yes, Josefina! *Por dios!* She'll be needing somebody now. *Ay de mi!* I wish you were mine but if you were I'd probably never sell you. I nearly forgot. You haven't had your breakfast. Go, boy,' he motioned to Pajarito, 'go and fetch don Stallion's breakfast and hurry back with it.'

The boy left, but returned in a moment with a bowl of some grey cereal, cold and greasy, with clots of blackened meat in it. 'Hand it to don Jackass, Pajarito. He needs nourishment after what just happened.'

The boy hesitatingly placed it in Miguel's hand, essaying a shy smile which seemed to link them together as victims of Solano's prurience.

Miguel looked at it and slowly raised the bowl, the better to assess its contents. He sniffed at it and then regarded Solano for the first time. Words, almost unintelligible, came from his cracked lips. 'For me, you fat sow? For me? Ah, there you are mistaken. It's for you, damn you!' With his last ounce of strength he flung the bowl in Solano's face.

A cataract of greasy gruel cascaded down his chins, over the curves of his bellies and onto the ground. Solano waved his arms blindly, clutched at the boy beside him, his hands groping blindly for the towel. He tore at it; it came apart; and he wiped his face with it.

'That's enough from you, you stinking nigger buck,' he screamed at Miguel. 'Take him, Babu, take him and rope him to the whipping post. I'll teach him a thing or two, goddamn his soul; but I forgot, he doesn't have a soul, does he? Every slave in this compound who saw it is laughing to himself. But they won't laugh when they see what happens to him. Tie him up, Babu, and you, you little slut,' he turned, slashing at the boy's bare rump with his hand, 'go and get something to cover your nakedness. I'll not have you exposing yourself to these black beasts in the cages.'

Babu dragged Miguel across the courtyard without Miguel's making any resistance. Tying a thin rope around his wrists, he looped the end up over an iron hook in a tall pole and pulled, lifting Miguel's body straight up so that only his toes touched the ground. With another rope he bound his legs to the post, testing the knots to see that they would hold.

Solano observed from the other side of the patio, shouting orders to Babu. 'Higher! Don't let his feet touch the ground. Tighter! Truss him up well. That's better. Now the whip! Well, find it! I want to see this stubborn nigger taste the leather and when he gets through, Babu, see that he kisses the whip and thanks me for teaching him a lesson. Lay to it, Babu! Give it all your strength. Twenty lashes!'

The black lash curled through the air and wound itself around Miguel. It seemed like a live thing as it came swishing around his shoulders like an infuriated snake. Each time it landed, Miguel screamed, and the red welts were soon crisscrossed into bloody patches on his back. With the dull thud of the whip on his flesh he could hear Solano counting. Ten! He could never survive another. Eleven! This was worse as it cut into the tender flesh of his buttocks. Twelve! Thirteen? No, there was no thirteen. Instead there was a furious banging on the gate. Babu dropped the whip and looked to Solano for instructions. A wave of his pudgy hand directed the slave to go to the gate. He abandoned Miguel.

Enrique rushed in, took in the scene at a glance, then walked quickly to where Solano was sitting. 'Fool,' he cried angrily, 'utter fool that you are, what are you trying to do? Do you want to kill my slave? Imbecile! If you have maimed him, if one scar remains on him, you will pay for it. What do you think I want him for? I want to sell him and who in hell would want a cripple. Cut him down. Untie him. Carry him to one of your rooms upstairs and get someone to tend his wounds. You are a fool, Solano, a blasted idiot and if you've ruined my slave for your own pleasure, I'll kill you.'

'Softly, don Enrique!' Solano squirmed in his chair. 'Your pardon. Your instructions were to treat him as any other slave and that I did. You said to show him no favours. I didn't. The bastard threw a dish of stew at me and I had to punish him as I would have punished any other buck.'

Enrique ran across the courtyard to find Miguel unconscious. His hands assayed the damage to the bloody back, and the knife that Babu handed him, slashed at the bonds that tied Miguel to the post. With Babu's arms open to receive him, Enrique cut through the cord that held him up, and Babu supported Miguel's senseless form.

'All Havana knows your reputation, Solano, and if you've done anything else to my slave, you'll suffer for it. I'll report it to the Bishop and you know what that will mean. Now, have him carried to one of your upstairs rooms. Have his wounds dressed, treat him well and, by God, Solano, if I ever hear from Miguel that you have misused him in any way, I'll do what I threatened. I'll be back later to see that he will be well cared for.'

'I did nothing to him, nothing, don Enrique. You misjudge me. I'll do as you say, just as you say.'

'And remember this, you miserable *maricon*. He still has friends. If you are bribed to let him escape I'll pay you double to keep him. But if he does escape, I'll take the whip to you myself.' Without looking again at Miguel, he turned and left the courtyard.

Slinging Miguel over his shoulder like a bag of meal, Babu toted him up the rickety wooden stairs at the corner of the patio. He went along the gallery and down the little hall to an empty room at the corner – the same room in which Antonio and Fidel had stayed. He laid Miguel down on the cot, then called for the boy Pajarito and together they sponged off Miguel's back and the torn skin of the wrists where the rope had encircled them. When his wounds were cleaned, Babu spread a thick black ointment over them. He and the boy tiptoed from the room.

'Better yo' says nothin' 'bout what the *amo* did ter that boy,' Babu cautioned Pajarito on the way downstairs.

'All the niggers seen him,' the boy countered.

'Yes but they ain' a-goin' ter talk. But yo' better not tell don 'Rique what yo' saw. Git's yore ass paddled if'n yo' do.'

'Won't,' Pajarito agreed. 'Didn' see nothin' nohow.'

Miguel lay still; bubbles of bloody saliva drooled from the corners of his mouth. His thoughts were a phantasmagoria of the real and the unreal, and then even those vanished. He remembered Babu and the boy Pajarito coming to him and Pajarito's spooning a rich chicken broth into his mouth. Babu was saying something and he roused himself enough to comprehend the words the big black was speaking. 'Don Solano, he say if'n yo' do'n tell yore *amo* 'bout what he did, he see yo' git treated better. Seems like'n he mighty afeerd o' yore *amo*.'

'Enrique would be the last person I would ever tell. Solano need have no fear.'

After Babu and Pajarito had left, Miguel again drifted into an oblivion of dreams and fantasies. He seemed to see Enrique enter his cell and bend over him. He felt his fingers on his body as they lightly traced the welts. Later on he thought he saw Margerita kneeling beside him and felt her cool hands on his forehead. He heard her pledges of love and although he tried to deny them, they gave him assurance. Then she disappeared and he saw Fidel sitting beside him on the cot – Fidel without the suit of amber satin, clad only in ragged trousers such as he had worn when Miguel first saw him. He slept and at length there were no more dreams, only cups of water that came to his lips from nowhere when he was thirsty, soft hands that changed the poultices on his back, brushed his hair from his eyes and kept the flies from bothering him. He slept, and as he slept the room grew dark, then light and dark again until the sun had risen three times before he awoke. Lifting one arm slowly to shield his face from the light, he saw Fidel seated at the foot of his bed. He slept again.

Chapter Twenty-two

ALTHOUGH THE GOVERNOR had been absolutely convinced on the night of the trial, at Margerita's importunings, he spent the day following Miguel's arrest in reviewing the case. La Clavelita might be only a dancer but she had important friends in Spain so the Governor yielded. He called at don Francisco's office and they poured over the evidence together. To give the Governor credit, he was a fair man and, for that matter, so was don Francisco, although the latter's judgement was often swayed by a meticulous respect for the fine points of the law and a conscientious regard for its obtuse meanderings. Together they examined everything pertaining to the Santiago case and, the more they pondered over it, the truer it became to them. There was much against don Miguel and not a single thing in his favour.

The leading piece of evidence, however, remained the entry in the old priest's book. Don Francisco had the complete set of books in his office. Between their worn leather covers, they carried a record of the vital statistics, not only of the *finca* itself but of the surrounding countryside. The records started at the time when, as a young man, Father Eliseo had come to the little chapel at Estrellita and continued until a few days before his death. Every birth and death, slave or white, was set forth in the painstakingly precise handwriting of the priest. The yellowed pages of the books contained a record of all the years' happenings.

The book which had to do with the birth of the Santiago heir and the birth of Rodana's child was examined closely to be sure there was no forgery but the page on which the damning entry had been made was untouched. There was no sign of an erasure, no evidence of any tampering or falsification. Nor was there any evidence of a page having been inserted. That particular page was one of an *octavo*, bound into the book, every other page of which was covered with entries. The only thing that their careful examination discovered was, that at one time, the binding of the book had been repaired but, as the book was old, this might be expected.

It was an important matter – this matter of having condemned a man, particularly a man of Miguel's importance, to a life of slavery. Much of the story they had to supply themselves but much of it they had before them in black and white. Both of them had known the Señora de Santiago; her hatred of the girl from Josefina's house that her son had married in a drunken stupor; and her unrelenting hatred of the issue of that unfortunate marriage – Enrique. After much serious consideration, the Governor agreed with don Francisco that the old señora had committed a great crime, had denied Enrique his birthright and had foisted an impostor, a Negro slave on the people of Havana for twenty-two years.

And so the Governor, with don Francisco to confirm his words, informed a tearful Margerita. There was nothing they could do. According to law this Miguel had been born a slave and still was. As Enrique was the señora's only heir, Miguel like all the other Santiago slaves now belonged to him. That was the end of the case. Margerita was forced to accept their verdict.

The story of the señora's death; Enrique's inheritance; and Miguel's status as a slave was the leading conversation piece in Havana. Men met each other in cafes and cantinas throughout the city; women met in patios and boudoirs; and everywhere the same topic was paramount. Miguel de Santiago, *The* Santiago, a slave! The more it was gossiped about, the more it rapidly gained supporters.

'I'd always suspected it. He *was* dark you know.'

'I forbade my daughter to go out with him. I can always

spot a nigger when I see one.' This from a fond mama who had used every device to lure Miguel for her daughter.

'Now you can't say you haven't been laid by a nigger.' From one of Josefina's whores who had been jealous of Miguel's fondness for another girl in the house.

'Of course, I had heard rumours of the substitution of the child.'

'My cousin says he knows somebody who was there at the time and saw the old señora put the child in the chest.'

Many there were who suddenly found that they had never liked either the señora nor her grandson, Miguel. 'More Spanish than Cuban, they were, with their airs and manners.'

The great planters sighed in relief now that the Santiago slaves were not to be freed. The social climbers who had been snubbed by the señora sniggered behind their fans. The young men who had been jealous of Miguel's good looks and his wealth were only too willing to condemn him and fingers of scorn were pointed at those unhappy señoritas who had thought themselves so fortunate as to be escorted to a *baile* or a *tertulia* by the once dashing don Miguel.

Suddenly many discovered Enrique.

'That poor Enrique de Santiago! How he must have suffered all these years.'

'And how handsome he is! Far better looking than Miguel ever was. So distinguished!'

'And rich! We must invite him to dinner to meet Alicia.'

'By all means!'

'I understand that La Clavelita has cancelled all her appearances in Havana.'

'She's left for Spain.'

'No, she's gone into a convent in Santo Domingo.'

'I thought it was Panama.'

'It doesn't matter. Her career is ended. Imagine, a nigger for a lover! She'll never be able to hold up her head again. It's a wonder that any convent would take her.'

'Oh, there's don Enrique riding his horse in the paseo! Smile at him, Inez, but discreetly, behind your fan.'

Enrique soon occupied first place in Havana but of Miguel

there was only a whispered memory among those who had loved him and those were very few.

*

To Miguel himself, struggling back over the long road to consciousness in the little cell of Solano's, no knowledge of the outside world had penetrated. Automatically he opened his lips as the cups of water, freshened by the juice of limes, were passed to him. His eyes opened but he did not see – he sensed only the pain of his body and the tortured images of his mind. He was grateful for the cool hands that changed the bandages on his back, for the soothing ointment and for the tender care. Gradually his senses returned to him. The mean little cell took shape slowly – the barred window, the rough cot, and Fidel, seated on the couch brushing away the flies.

Miguel struggled to speak; his words came slowly and thickly as if his tongue were too big for his parched mouth. 'You, Fidel? I dreamed you were here but … is it really you?'

'Yes, don Miguel, it is Fidel,' the boy's answer was calm and reassuring. 'Do not disturb yourself; you must keep quiet. Sleep again, don Miguel, I will not leave you.'

Miguel closed his eyes wearily but struggled to open them again. 'Tell me, Fidel, tell me all that has happened,' he begged.

'When you are stronger I shall tell you all.'

'No, now. I must hear it. I must hear everything that has happened since I came here. How long have I been here? How long have you been here? And Margerita? Tell me about her.' Miguel half raised himself from the cot. His hands clutched at Fidel with frenzy. 'Tell me, *chico*, tell me all.'

Fidel forced him gently back on to the cot. 'Will you promise to be quiet and not get yourself excited if I tell you all that has happened – at least all that I know. I'm afraid it will disturb you but perhaps it is better that I tell you.'

'Yes, yes, go on.'

'*Bueno*, but you must promise to be quiet and not excite yourself.'

Miguel smiled wanly and nodded his head.

'Well then, when the señorita came home the night you were taken, I was awaiting her. She came to me immediately and told me what had happened and I decided to get Antonio. I found him at the Casa de Santiago; there was much excitement there and nobody noticed me in the confusion as they were just bringing old Tomas home and he was badly injured from the torture. Antonio got his papers of freedom from his room and together we slipped out the back door and went to the señorita's house. The three of us sat in the patio all the rest of the night, going over the evidence again and again and making plans for your escape. She refused to believe that you were a slave.'

Miguel's head stirred on the pillow. 'But I believe it, Fidel. I know it must be true. Poor Margerita! How I have wronged her.'

'But she still loves you. Now, you must not talk. You promised to be quiet.' Fidel waved the tattered palm leaf fan. 'Where was I? Oh yes. Finally I had an idea which both Antonio and the señorita thought had merit. You see, I knew what this place was like. I knew how unbearable it would be without Antonio so I begged the señorita to arrange for me to come here and stay with you. Antonio saw that it was a good idea and he insisted on coming himself. But doña Margerita said that it was my idea so I had the right. The three of us came early the next day but we saw Enrique going in to Solano's so we waited until he came out.'

'Enrique was here?' Miguel asked. 'I don't remember seeing him but then I can't seem to remember anything.'

'As soon as we saw him come out, all three of us came in and talked with Solano. At first Solano would not listen to my staying but he needed someone to take care of you and he was afraid of Enrique if anything happened to you. Then doña Margerita gave him some money – quite a lot of money – so he agreed.'

'Poor Fidel, a slave again,' Miguel interrupted.

'Not really a slave because doña Margerita holds my freedom papers and Solano knows I am a free man. As long as you remain here I am allowed to stay with you. If Enrique comes, I am to pretend I am just sweeping the room; he does not know me.'

Miguel's eyes closed and he seemed to drop off to sleep. Fidel stood up and walked quietly to the window, hoisting himself so that he could peer into the street below. He waited for a moment, scanning the street, then let himself down, dampened a cloth with water from a porous jar and placed it on Miguel's forehead.

'Did I dream it,' Miguel opened his eyes, 'or was Margerita really here in this room?' he asked.

'It was no dream. She came here to see you but you did not know she was here. She sat right here on the edge of the cot and cried. Antonio was with her. He walked up and down the room and vowed revenge on your cousin. I hope that no one ever has such terrible thoughts about me as Antonio had about Enrique. He swears he will kill him.'

Miguel studied the boy's face a long moment. Behind the softness of adolescence, there was a look of grim hardness mingled with strength and perseverance. 'You have given up your liberty for me, *chico hombre*? You have come back to this place you hated just to be with me.'

'For you and doña Margerita and Antonio,' he replied.

'Now tell me more,' Miguel begged.

Fidel related the details of their visit. How Margerita, still in her ball gown, the scarlet carnations in her hair dry and wilted, had knelt on the floor of the miserable room, her arms around Miguel. And then again, he told of how she had arranged with Solano for Fidel to stay. He told of the guards that Enrique had posted under Miguel's windows and how they walked the pavement twenty-four hours a day to make sure that Miguel did not escape. Then he added reassuringly, 'Never fear, the señorita will find a way for you to escape. She is clever, that one. She is making plans now.'

Miguel raised himself on his elbow, a look of real terror in his eyes. 'Fidel,' he begged, 'don't let her do that. I must not escape for if I do, I cannot trust myself with her and I must not spoil her life. We are separated now by more than iron bars but let it be the iron bars that keep us apart. Nothing must ever bring us together again.'

'Let doña Margerita arrange it, Miguel. Money will buy many things.'

Miguel sank back on the thin mattress, suddenly aware that this body of his of which he had always been so proud; this spirit of his which had been so arrogant; this soul which he now possessed no longer, were all for sale. 'Yes, even me! Her money could buy me – anybody's money can. But she must not bother about me. She must forget me: I must be no more to her than a dog she patted on the head, a kitten she held against her breast or a horse whose neck she stroked. If I could just get one word to her and tell her to forget me.'

Fidel arose from the couch, lifted a corner of the straw mattress and fumbled under it for a second. Then he drew forth a ball of stout cord with a small lead weight fastened to one end. He placed his fingers to his lips and walked to the little window. Kneeling down, he took from under a loose board in the floor a little box which he opened and showed to Miguel. It contained paper, pen and ink. Still cautioning Miguel not to make any noise, he went back to the bed and whispered, 'You see, having spent much time here, I know many secrets of this room. Antonio and I discovered the loose board in the floor. Antonio always said it would be a wonderful place to hide a file and a length of rope if we had them but, alas, nobody ever brought them to us. But see, now we write on this paper, attach it so,' he looped the cord in a half knot over the paper, 'and then we lower it out the window.'

'To Enrique's guards, I suppose, who are waiting there to take it.'

Fidel shook his head. 'Enrique has told them they will be bribed to allow you to escape so he informed them that if they have an offer of a bribe to come to him and he will double it. Therefore they cannot be bought. But you forget Antonio.'

'Is he one of the guards?'

'*Ay de mi!* 'Twould be simple if he were, but he is not.

But he is clever, my Antonio. He has watched them carefully. The one in the daytime is scarcely human. He must have a bladder made of cast iron for he never leaves. But the one at night! Ah, he is different. Once in a while he goes up in the alleyway to take a piss, being a modest soul and not wanting to do it in the street. Antonio is hiding behind a pillar of the building across the way. He throws a little stone into the window and I throw the lead weight out with the letter attached to it. It's all done in a moment. Then, if Antonio still has time while the stupid guard is buttoning his britches, Antonio attaches another letter, gives the string a little tug and I yank it back. Antonio thought of the whole idea and we have tried it several times for the señorita wants to know exactly how you are. See, she even sent you this. I have been keeping it for you to read.'

He reached in the pocket of his ragged trousers and drew forth a little piece of folded paper which he handed to Miguel. It contained only the words, 'Whatever happens, trust me and always love me.'

Miguel folded the note and handed it back to Fidel. 'Keep it safe for me, Fidelito. Strange that in all of Havana I have only you, Margerita and Antonio.'

'Don't forget don Julio,' Fidel added. 'He is still your friend. Old Solano does not dare to keep him out. He has been here several times but you were too sick to know it. He brought ice and wine for you. Now, Miguel, you are too weak to talk more. All my nursing will be undone if you allow yourself to get excited. The fever will return. Let me fix your bed so you will be comfortable and then you must rest.'

With tender fingers, he undid the bandages from Miguel's back, removed the sticky ointment and washed the sores clean. The ugly gashes were beginning to heal. After applying a fresh dressing, he bound it on with strips of clean worn linen. Then he attended to the cut on Miguel's head and after that applied clean bandages to his torn wrists, smoothed the ticking of the mattress and applied a fresh cool cloth to Miguel's forehead. The bandage on one of his wrists caught Miguel's attention – a portion of the Santiago crest was embroidered on one of the torn strips.

'Who sent these bandages?' he asked.

'They come from Enrique. Solano sends them up each morning. He cannot get over the stairs, thank God, but he is much disturbed over your condition. Seems that Enrique has threatened to kill Solano if you do not recover without a scar on your back.'

Miguel pondered the matter and shook his head. Enrique's solicitude was hard to understand but, of course . . . the better a slave's physical condition, the freer his body from whip marks, the more his value.

'That's why Solano let me come, I think,' Fidel said, 'so that I could nurse you. That foolish little *maricon*, El Pajarito, who beds with Solano was trying to take care of you but he is a stupid thing. *Que maricon el!*'

Miguel looked up at Fidel hardly able to suppress a smile at the pot calling the kettle black.

'Well, at least I can act like a man if I have to,' the boy asserted, 'and I don't mince around like a two-peseta whore and paint my cheeks and sleep with Solano.'

'Maybe Pajarito doesn't enjoy it.'

'No, he hates it and he hates Solano too. He told me so. He longs for the day he will be sold. He says anything would be better than having to do the things Solano makes him do, but he's been here for six months now.'

Six months! Six months in this hell hole! And how long had he been here himself, Miguel wondered. He asked Fidel.

'Ten days in all.'

'Then it is ten days since I have been a slave. Ten whole days! Ten days a slave and ten days without a woman! *Por dios,* Fidel, you tell me not to excite myself and yet just thinking about it excites me. Since I was fourteen and first tumbled a wench in the high weeds behind the stable, I have never been ten days without a woman. Once I went three days and nearly busted my britches. And now, what am I to do?'

Fidel sat down on the floor beside the cot. His hand

touched the bare skin of Miguel's shoulder and slipped down his arm slowly.

'Antonio had me, don Miguel, and now you have me,' the boy lowered his head, not daring to look at Miguel.

Miguel's hand reached for that of Fidel, took it and gripped it tightly. 'I appreciate your offer, little fellow, because I know it is made out of real love for me but I cannot accept it. Everything in me rebels against it. True, right at this moment I love you far more than the brother I never had. Believe me, Fidel, I do. But if we stopped being brothers and became something else, my feeling for you might change and I don't want it to change.'

'And neither do I, don Miguel. But if you ever want me, you need only ask me and yet I do not think that will be necessary.' Fidel pointed to the remains of Miguel's breeches which he had rolled up to make a pillow for his head on the floor. Without standing up, he hitched his body across the floor and reached into one of the pockets. From it he drew forth two rings which he handed to Miguel. One was a huge emerald surrounded by diamonds and the other a golden sapphire with the Santiago crest. He reached in the pocket again and brought out several gold pieces.

'These were in the pocket,' he handed Miguel the rings, 'and don Julio gave me these in case you needed something,' he put the gold pieces in Miguel's hand.

Miguel remembered slipping the rings off his fingers the night of the *tertulia* and putting them in his pocket. Their size had bothered him and they felt hot and clumsy on his fingers. He handed the rings and the coins back to Fidel.

'Keep them,' he said. 'Enrique does not know about them. Some day the emerald will be worth much to you. Take it to Julio and he will give you money. Give the one with the carved birds on it to Margerita, but keep the emerald for yourself. I'm glad you found them but I can't see how they are going to produce a woman for me.'

'This,' Fidel held up one of the gold pieces. 'Babu can be bribed. In one of the cells up here there is a girl and a pretty one at that. She saw them carry you by her cell the first day you were here and she has sent messages every day by Pajarito to find out how you are. Since that one quick glance she's been in love with you, or so she says. So, when you get to feeling better and when your back has healed, we'll bribe Babu and he'll bring her here after everyone's asleep. But you'll have to wait until your back heals.'

Miguel started to laugh. 'Chico, if it was her back that was bandaged there might be some reason for waiting, but as it is my back, there is none. Arrange it for tonight, Fidel, because, as you can see,' he turned over carefully, 'I cannot wait any longer.'

Chapter Twenty-three

Enrique de Santiago let his hand rest caressingly on the smooth marble balustrade as he slowly ascended the stairs to what had formerly been Miguel's room in the Santiago palace. The marble was warm where the sun touched it and its very smoothness confirmed the fact that it belonged to him. He looked down over the patio. His fountain! His roses! He raised his eyes to the galleries. His, all his! For a moment he was almost overwhelmed by the sense of possession – he who had never had anything but his own body and not even that when he had rented it out to whatever man or woman wanted to pay for it.

Ignoring the doors of his grandmother's room – there were too many mocking ghosts among her Venetian glass and her tambour frames – he ran up the stairs to Miguel's floor. If he could only get it out of his mind that he was a stranger here; this was his home, all his.

Opening the door of Miguel's room, he stepped inside. There were no ghosts here because Miguel was still alive. No ghosts, but what a quantity of riches. Smiling in satisfaction, he flung open one of the doors of the massive carved mahogany *guardaropa* which stood solemnly in the corner of Miguel's room. Imagine one person having all these clothes! Despite the fact that he was an inch taller than Miguel and somewhat slenderer, he knew Miguel's clothes would fit him, at least until he had time to have a tailor make some new ones or, better still, send his measurements to Madrid for a complete new wardrobe. Hitherto he had considered himself fortunate to have at the most two decent suits.

Hastily he tore off the blue suit that Inocencia had given him – a shoddy thing, carelessly tailored and a bit thin as to material. With a gesture of impatience he bundled it together, added the cotton undergarments he was wearing and strode through the door to the edge of the gallery.

'Juan,' he yelled, 'come here you lazy black bastard.'

As the boy came running across the patio, he threw the bundle down to him.

'Burn them, boy, or wear them yourself if you want them.'

Juan bowed meekly but there was a surly look on his face and he crossed the patio holding the bundle at arm's length as though it might contaminate him. As he was about to disappear through the kitchen door, he called to Enrique.

'I'll burn them. I'll be happy to carry out your wishes,' and then after waiting a second, he added, '*amo*.'

Enrique frowned. He could hardly discipline the slave for overpoliteness even though he recognized the hidden contempt in the boy's words.

'These Santiago slaves – bah – they'll need a lesson. And I'm the one that can give it to them. I'll not send them to the public whips. No! It will give me too much pleasure to do it myself. But later. Now that I have shed every trace of Josefina, let me become a real Santiago.' He went back to the wardrobe and pushed through the clothes with the enthusiasm of a small boy. Snatching a coat from its thickly padded hanger, he would try it on and then discard it in favour of another which seemed even more resplendent. One by one he threw them from him and in his haste to reach another, he carelessly flung them on a chair until the very weight of them toppled the chair over and tumbled them onto the floor – a glittering silken pile of vivid colours.

One had struck his fancy more than all the others and he rummaged through the pile until he located it. It was an elaborate affair of peacock velvet, heavily encrusted with gold which Miguel had once worn to a fete in honour of some visiting grandee of Spain. Enrique donned it and paraded in front of the long mirror, his bare legs grotesquely inadequate under the elaborate richness of the coat.

The matter of a coat settled, he chose a pair of cream-coloured satin breeches and then – even more exciting than the clothes – came the choice of the Santiago jewels. He had previously procured the key to Miguel's strong box from old Andreas and, as he opened the lid, he could scarcely believe that any one person could have had as much as Miguel had had – no, damn it, as he himself now had. The watches, the fobs, the snuff boxes, the seals, the rings! How they fascinated him and once again he had to remind himself that they all belonged to him. He picked out an enormous sapphire, slipped it on his finger and turned toward the mirror, holding his hand up before his face so that the blue light of the stone was reflected in the mirror.

'*Caramba!*' he grinned at his own reflection. 'Why did I wait so long?'

Suddenly the reflection in the mirror was not of himself alone. He could see Juan's face as he slowly opened the door.

'*Amo,*' the slave began.

'Yes, out with it, boy.'

'There is a woman downstairs; she says she wishes to see you. She gave me this note for you.'

Enrique took the folded slip of paper, opened it up and recognized Josefina's cramped handwriting.

Enriquito,

For several days you have not been to the Casa Josefina. Methinks you might be a trifle hungry for attention. And so I have sent Elvira to keep you company for a little while. You are never far from the thoughts of

Josefina.

Bah! Just as he was about to shed Josefina, she had to remind him. That Elvira! He remembered the circus he had performed with her and two others not more than two weeks ago before some of Havana's young fops. The memory of it made him shudder. He tore the note in pieces.

'Go,' he said to Juan. 'Tell the girl to go back and, boy, give her this message to deliver to her mistress. Say that from now on Enrique de Santiago picks his own wenches and he aims a bit higher than those at Josefina's.'

He started to dress and before he had pulled on the white silk stockings, he heard the heavy entrance gates bang open and then shut. By lifting a corner of the *persianas* he could see the little red combs in the shining black of the girl's hair as she walked to Josefina's doorway. The way she twitched her hips told him that she was angry at having been sent away. Well to hell with her! He had suddenly remembered the little gypsy who sang at the *cantina*. Ah, there was a wench to make a man forget he had been the centre of attraction in Josefina's circuses. All wild fire and abandon. He must remember to stop there on his return from Inocencia's. Slowly and carefully he finished dressing.

Juan stood at the side of the *volanta* as Enrique took his seat under the wide hood. The boy's lip curled as he waited for Enrique to settle himself and then he leaped up and took the reins for old Tomas had not recovered. Had it been Miguel, Juan would have been all white-toothed grin, as it was he merely nodded in acquiescence at the order to drive to the Gonzalez house. He flicked the whip at the horses, causing them to start suddenly and throwing Enrique back against the cushions.

'You're itching for the whip, boy.' If Enrique had had one in his hand he would have brought it down on Juan's shoulders. But Juan turned, half apologetically, 'A thousand pardons, *amo*, it is that I am not used to the horses. Tomas knew how to handle them but with his poor arms broken, he'll never be able to drive again.'

'Enough! A few turns around the Plaza and then out to the Gonzalez house.'

It was the hour of the *paseo* when all the carriages in Havana, from the *quidrine* of the Governor to the meanest hired *volanta*, made the slow, sedate circle around the Plaza de Armas.

The Santiago *volanta*, smart with its shiny varnish and the gay emblazonment of arms, its silver harness jingling, awaited its opportunity and passed into the procession. Enrique, alone on the seat, caused more attention than Miguel ever had. Fluttering mamas, their parasols tilted so as not to hide their daughters' charms, bowed low in his direction as the carriage passed. The daughters, urged on by hearty maternal nudges, glanced invitingly sideways over their fans at him. In turn, he smiled and bowed to them, greeting the men with a pleasant nod but favouring the ladies with his most charming smile. A few he had known through the back door of Josefina's but his greetings to those were as impersonally charming as they were to the others.

At last he had come into his own and what a wonderful sensation it was. After all these years *he* could sit in the Santiago carriage and bow and smile to those in passing carriages as an equal. Gone were the days when he ran, as a ragged urchin, on the outskirts of the crowd or dragged his worn *alpargatas* over the path as a youth. Then there were no smiles for him, no courtly bows from scheming mamas. Many times he had seen the carriage pass with Miguel and his grandmother in it. But they had never noticed him. Now the señora was in her tomb and Miguel was in Solano's barracoons. How times had changed.

Juan, driving circumspectly now, circled the plaza three times, turned and drove up Obispo Street, then turned to the right and soon left the city gates behind him. Old Pepe Gonzalez, with his usual business acumen, had bought a vast tract of land in the hitherto worthless Vedado – that section of overrun jungle outside the city gates. There by building roads, by clearing away the dense growth and by employing hundreds of slaves, he had erected a huge green and white confection of a house, looking for all the world like a poisonous wedding cake with its sugary plaster towers and its pseudo Moorish fretwork. Ill-conceived and dripping with ornament as it was, it still succeeded in creating the impression of opulence and proclaimed the millions of its owner.

When Enrique's carriage arrived, Inocencia was waiting on an upper balcony. She leaned over and waved to him as he descended. Then, detaching a full blown rose from the lace of her mantilla, she brushed it with her lips and tossed it to him as he ascended the marble steps. It fell at his feet and he made no motion to retrieve it. Instead he frowned at her and put his finger to his lips. His manner of caution spoke more than words.

'Remember,' it said, 'we have never seen each other before.'

The door was opened by a female slave who relieved him of his hat. Then, as though having been advised of the nature of his call, she conducted him down a seemingly endless corridor, bordered on one side by windows of varicoloured glass, to a high closed door at the end. At her soft rap, the door was opened by a nun, whose austere black and white seemed a welcome contrast to the gaudy spendour of the hall. She too had been expecting his visit. She ushered him into the room, placing a chair for him beside the bed.

The shrunken face on the pillow stared at him with half-closed eyes. Old Pepe had been dying for months but the same stubborn tenacity which had made him the richest man in Cuba, made him refuse to let go of life. He hung on, clutching at the feeble thread of his existence. His rheumy eyes followed Enrique's entrance into the room and watched him advance to the bed and seat himself beside it. At a slight movement of the old man's hand, the nurse placed another pillow under his head, raising the emaciated body to a sitting position.

'So, you have come, don Enrique.'

'I am here,' Enrique answered.

'Your lawyer gave you my message?' Old Pepe smiled a toothless smile and rallied his strength. 'Damn it, boy! I almost married my daughter to a nigger slave.'

'It would not have been your fault, señor. All Havana accepted him until I exposed him.'

'*Ay*, you're a smart lad! Must take it from old Elena. At least I beat her in one thing. I outlived her. Well, what do you think? Can you handle my money?'

'I thought we were here to discuss your daughter, señor.'

The old man cackled. He pointed to the portraits of his late wife and Inocencia on the opposite wall. Inocencia favoured her mother in the multiplicity of her chins. He could see Enrique's reaction to the portraits.

'Bah, my daughter! You're not marrying her. It's my money you're marrying. Have you seen her?'

Enrique shook his head.

'She's not much to look at. But she's got a kind heart and she's gold-plated. Yes, overlaid with pure gold. The Gonzalez money makes a peacock out of my little guinea hen. All those English pounds; those French francs; those Dutch guilders! No, boy, don't protest. I've always been a man of business and this is business too. All my life I've had everything I wanted but one thing. Do you know what that is?'

'No, señor.'

'I've always wanted an invitation to the Casa de Santiago. I wasn't good enough to go there and neither was my one chick. Oh, yes! I tried to buy her way in but she didn't get far. I'll soon be dead and with me ends the Gonzalez name. Good riddance to it. Yet there is something I want. I want my grandsons to be Santiagos – rich and proud with every door in Havana open to them. So, don Enrique, here's my proposition: my money for the Santiago name and my daughter thrown in. How about it?' he stretched forth a withered yellow hand.

Enrique took it and clasped it solemnly. 'I accept, señor. I will marry your daughter and, God willing, we shall spawn a brood of Santiagos that will spread all over Cuba.'

Old Pepe's laugh rattled. He slowly closed one eye and winked knowingly at Enrique as he whispered, 'She'll be willing, that one. She'll be like a brood mare – always willing for a little exercise.'

A little silver bell, sewed to the counterpane, tinkled as the old man clawed at it. The faint jingling brought the nun to the doorway. At a nod from the old man, she disappeared again. Inocencia walked into the room, her white mantilla hiding her eyes. Following her came the Sister who carried a large tray, complete with silver inkwell, paper and quills. Enrique stood up and bowed to Inocencia. Together they stood by the old man.

'*Chiquita*,' old Pepe began, 'this is don Enrique de Santiago who is to be your husband. Be grateful it isn't the don Miguel I originally intended.' He turned to Enrique. 'Don Enrique, this is my Inocencia, a name well chosen for she has led a sheltered life. A true pearl of innocence. Now, my children, join your hands together. There,' he said as they clasped hands, 'my blessing on you. It is done. You are betrothed. Let go of his hand, Inocencia – you'll find plenty of time for that later. And you, don Enrique, sign here, then Inocencia will sign and I'll sign and the good Sister can be a witness.'

Inocencia released Enrique's hand reluctantly while he read the paper and scratched his name on it with a quill. Then she added her name boldly beneath his. Old Pepe scratched his faint signature and while the nun was signing, Enrique bowed low to Inocencia.

'A comely man!' Old Pepe seemed relieved to sink back into the pillows. 'A hell of a lot better than that goddamned mulatto Elena would have foisted off on us. I can call her Elena now because she can't hear me.' He held up his hand in a gesture of farewell to Enrique. 'You've got yourself an armful, my son, but it's much softer lying on a featherbed than a bag of bones, eh?'

Enrique took his leave of the old man, backing slowly out of the room. After he had closed the door and started down the hall, Inocencia came out and ran after him.

'Kiss me, Enrique. It's quite safe.'

He held her at arms' length. 'Better not. We should be down on our knees thanking God things have gone the way they have. Let's not take any more chances until we are married. Shall we miss a million kisses for one? Remember, we've never seen each other before today.'

'But nobody will see us,' she was edging toward him until she noticed the look in his eyes. 'As you say, Enrique. 'Tis better so, but oh, Enrique,' her hand slid under the edge of his coat but she drew it away.

'Our wedding day will come soon, Inocencia.'

'I don't know what you did or how you did it, but it has all turned out so wonderfully. You are *The* Santiago now and I shall be the envy of every woman in Havana. Poor, fat Inocencia Gonzalez; the Señora Enrique de Santiago. *Ay de mi!*'

He pushed her away gently but firmly but she followed him down the long hall. Just before they reached the outside door, she clutched at his hand, carried it clumsily to her lips and then fled into a nearby *sala*. He straightened his shoulders and let himself out, as there was no servant around to open the door for him. Juan was waiting at the foot of the steps, perched on the coachman's box. He made no move to get down and help Enrique in and for once Enrique did not notice his lax manners. He was thinking of the red lips and the round breasts of the gypsy girl. For once, he'd have a girl of his own choosing. With a lifetime of trying to fend off Inocencia's pawings ahead of him, he'd better not waste any time.

'To the Cantina Neptuno,' he called to Juan, 'and hurry.

Chapter Twenty-four

IN THE STAGNANT backwater of Solano's barracoons, the tortuous procession of seemingly endless days marched slowly on into weeks. Each day helped to erase the red welts and angry wounds from Miguel's body and his own natural strength and vitality brought him back to health. Each morning he awoke to the misery of confinement and each night he sought sleep within the same barren walls which enclosed his cell. Once a week, Babu conducted the girl, whose name Miguel discovered to be Esmeralda, from her cell to his and locked her in until morning. She returned Miguel's stored-up ardour in kind, for the girl was really in love with him, and after the first night, Miguel forgot Fidel's presence on the pallet on the floor. Just having these weekly visits to anticipate eased the tension for him and helped him build slowly, day by day, the bridge between the life he had left and the great uncertainty that lay ahead of him.

At first, physical pain predominating, he had been willing and only too contented to lie on the narrow cot, seeking oblivion in his pain and Fidel's patient administrations. Then with the gradual return of strength, he found his imprisonment becoming more and more difficult. His mind, released from the pain of his body, began to question Enrique's purpose. The enforced inactivity and doubt caused him to long for a change, even a change for the worse would be preferable to this doubt and uncertainty. He found himself longing for the day when he would be sold; anything, any form of slavery seemed infinitely better than the tedious boredom of never-ending confinement. Yet, he tried to assure himself, he had little to complain about; their cell though small was sunny and well ventilated; his meals were furnished from Solano's own table which guaranteed their quality; he had Fidel for companionship – *gracias a dios* – and the realization of the boy's sacrifice and his unfailing generosity and sympathy kept Miguel from entirely losing his mind.

At first there had been contact with Margerita and through her with the world outside. At least once each night the cord had been lowered and a message had come to him. But now even this had passed. Margerita had left Havana and had taken Antonio with her. Where she had gone or what had impelled her to leave so suddenly, he did not know. One night he had waited long for Antonio's signal and when it had not come, they had resigned themselves to sleep. But a pebble had finally rattled through the window and awakened Fidel who had lowered the cord. It brought up a note almost cryptic in its brevity. The few written words had said, 'Have faith in me, dear heart. Antonio and I leave Havana tomorrow. We shall return as soon as possible, but never cease to love me, as I am always loving you. Trust me, *querido*, and know that I shall be thinking of you every moment I am away. M.'

Since then there had been no news except that which had filtered to their room during the daily visits of Babu – who was never very communicative – or the frequent calls of Pajarito who, whenever he could, sidled up the stairs and sat at the door of their cell. Gossip and rumours occasionally reached them. They heard of Enrique's betrothal and Miguel averred that he had rather be a slave in Solano's than married to Inocencia. The actuality of life in Havana, however, scarcely existed for them. Their life had narrowed itself to the four walls of their cell and, as any life does, no matter how terrible, it took on its daily pattern of routine. They slept late, as Solano's love of sleep did not encourage early rising in his establishment. Babu came with their meals which they enjoyed. Fidel, remembering the filthy slop that he and Antonio had eaten, assured Miguel that both Margerita and don Julio had paid Solano for this extra food. He was getting paid twice for it, as he had not mentioned to either of the donors that there was another, so he could well afford to give Miguel and Fidel the best. Then, according to Babu, Enrique had ordered special food for Miguel, specifying that he wanted no emaciated wretch on the block when it came time to sell him.

Food therefore was plentiful for both of them; food cooked as only an epicurean like Solano would have it cooked. They had wine and occasionally rum to spike it with and although the wine was not of the best, it served to spice their appetites.

After they had breakfasted and cleaned their rooms, the bleakness of the day, with its increasing boredom, was all they had to look forward to. Although the other slaves were released from their cages to tramp around the patio for a few rounds of exercise, even this was denied Miguel. Hearing the rhythmic clank of the slaves' shackles in the courtyard below made him envy them momentarily for their brief respite but he consoled himself with the realization that neither Fidel nor he had to wear the cumbersome shackles. Physical exercise had become a problem until Pajarito found two slender poles for them. Miguel whittled them to the proportion of rapiers and with these he taught Fidel how to fence. Miguel also taught Fidel to wrestle and their thrashing about on the floor of the cell, together with their fencing, kept them in good condition. Fidel even began to find muscles under the adolescent smoothness of his limbs and a heavy padding appearing on his chest.

There was nothing else to do but talk. Gradually, Miguel, drawing from his wealth of experience, found himself in the role of a teacher and Fidel became an apt pupil. After a few weeks he was able to converse with Miguel in French – haltingly to be sure – and the acquisition of a few words each day became a real event to both of them. Miguel, although he had never been much of a student, dipped into his knowledge of history and geography, only to find that Fidel, who had been instructed by Antonio, knew more than he did about such matters. But it was in certain lessons of deportment and etiquette that Fidel was most interested. He wished to acquire the *savoir faire* of a gentleman, and here was a field in which Miguel was an expert. He instructed Fidel in such things as how to ask a lady to dance; what clothes to wear at an afternoon reception; the banalities of small talk and how to keep a conversation going without really saying anything; and such inconsequentialities as how to dip one's fingers in a finger bowl and wipe them on a napkin, with the end result that Fidel became the most polished *mestizo* in Havana.

At times, Pajarito was able to escape from Solano long enough to come and sit quietly outside the bars of their door and listen with rapt attention. He was a pathetic youth, thirteen or fourteen years of age, but more of a child in looks. He was delicately made with graceful arms and slender legs. One might mistake his smooth bronze cheeks and long wavy black hair for those of a girl. Solano seemed to delight in rewarding him with kicks or curses and reproving him with loving blandishments. The lad had formed a silent attachment for Miguel and Fidel, worshipping them with his eyes. They, in turn, treated him kindly. He would remain outside the grating, drinking in their conversation and treasuring their words to him. Then the high soprano shrieks of Solano would send him scurrying back down the stairs as silently as he had come.

One morning when Babu lumbered up the stairs with their breakfast, he lingered for a moment as he placed the food on Miguel's bed. 'You are to come with me when you are finished,' he said gruffly, 'I'll be back to fetch you.'

'Am I to be sold?' Miguel had difficulty in framing the question, wondering whether he hoped for 'yes' or 'no' for an answer.

'No, not today at least.' Babu tried to show some reassuring sympathy in his words.

'Then what?'

'Don't worry, boy. Eat your breakfast.'

Miguel realized that there was no use in questioning him further. But he had to know one very important thing. Babu saw him look at Fidel and, sensing the question that was forthcoming, answered it before Miguel asked. 'The boy'll be here when you get back and,' he hesitated as though considering the matter, 'tell you what I'll do. I'll bring that Esmeralda wench here tonight after Solano gets to bed. Won't charge you nothing for it this time. Never forgot that time when you was the high and mighty don Miguel that you pinked old Solano and neither has he.' He locked the door of the grating and went down the stairs.

Miguel ate the fruit and drank the coffee, then waited for an hour or so before Babu's return, his tension mounting with each minute. As much as he had longed to quit the little cell, now he found he was afraid of the outside world. Here he was safe. What might happen on the other side of the grating and down in the courtyard he could not imagine but he sensed it would not be good. He heard the key grate in the lock and saw the grating open. Babu was awaiting him.

It was the first time he had crossed the threshold for over a month. Despite his sense of apprehension it seemed good to walk more than a few steps in one direction and when he passed the grating of Esmeralda's cell, she reached out her arm to touch him and whispered, 'Tonight, Miguelito, I'll make you forget everything.'

'And I'll give you something to remember,' he winked at her and found that he was recovering his courage.

Babu followed him out onto the gallery and down the steep wooden stairs. Solano was at his usual place in the awninged corner of the courtyard. He was seated in his heavy wooden chair, from which he never stirred except to roll into bed. The table in front of him was piled with food and he was busy with a plate of fried eggs, soaking great chunks of bread in them and conveying them to his mouth with his fingers. He looked up, gestured to Pajarito to wipe his mouth with a stained napkin and then rubbed his dripping fingers on his shirt. As he leaned back in his chair, Miguel saw the figure of a woman a little behind him. She had been hidden by Solano's bulk but now he saw that it was Josefina.

Solano spoke with a mincing mockery. 'Ah, Don Negrito, I do believe. Have you come to have breakfast with me? No, of course not. I seem to remember that you have no liking to partake of food with me. Tell me, don Pericon, how do you enjoy my hospitality?'

'Need I tell you?' Miguel felt Josefina's eyes on him but did not look at her.

'Come, come now,' Solano seemed to be in the best of humour. 'There are worse places than Solano's.' He shifted his weight so that he could address Josefina, 'You have no idea, doña Josefina, the care I have taken of this fellow. He's had his own cell, the best of food, and even a nurse for his wounds.'

'Which you caused, Solano,' Miguel spoke.

'*Que lastima!* But you were a bad boy, don Esclavo. Bad, bad, bad! I had to discipline you.' Again he turned to Josefina. 'But not much. I do believe there's not a scar on him, doña.'

''Twould spoil his value if there was. But that's what I'm here to find out about.'

'Of course, of course, my dear doña Josefina.' Suddenly his voice changed and he snapped at Miguel. 'Shuck off those pants, boy. Quick! Out of them!'

'But . . .?' Miguel looked at Josefina who stared back at him.

'A naked man's no novelty to me, boy,' she said. 'Come, off with your britches and come over here.'

This was even worse than the night he had been compelled to strip before the Governor and don Francisco. At least there were only men present, but now . . . he knew it was useless to resist. He walked around the table to where Josefina sat, so close that he could touch her, and standing straight and tall he undid the wooden button at his waistband and let the ragged trousers fall to the floor. For a long moment, he stood there while Josefina inventoried him. She nodded her approval to Solano.

'A prime specimen, indeed, don Solano. I don't know if I ever saw a finer specimen. He's good looking, nay, he's downright handsome. Good broad shoulders, fine physique, good legs and nearly white. Actually I don't see even a trace of colour. His hair is straight, his lips are good and so are his nostrils. And, of course,' she reached forward, her hands clutching at Miguel's crotch, 'he's well equipped – most exceedingly so. Turn around boy!' She waited for Miguel to turn his back to her and he could feel her fingers stroking his back. 'No scars, fortunately. Here boy, jump!' she opened her reticule and threw a copper centavo high in the air. Miguel leaped up and caught it.

'A real fancy, doña Josefina. A buck like this comes on the market once every hundred years. Don Enrique's got a small fortune wrapped up in him. That's why he's been so solicitous about him. I do declare, doña Josefina, no slave ever had better treatment. If I'd had my way, young don Mulatto here would have had far different treatment but don Enrique said, "Treat him well, Solano, treat him well. Feed him, take good care of him and pamper him because he's got to make a good appearance on the block."'

'Don Enrique's a real *caballero*,' Josefina arose from her chair. 'Well, breeding will tell and one can see the difference now between this slave and his *amo*. I'll take my leave of you, don Solano. And, I'll report to don Enrique that his boy is in good condition. The package that don Enrique sent I'll leave with you and now, *hasta luego*, don Solano. You'll keep me advised?'

'*Por supesto*, doña Josefina, and if you'll pardon me, I'll have my boy, Pajarito, show you to the gate and you, Pajarito, tell Babu to come back here. *Buenos dias*, doña Josefina, *buenos dias*.'

Picking her skirts up to avoid the soil of the courtyard, Josefina left and as she turned to go, Miguel reached down for his pants.

'Hold there, don Asno,' Solano barked, 'nobody told you to get dressed. You might as well learn now as ever that you do only what you are told and when you are told. Drop them! Turn and face me. My, my Josefina was right! What a specimen you are! I'm the best judge of nigger flesh in Cuba and I say you are the finest I've even seen. How lucky don Enrique is! And, speaking of your *amo*, I have a little present here for you which he just sent. He would have brought it himself but a man about to be married has little time for running errands so he sent it by doña Josefina. *Ay de mi!* The old girl must miss your patronage, don Diablo. And you must miss all those pretty little sluts of hers too but then of course you've got that Fidel and there are those who say that the back door is even better than the front door, even if it is harder to enter,' Solano giggled. With a great effort, he bent over and fumbled under the table to bring out a long narrow bundle, crudely wrapped in heavy brown paper and securely tied. With a mighty effort he hurled it at Miguel. It fell short and landed at Miguel's feet with a muffled metallic clang.

'Pick it up and open it, you goddamned nigger!'

Miguel stooped to pick up the package. Strange thoughts went through his mind. Could Enrique be offering him his freedom? Could this be a sword? The shape suggested it. Or it might be some instrument to pry apart the bars of his cell and escape silently into the darkness thus relieving Enrique of further responsibility. Perhaps the Gonzalez bitch wanted him out of the way. With eager fingers, he untied the knots and unrolled the paper. His face blanched as he reached the object inside. For a fleeting moment he had credited Enrique with some degree of charity but now he realized how wrong he had been. He recoiled from it and as his fingers loosened it dropped to the tiles, this time with a clearer note.

'Ah, you do not seem pleased with your *amo*'s gift, don Lucifer,' Solano pointed to Babu to pick it up. 'Perhaps you do not recognize it, don Medianoche. I believe it was once your property. Came from the *finca*, didn't it? Something you've used hundreds of times.'

'I never used it myself, Solano, but I suppose it was used through my authority. I recognize it well enough. It is the branding iron that was used for the Santiago slaves. It has the Santiago arms on it.'

Babu handed it to Solano who examined it carefully. The brand was small and delicately made with a long iron handle.

'So that is what my cousin wants. I am to be branded.'

'But of course, don Pinga. Didn't you always brand your own slaves? How much more important for don Enrique to brand you. Didn't you expect it?'

Miguel shrugged his shoulders. 'It's my final humiliation I suppose.'

Solano snickered as he toyed with the iron. 'Final, did you say? Oh no! You're young yet. You've plenty in store for you, don Bicho. Plenty!' Solano handed the iron to Babu. 'Heat this up! Remove the coffee from the brazier and you, Pajarito, exercise your lungs on the charcoal. Blow on it. It needs to be white hot, you know. Our young stallion has a tender skin and we must remember his master's instructions. A clean brand, on his left shoulder. Those were his *amo*'s orders. Now, while we wait for it to heat, better tie him, Babu. But remember, no violence.'

Solano lolled back in his chair, his hamlike hands almost meeting across his gross belly. This was something he had been anticipating and he watched with hate-glazed eyes as Babu, a leather thong in his hands, advanced to where Miguel stood.

Resistance was futile. He was a slave, therefore he must be branded. Furthermore he realized that Babu was hoping for resistance so that he might have a valid excuse for punishing him.

'Draw it tight around the knees, Babu. He mustn't move or it won't be a clean brand. That's fine! Now his hands.

Tie them behind his back and then tie his hands to his ankles. Truss him up like a pig on a pole.'

Miguel felt the thongs bite into his ankles and then his wrists. His hand in Miguel's hair, Babu pulled his head back so that he could join wrists and ankles together. With Miguel unable to move, the huge black tipped him over onto his side and pointed to a spot on his shoulder.

'Here, *amo*?'

Solano pursed his lips, moving his head from side to side. 'Up a bit. No, over to the left. Down a little. There!'

Miguel closed his eyes and clenched his hands, already so tightly bound together. He could feel the warmth of the sun on his bare shoulders. He could hear the soft thud of Babu's bare feet as he walked to the brazier. Pajarito's huffing stopped and there was a faint crunch as the charcoal fell to the bottom of the brazier after the iron was removed. He heard the sizzle of Babu's spit on the hot iron and then the footsteps returned.

Miguel took a long breath and gritted his teeth. Seconds passed while he waited – seconds that seemed like cold grey hours. Sweat broke out on his forehead and ran down into his eyes.

Then suddenly it was upon him and the fierce sting of the hot iron swept through his body. He fought back a scream of terror. Damn Enrique! Damn Josefina and her caressing fingers! Damn Solano and the pleasure he was getting from this! Damn that nameless black who so long ago had polluted his white blood and damn the white men who had so carelessly polluted his black. Damn Rodana for letting a white man impregnate her with his callously shot sperm! Damn the woman who had passed herself off as his grandmother! Damn Cuba and the whole rotten system! Damn them all! Damn them, damn them, damn them!

He lay there for a moment in a world of pain and anger, hearing, as if at a distance, Solano's falsetto giggles. The thongs were loosened and Babu lifted him to his feet. Leaning on Pajarito, he picked his way over the offal of the patio and up the rickety stairs to stumble into his cell.

Fidel's hands supported him and guided him to the cot.

'I know how it hurts, Miguelito. I had it once but the pain will not last long. A day or so and it will go. It will blister and puff up and be sore but then it will form a scab and heal. See, Miguelito, mine healed and it is much larger than yours,' he pointed to the scar on his shoulder.

'This will never heal,' Miguel muttered through clenched teeth. 'Never! The skin will heal yes, but it will always remind me of what I am. What did Solano call me? *Don Asno!* Sir Jackass. Don Pericon! Sir Stallion. Don Pinga! Sir Prick. Well then, let me be that. Slap some of that ointment on my shoulder, little brother, to take the sting out so that when Babu brings in that Esmeralda tonight, I can prove to them all what a jackass, what a stallion, what a prick I really am. Oh, Fidel,' he sought the shelter of Fidel's comforting arms and sobbed.

Fidel applied a poultice of the healing ointment, pillowed Miguel's head in his lap and let him find consolation in the paroxysms of his grief. He leaned over and planted a kiss on Miguel's hair.

'It would have been better had you been raised a slave, my brother. You would have suffered longer but not so much.'

Chapter Twenty-five

IT WAS PAST the hour of the siesta but Miguel was still sleeping when the rattle of the key in the lock awoke him. He wondered what new indignity he might be forced to suffer but his fears were allayed when he heard Fidel's joyful 'don Julio' and turned to see his one-time friend standing in the doorway. He scarcely knew now, in his position as a slave, how to greet this life-long friend but he could see no difference in Julio's attitude toward him; he was smiling as friendly as ever. There was, however, a look of annoyance on his face as Babu closed and locked the door after his entrance but it faded quickly when he approached the cot.

'I suppose I should get up and make a bow, my lord, seeing as how I am no longer what I once was, but I'll be damned if I will.'

'And if you did it would be the last bow you ever made. I'll never believe what they say about you, Miguel, and even if it is true, it would make no difference in my feeling for you. We've been friends too long for that.'

'I should thank you but I won't because I know you do not want thanks and yet I do not know how safe it is for me to lie here with you towering over me. A long time ago in another life, you once came in and found me sleeping and dosed me with hot ashes in the middle of my back. Thank you, *amigo mio*, for not repeating the treatment today. I've already been burned by experts,' Miguel turned so that Julio could see the healing brand on his shoulder. 'Well, I suppose I deserve it. Now I can't forget what I am – a nigger slave, and neither can you.'

Julio leaned over and peered at the scarred flesh. His face became grim and bitter and although he pressed his lips tightly together, a nervous twitching in the corner of his mouth betrayed his anxiety. His anger prevented him from speaking, but he motioned to Fidel to open the wicker hamper which Babu had left inside the bars. Reassuringly he placed his hand on Miguel's bare arm.

'I've tried to visit you before, Miguelito, but since the first few days, Enrique has forbidden you to have any visitors. I've sent a few pesos, however, hoping that they would help you out with some little luxuries.'

'Little luxuries! Julito, you'll never know what those pesos did for me. There's a girl down the hall, a pretty one too, and those pesos you left bribed Babu to bring her here from time to time. That's been the greatest luxury of all but tell me, if my master, the all powerful don Enrique, says that I may have no visitors how come you are here today?'

'*Ay*, you'll have visitors from now on! So many that you'll wish Enrique had maintained your seclusion. They'll be here in droves, pawing you all over. But more about that later. Just now let us forget it, forget all that has happened, forget these surroundings, forget everything. We're going to have a picnic here, you and Fidel and I. It's been a long time since we have eaten together. But while Fidel is unpacking the hamper, I do have news for you. There are two items – one concerns yourself and one Margerita. Which do you want to hear first?'

'For the love of God, tell me about her.'

'There's not much to tell you really. Only this: a letter came this morning from our factors in New Orleans, enclosing a draft for one thousand Spanish reales, drawn on our bank by Margerita. It is the first inkling we have had of where she is.'

'New Orleans? In America? But was there no message, Julio?'

'None,' he answered, shaking his head.

The look of eager anticipation faded from Miguel's face as he watched Fidel unpack the basket. Taking out a fringed cloth, he spread it over the foot of Miguel's cot. On this he placed the dishes of food, glasses and a bottle of wine which had been packed in snow in an earthenware *olla*. There were cold chickens, pink slices of Spanish ham, a salad of avocado and crisp onions and to top it off a deep dish of Spanish custard, rich with caramel.

Miguel gnawed at a chicken leg, trying to discover some reason why Margerita might be in New Orleans. He was sure that she was not appearing there professionally but he could think of no other reason and his conjectures led him nowhere. Then he remembered that Julio had other news – about himself. He asked Julio but instead of answering him, Julio drew a folded sheet of heavy paper from his pocket and handed it to Miguel. Miguel opened it and glanced at the heading. It was a printed handbill. He read it carefully.

IMPORTANT NOTICE

To the Illustrious Citizens of His Majesty's City of Havana

SALE SALE SALE SALE SALE SALE SALE

EXTRAORDINARY!!!!!

On Saturday at noon, there will take place at the establishment of don Solano – known as the Mercado de San Martin – an important sale at public auction of all the slaves on the premises, both those belonging to the estate of the late don

Diego Alvarez and those consigned by various owners and estates. Included in the lot are the following

162 male slaves from the Alvarez estate to be sold in lots of 10 according to age.

84 female slaves, 8 with infant sons and 12 with infant daughters. From the Alvarez Estate. Sold singly or in lots of 5 according to age.

64 young healthy bucks, recently arrived from Africa. All are strong and healthy in good condition. Sold in lots of 10 or singly if desired.

52 male slaves of various ages, field hands, and 12 females (house servants) from the estate of don Raimundo Almendares.

1 male, Roberto, about 40 years of age, former valet to the Conde de Aguero. Sold by his order.

Female, Alicia, quadroon, 18 years of age, trained as seamstress, sold by order of Señorita Lelia Estevez.

Female, Esmeralda, octoroon, by order of don Carlos Lopez. Must be seen to be appreciated.

AND . . . OF SPECIAL INTEREST!

EXTRAORDINARY EVENT!

THE MALE SLAVE *MIGUEL*

Age 22 years. A fine mestee. Strong, vigorous and healthy. Recommended for breeding. Formerly known as Miguel de Santiago of this city. An unusual opportunity to acquire the most valuable slave ever sold in Cuba and undoubtedly the finest ever sold in the world.

NOTICE! The above stock may be examined three days previous to sale at the Mercado de San Martin. Examinations of the slaves Miguel, Esmeralda, Alicia and Roberto by appointment only.

NOTICE TO ALL INTERESTED PARTIES . . . SEE THESE SUPERB FANCIES BEFORE PURCHASING ELSEWHERE.

Miguel flung the paper to the floor. 'I resent the word "undoubtedly". I prefer to be the best in the world without any question. Well, so be it! I've been the best fencer, the fastest swimmer, the most accomplished dancer, the most proficient rake-hell, and the best primed whoremonger in Havana. Now I insist on being the most valuable slave in the world.' He took a bite from a piece of ham, 'Delicious, Julito.'

'Are you trying to fool yourself or to fool me, amigo?' Julio asked.

Fidel picked up the handbill, read it and seemed ready to burst into tears. Miguel grabbed it from him, smoothed it out and reread it.

'No tears!' he said to Fidel. 'Why should we weep about it? So I'm black, so I'm a slave, so somebody will buy me. Look! "Recommended for breeding." See! They'll put me out to stud like a prize bull. All I'll have to do is knock up six wenches a week and mayhap they'll let me rest on Sunday. Look, Julito, why don't you buy me and rent me out. You'd make money on me. You could hire me out to a plantation for a month and let me get all the wenches knocked up and then send me to another. I'm a good investment. Buy me!'

Julio leaned toward Miguel. 'That is what I intend to do. We held a meeting at my house last night – Oswaldo, Juan Bobadilla, Jose Aredondo and Enrique Arango. We have formed a society.'

'Whose object, I suppose, is the deflowering of any virgin who has reached the age of fifteen with her virginity still intact.'

'Whose object is the purchase and manumission of him who is undoubtedly the most valuable slave in the world.'

'Again I resent that word "undoubtedly".'

'*Caramba!* Will you keep quiet? Listen to me! Each of us has contributed 2,500 pesos. That's 12,500 pesos in all. As far as I can recall the highest price ever paid for a slave in Havana was 5,000 pesos for the octoroon girl Adelaida that Serafino Bosques bought and took to Alabama in *los Estados Unidos*.'

'Do you think Miguel will bring as much as that?' Fidel asked.

Julio laughed. 'I hope not. After all, Adelaida did have certain charms that Serafino was willing to pay for. Leandro Jiminez wanted her too – that's why the price went up.'

Miguel's answering laugh had a hollow sound. 'Old

Señora Gutherez might want me; you know how she's always had a male harem of handsome footmen. Young Caradonga might be interested too. He supports another male harem and he's certainly got money enough to buy me. Why even Josefina....'

'Nobody will buy you but me,' Julio was deadly serious. 'We will top every bid and with what money we have left over, we are going to send you to the States as a free man. There should be enough left to give you a start. My father is doing much business these days with a firm in Boston that is shipping ice to Cuba. I've written them, asking them to employ you. Or you could go to New Orleans where many people speak Spanish.'

'Anywhere but New Orleans,' Miguel shook his head and sighed. 'That's where Margerita is.'

'Boston would be the best place. They have few slaves there. Now, it's all settled, Miguel. You have nothing to worry about. Let us enjoy our picnic and these few minutes we have together.'

'First, Julito, there is something I want to say but somehow I cannot find the words to say it.' Miguel searched Julio's face earnestly. 'Perhaps you know what it is.'

Julio nodded. 'Yes, I think Margerita still loves you. I think that is why she is in New Orleans. She did not want to remain in Havana but she did not want to return to Spain and be so far away from you so she went to New Orleans which is nearer.' He took the cork from the bottle of wine and motioned to Fidel to hold the glasses. The wine splashed clear and cold into the crystal and Fidel passed one to Julio and one to Miguel and then poured one for himself. As they started to drink, he held his glass high.'

'May I make a toast,' Fidel asked.

'Why not?' Miguel winked at Julio. 'This ought to be good; the boy's an actor you know.'

'I'm not acting, Miguel. This comes from the heart. Let us drink to your freedom, Miguel, and to our new life in – where are we going?'

'Boston,' prompted Julio.

'To our life in Boston, wherever that is,' Fidel added.

'You would go with me, Fidel?' Miguel asked.

'And why not? You'll need me, Miguel.'

'Thank you, little fellow. Thank you.'

The glasses clinked and they drank slowly. Miguel tossed his empty glass to the wall but his injury prevented his aim from being true. The glass sailed out the window.

'I hope it lands on Enrique's guard,' Miguel laughed. Suddenly he felt a great weight off his mind. He would no longer be a slave. True, he would not be white, but he need fear being a bondsman no longer. Perhaps in this far-away Boston he could start a new life. True, he could never marry because he could not marry a white woman but then, he could never love another woman after having loved Margerita. At least he had discovered what true friends could be. Julio here, Oswaldo, Juan Bobadilla, Jose Aredondo and Enrique Arango. They had not forgotten him and together were willing to pay a small fortune for him. And even poor Fidel, offering to accompany him. Yes, he had friends. *Gracias a dios!*

And then they talked, the son of Havana's wealthiest banker and the two *mestizo* slaves. Oh, it was good to hear all the latest gossip as to who was sleeping with whom and who was putting horns on whom else. And during all the conversation Miguel had the comforting thought that soon he was to be free. He could stand all the curious pawing that he would be subjected to; he could brave the stares of the buyers as he mounted the block; he could tell them all to go to hell once he was free and on the ship to the States. To be free again! To call his soul his own! Yes, when he was free, he would once again have a soul.

The heat of the afternoon diminished and the shadow of the bars on the window crept over to the opposite wall. The chicken bones had been gnawed clean, the wine bottle was drained and the snow in the *olla* had melted. Fidel repacked the hamper for Julio's departure. He went to the door and yelled for Babu and his cry was relayed by the occupants of the other cells. In the midst of his farewells to Julio, Miguel suddenly thought of something.

'There is something you can do for me, Julio.'

'Anything I can,' Julio nodded in agreement.

'Before this happened, I left a gold toilet set at the house of Rodriguez, the penman. Enrique does not know about it – at least I can't imagine that he would. It was to be engraved for Margerita and no doubt she forgot it too. Get it for me, Julio, and give it to your *novia*. It is quite valuable.'

Julio shook his head. 'That is something I cannot do for you, Miguel. Rodriguez disappeared some time ago. No one knows where he went. The school is closed and the house is vacant. I'm afraid our little señoritas will return to their usual illegible penmanship.'

'*Ay de mi!*' Miguel sighed. 'Nobody will ever be able to read a damn thing they write from now on.'

Chapter Twenty-six

ALTHOUGH MIGUEL had steeled himself for the indignities of those three days before the sale, the ordeal was even worse than he had anticipated. From early morning until late at night there was a steady procession up and down the stairs of the Mercado de San Martin. For every genuinely prospective buyer, there was a hundred who were impelled merely by curiosity, animosity or mere thrill seeking. The fact that at one time, most of them had been friends or at least speaking acquaintances of Miguel's made it even worse. A few, but only a few commiserated with him and he found their pity almost harder to bear than the peeping-Tom curiosity of others. Why the secrets of his body had become such a magnet of attention for all Havana, he could not understand but had he known, it had become the fashionable subject of discussion, at least among the male population of Havana, to mock, snigger and nod one's head wisely about him. He was as popular as a dancing bear or a raree show. To have seen him and been able to discuss him was a *cachet* of distinction. He had been a subject of conversation for so long that now to see him in the flesh and to be able to run one's hands over him offered an opportunity that nobody wanted to miss.

So they came! Rich plantation owners who had been his friends and neighbours; casual acquaintances who had once so eagerly sought his favours; anyone who had a decent suit of clothes and some air of affluence. There was nothing he could do but obey their commands while fingers poked in his mouth, spread his buttocks, cupped his testicles and, in some instances, remained far longer than necessary in making their examination. Still he could not resist, even by so much as a word. He was up for sale and certainly prospective purchasers had a right to examine what they were subsequently to bid on. Even Fidel had been removed from his cell and his only protection was the stolid Babu who stood guard at the door and hustled the quidnuncs in and out. The ordeal conditioned Miguel for the day of sale. Now he anticipated it knowing that through the surviving friendship of a few, he would be free. It was this thought that gave him strength and kept his temper in check even when sweaty hands became too familiar.

The day of the sale finally arrived.

Long before noon, a procession of carriages, *volantas*, and coaches began to swell the narrow streets near the Mercado. By the time the sale was about to begin, the streets were impassable to all but pedestrians. People were forced to leave their carriages as far away as the Plaza de Armas and brave the heat of the sun to walk over the rough cobbles to the Mercado. For once Cubans were on time. Most unusual of all, the crowd was not an entirely masculine one. For the first time, the ladies of Havana attended a slave auction. It was unprecedented! Husbands had stormed and raved but in the end the señoras had won, with the tacit understanding that after Miguel had been sold, they would leave and allow the auction to become a purely male affair.

They picked their way daintily through the debris of Solano's patio, waving their perfumed lace handkerchiefs to dispel the ever-present slave odour or holding silver-filigreed pomanders to their noses to alleviate the accumulated musk of Negro bodies. Neither the heat, the discomfort nor the odour could keep them away. They came to see the slave Miguel sold – he who had so lately danced with them, flirted with them and, in so many cases, had slept with them. So many of them could have told their husbands or their brothers certain things that the latter had been forced to discover only a day or so before. To them, Miguel's body held no secrets. They all entertained fantasies whereby they purchased him for themselves. How nice it would be to have him for a footman, a coachman, or even for their husband's valet. 'Do buy him, darling,' they urged, 'we'd be the envy of all Havana with Miguel de Santiago to answer the door bell.'

The crowd inside the Mercado taxed the jerry-built old building. Rough planters from the provinces who were more interested in getting ten rough bozals for field hands than Miguel crowded against the high-born señoras of the city. Mantillas caught on the buttons of coarse cotton suits and the wires of lacy parasols were bent and twisted in the melee. People were wedged together in such a mass that there was no room even to spread the sticks of an ivory fan but nobody minded. An air of expectancy repaid them. Some had even brought little folding chairs; others had lunch hampers and *ollas* of cool drinks.

Enrique was there, his face pale against the starched linen of his coat. His chair was conveniently placed under an awning in front. Standing, directly across from him, was a little group of Miguel's friends – Julio, Oswaldo, Juan and others.

Josefina's entrance caused an audible stir in the crowd. She came alone and unattended; her virtue certainly did not require the companionship of a dueña. A place was made for her near the platform and at Enrique's whispered words to one of the Santiago servants in attendance on him, a camp chair was carried over and placed for her. She looked across at Enrique as though to thank him but the nod she gave him was more an affirmation of understanding than of gratitude. Her arrival and the seeming *rapport* between them seemed to give Enrique confidence. He leaned back in his chair. This was his day! Triumph, at last! All the poverty and degradation of the past years were as nothing. He was *The* Santiago and he was soon to witness the supreme humiliation of him who had occupied that position. Revenge was sweet! It was something to sit back in one's chair and accept the looks of admiration of *todo del mundo*. Well, he had planned for this; now it was here.

A path was cleared leading from the far side of the patio to the platform. Four husky Negroes appeared, lugging Solano in his ponderous chair. With great difficulty they hoisted him up onto the platform where he squatted like an obese heathen god. In deference to the leading role he was to play, he had changed his clothes and for once, he appeared clean. The many coloured gems on his fingers glinted as he languidly waved a large painted chicken skin fan and signalled out certain persons in the audience whom he favoured with his greetings. Two of the monumental Negroes remained behind his chair, their bodies immovable, their faces expressionless as they held an awning over him.

The top of the platform was large enough to accommodate Solano and his attendants in one corner and a pulpit-like arrangement for the auctioneer in another. The centre was occupied by a square wooden block. It was barely large enough for a man to stand on – raised about two feet from the floor of the platform.

The auctioneer, a calm and disinterested looking person, followed Solano onto the platform and stood behind the desk. He pulled a number of papers from his pocket and adjusted them carefully on the desk; wiped a pair of steel-rimmed spectacles with his handkerchief and settled them on his nose. Only then did he deign to notice the restless crowd beneath him. It was the largest assembly he had ever faced and the presence of women in the crowd warned him that he must refrain from the usual obscenely humorous comments he was in the habit of making in connection with the stock he was to sell. Usually he relied on these stale pornographic jokes to get the crowd into a good humour; a laughing crowd was wont to bid higher.

Three quick raps with his gavel silenced the hum of conversation. All eyes were turned toward him and in acknowledgement he inclined his body stiffly at the waist and bowed to the front and to both sides; then he made a deeper bow to Solano who answered with a coruscating wave of his hand. Peering over the edge of his glasses, the auctioneer scanned the crowd carefully until he located Enrique, then bowed again but Enrique was indifferent to the salute. Once more the auctioneer rapped with his gavel.

'Señores and señoras,' he began in a booming theatrical voice that seemed inconsistent with his dignified and almost scholarly appearance, 'this day we are to sell at public auction a number of particularly fine slaves. In each case, the slave up for sale will be sold to the highest bidder. The rap of the gavel for the third time will close each sale. Buyers will give their names when the sale is made and will make their financial arrangements with don Solano after the sale. All slaves must be removed from the premises by midnight or there will be an additional charge for their board and lodging. All slaves are sold without any guarantee as to physical fitness, health or condition but don Solano wishes to advise that, to the full extent of his knowledge, none of the stock offered today have any illnesses. And, I shall remind you that for the past three days, you have all had an opportunity to examine the stock to be sold. Now, if the conditions of sale are understood, we shall proceed.'

He wiped his face, sipped from a glass of water, adjusted his glasses and turned to await the arrival of the first slave to be sold. She ascended to the platform carefully, a delicate girl, probably a quadroon, for her skin was only slightly bronzed and her hair was long, dark and wavy. She was dressed in stiffly starched white muslin with a wide blue sash and wore a blue ribbon in her hair. Babu, who had escorted her up to the platform, assisted her to mount the block. She stood there, trembling visibly, her head bowed in humility.

The auctioneer appraised her for a long moment, glanced at the paper on his desk and cleared his throat.

'Here, señores and señoras, we have the slave Alicia. Ah, what a tender morsel, a young lass just emerging into the full bloom of womanhood! Isn't she lovely? And, she's more than lovely; she's well educated. Speaks perfect Spanish and has been trained to be a lady's maid. She has been the property of the distinguished Señora Estevez who is broken-hearted at parting with her but is forced to do so as Señor

Estevez is returning to Spain. *Miré, miré, miré!* With all this beauty, she also has remarkable talents; she plays the guitar and sings. Here, Tito,' he beckoned to a boy at the foot of the platform, 'fetch a guitar for the wench to strum.'

The boy dashed away and returned in a moment with the instrument. He carried it up the stairs and placed it in the girl's hands. She regarded it listlessly, strummed the strings and then broke into a plaintive song. While she was singing, she appeared not to notice the crowd and once she had finished, she stood again with downcast eyes. The auctioneer, at a nod from Solano, walked over and lifted her chin in his hands, so that her face could be more plainly seen.

'Smile, you little bitch,' he threatened, whispering the words while he himself smiled, 'if you don't I'll see to it that you get a good switching on your legs as soon as you're led down.' She lifted her face and forced a smile. He returned to the desk.

'Now, how much am I offered?'

'Two hundred pesos,' it was a planter in the rear whose friends nudged him with their elbows and laughed uproariously at his bid.

'Two hundred pesos?' The auctioneer spat out the words as if they were poison. 'Well, it's a bid and that's all I can say. Surely there must be some lady in this gathering who is in need of this girl's services or some man who would like to make a present of her to his wife.'

The men laughed and the women hid their smiles behind their fans.

'Well, then, señores, if not a present to your wife how about one for yourselves. Come now! Another bid!'

The bidding went slowly at first, then started to gather speed and went forward fifty and a hundred pesos at a time. It stopped momentarily at five hundred pesos. For a while it looked very much as though old Alfonzo Ramirez would own her. But just as the auctioneer's hammer was ready to descend for the third time, young Tomas Robledo, who owned a big plantation near Camaguey, raised the bid another hundred. The girl looked out over the sea of faces at him and saw that Tomas was young and handsome and that his black hair curled over his forehead. Her expression changed. She smiled and waved in his direction. Her hand swept across the strings of the guitar and she commenced to sing a gay and provocative little tune. Old Ramirez bid hopefully once more but again she looked at Tomas – this time imploringly. He quickly raised the bid. The sale hung in suspense while old Ramirez chewed the ends of his moustache but his miserliness won out over his lubricity. The gavel descended for the third time and she became the property of Tomas. Babu ascended the platform to help her down the stairs and Tomas, unwilling to wait until the end of the sale to claim her, handed over the money to Babu and escorted her back. His friends crowded around them both, slapping him on the back and appraising her until the noise of the auctioneer's gavel brought everyone to attention again.

Another slave had been led up the stairs and onto the block. It was the young Octavio who had been in the service of the Marquesa d'Ona – she who had but recently been buried with full honours from the Cathedral. There was a buzz of excitement among the ladies. Fans clicked open and shut. Whispered conversations took place behind them. Few there were in Havana who were not aware of the old Marquesa's eccentricities.

Octavio stood on the block, nude to the waist, a very brute of a man. His shoulders had been rubbed with oil and the sun highlighted the muscles, making them shine like polished black steel. His white pantaloons were rolled up to the knees and his bare toes curled over the edge of the block. He swept the audience with an insolent stare. The auctioneer advanced toward him, ran his hands over the man's arms and slapped the muscles of his thighs. He started to extol the virtues of the man, telling how he had served the old Marquesa so faithfully, which elicited a few snickers from the assembly. He told how he had carried the old lady in his arms after she had become unable to walk; of his superiority as a coachman and his uncanny ability to handle horses; then dwelt at length on his strength and brute good looks. Bids were not long in coming. The price climbed rapidly, exceeding that paid for Alicia. At first there was a craning of necks to see who was bidding. Eventually it was discovered that it was a contest between the agent of the Señorita de los Reyes – a spinster who lived in great state on a *finca* not far from Havana – and the agent for the young Conde de Caradonga – a blond and perfumed youth who nodded his head almost imperceptibly when it was time for his agent to bid. Having reached his limit, the señorita's agent was forced to stop. But a higher bid, from the Caradonga man, closed the sale and the young Count sat back, beaming with satisfaction.

A long pause followed the sale of Octavio. The spectators sat in nervous silence, staring at the empty block. The actioneer paced back and forth on the platform, looking up every few minutes to see if anyone were approaching. His patience finally exhausted, he went over to the counter where Solano was sitting and conferred with him in whispers, then bowed to Solano and climbed down the ladder. As the minutes dragged along, the tension in the crowd increased. Whispers became murmurs and the murmurs became more and more audible. Solano smiled with satisfaction; he was a master of stagecraft and he could gauge the mounting tension in the crowd. Finally when he felt it at a peak, he rose from his chair with great difficulty, steadied himself on the massive arms and raised a ham-like hand for silence. There was a sudden and complete hush. It became so quiet that one could hear the breeze rustling the palm fronds in the little square outside. Solano started to speak.

'Illustrious señores and señoras. I, don Solano, bid you welcome to my Mercado. Never before have I been so honoured but never have I had so much to offer you Habañeros. This is a very special sale and a very special day. Today I, personally, am going to sell the most distinguished slave ever sold in Cuba. Ah, you ask how a slave can be distinguished. Yes, that is a moot question. But I am sure many of you *caballeros* possess a stallion which, in your opinion, is a distinguished horse. Or you may have a prize bull which you can well consider distinguished. You ladies may have a spaniel dog or a Persian cat which you consider distinguished. So, I feel that I can truthfully call the next item in our sale *distinguished*.

'Many have stood on that block there,' he pointed to the heavy piece of wood, 'and many have been sold. Thousands have come and gone and each has had his brief moment and has then been forgotten. Many of these slaves have been unusual and a few have been exceptional. What I have to offer you today far surpasses any slave who has ever stood on that block. He will be one whose presence on the block will never be forgotten. Today I offer you him who was, until so very recently, the handsomest, the richest, the most sought after in all Cuba. *Señores y señoras*, it is my pleasure to offer you the slave Miguel.'

He turned his huge body slightly as Miguel was led up the stairway by Babu and another man – each holding one arm. No one could mistake the look of distress on Miguel's face – distress partly hidden by anger and shame. He was resplendently attired in ivory coloured satin, embroidered in scarlet – one of his own suits which had been sent to the Mercado by Enrique. The tan of his face had paled under confinement and his skin was now the same ivory colour as the coat. His face contorted as he tried desperately to free his hands but the men had a strong grip on him, and his efforts availed him nothing. They forced him to mount the block but once he was there they released him. For a long moment he stood, without moving, expressionless except for the fire of anger in his eyes which surveyed the sea of upturned faces below him with utter contempt. He held up his hand and the crowd became quiet.

'I shall speak,' he said, 'and if my words merit lashes from my next master, so be it. I am a slave, so let me be a slave. As such I have no need of these gaudy trappings.' He tore off the satin coat and hurled it at Solano. With frenzied hands he unbuttoned the waistcoat, tore off the fine linen shirt and dropped them at his feet. The buttons on the satin breeches caused some difficulty, while the women gasped and raised their fans, but Miguel ripped them off, kicked the shoes into the crowd below and stood erect, clad only in his short linen drawers with the Santiago crest embroidered on them in red.

'Yes, I am a slave,' he said, 'and whoever saw a slave tricked out like a *caballero*. If I am a slave, let me stand here as my brothers have stood, clad only in a breech clout. A Negro has no need for satin. So buy me, masters. I am strong and I will make a good field hand. I can chop cane and I can work in your tobacco fields. So, buy me as a man to work, not as a dressed-up puppet to decorate your drawing rooms. I am a slave but I am still a man, so buy me as one.'

The crowd roared its applause until silenced by Solano. He smiled indulgently at Miguel.

'Have you finished? For if you have come to the end of your little oration, I shall proceed. It is not often that I deign to sell a slave myself but this time I shall take a certain pride in conducting the sale. You are no ordinary slave: I am no ordinary auctioneer. And now,' his voice grew louder, 'I offer you for your bids the slave, Miguel. Whoever bids the highest will own him.'

He was greeted by a deep silence; not a hand in the audience was raised, not a voice spoke. Solano looked from one to the other. He realized that the spectators were momentarily stunned. Instead of bidding, they were staring at Miguel standing straight and immobile on the block, naked except for the thin drawers of white linen which, unbeknownst to him, revealed more than they concealed. All eyes were on his rounded calves; the swelling thighs, the narrow hips and the flat belly. They traversed upwards to the swelling shoulders and the paps which were like round copper pennies against his chest. They took in the columnar neck with the throbbing artery in its side and the face above it, as proud and arrogant as when it had accepted their homage as *The* Santiago.

Josefina exchanged a look with Enrique and he nodded.

'I will bid five hundred pesos for the fellow,' she said, closing her fan with a snap and sitting forward in her chair.

Miguel glanced down to see from whom the bid had

come. Recognizing Josefina, his lips set in a grim line, but he relaxed when he heard Julio's voice.

'One thousand.' Julio's voice was loud and clear and all heads turned in accord to look at him.

'Fifteen hundred.' The young Count de Caradonga was bidding himself this time and, although his lisp made the words hardly audible, Solano recognized the bid.

'Two thousand,' Josefina spoke the figures without a trace of emotion.

'Two thousand five,' Julio was prompt and Solano, realizing that he had nothing to do, extended his hands in a gesture of helplessness.

'Three thousand!' Caradonga spoke louder this time.

'And five hundred more.' It was Oswaldo who bid.

'Four thousand.' Josefina was not to be outdone.

'Five!' Caradonga was standing up.

'Ten thousand pesos.' Julio's voice trembled and he steadied himself by placing his hand on Oswaldo's shoulder. Still Solano stood with outstretched hands. There was no need for him to speak. The auction was conducting itself. Caradonga slumped back in his chair, a pout on his pretty lips.

Josefina glanced at Enrique and saw that he raised his finger ever so little. She stood up and faced the crowd. In an even voice, carefully measuring each word, she announced, 'I will bid fifteen thousand pesos for the slave Miguel.'

Pandemonium broke loose. The crowd surged toward the platform. Julio conferred in rapid whispers with Oswaldo and Juan. Solano raised his hands and cried excitedly, 'Fifteen thousand pesos has been bid for this man. It is the highest price ever paid in Cuba – probably in the world. Fifteen thousand pesos and the slave Miguel is sold to doña....'

'Wait!' Julio waved his hand wildly. 'The bidding has *not* stopped. I will bid fifteen thousand five hundred.'

It was too much for Solano. He beckoned to a slave to wipe his face. His lips formed the words 'Fifteen thousand, five hundred,' but no sound came. Feebly he waved one hand in Julio's direction. He struggled to speak and make himself heard above the shouting. But as he did so, Josefina arose, walked to the platform and stood directly beneath Solano. 'It seems I have opposition,' she shouted up to Solano. 'Someone has bid against me. *Bien!* I bid sixteen thousand pesos.'

The crowd was now beyond control. Women wept and men threw their hats in the air. In the confusion Miguel stepped down from the block and leaned forward, his hands supplicating Julio but Julio shook his head sadly. He had far exceeded his limit and he could do nothing.

The auctioneer came up the steps and rapped on the desk with his gavel. Three decisive knocks added emphasis to his words.

'Sold! The slave Miguel becomes the property of doña Josefina for sixteen thousand pesos. Let us now proceed with the sale.'

They led Miguel unprotestingly away. He stepped down from the platform and followed Babu across the patio, slowly ascending the stairs to his cell. Josefina gathered up her skirts and swept majestically from the Mercado. Men looked at her with awe as she swept by but the women moved away so that her skirts would not brush against them as she passed. Her leaving was the signal for a general exodus. The women gathered up their fans and their parasols and left. So did the young Count of Caradonga, his lips still pouting. Most of the men remained until after the women had left. Esmeralda was now standing on the block and the auction would proceed like all slave sales. The auctioneer rapped with his gavel, the crowd became quiet and once again the bidding started.

Chapter Twenty-seven

MINDFUL OF HIS promise to Margerita, Julio had arrived at Solano's the morning after the sale to arrange for Fidel's freedom. He found Fidel pacing the floor of his cell, desperate in his loneliness. He had bid farewell to Miguel just before he had descended the stairs for the sale and had not seen him since although he had learned from Pajarito that Miguel's purchaser was Josefina. He realized that Julio's plan had come to nothing and that instead of being on their way to that city in the north, Miguel was now in Enrique's old place at Josefina's house and he....? For the first time in his life he was on his own. He was glad to see Julio and walk with him through the gates of Solano's but once on the street, conscious of his own freedom, he declined Julio's offer to give him employment and watched Julio get into his *volanta* and drive away. But before the carriage had turned the corner, Fidel remembered something very important and sped off after the carriage. Only the uneven cobbles of the street prevented Julio from being out of sight, but Fidel managed to catch up with him.

Julio spied him, running breathlessly beside the carriage and ordered the coachman to stop. He motioned Fidel to jump in and sit beside him.

'Changed your mind? Going with me?'

Fidel shook his head. He was panting so hard it was a moment before he could speak. '*Gracias*, don Julio, I cannot come with you now as there is something I must do but perhaps later if you will still accept me.' He reached in his trousers pocket and drew out a little cloth bag. 'This,' he said as he passed Julio the emerald ring which Miguel had given him. 'Will you take care of this for me? Miguel gave it to me and I fear to lose it and, don Julio, if you would advance me a few pieces of gold on it, I could use them.' He pointed to the rags he was wearing.

Julio recognized the emerald and promised the boy that he would keep it safe. Drawing a purse from his pocket he took out several gold coins and handed them to Fidel with the assurance of more whenever Fidel needed them along with the assurance that Fidel would always find a welcome in his home.

The coins clinked musically in Fidel's palm. He waited for the carriage to stop and jumped out. Shaking his head wisely he looked up at Julio. 'Don Miguel's gold freed me once, don Julio, and yours will free me a second time and some day soon I shall come to you and ask you for a job. In the meantime, *hasta luego* and many thanks for all you did for Miguel and for me.' He watched the carriage turn the corner and heard the noon chimes from the church of San Francisco. Glorying in his freedom, Fidel whistled as he walked along and when he arrived at the Plaza, he sat down on an empty bench. The vague idea that had been forming in his mind was becoming clearer but he needed a few minutes to think it out to completion. He had never thought for himself before and it required some scratching of his head, frowning and knitting of his brows but at length he arose resolutely from the bench and turned up Obispo Street, his eyes searching for a particular shop. It was only a few steps away and when he reached it, he studied the meagre display of hardware in the window – locks and keys, machetes and knives.

Inside the shop it seemed dark after the brilliant whiteness of the sun. He had to close his eyes for a moment before he could see. In a display on the counter, he found what he was seeking – a number of thin blades of Toledo steel. He tested various ones by bending the blades. The proprietor, certain that Fidel's clothing discounted any possibility of a sale, demanded that he leave but the ring of the gold coin which Fidel dropped on the counter changed his mind. Fidel chose one of the blades, slipped it into its leather sheath, pocketed the change and left the store. A few doors farther up the street, he stopped at another shop. Here he selected a pair of white cotton pantaloons and a loose shirt – a *quayabira* – such as the farmers wore. The proprietor, with a gesture towards the back room, gave him permission to change.

Fidel had made the greatest decision of his life – a life which had heretofore been devoid of decisions. It had been hard for him to make up his mind but as he rolled up the discarded garments and dressed himself in the clean new ones, he straightened his shoulders, lifted his head and marched out of the store with purposeful intent, not however without politely asking the proprietor if he would throw away the old clothes. His steps led him toward the waterfront and he stopped in at the first *bodega* where he ordered a glass of rum. The first glass disappeared slowly as its fiery rawness choked him but he tossed off the second and third with impatience.

The rum made him a little lightheaded but gave him courage. He was a free man and no *amo* could tell him what to do. Damn it to hell, no! He strutted a little as he followed the waterfront, passing the water steps where the boats left for Regla, then turning to the right towards the Street of the Sun. The street stretched out almost deserted in the siesta hour and as Fidel walked along, his shadow made a lonely blot on the narrow pavement. There was no stir around the Casa Josefina or the Casa de Santiago. Boldly he marched up to the door of the Casa Josefina, which was closed, and clattered a loud tattoo with the iron knocker.

After several moments, the door opened and Josefina herself greeted him but one look at his features and his unprepossessing clothes and she was about to shut the door in his face.

'*Un momento*, señora.' He edged his body into the opened doorway. 'This is the Casa Josefina?'

'It is. Hurry, what's your business?'

'I come as a customer, señora.'

A loud peal of laughter broke from Josefina's grim lips. 'My girls would make short work of you, lad, and besides, we do not accommodate men of colour. Better that you go to the Casa Ana down on San Isidro. Her girls will take anything.'

Fidel reached in his pocket and drew out two of his gold pieces, tossing them from one hand to the other. 'I did not say anything about girls, Señora.'

Her eyes on the gold, she motioned him to come in and closed the door behind him. Two pieces of gold were worth considering.

'Come lad, what are you looking for then? Don't be bashful. Every man has to have his first experience sometime and you're a nice looking fellow so mayhap one of my girls would be willing to help you out.'

Fidel shook his head, averting his eyes and looking down

at the floor. He was a perfect picture of confusion, shame and indecision. Actually he had never played a part better. He even stuttered when he spoke.

'Hear me out, señora. Yesterday I was at the Mercado when you purchased the slave Miguel. Once when this Miguel was the grand Santiago, he mistreated me. I was a waiter at the café on Obrapia. In serving him, I spilled some wine on his coat. He dashed at me in a rage and beat me, then had me discharged. Oh, I got another job all right but I have always hated him ever since. Yesterday I took the day off and went to the Mercado to see him sold. Seeing him a slave and knowing myself free almost paid me for what he did for me. But not quite! No, his humiliation was public and he didn't even see me and probably if he had, he would not have remembered me. Now I want my revenge. Therefore, señora, I do not ask for the services of one of your women. Oh no! I ask for the services of your slave Miguel. I am willing to give you these two pieces of gold which it has taken me a year to save out of my earnings. This Miguel is your slave. He must do your bidding. Therefore, I would buy him for half an hour or an hour because I suppose that is what he is here for. I believed that as you sold the services of your girls, so would you sell his.'

Josefina stared at the boy in astonishment and then started to laugh. She laughed so long that her eyes grew red and perspiration formed on her forehead but she did not forget to hold out her hand for the gold pieces.

'What a beginning! Oh, *dios mio*, what a beginning! The first day that he is here. A mulatto *mozo* marches up to the door and pays royally in gold for him. I couldn't have planned it better. Miguel de Santiago bought for an hour by a nigger waiter!' She slapped Fidel on the back. '*Hola, muchacho!* You shall have him and if he doesn't do everything you want him to do, you let me know, and we'll give him a taste of the whip. *Por dios!* He's got to learn sooner or later and he might as well start now.'

He followed her across the patio to the room which Enrique had formerly occupied – the room with the little door that led to the back street. When they entered, it was cool and dark in the room and Miguel was stretched out on the bed. He was wearing a pair of his own white pants for he had found some of his clothes at Josefina's – a fact which bore out what he had suspected, that Enrique had financed the entire deal. He glanced up as Fidel entered with Josefina. He started to speak but noticed the warning look on Fidel's face.

'Ay, Miguel,' Josefina was still chuckling, 'you are already starting to repay me your purchase price. Today I have received two pieces of gold for an hour of your time and if this keeps up, I shall make a profit on you. I anticipate good business from you, Miguel.'

Miguel stood up. 'Who is this person?' he pointed to Fidel.

'A patron of my house. That is enough. It is not up to you to ask who he is but to do whatever he wants you to do.' She took a step nearer to him. 'And see that you do it.'

'Do what?'

'Perhaps Enrique should have given you a few instructions before you took his place. Do what? Whatever this fellow requires. He has paid his money and he sings the tune. You'll do as he says. Remember one thing! If you don't, I'll send you to the public whips every day of your life. Here you do as I say and my patrons say. Refuse and it's the whips for you every time you do. Try to escape and I'll have you brought back. Do you understand?'

Miguel bit his underlip and nodded his head slowly. 'Unfortunately I do, señora. It is easier to obey than be whipped and as for escaping, what good would it do me? Everybody in Havana would recognize me.'

She relented and her voice lost its bitterness. 'That's my boy! You'll find it easier in the end. So now I'll leave you two together and you, Señor Mestizo, stop on your way out and tell me, in all truth, if your gold pieces were well spent.' She walked out and closed the door behind her.

Fidel ran to the little window to watch her until she had crossed the patio.

'I've come for you, Miguel,' Fidel whispered. 'We are going to leave together, you and I. Cuba is big. We can get away to some place in the mountains where we can be free. There are many runaway slaves in the mountains near Matanzas.'

Miguel shook his head.

'No, and why not?' Fidel begged. He examined the room and his eyes rested on the door. 'What is that? A door? With a key in it?' He seemed incredulous. 'It leads to the street in back. Ah, it is simpler than I had planned. We can slip out, you and I, and go to Julio's house. The streets are deserted now as it is the hour of the *siesta*. Besides, nobody would think of your running away in the daytime. Josefina will not miss you as she believes I shall be here for an hour or so. We would get a good start, hide at Julio's house until nightfall and be miles away from the city by morning. Perhaps Julio could provide us with horses. Come, let's not waste time.'

Miguel paced up and down the room, returned to where Fidel was standing and placed his hands on the boy's shoulders. 'I don't know how you got here, *chico hombre*, but the fact that you are here proves how faithful you are. Your plan sounds tempting but it is impossible. Don't you realize just how impossible it is?'

'But we can try.'

'And it would be only a trial. Look, everyone knows that Julio bid to buy me. The minute Josefina found that I was missing there'd be a hue and cry after me. The first place they would seek me would be Julio's house. He'd be implicated and so would you. Helping a slave to escape is a serious offence. And as for me, I'd be dragged back here and sent to the public whips and no doubt all of Havana would congregate again to see the meat sliced off my back. No, *chico*, that door does not lead to freedom. No door ever will for me. I'm the most notorious person in Cuba today. There is nobody but what has heard of the sale at the Mercado. If Enrique was willing to pay a fortune to purchase me, he'd pay another fortune to get me back. He'd offer such a big reward that every hand in Cuba would be against me. So, there is nothing I can do. Josefina knows this. Now that I am sold I am not even guarded. I am too well known and, remember, I've got this,' he pointed to the brand on his shoulder, 'and I can always be identified.'

Fidel bowed his head in acknowledgement. 'Then you must stay here?'

Miguel nodded.

'But you can't. Do you know why you are here?'

'I suppose I am here to take Enrique's place.'

'Yes, and to do what he did. Do you know how I got here? No, you said you didn't. Well, I'll tell you. I offered Josefina two pieces of gold for an hour of your time. Yes, even I, a *mestizo*, can buy you for gold.'

Miguel shook his head slowly. He had already guessed Fidel's subterfuge to gain entrance. 'They can only buy my body, Fidel. I have to realize that it does not belong to me any more. So, it is for sale to anyone who can put a few pieces of silver in Josefina's hand. So be it! I'd rather chop cane all day under the hot sun or work in the *central* with the boiling vats but I have no choice. Perhaps this is no worse. Who knows,' he essayed a weak smile, 'perhaps in time I'll come to enjoy it. Enrique did not seem to mind; he did it voluntarily.'

They sat in the room, neither of them speaking until the shadows lengthened on the floor and the silence endured until Fidel arose.

'I must leave you now and my heart aches for you. If only Antonio were here, he would know what to do.'

They clasped hands and Fidel opened the door to the patio. He did not turn around as he walked across the courtyard to where Josefina was standing in her little office off the corridor. He swaggered up to her, threw his shoulders back and grinned broadly.

''Twas money well spent, señora. There are still some things the whoreson could do better but I gave him a good lesson. You should pay me for teaching him.'

'Maybe the next time you come I will,' she waved him out the door, 'if you tell your friends who might be interested.'

Outside the white walls of the Santiago palace blinded him with their brilliance. A pull on the bell chain brought old Andreas but his sight was so poor he did not recognize Fidel as he opened the gate.

'I have a message for don Enrique,' Fidel said.

'A message for the *amo*? But can't it wait? He is sleeping.'

'A most important message. It's not written on paper. I must repeat it to him,' his voice sank to a whisper, 'it's from a lady.'

'But I don't know, I don't know,' Old Andreas stammered in indecision.

Fidel brushed past him. 'Better to let me by than have don Enrique send you to the whips as he surely would if he missed what I have to tell him.'

Andreas, still in doubt, conducted him up the stairs to Miguel's room and started to rap on the door, but Fidel silenced him and dismissed him. 'Don't wait, *viejo*. The message I have is for don Enrique's ears alone so don't try to listen through the keyhole.'

As Andreas turned to leave, Fidel lifted the latch on the door carefully and quietly so that no tell-tale click would betray his presence. The door opened silently on well-oiled hinges. Inside there was partial darkness as the *persianas* had been drawn against the sun but Fidel could see Enrique sleeping on the huge bed, veiled in netting. He stood still, watching for any movement from the sleeping form. Drawing the thin blade from its leather sheath, he clutched it tightly in his hand and advanced cautiously, step by step, across the tiles. Once he stopped in an agony of fear as a tile, somewhat loosened, creaked under his weight. Not daring to breathe, he stood poised for a moment as the sleeper turned uneasily on the bed and then rested quietly.

Slowly he approached Enrique, like a cat gliding across the floor. He gained the bed and reaching down with his left hand to raise the thin netting, he lifted the blade in his right. Still clutching the netting, he drew back to strike and lunged forward, the blade aimed at Enrique's heart. There was a sound of ripping cloth. The dagger had caught in the netting, causing Fidel to slip, and the blade was buried to the hilt in the mattress. Enrique awoke with a stifled scream and grappled with the form bending over him. As Enrique extricated himself from the folds of netting, he grabbed Fidel by the throat. Fidel's adolescent strength was no match for that of Enrique who knew he was fighting for his life. His fingers closed around Fidel's throat so that the boy could not speak. He could not breathe, not even gasp for air. The fingers grew tighter around his throat until he no longer felt them. His face became empurpled, his eyes bulged and his tongue hung from his mouth.

Enrique released his grip, certain that Fidel would never breathe again and pushed Fidel's lifeless body onto the floor. He turned the body over with his foot. No, he did not recognize him as anyone he had ever seen before. Coloured – probably an octoroon; a rare type with blond hair. He opened Fidel's shirt and saw the brand on his shoulder but did not recognize the crest. It was sufficient to identify him as a slave. In searching the boy's pockets, he found the other ring and saw the Santiago crest. It was the only identification he could find but it proved that he had some connection with Miguel. Well, his erstwhile cousin must be pretty hard up if the only one he could send to avenge him was a *mestizo* boy and a slave at that.

But now, what could he do with the body? It must be removed. He did not want to give whomever had sent the lad, probably Miguel, the satisfaction of knowing that their plan had almost succeeded. Furthermore, he wanted to avoid the embarrassment of any gossip about the matter. Better by far that the Santiagos dropped out of the limelight now that he was about to marry Inocencia and furthermore, he didn't want all of Havana to know that whoever had tried to assassinate him had thought so little of him that they had sent a slave to murder him.

The street in back of the house! It was lonely and deserted with only the blank walls of houses lining its narrow roadway. It would be empty now. He would place the body in the doorway of Josefina's house, the door that led to his former room which he knew Miguel now occupied. When it was found, people would connect it with Miguel and not with himself. He realized that whoever had sent the slave would never mention the matter.

Fidel's body weighed more than he had judged, but he managed to pick it up and carried it down the gallery stairs. As he reached the bottom, Juan crossed the courtyard. The boy stared in terror for he had recognized the purple face.

'Come over here,' Enrique commanded.

Juan walked toward him, his eyes still on Fidel's face.

'Do you know this fellow?'

'No, *amo*.'

'Help me carry him out the back door and place him in the next doorway. Ask no questions. Let one word of this escape your lips and I promise you you'll be in the same condition. Here, take his feet.'

They struggled along with Fidel's body between them, reached the door and put Fidel down. Enrique opened the door and looked out. It was as he had expected – the street was deserted. Again they picked up the body and carried it down the street to Josefina's house.

'Leave him in the shadow of the doorway,' Enrique whispered.

They dumped Fidel's body on the threshold and ran back. But, as the door of the Santiago house slammed shut, the door of Josefina's house opened and Fidel's body sprawled on the floor at Miguel's feet. He lifted it, brought it in and deposited it on his bed. Tears welled up in his eyes as he stared down at the youthful face and he knelt on the floor, placing his head on the still warm chest. For a long moment his head remained there then he sprang to his feet and ran to the door. He too looked up and down the street. *Gracias a dios*, it was empty.

Chapter Twenty-eight

To some extent Enrique had taken Miguel's place in Havana. True, he was *The* Santiago now but the first flush of his popularity had become somewhat tarnished. There were those who remembered that he had been not only a pimp but an entertainer in Josefina's house and there were also those who, having met him and become acquainted with him, decided that they didn't like him, despite all he did to curry their favour. With the official announcement of his betrothal to Inocencia Gonzalez, anxious mothers who had hoped to snare him saw no further reason to invite him to their homes. Yet, despite the not inconsiderable number of snubs he had had, he still held an important place in Havana society.

Each afternoon, his carriage appeared in the *paseo* and each day he relinquished his solitary seat to share the damask upholstery of Inocencia's *volanta.* Hats were raised and parasols dipped in their honour as they made the slow circuit but after it was over, Enrique kissed Inocencia's pudgy hand and departed. His evenings were far too precious to waste in her company. He preferred to be with his friends and friends he had aplenty. Being a free spender, he had gathered a group of sycophants about him – a rash crowd of young rakehells who were all too willing to flatter him. None of them had been friends of Miguel's although some of them had been acquaintances who had desired his friendship. They had discovered that the easiest way to gain Enrique's favour was to disparage Miguel and this they did on every opportunity, realizing that it opened his purse strings still wider.

As the days passed into weeks and the first thrill of the *lance de Santiago* palled as a matter of gossip, Miguel's name passed into limbo. It was unfortunate that it had happened to him, people said, because he had been handsome, witty and altogether charming but what an evil thing the old Señora de Santiago had done to pass him off on them as a white man. Where was he now? But, of course, a slave in the house of Josefina! *Ay de mi!* Best that he be forgotten. There were those, however, who were frequent visitors at the house of Josefina and saw him but never recognized him. Others, who saw him often, never admitted it. Thus, as the days passed, his name was mentioned less and less and only a few cared to remember that there had once been a Miguel de Santiago among them.

But, although he had nearly died in the memory of the city, he still lived. Yes, he lived but life meant very little to him. From that first day at Josefina's when Fidel's body had fallen at his feet and he had dared everything to run to Julio's house to fetch him, life had been only a succession of miserable and unhappy days, followed by still more miserable and unhappier nights. During the day he did many of the menial tasks around the house. He waited on the other slaves, he swept, he polished, he washed the soiled linen, and scoured the kitchen pots. The pampered life that Enrique had led with Josefina was not for Miguel. The only kindness he ever received was a chance word from one of the girls – carelessly tossed to him as a sop to her own conscience. His days were filled with hard work but it was not so degrading as what he was forced to do at night. Josefina would appear at his door with a curt summons and bid him go to one of the upstairs rooms where he would be one of the principal performers in her famous circus. Failing that, there would come a knock on his back door and he would open it to admit a veiled figure or Josefina would usher in some male patron, like the young Conde de Caradonga, who had become a steady patron of Josefina's now that Miguel was there.

Of course he had rebelled against it even to the extent of pushing one old beldam with stinking breath out the back door but it had availed him nothing. Each time he had refused he had been sent to the public whips the next day. After the third time, he realized that there was nothing to be gained by refusing except the agony of working with blood encrusted welts on his back. Better to submit. Better to force his body to go through the motions that were expected of him, to feign desire and then feign repletion. The sooner he could cause his unwelcome partner to believe that he could do no more, the sooner he would be free to lie on his bed alone and think.

Thinking meant freedom. Over and over again he made plans for escape. On the face of it, it seemed simple. He had the run of the house and even the streets of Havana when he went to the market. But wherever he went the chain of bondage held him. His only hope lay in stowing away on some vessel which was leaving Havana but that too involved a risk. If the vessel took him to Spain, Enrique's power would bring him back again; if he went to any of the southern ports in the States, he would stand a chance of being taken as a slave and sold again. As for fleeing to any part of Cuba, that was impossible because he knew that the reward Enrique would offer would be too much of a temptation for anyone to resist. Yet even faced as he was with the utter futility of escape, his thoughts revolved around it like a squirrel in a cage. Yet with all his thinking, he always returned to the same damnable conclusion. It would avail him nothing. Then, in his utter despondency he would consider killing himself. He had even stolen a knife from Josefina's kitchen and sharpened it so it cut like a razor. He would sit with it in his hands and stare at his wrists but never quite dared to make the decisive cut. Better to go on. Better to pant and thrust and gasp and pretend it was all over and see another patron leave. At least he was alive, and as much as he hated his life, he could not bear to part with it.

Of Margerita he had heard nothing; nor had he had any word from Antonio. Once on the way to market he had passed the Quesada but when he spoke to her, she had stared through him blankly without the slightest sign of recognition. Since his last sight of Fidel, he had had no contact with his former life except occasional messages from Julio. Often on his way to market, he would stop at the door of Julio's house and if Julio were in, the cook would send a servant for him and they would talk for a few moments. More and more their conversation had deteriorated into mere inquiries as to each other's health. It was not that Julio's friendship for him had lessened, merely that they now lived in such entirely different worlds that there was no common ground on which they could meet. This new life was entirely devoid of friendship and affection although filled to sorrowful repletion with lust and passion which masqueraded, for the moment, as love.

This day had been a particularly difficult one. With little sleep the night before, he had spent the morning and afternoon scrubbing the marble tiles of the patio. First a black one and then a white one, stopping only for a moment to wipe the sweat from his eyes as one of the girls walked across the tiles and he had to pause in his scrubbing. Even these momentary pauses brought a shrill rebuke from Josefina if she happened to be near and he would return to his task. Throughout the day he had longed for sleep and when the time came for his evening meal, he had crept away to his room too tired to eat. Sleep was more important than food.

It was cool in his room and well ordered for it was not his room alone. All of Josefina's rooms were a part of her business and each must bring in a profit. A straw tick under the gallery stairs would have been more to his liking than the soft whiteness of Enrique's bed. Tonight he was too exhausted to think. He fumbled at the buttons of his shirt with fingers which were puffed and white from long soaking in water. It fell from his shoulders and with his remaining strength he loosened the wooden buttons of his pants and let them fall to the floor, staggered across the room and fell across the bed. How long he slept, he did not know but when he awoke it was dark and a cool breeze blew in the window. A desire to move, to change his position, came over him but the ever-present ache in his muscles made it easier to stay still. With an effort, he raised his arm to shade his eyes from the lamp that burned in the patio and shone wanly through the grating on the wall. He stretched his muscles on the cool linen, getting the kinks out of his legs and arms. Sleep! To be able to sleep forever; to forget everything and never know the reality of awakening. Sleep, the only pleasure he had left! His hands groped under the mattress and found the knife. The smoothness of its wooden handle felt reassuring in his palm, but no, there would always be that. Better to live another day; perhaps tomorrow would be better. *Quien sabe?*

He heard steps outside and without knocking Josefina opened the door abruptly and called out his name. He opened his eyes with difficulty to see the bulging curves of her figure silhouetted in the doorway. Then he closed them, feigning sleep. Let the old bitch call. She did and with each repetition of his name her voice became louder and more demanding. Finally he mumbled an acknowledgement.

She stepped inside, screaming now. 'Wake up, you lazy bastard, you good for nothing *maricon*!'

'If I am, it's you that made me,' he was in no mood for her abuse.

'Don't sauce me with your black mouth. Get up! Wash the stink off your body. There's work to be done. Dress in your best shirt and pants and come to my room. I'll give you ten minutes.'

He raised himself on one elbow and stared up at her. 'What if I refuse?'

'You? Refuse?' Her laugh had no humour in it. 'Go ahead! Refuse if you want. Yes, refuse and as God is my witness, for every peso I lose on you tonight, you'll have ten stripes on your back tomorrow. Enough! Why should I bandy words with a slave. Be at my door in ten minutes and mind you, I want no snivelling slave, no sweaty drudge, no dragging feet and hang-dog look. I want a man, handsome and immaculate. There's work for you to do.'

The door closed with a finality that shook the iron gratings in the window. For one long moment he lay there, gathering strength and courage to get up. Could he have a choice, he hoped it would be Caradonga who was easily satisfied and not the nameless woman with the hennaed hair whom, he was certain, no man on earth could ever satisfy. With an effort, he lifted himself from the bed and walked slowly to the door in back, opened it and peered out at the empty street. Freedom? No, even in the dark he could not be free. Closing the door with a sigh, he lit the candle. The cool water refreshed him as he splashed it over his body and the handful of lemon verbena leaves with which he scrubbed himself removed the sweat of the day. He lifted one arm and sniffed of his armpit. Did he really smell like a slave or was it the odour from Solano's that lingered in his nostrils? With towel in hand, he sank back on the bed to steal another moment of rest but realized he would succumb if he remained there. He forced himself to his feet before his eyes closed. Oh, let it be Caradonga and it would be over in a half an hour! From the *guardaropa* he took out a shirt of thin cotton and a pair of clean white linen pants, both of which he had worn before in another life. This time he had washed and pressed them himself. No use to bother with underclothes, stockings or shoes. He'd be undressing in a few minutes and the more clothes he wore, the more it complicated things. Running a comb through his hair, he tied it in back with a worn black ribbon and stepped out into the patio, feeling the cool marble under his bare feet.

Josefina met him at the entrance to her room. She rarely looked at him but tonight, as the light fell full on his face, she scanned it carefully. The lines on it were noticeable – those heavy lines of fatigue and the finer ones of sorrow. He had aged since he came there; not noticeably of course but only on close inspection. While she looked at him, she found herself fighting a strange emotion. She had never allowed herself the luxury of pity but now the sensation was too strong to ignore. When she spoke to him, her voice had lost its usual grating harshness. There was something almost kind in her inflection.

'You are on time; the ten minutes is just up.' Then, as an afterthought which surprised even herself, she added, 'A glass of wine, Miguel?'

He stared at her in astonishment and nodded. She poured the wine from a decanter and handed the glass to him. He gulped it down, questioning with his eyes.

'Old Josefina's a pretty hard taskmistress, isn't she?' she managed an indulgent smile.

'No, señora, the work is not too hard.'

'Come, come, of course it is. I've just realized that I'm ruining my investment. I'd better take care of you; treat you better; give you more chance to sleep. Even a stallion gets turned out to pasture, *verdad?*'

'It is not the work I mind, señora. I'll work from the time the sun comes up in the morning until it sets at night. I'll do anything you want if you will not make me . . .'

'Don't be stupid! I can get some dim-witted nigger to do your day-time work. I can buy one at Solano's for five hundred pesos. But the other – ah, that he could not do,' she advanced toward him and looked at him, her eyes flashing under her heavy brows. 'Nobody else can do that. Nobody! You are *The* Santiago. You've got what few men have and what everybody wants. They're willing to pay for it – good solid yellow gold with the King of Spain's picture on it. Here, have another glass of wine; I'll even put a shot of rum in it. It may give you some spirit. There's an important party on tonight. It is a party I owe to somebody and it must go off well. Do you know what that means?'

'It means I must perform like a dancing bear.'

'. . . at the circus! Yes, that is what they call my little entertainments. You can either do it well, with fire and abandon, or you can merely go through the motions like an automaton. Tonight I'd like fire and not just a smouldering flame that could be put out with one blow.'

He gulped down the wine and stared back at her without answering. She put her hand on his shoulder and he could feel the warmth of her palm through the thin fabric of his shirt.

'Look, Miguel, you have no reason to do me any favours. You hate me and God alone knows why you shouldn't. But I'll make a bargain with you. Tonight if you do as I want and cause me no trouble, I tell you what I'll do. From now on, no work during the day. Life can be easy for you, if you'll but let it. Come, Miguel, life has thrown us together and life is cruel. It's been cruel to me and I've had to fight to get where I am. You'll have to fight too but there's no need of your fighting me. Look, *chico*, we got off to a bad beginning and I'll confess, it was not all my fault. I'll do the best I can for you from now on if you'll work along with me. How about it, lad?'

Miguel continued to stare at her. Could this be Josefina talking? Could she, who had never done anything but scream vituperations at him, actually possess some shred of feeling? *Por dios!* The old girl had showed the chink in her armour. He remembered an old saying of Pepe's back in those days at Estrellita when he had done something wrong and came up before his grandmother for punishment. Pepe had always whispered as he led him to his grandmother's room, 'you can catch more flies with sugar than with vinegar, Miguelito.' And . . . it had worked. Instead of defying his grandmother, he had pandered to her with flattery and glossed her with blandishments until, completely charmed by his pretty words, she had forgotten the punishment she had intended. If it had worked then, it might work now. It was worth trying. It might eventually lead to freedom.

He put his hand over the hand that was on his arm and took it in both of his. For a long moment he looked at her and then lifted her hand to his mouth and kissed it, then, with his lips in her palm, he drew it up to his cheek.

'*Mi ama,*' he whispered. 'Know you not that there is but a very thin wall between love and hate? You were right, I have hated you and methinks you have tried hard to hate me. Yet tonight I find that you do not hate me and I find that I do not hate you. Listen, *mi ama*, once I had many people to love me; today I have nobody. If I felt that somebody cared a little about me, I could love that person in return. There is only one desolation greater than not being loved and that is to have nobody to love. May I have that privilege, *ama querida*?'

Her hand patted his cheek, then suddenly her manner changed and she was all business.

'Then you will do your best to put on a good performance tonight?'

'With fire and abandon!' he winked at her, 'and after all, why not? It is work for which your Miguel is well fashioned, *verdad*? As you yourself said, I have what they want and are willing to pay for. Tonight, I promise you, your patrons will not be cheated. The bigger the audience, the better the performance. And where do we go, *mamacita*, to the big *sala* upstairs?'

She shook her head. 'Tonight, *chico*, we go next door, to the Casa de Santiago.'

For a moment he felt he could not go through with it; not in his own home with all the memories it contained. What was it Josefina had said? She'd had to fight to get where she was. *Bien!* he would fight too. He grinned down at her.

'And why not? That means my cousin Enrique will be there. I could not have wished for anything better. I'll show all his guests that the slave Miguel is more of a man than poor Enrique can ever hope to be. *Vamos, mamacita! Vamos!*'

Chapter Twenty-nine

HAD IT NOT been for Josefina and five of her girls who were behind him, Miguel could well have imagined that no change had ever taken place in his life. The wrought iron gates of the Casa de Santiago swung open as easily and as silently as ever at Juan's touch and the boy ushered them inside with as much grace as if they had been the late señora's invited guests. The hurricane-shaded lights of candles in the patio showed the plants to be as lush and blooming as usual; the fountain dripped with the same musical cadence; and the white pillars of the galleries shone in the dim light. As they crossed the patio, Juan stepped up alongside Miguel and whispered to him.

'We miss you, don Miguel.'

Miguel steeled himself against the sympathy and friendship in the boy's words. Tonight he could not indulge in the luxury of nostalgia. Tonight he must cram all his feelings down into some obscure corner of his brain and let none of them escape. He could not let Juan commiserate with him.

'How are you getting along with Edita, boy?' It was far safer ground than disturbing remembrances of things past.

'*Caramba*, don Miguel! If you could see her you would know. Her belly's bigger than a barrel and don Enrique sent her to Estrellita. Now it's Evelina that lingers in the pantry with me.'

'*Que hombre!*' Miguel sensed the subtle difference in Juan's attitude toward him. He spoke with the camaradie that existed between slaves, not between slave and master.

But, why not? He followed Juan across the patio into the big first floor sala which was brilliantly lighted but deserted. Juan indicated chairs for Josefina and the girls to sit and then left them. Miguel looked around. The new damask that Antonio had picked out was on the chairs; there was a big wine stain on the Aubusson rug and the vases were filled with wilted flowers. A film of dust obscured the brilliance of a satinwood table and a crumpled pair of men's drawers reposed on one end of the long French sofa. From the big double doors that closed off the dining room, there was the sound of music and laughter. An orchestra was playing a lilting Spanish dance and above it, Miguel could hear the clicking of castanets and the staccato tattoo of heels. The music stopped, was followed by a loud sound of clapping hands and shouted '*ole*'s' and then a louder-than-before burst of conversation.

Josefina stood up, made a quick eye-searching inventory to determine that her girls and Miguel were all there and then crossed the room to knock on the big doors. She had to knock several times to make herself heard, and when the door was opened Miguel recognized a certain Alfonzo Real, a swarthy lout who had somehow managed a precarious toe-hold in Havana society.

'*Hola,* it's Josefina!' he called out to those in the room behind him. 'Old Mama Josefina's come over to get all her boys and take them over to her house and put them to bed with her pretty little whores. Have a drink, *vieja,*' he lifted a wineglass to her lips but she pushed his hand away.

A voice from inside, not as drunkenly boisterous as Real's called out, 'Come in, doña Josefina.' Miguel recognized it as Enrique's. Josefina stepped inside and closed the door behind her while Miguel and the five girls sat and stared at each other.

'You used to live here, Miguel?' one of them asked.

'*Por supuesto!*' he shrugged his shoulders. 'It wasn't a bad place to live, Perla, but it wasn't as exciting as living at Josefina's. Something different every night there.'

'If you like something different every night,' the girl

answered. 'As for me I'm getting sick of it. I'd like the same one every night . . .'

'And a little *casa* of your own where you could entertain him,' one of the other girls said. '*Ay de mi*, Perla, no man's going to set you up in your own establishment at your age. You must be almost twenty.'

Perla turned to answer the girl, her hand raised to slap her but Miguel intervened. 'Come, girls, no fighting! Look, we're all in this together. Let's enjoy it. Time was when I paid ten gold pieces to see an entertainment such as we are going to put on tonight. After all, we are the ones who should get the fun out of it. It's a hell of a lot more fun doing it than just watching. What's the routine tonight?'

'The same old one they always want,' another girl smoothed her hair back and reset the little combs in it. 'You stand up and we all fight over you to see who can get you first. That's why we're wearing old clothes. And you, Magdalena, don't you dare to pull my hair tonight. If you do,' she doubled up a fist and shook it.

'No fighting, *putas*! We're going to have fun and I'll promise you, the first one that gets me won't be sorry. I hope Josefina brought an extra pair of britches for me so I won't have to go back naked. And, girls, no scratching. I don't want to come out of this looking like I've been in a tiger's cage.'

'You're different tonight, Miguel,' the girl called Perla smiled at him. 'It's fun being with you. Be like this all the time. We like you better this way. You're cute, Miguel. I hope I get you tonight.'

'You're cute, Miguel,' they all echoed but one of them held up her hand for them to be quiet. She had seen the doorknob on one of the big doors turning. 'Sh-h-h! Josefina's coming back.' They all sat up straight in the chairs as the door opened and Josefina came in.

'You will all go in now. Miguel, you stand in the middle of the big table. Girls, you know what to do. They want to see a good fight. The one that gets to Miguel first will get a gold piece for herself and she can keep it. That ought to liven things up a bit. After it is over, you, Miguel, can come back. I doubt if any of the men here tonight are the kind who will want your services and even if they do, you'll be in no condition to give them. You girls will remain here until morning. If they require any more girls, you, Magdalena, skip out and come over and let me know. Now, any questions?'

'Yes, *ama mia,*' Miguel grinned at her. 'And if my pants get torn to rags as they usually do, how am I going to get home?'

'Damn!' Josefina snapped her fingers, 'I forgot to tell you to bring an extra pair. Tell you what you do. The door of your room will be unlocked. Slip out the back way. There won't be any *guardias* out back at night. It will only take you a minute boy. And,' she smiled at him, 'let me know when you get back.'

'That I will. Come on girls!' Miguel led the way. 'Which one of you will be the lucky one to get the gold piece . . . and me?'

Miguel swaggered over to the big double doors. For one small moment, while his hand remained on the doorknob, he recalled how many times he had walked through these same doors with his grandmother on his arm. He could never bring himself to hate her, never, even though it had been she who had brought him where he was. But this was no time to remember such things. *Caramba!* He'd put on such a performance tonight as Havana would never forget. He straightened his shoulders, threw out his chest and lifted his chin. He grinned and called back to the girls. '*Vamos, putas. Soy el mas putesco que todos.*' He flung open the doors and marched in.

The air was blue with tobacco smoke. Some twenty men sat about the room, their chairs pushed back from the long dining table. One of them was fondling a half-naked gypsy girl – evidently she who had been dancing. The table was strewn with wine bottles and glasses and in the centre was the remains of the big cut glass epergne which had always graced the table on formal occasions. Now it was broken, the flowers strewn over the table in a puddle of water. At Miguel's entrance there was a sudden hush. Even the fellow who was fondling the gypsy girl looked up and pushed her off his lap. Enrique sat at the far end of the table, facing Miguel. Their eyes met and Miguel bowed low, exaggerating his genuflection with low comedy.

'*Hola, señores,*' he said, 'and you, Excellency', he bowed a second time to Enrique. 'We are a band of strolling players and we have come to entertain you tonight. We have a very special little play to perform for you tonight. Mayhap some of you felt it would be a tragedy but no, it is a comedy, designed to make you split your sides with laughing.' Through the cigar smoke, he could see that Enrique was nonplussed. Whatever it was that he had expected, it was certainly not Miguel's gay insouciance. Let the bastard be surprised, Miguel thought, as he continued. 'Yes, señores, this is a comedy. We call it "Catch the Black Rabbit". Once I called it "Catch the White Rabbit" but that was before I found out I was black and not white. And so, señores, the name has been changed but that is all. *Hola, señores!*' He vaulted up onto the table and stood in the centre, bare feet wide apart on the polished wood, his hands on his hips and his shoulders thrown back. '*He aqui!* The black rabbit! Once when I was a white rabbit, I was flattered if two girls fought over me but now, behold, five young and charming girls will stage a battle royal to see which one gets me and it is you, Señor don Enrique de Santiago, or should I say *mi amo querido* that I have to thank for all this and I do thank you. Life in this house was never as exciting as it is in the house next door. There I am never bored; here I often was. *Muchas gracias,* don Enrique! And now a glass of rum for the black rabbit, señores, and rum for the pretty girls who will fight to get him.' He reached down and took the glass of rum which a hand held up to him, downed it and tossed the glass to the floor and then, noticing the broken glass on the table he called out to Juan whom he saw hovering in the background. '*Hola,* Juanito, sweep up this broken glass and wipe the table clean. My girls have tender backs and I would not want anyone of them injured.'

He waited for Juan to clean away the debris. Enrique looked crestfallen; things were not going the way he had expected them. This young cock-o-the-walk was a far cry from the crestfallen slave which had been auctioned off at Solano's. Could it be that he was actually happier in his new role? He looked it. But then, Enrique did not know that Miguel had suddenly discovered a talent for acting. Now, with the table clean, Miguel took up his stance again and called out to the girls.

'Come, my pretties, let's see which one of you can claim the black rabbit. It's worth fighting for, *chiquitas*, and we shall teach the great don Enrique a lesson which he perhaps needs. He is to be married soon. Bien! Then we shall show him the best way to entertain his bride. Watch, don Enrique! Watch and learn!'

Enrique half rose from his chair, but drunken hands pulled him down. The five girls circled the table warily. As one started to hoist herself up, another was upon her, yanking her back, but the first girl turned and with a resounding slap floored the one who had pulled her. The fight began. The girls had been through it so many times, they had perfected their technique and at first they treated each other with some degree of gentleness, pushing and slapping but gradually tempers were aroused and they pitched into each other, pulling hair, screaming, ripping dresses, tripping, shoving, and mauling each other while Miguel from his perch on the table looked down and smiled.

The audience rose to the fight, claiming favourites and betting on them, encouraging one and denouncing another. Now the five were in one snarling group, like a bag of cats, scratching and clawing. One of the girls – it was Perla – her hair streaming down her back, her gown hanging from her in rags, managed to get one knee up onto the table, then flung herself onto it, rolling over until she came to Miguel's feet. Hooking her fingers into his waistband, she started to pull herself up, but the buttons gave way and she fell to the floor again while Miguel sidestepped, freeing his ankles from the confining cloth.

Another girl, she who was called Magdalena, had now gained the table and she crept over to where Perla was trying to stand up, her arms around Miguel's thighs. Magdalena, her hand gripping at Perla's hair, pulled her away and threw herself into Miguel's arms but Perla was too quick for her. She got to her feet, circled Magdalena's neck with her arms and pulled her back and as the girl stumbled and fell, she dragged Miguel's shirt with her. Now Perla had the field to herself and she was upon Miguel and he, giving her the victory, claimed her, forcing her back down onto the table.

For a few moments there was silence, broken only by Miguel's breathing. Every pair of eyes in the room was upon him and he found himself forgetting that he was playing a role. Now he was in earnest and despite the moans and entreaties of the girl under him he continued with such brilliant bravura that along with his mounting fire, he was conscious of the '*ole*'s' and '*bravo*'s' of the men crowding around the table. Then it was over and for a second, he slumped over the girl, gasping for breath. Slowly he got to his knees and then stood up. Reaching down, he gathered up his trousers and the rags of his shirt.

A shower of gold pieces spattered onto the table but Miguel ignored them while he pulled on the rags that were his pants and then jumped down from the table.

'The gold, señores,' he waved toward the table where Perla was struggling to sit up, 'is not mine to claim. A slave, you know, can possess nothing. But, if my performance tonight has pleased you, you can reward me by telling my mistress, doña Josefina. Perhaps she will let me entertain you again. *Muchas gracias, señores.* You will have no further need for me. Being men, you will understand why I cannot repeat my performance as much as I would like to. *Buenas noches, señores,* and you too, don Enrique. I thank you and all Havana thanks you for if it had not been for you, a great artist would never have been discovered.'

He started to leave, but two of the men hoisted him up on their shoulders, carrying him out the door. One by one the rest followed, leaving Enrique sitting alone. Even the girls, clutching their rags around them, followed the procession which wound out through the patio through the big gate and onto the street, then along the middle of the street until they reached the door of Josefina's house. The door was opened and they carried Miguel inside, although he could hardly bend low enough to get his head under the doorframe. They carried him to the middle of Josefina's patio, still cheering and calling his name. Josefina appeared from her little office, and now her name was added to their cheers.

Alfonso Real, on whose shoulders Miguel was being carried, eased him down to the floor. With a deep bow to Josefina and with one arm still around Miguel, Real spoke.

'Doña Josefina! When a *torero* in Madrid wins the ears and the tail, he is carried back on the shoulders of his *aficionados*. When a flamenco singer in Sevilla stirs his listeners with the depth of his singing, he is given a like honour. Tonight we have seen a great performance. This, our Miguel, is greater than any *torero* so we have brought him back to you in triumph. Guard him well, doña Josefina, he is a true artist.'

With their arms around the girls, they drifted back to the front *sala*, leaving Miguel and Josefina alone.

She came up to him, put her arm around his waist and led him to his room.

'You are tired, Miguel,' she said softly.

'Tired, *mamacita*.' He nodded.

'Then you shall sleep. Sleep as long as you wish. Sleep around the clock if you want.'

'Gracias, mamacita.'

'My thanks to you, Miguel. There is food on a tray in your room, and wine too. If you would like one of my girls to keep you company, you have but to ask.'

He shook his head. 'Fire and bravado, *mamacita*! That's what you asked for.'

'And it seems that's what I got. By tomorrow you'll be even more celebrated than the Miguel de Santiago who strutted the streets of Havana or Miguel the Slave, who was sold at Solano's. Tomorrow you'll be El Macho, the champion of Havana,' she patted his shoulder. 'I must get back or those bastards will drink all my wine and get all my girls without paying a *centavo*. Good night, Miguel.'

'Good night, *mamacita.*'

A candle was burning in his room. He closed the door, let his pants fall to the floor and fell on the bed. Lazily he reached over to the tray on the table and chose a chicken leg. He tore the meat from the bone and chewed it, then poured out a glass of wine, drank it and blew out the candle. He could sleep and how he would sleep. Good old Pepe! It was still true, one could catch more flies with sugar than with vinegar. He had been wise.

A cool breeze passed over his sweaty body and he punched the pillow into a more comfortable position. He was just dropping off to sleep when suddenly he stirred.

Damn those bastards for breaking his grandmother's epergne! She had set a big store by it. But then, she was not his grandmother and the epergne belonged to Enrique. To hell with it! To hell with everything! From now on he would live one day at a time and if a few soft words and a few gasps and thrusts would make life easier for him, so be it. For the first time since that night he had been taken to Solano's, he slept soundly.

Chapter Thirty

INOCENCIA SMILED CONTENTEDLY as her *volanta* turned into the Street of the Sun. How pleasant, she thought, to be able to arrive in daylight, unafraid and unashamed; to drive up to the Casa de Santiago and entirely ignore the Casa Josefina; to be announced by old Andreas and to see Enrique without stealth or deceit. It was all so much different than having to sneak into the back door of the Casa Josefina. Now Enrique was hers and soon he would be hers forever.

To be in love! To be in love with no obstacles in her path! To know that Enrique would be her husband. Her happiness made her almost beautiful. She had nearly succeeded in forgetting that as much as she loved, she was not loved in return.

Each time they met, she hoped that he would be pleased

to see her; that there would be some sign in his greeting to prove that he really wanted her. If only once, just once, he would say some word or make some gesture. How she would treasure it in her heart; store it away and take it out and relish it over and over again. Just suppose he were to say 'Inocencia' and come running across the patio to meet her, his arms outstretched to enfold her and his lips warm and wet with desire. How wonderful it would be! But why desire the impossible? Wasn't it enough to know that he would be her husband?

Enrique was waiting for her in the patio. She glanced up at him hopefully but he merely raised her hand, brushed it fleetingly and lightly with his lips and let it drop. 'You are late, Inocencia.' His tone was like a slap in the face.

'I am sorry, Enrique. It was not my fault. I was delayed.'

'It doesn't matter.'

'There is so much to do,' she continued to excuse herself. 'I stopped at the bootmakers to see about my wedding slippers. They are nearly finished and I left Gertrudia there to fetch them. Enrique, *querido*! Wedding slippers – my wedding slippers! Just thinking about them makes me happy. They are embroidered with real pearls and Persian turquoises. Our wedding, Enrique! You and I – married in the cathedral with the Bishop himself there. Oh, Enrique, you are happy too, aren't you? You do love me, Enrique. You do, you do, you do! Kiss me, Enrique.'

He sighed and shrugged his shoulders.

'Just one kiss, my love?' She could see that he was annoyed but her desire for some show of affection was more important to her than his displeasure. She moved closer to him.

Sighing again, he pecked at her cheek. 'The servants, Inocencia.'

She was near to weeping but she controlled herself. Better to laugh it off. 'Of course the servants! Or else you are too warm; or you are too tired; or your dinner has upset you. Your excuses are always so logical that I cannot accuse you of not wanting to. Oh, how practical you are, Enrique! But love is not practical. Love does not mind servants or hot weather or a hearty dinner. I wonder what would happen if just once you were to open your arms, hold me willingly and kiss me so I struggled to breathe.'

'That will come later, Inocencia.'

'Of course! How stupid of me! Later when we are married. Then let us discuss our wedding.'

It was a safer subject by far and he welcomed the change. A clap of his hands brought Juan who placed a chair for her.

'Yes, Inocencia, let us discuss our wedding – the wedding of Inocencia Gonzalez and Enrique de Santiago. It will be a wedding that the *Habaneros* will never forget. For once, you and I, Inocencia, will occupy the centre of the stage. We have both stood too long in the wings, waiting for our cue. Now, every eye in Havana will be upon us.'

'Even the Bishop will be in the background.'

'Yes, even the Bishop.'

'And the Bishop's new robes which my father has given him will not compare with my wedding dress. Wait till you see it, Enrique. It's like a white cloud, all embroidered in gold with pomegranates and you know what they signify.'

Some of the strain had disappeared between them. Enrique even smiled. 'Should I?' he asked.

'Fertility,' she lowered her eyes and whispered, 'that we may have many sons.'

The shadows lengthened while they talked under the striped awning. During a lull in their conversation the big green parrot which had been trying to make himself heard above the chattering of the parakeets, screamed out, 'Miguel! Miguel! Oh, Miguel, you are a pretty boy! Miguel!'

Enrique bit his lips in exasperation. 'Remind me to have someone wring that goddamn bird's neck. Miguel, Miguel! It's all I hear. Each time I try to humiliate him, he comes out on top. Why only last night . . .' he stopped suddenly, remembering that the party at his house last night was certainly not for Inocencia's ears.

'Last night?' she questioned.

He leaned over and took her hand in his, knowing one sure way to change the subject. 'Inocencia, my love . . .'

She leaned forward expectantly but the loud ringing of the outside bell silenced his words. She was disappointed at the interruption and she resented old Andreas as he came hobbling across the patio.

'Yes,' she whispered, 'you were about to say . . .'

'It was of no import,' he said, his eyes on the door, his ears straining to hear the conversation at the entrance. The few words that were spoken were loud and acrimonious. Josefina strode into the patio. She walked straight to Enrique, her face purple with rage.

'Since when, Enrique, am I denied entrance to your house? Time was when you were always welcome in mine.' She became aware of Inocencia. 'Oh, your pardon, don Enrique, I did not know you had a guest.'

Inocencia lowered her eyes, drawing a fold of her mantilla across her face.

'Ah, this might be your affianced?' Josefina asked.

'It is,' Enrique answered. 'It is the Señorita Inocencia Gonzalez.'

The stiff steels in Josefina's corsets creaked as she attempted a curtsy. 'I am so happy to see you, señorita. I have heard much of your charm and beauty but you far exceed all reports. Your marriage is to take place soon, I understand. My best wishes for your future happiness.'

Inocencia answered without raising her eyes. 'In two days.'

'What a wonderful couple you will make. Will you pardon me, señorita, for coming in like this? The trifling business I had with don Enrique can wait until some other time. I bid you good evening and hope that you will accept my apologies. But tell that old buzzard at the gate that the next time I ring, I do not expect to be kept standing like a street hawker.'

She walked toward the gate; her figure erect and her black skirts brushing the flowers that lined the walk. Enrique called to her.

'*Un momento*, Josefina.'

She stopped and turned to face him.

'Day after tomorrow,' he continued, 'I am to be married. In all the cathedral I shall have no relative. There will not be one single person related to me either by blood or by bonds of affection. I doubt if your name has been put on the invitation lists. Inocencia probably forgot it but, Josefina, I want you to be there. Will you come?'

For a long moment she was silent. 'You really want me to come, Enrique?'

'I do.'

'Then thank you, I shall be there.'

He smiled at her – a kindly smile which seemed out of place on his countenance. 'Believe me, Josefina, I am sincere. I want you there because you know me better than anyone else, even Inocencia. Yet you cannot go to the cathedral alone. Someone must accompany you.'

'One of my young ladies?' she suggested.

Enrique laughed. 'Heavens no! You will be enough of a shock to Havana without bringing one of your girls. I have it! My former cousin, Josefina! Have Miguel accompany you. What more fitting than to have your servant attend you and besides, he is almost my family. At one time he bore the name of Santiago.'

She shook her head emphatically. 'Not Miguel, please. No, Enrique, not that.'

Inocencia stood up. She spoke very calmly but her words were trenchant and bitingly clear.

'This is my wedding, Enrique, and I'll not stand for it. Invite Josefina if you will but not that Miguel. There are limits. I'll not have it, do you understand?'

As he stepped menacingly toward her, she sank back into her chair. He grabbed her wrist.

Josefina plucked at his sleeve. 'Take care, Enrique,' she cautioned.

He gave Inocencia's wrist a vicious twist and she cried out with pain. 'You'll not have it?' he asked, 'you? who are you to say? I'll have it! Yes, by God, I will. Not another word out of you.' He turned to Josefina. 'See to it that my wishes are carried out. Drive to the cathedral in a coach. Have Miguel sit on the box with the coachman. Have him open the door of the coach for you. Have him follow behind you as you enter the cathedral. Have him carry your shawl and your purse. Dress him neatly but leave no doubt in anyone's mind that he is a slave – *your* slave, Josefina. I'll humiliate the bastard if I have to make him eat dung in the streets. Each time he gets the upper hand of me. Even last night!'

'He merely carried out your orders, Enrique. What more could he do? But he will be at your wedding. I promise you that.' Her skirts whirled about her as she turned quickly and strode across the patio. As she reached the passageway, she spat upon the tiles. 'God damn it!' she said half aloud as Andreas opened the gate, 'I could have made a mistake. Miguel's twice the man Enrique will ever be.'

Chapter Thirty-one

JOSEFINA APPEARED AT Miguel's door early on the morning of Enrique's wedding day. She knocked and receiving no answer she opened the door to find Miguel sprawled on the bed still asleep. She stood there, staring at him, revelling in the pure masculinity of him as he stretched unconscious before her. *Por dios!* He was handsome! He was worth every cent she charged for him. More! From now on she would raise her prices; where else in the world could anyone find anything to equal *that*? Quietly she walked across the room and draped the clean white suit she was carrying over the back of a chair, then came to sit down on the bed beside him. Her weight on the mattress caused him to awaken. He opened his eyes cautiously and seeing Josefina sitting there, he smiled.

'It will cost you a gold piece, señora, nay, even two. My *ama* does not sell my favours cheaply.'

Her hand reached out to tousle his hair. 'I think we'll go up on our rates, *hombre*. I've been taking inventory and I think the price should be raised.'

'You took inventory before,' he reminded her.

'Ah, but then it was different. This time you were sleeping and no doubt you were dreaming. I didn't fully appreciate you before. The black rabbit grows when he sleeps, *verdad*? I'm sorry to rouse you,' she apologized. 'I had told you you might sleep as long as you wished but this one day is different. We have something special on this morning.'

He raised himself on one elbow. '*Hola*, am I to be married today along with Enrique? Today is his wedding day and I understand all Havana is to be there. All except you and me.'

'Even us.'

'No! It's not possible. Look, *mamacita*, you may keep the best whorehouse in the city; your girls are the youngest and the prettiest and your stud, Miguel, is the most upstanding and proficient, but that hardly constitutes your *entre* into society. Don't tell me the fat Gonzalez sent you an invitation?'

She shook her head.

'Then Enrique invited us?'

'Yes.'

'He should know better. More people will be interested in doña Josefina and her slave Miguel than in the bride and groom. *Caramba!* I don't envy him. Believe me, *mamacita*, I'd a damn sight rather be your slave than Inocencia's husband. Do you suppose she'll shave for the wedding so as not to scratch Enrique's face the first night? Yes, *mamacita*, I mean it. I like you. It took us a little time to get acquainted and at first you were an old hellion but the longer I know you the better I like you. In fact I almost love you, old girl. When do we leave?'

'The ceremony is in an hour. The coach will be here soon.'

'Then tell me, which do I do? Eat breakfast or take a bath? I haven't time to do both and,' he screwed up his nose, 'I stink like Solano's barracoons. I suppose it's the nigger blood in me but I never used to notice it. Look, *mamacita*! Have old Amistad fry up some eggs and make me a pot of coffee. Then rout Perla out of bed and send her in with them. While I bathe and dress she'll feed me.'

'If she saw you looking like you looked five minutes ago, she'd forget all about feeding you.'

'She has, *mamacita*. Remember, I have no secrets from Perla, or Magdalena....'

'Or Elenora or Rosita or Flor de Oro or even poor old Josefina. Come, *hombre*! While we're gabbing away you could be up. I'll send the coffee and the eggs and Perla too but hurry.'

He reached out and grabbed her hand and placed it on his forehead. 'You know, *mamacita*, I never had a mother. I had a grandmother or at least I thought I had, but it seems she wasn't a grandmother at all. Having you is almost like having a mother.'

She twisted a lock of his hair between her fingers and shook her head. 'Believe me, Miguel, I tried to dislike you, nay even hate you. I was supposed to. But I couldn't. You've got a way with you. Try as I might, you crept around me and, fool that I am, I let you. Now, I'm going to be cross. Get up!' She stood up and without looking back, left him.

He jumped up from the bed, filled the copper pan with water and grimaced as he stepped into it and splashed it over him. The soap was French and scented with lilac and it removed the sweat of the night. He was scrubbing himself with a towel when Perla entered with his breakfast. In the morning light, she looked haggard and worn and her wrapper was draggled and soiled, but she spooned the eggs into his mouth, alternating them with freshly buttered bread and sips of coffee, until he was both dressed and breakfasted. Then she combed his hair, her comb snagging in the snarls until she had it smooth and nicely clubbed in the back. As he passed out into the patio, all the girls were on the balconies, looking down at him and he had a greeting for each one which they returned. They liked him, this Miguel! They liked him as much as they had disliked Enrique who had always treated them viciously. Even when he was rough Miguel was kind, whispering little endearments to them which the audience could not hear.

He waited at the door for Josefina. When she appeared, she was dressed as fine as became the most important *dama* in the city. Her black dress was encrusted with jet, her black mantilla was caught back with jet pins and diamonds sparkled on her fingers and in her ears. She made a motion to hand Miguel the shawl of heavy black silk and long fringes, then thought better of it and draped it over her arm.

'You will ride inside with me and not up on the box with the coachman. But first turn around and let me see how you look,' she shook her head. 'No, go back and put on the black stock. Only slaves wear open-necked shirts but run.'

He was back in a moment and he helped her into the carriage as gallantly as ever he had the old Señora de Santiago. It was stuffy in the hired coach so he purloined her fan and fanned the both of them as the coach covered the short distance to the cathedral. The square before the church was filled with carriages and when they arrived, Miguel again helped her to alight. This time he himself reached for the shawl but she shook her head and carried it herself.

Inside the old church it was darkly cool and the walls shone almost phosphorescent in their whiteness. The pictures in their dull gold frames glowed in the subdued light. Although they were early, there were already many people in the church and as they walked down the aisle, there was a hush. Suddenly every fan in the church stopped in its lazy arc and those sitting in front of them, nudged by those in the rows behind, turned to stare. Then when they were seated, like a rush of wind after a moment's calmness, the whispering started. One or two old dowagers in rusty black lace, who were near them, made a show of moving, staring at poor Josefina as if she had the plague. Others, taking the cue, moved until they were alone in a little island of emptiness, Miguel sitting on the aisle and Josefina beside him – two outcasts in their loneliness. He could see that she was hurt and his hand crept down onto the seat, reached over and squeezed hers. It gave her courage to open her fan and wave it languidly while she smiled and whispered to him.

Old Gonzalez dragged his feet down the aisle, supported by two servants to sink exhausted into one of the chairs near the altar. A fatuous look of satisfaction betrayed his accomplishment of his ends. The next generation of Gonzalez would be Santiagos.

Miguel glanced around the church. Most of the faces he

saw were familiar. He could name practically everyone there. Many stole glances at him; some even caught themselves bowing and then looked shamefacedly the other way. The church filled slowly but the few seats near Josefina and himself remained empty. Her hands, nervously slipping the beads of her rosary, were the only indication that she was aware of her ostracism.

A whir and a wheeze sounded from the depths of the organ and signalled all heads to turn, like a thousand-headed hydra, as Inocencia entered on the arm of old don Lorenzo de Riojas who was substituting for her father. The wedding procession formed behind her and then she started with slow steps toward the altar. In the dim light, under the thin veil of lace, Inocencia looked almost beautiful. The golden pomegranates on her dress glowed and twinkled as she proceeded slowly up the aisle. Enrique, as pale as the white satin suit he wore, appeared from beside the high altar and the bishop, with silver embroidered robes, took his place. There was a momentary hush and the service began. From where Miguel was sitting he could not hear the words of the Mass. It was only an impression of shimmering candlelight, tinkling bells and figures that moved like puppets on a string. Strangely enough it seemed to be all over in a few moments and, he thought, how little time it took to marry – to join a man and woman together for a lifetime.

Enrique and Inocencia arose from the satin pillow on which they had been kneeling, the organ wheezed out a tune and the procession formed again. Miguel wondered if Enrique would notice him as he passed. As the couple approached, Enrique did look at him. A triumphant glance! They passed Miguel on toward the square of brilliant sunlight which was the door. Miguel, like all the others, turned to watch them.

Suddenly the square of white light that was the door was changed. It was no longer a square. Black silhouettes of human forms blocked it and then the pattern shifted and a figure disengaged itself from those at the door and started down the aisle to meet Enrique and Inocencia. The slow recessional halted although the organ wheezed on. Something was happening. Miguel did not know what and apparently nobody else did for now the congregation stood up and then jammed toward the aisles. The crowd pressed behind Miguel and Josefina, no longer afraid of contamination from either of them, in an anxiety to see what was happening. Miguel and Josefina were separated and he found himself pushed along until he was near the little knot of people who were talking in loud voices.

He heard his name mentioned, then again in an even louder tone. Slowly the crowd pushed out onto the steps, then down the steps to the pavement. Everyone was gesticulating excitedly and then as if in one voice, they all started shouting his name. He edged through the press and willing hands made an open space for him. As the crowd parted he saw Antonio and beside Antonio....

'Miguel!' It was not a scream. It was not a cry. It was the Angel Gabriel blowing his horn; it was the music of the spheres; it was Margerita. He felt her arms around him and her lips on his. She clung to him so tightly he could not push her away and yet he knew he must. She must not touch him. Like a leper, he shunned contact with her. But it availed him nothing; her arms were around him.

'Oh, my darling!'

He started to speak but she placed her fingers on his lips. 'Later,' she whispered. Then in a loud voice she demanded, 'Where is the Governor? I must see him! Will somebody summon him?'

'Stand aside, woman, and let us pass,' Enrique tried to force a passage through the crowd to the Santiago coach but Antonio grabbed the neck of Enrique's coat and yanked him back. Inocencia was sobbing and screaming in the same voice.

It was then that Miguel saw the cringing figure of Rodriguez the engraver. Certainly he was the last person Miguel expected to see, especially shackled and handcuffed. Rodriguez seemed smaller and greyer than ever. A man was struggling to get through and when the crowd saw that it was the Governor, they grudgingly made room and His Excellency appeared with don Francisco behind him. Antonio released his hold on Enrique's coat and the Governor frowned at him; it was presumptous indeed for anyone to collar the bridegroom on the very steps of the cathedral.

'What is happening here?' The Governor had finally found his breath. 'This disturbance is unseemly. Break it up or I shall call out the *guardias*.'

'Yes do,' Margerita abandoned Miguel and stepped before the Governor. 'Never in the history of Havana were they needed more. But first, hear this man. He has something to tell you. Speak. Rodriguez, speak!'

Rodriguez fell on his knees before the Governor, lifting his manacled hands. 'I am innocent, your Excellency, innocent,' he pleaded, then, noticing Antonio's upraised fist, he changed his tune. 'Mercy, your Excellency, mercy. I did not know. It was not my fault. A great wrong has been committed.'

'A great wrong? What great wrong?'

Rodriguez continued. 'That man there,' he pointed to Miguel, 'is not a slave, nor is he a *mestizo*. He is the true Miguel de Santiago.'

'It's a lie,' Enrique's voice had a trembling bravado. 'Some story hatched up by that woman, that dancer.'

'You speak of lying?' Margerita turned quickly from Enrique to the governor. 'I speak only the truth, Your Excellency, and furthermore I can prove what I say and this time, the proof is genuine. Here, Your Excellency, and you too, don Francisco, here is all the proof you will ever need.' She handed them a package wrapped in paper.

The Governor ripped open the paper and took a quick glance at the contents. He handed the package to don Francisco who had to don his spectacles to examine it. He shook his head as though he could not believe what his eyes saw.

'Let us repair to my office where we can examine this in more detail. You, señorita, and you, Miguel, and you, don Enrique.' He beckoned to them to come but when he looked at the place where Enrique had been standing, he did not see him. 'Don Enrique,' he called out, 'where is don Enrique?'

'My husband!' Inocencia collapsed in a pile of golden pomegranates.

Everyone stared at his neighbour and received a vacant stare in return. Someone pointed down the narrow street that ran alongside the cathedral. A boy came running toward them, waving his arms and shouting. 'There's a dead man down the street,' he yelled, his eyes popping out of his head, his face blanched with terror.

Again the crowd surged forward, sweeping Miguel and Margerita with them. Rodriguez stumbled on his chains and fell but Miguel lifted him by the collar and did not relinquish his hold on him. They turned the corner and halted. There, lying on the cobbles, was Enrique, his neck curiously twisted, his head against a curbstone and his white satin suit slowly turning crimson. A dagger was plunged in his heart.

Antonio was suddenly beside Miguel. 'We got separated in the crowd,' he said, 'I'll take care of Rodriguez here. Come, let us proceed to don Francisco's office. Juan is waiting in *your* coach, don Miguel.'

Chapter Thirty-two

THE BIG ROOM in the Ministry of Justice that was don Francisco's office seemed even larger to Miguel with the sun streaming through the windows than it had on the night when he had visited it before. Perhaps it was because there were so few people in the room, only His Excellency, don Francisco, Antonio, Rodriguez, Margerita and Miguel himself. Don Francisco had invited Inocencia to come but she had been taken away in hysterics, her fingers plucking the embroidered pomegranates from her dress. This time a chair was placed for Miguel and he sat between Margerita and Antonio, facing don Francisco and the Governor across the table. The only one standing was Rodriguez, who sagged beneath the weight of his irons.

Don Francisco placed the package Margerita had given

him on the table before him, once again adjusted his spectacles and peered over them, addressing Miguel.

'I imagine, *don* Miguel,' he put a special emphasis on the title, 'that you know as little about this as we ourselves. It is evident that this man Rodriguez knows more about it than anyone else and I shall question him in time, but suppose we give precedence to the lady and let her speak first. My dear señorita, would you be willing to tell us what you know?'

Margerita began with the day that she and Miguel had gone to Estrellita. She told about his gift to her of the toilet set and the monograms and his insistence that they be changed. From that she told of their drive back to Havana and their stopping at the house of Rodriguez. She turned to Miguel.

'Remember how distraught the man was when he saw you. He was scarcely civil until he discovered that your reason for being there was concerned only with the changing of the monograms. Had we but known it, Enrique de Santiago was there in the house at the same time we were. That's why Rodriguez stood in the door to the back room. He was afraid we might enter.' She turned to him for confirmation and he bowed his head in acquiescence. 'Also you will remember, Miguel, he said that he had a very important job to do before he could undertake the monograms. We had interrupted him and Enrique who were at that moment working your destruction. You must have been the last person in the world he expected to see. No wonder he was struck dumb.'

She skipped over the matter of the señora's sudden death, Miguel's imprisonment at Solano's and his slave status and returned to her story.

'A few days after Miguel was taken to Solano's, I remembered the toilet set. It was Miguel's last gift to me and very precious to me. Whether it was finished or not I decided to get it. Antonio had come to my house when Fidel left to be with Miguel and together we went to Rodriguez's house. It was nearly dark when we arrived and although we knocked several times no servant came. We found the door to be unlocked, so we walked in and sat down in the schoolroom to wait. Antonio and I could hear voices and although we could make out the words, I shall leave that part of my testimony out as I think it hardly fitting that I repeat it. Rodriguez can tell you later.

'Sufficient to say one voice was angry and one voice which I recognized as that of Rodriguez was pleading. Then the voices stopped and for several moments we heard nothing until the door of the back room opened. We were sitting in the darkness of the schoolroom but by the light streaming through the door I recognized Enrique de Santiago talking with Rodriguez. Fearful that we might be seen, Antonio and I crouched down behind the desks. The pair were arguing. I heard Enrique say, "Look you, I've more than paid you already but you've got to get out of town and not only out of Havana but out of Cuba. I'm going to give you one hundred American dollars. There's a boat leaving for New Orleans tonight. It is the American schooner "Lucy", tied up at Machinas wharf. Be on that boat, Rodriguez, tonight! If you want to live. You are in this as deeply as I am."'

The Governor groaned and wiped his face with his handkerchief. Don Francisco flipped over the pages that were in the package.

'Enrique walked out and closed the front door,' Margerita continued, 'and then Rodriguez started to sob. "I didn't want the money, Enrique, I didn't want the money. One hundred dollars! And I must leave everything behind. You've got the Santiago millions and I get one hundred dollars. Oh, Enrique! You promised so much – so very much." He stumbled back into the other room and Antonio and I waited a few minutes, then slipped out to the street. Again we rapped and rapped on the front door and finally Rodriguez came to the door. When I asked for the toilet set, he denied that he had it. He said that somebody from the Casa de Santiago had come and called for it and he had given it to them.

'When Antonio and I got home, we started to think about the matter. I sent Antonio to the docks where he found that there had been an American schooner 'Lucy' there but that the ship had sailed. One of the hangers on at the dock remembered earning a peso from a man who fitted Rodriguez's description. He had carried a heavy trunk on board for him. True, we had little to go on as far as real evidence was concerned; perhaps it was merely a woman's intuition and my intense desire to see Miguel vindicated but Antonio and I felt we should act.

'Although I hated to leave Miguel alone in Havana, I had confidence in Fidel and I knew that Señor Castanero was still Miguel's friend. I needed to have a man with me and Antonio insisted on going anyway. So, we resolved to go to New Orleans. As soon as it was light, Antonio went to don Julio's house. It is always fortunate to have friends who are bankers.' She smiled. 'I needed money – much money – and in a hurry. We hired a boat and managed to get to New Orleans where I went to an influential friend, whom I had known in Paris – a cotton merchant – who immediately put me in touch with the Prefect of police. His wife offered me the hospitality of their home.

'The Prefect had some difficulty in locating Rodriguez but eventually they found him in a little rented room on Bourbon Street. We laid our plans well and early one morning, the Prefect sent the police and arrested Rodriguez on a charge of smuggling. They dragged him from his bed and saw to it that he had no opportunity to take anything with him. Antonio and I with the Prefect were waiting around the corner. As soon as we saw them taking Rodriguez away, we entered and searched Rodriguez's room. In the bottom of his trunk, whose lock we had to force, we found a package – that package,' she pointed to the one on the table before don Francisco. You will see when you come to examine it fully that it contains a book – a book minus its covers. You will see that the pages are old and yellowed, the writing cramped and faded. Yes, señores, it is the *original* parish register of the old priest at Estrellita. And,' here she paused that her words might take effect, 'in it is the correct entry of Miguel's birth and also the entry of the death of Rodana's child and its burial.'

She looked to Miguel, her eyes brimming with tears.

'And now, *querido mio*, I am going to leave you for a little while. Although I am aware of Rodriguez's motives I do not want to hear his sordid story again.'

'Don't leave me, Margerita,' Miguel pleaded, 'it's been so long since I have seen you. I cannot bear to have you out of my sight.'

'And I,' she laughed, all traces of tears gone, 'cannot bear to be in your sight, darling. I've worn this same dress for five days. This morning I scarcely had time to run a comb through my hair. Tonight, at seven o'clock, I shall arrive at the Casa de Santiago and you will be there to meet me. In the meantime, you will send your coachman to every house in Havana and invite everybody whom you know to be there, including, of course, His Excellency,' she bowed to the Governor, 'and don Francisco,' she bowed again and then, before Miguel could offer any further objections, she was gone and Antonio with her.

Miguel and the two men looked at the wretched figure of Rodriguez. At first he was unwilling to talk, either surly and uncommunicative or pleading and cringing but with the Governor's offer of leniency if he would tell the truth, he suddenly became voluble. It was, as Margerita had said, a sordid story. Rodriguez, it seemed, had become deeply infatuated with Enrique, squandering all his money on visits to Josefina's house. His infatuation was so overpowering that Enrique came to realize the power he had over the little man and had gradually drawn his story out of him. Rodriguez was a man of some considerable education but his unfortunate penchant for sailors and struggling young *toreros* had landed him in prison in Madrid. While there he had met a notorious forger who had taught him his trade. When he was released from prison, by means of a forged draft he had obtained sufficient money to come to Cuba and, once in the New World, had decided to abjure crime and go straight. He had first set himself up as a public letter writer and then had founded the Academia for teaching penmanship. It was his very success that led to his undoing for with prosperity, he had enough money to satisfy his desire for Enrique. It was an expensive luxury because Enrique, aware of the hold he had on the man, bled him for all he was worth.

Finally Enrique had come to him with the suggestion that Rodriguez could do something for him which would not only gain his favours permanently but also reimburse Rodriguez for all he had spent. He explained the matter of the parish registers and promised Rodriguez a thousand pesos in addition to the other considerations which he knew would appeal to Rodriguez more than the money. His idea was merely to have Rodriguez erase the entries regarding Miguel and the child of Rodana and substitute the damning entries.

Here Rodriguez demurred. He pointed out that in such an important case, a thorough examination would be made for erasures, the substitution of a page or any falsification of the original book. He proposed to copy the entire book, making the copy on old paper and using a special ink to match the old priest's writing. To give the man credit he did a painstaking job, using only the covers of the original book and copying every entry from the old correctly with the exception of that of Miguel and the slave child.

The Minister of Justice interrupted him. 'At first I rather suspected something and when Enrique brought the book to me I studied it carefully but there was no evidence that there had been any tampering. Absolutely none!'

In this the Governor agreed. He too had examined the book with the same idea in mind. At a wave of his hand Rodriguez was taken from the room, his destination the dungeons of El Morro until such a time, and the Governor did not specify when that would be, he would stand trial with the certainty of returning to the same dungeons of El Morro.

Pulling a piece of paper toward him, don Francisco scratched a few words on it, signed it and passed it to the Governor, who read it over and also signed. Then don Francisco struck his tinder box, and lighted a candle. The hot wax spurted in the flame and he dribbled it onto the paper, pressing onto it the big brass seal that stood on his desk.

Standing up and with a low bow, he handed the paper to Miguel who read it.

'You cannot possibly imagine what this piece of paper means to me,' Miguel reached out to shake hands with the two men. 'It reinstates me as Miguel de Santiago; it returns to me the homes I have always loved and the fortune which rightfully belongs to me. But, señores, it does more than that. It gives me back the love of my grandmother and reinstates my love for her, may her soul rest in peace. And then, señores, it does even more than that. It makes me a free man and not a slave and it gives me, once again, the chance to marry the one woman in the world I love.' With the paper in his hands he walked to the door, bowed again before leaving and walked down the stairs and out the door to where Juan, blubbering so that he could hardly see to drive, helped him into the Santiago coach.

'Home, Juanito,' he said, 'let's go home.'

Chapter Thirty-three

THE NEWS OF Miguel's freedom had travelled fast. In fact it had reached the Casa de Santiago before Miguel did and when the coach drove up, old Andreas and every servant in the house were standing at the gate to welcome Miguel. Even old Tomas hobbled in on crutches. Each one, from the little slavey who scrubbed the kitchen pots to old Andreas, had to embrace him, kiss him, look at him and glory in his return. Not that they had all loved him before but now, it seemed, they loved him even more. They would have spent hours, just fighting each other for his affections had he not told them that on this very night, at seven o'clock, all of Havana would be at the Casa de Santiago. He wanted the house immaculate, a light collation prepared and, if they loved him as much as they said they did, they would have everything ready. That sent them scurrying in all directions. He had Andreas find his grandmother's guest list and sent the old man off in the coach with a young lad to drive him with instructions to stop at each house on the list and invite the occupants to the Casa de Santiago that evening. He sent another messenger to Julio's house with a special note and still another to Margerita's house with a note that said merely 'I love you, love you, love you, and if you love me, you'll send Antonio back as I need him for something special.' Then, having dispatched Juan to his room to see what clothes he might have left and to prepare his bath, lay out his razors, and await him there, he stood alone in the deserted patio.

He walked over to one of the marble pillars, warm in the sun, and embraced it, like a living thing. 'Home,' he whispered, 'home.' Slowly, so that he might touch each plant by the path, he walked across the patio, lingering for a moment to dribble his fingers in the pool of the fountain, then again across the patio to a door which led into a storeroom. Here, he touched the rough masonry wall, knowing that on the other side of this wall of coral rock and mortar, there was the headboard of his bed in Josefina's house. Only a few feet away! But what a long journey it had been! How often, at night, he had placed his hand against the smooth plaster of Josefina's room and pictured this same storeroom in the Santiago house. And now he was here and it was all over like a bad dream. It had been more than a wall of coral rock and plaster; it had been a wall of blood – a wall impossible to scale or penetrate. Now that too was over. He looked down at his hands and suddenly they seemed white again. He undid the cravat and opened his shirt, sniffing experimentally at his armpits. The odour of Solano's – the odour of slaves – had disappeared.

He sank to his knees, resting his elbows on an old chest, and for the first time he gave way to sobs. He knew what it was now to be a Negro; to be a slave; to be a paid stud in a whorehouse; to be humiliated, disgraced, dishonoured. He knew what it was like to stand on the auction block and hear men and women bidding for his body. He knew what it was to scrub floors and wash clothes; to sink exhausted onto his bed at night and hope that morning would never come. He knew what it was to have his body pawed at by lustful hands and to feign passion where there was only disgust. He knew the sharp, all-consuming moment of ejaculation and the subsequent disgust and horror that followed it. Yes, he knew all this and now he was Miguel de Santiago again but he would never be the same Miguel. And yet, as his paroxysms of sobbing ceased and he looked back on his nightmare, it had not all been bad. In the welter of degradation and depression, there had been one small bright spot – Josefina. From his initial hatred, he had developed a real affection, nay even love for the woman. She had been good to him in her own strange way and he had a feeling that she cared even more for him than he did for her. He jumped up from his knees and ran out of the room, across the patio and up the stairs to his grandmother's room. The door was locked. Evidently Enrique had had no desire to disturb the ghosts it contained. By yelling upstairs for Juan and downstairs for Andreas, he brought Juan running and he sought out the key from old Andreas.

Miguel unlocked the door and entered the room. Nothing had been disturbed and the ghost of his grandmother's perfume lingered in the room. He walked softly across it, through the semi-darkness of lowered blinds, and raised one. A small painting by some French artist, Nattier or Boucher, hung beside his grandmother's bed in an ornate gold frame. He stepped up to it, twisted one rosette in the frame and then another, causing it to open on hinges. Behind it was an iron door and when he opened that he was faced with row after row of velvet and morocco boxes. He had to open several before he found the two he was looking for – one was a parure of diamonds and rubies, and this one he put aside for Margerita. The other he sought was a similar jewelled set; tiara, necklace, earrings, and bracelets of fiery Mexican opals, the gift of a Mexican viceroy to his grandmother. She had never worn it, thinking it far too gaudy but he knew that Josefina would like it. Leaving the box with the rubies on his grandmother's bed, he took the other box and ran down the stairs, across the patio and out the front gate, then under the colonnade to the door of Josefina's house. His banging brought old Amistad.

'Yo' comin' back to us, Black Rabbit?' she grinned and

threw an arm around him. 'We glad yo' back. Old *ama*, she bin a-cryin'. Never thought I'd see old Josefina shed a tear but she comed back from the church a-snifflin' 'n a-snufflin' 'n she a-sayin' yo' ain' goin' to come back here no mo', 'n here yo' is, jes' a-bustin' out all over.'

'Where's Josefina?'

'She in her room a-lyin' down, sniffin' de camphor bottle 'n cussin' de girls 'n raisin' hell in gen'rl.'

Miguel put his fingers to his lips to quiet the old crone and went down the passage to knock at Josefina's door.

'Which one of you damned sluts is it now?' the voice came through the door.

Miguel opened it to see Josefina, her black dress discarded for a plain black wrapper, her hair loose on the pillow, a folded compress on her forehead and a string of rosary beads in her hand. She looked up, unable to believe her eyes.

'Yes,' he said, 'it's Miguel. You didn't think I'd forget you, *mamacita*?'

'Of course I did. Never expected to see you again and I certainly wouldn't blame you.'

'Oh, but there you are wrong, *mamacita*. You may see me more than ever now. I feel at home here. But listen! To-night all of Havana is to be at my house. They'll all come to see *The* Santiago again and everyone of them will be *so* happy to see me and not one of them will admit to ever be-lieving that anything that ever happened to me was true. They'll commiserate with me and congratulate me and leave early so they can talk about me and compare notes about me. To hell with them all, Josefina! I've come here to invite you to come to my house this evening too. The real friends I have in Havana I can number on the fingers of one hand, and you are one of those real friends, *mamacita*.'

She flung the folded rag from her head, placed the rosary beads on the table, replaced the cut glass stopper in the camphor bottle, without ever taking her eyes off him, and sat up slowly, pushing her hair back from her eyes.

'Well, I'll be god damned,' she said.

'Don't worry, *mamacita,*' Miguel laughed, 'you were long ago, but come to my party tonight, will you?'

For a long time she looked at him and then started shaking her head. 'No, Miguel, I'll not come but I want you to know how much I treasure your asking me. Let's not forget I am Josefina the keeper of Havana's best known bawdy house.'

'And I was Miguel, your stud. Surely if they can come to see me, they cannot object to you.'

Again she shook her head. 'There's a difference. You were here because of circumstances over which you had no control. I am here because I choose to be. No, Miguel, oil and water won't mix. I'd not only embarrass you and the lovely girl who worked so hard to free you but I'd embarrass myself. I tell you what. There'll come a time tonight when all your high and mighty guests will drive off in their coaches. There'll come a time when your sweet little lady will return to her own home. Then, Miguelito, when everyone has gone, slip out your own back door and into the little door of your room. I'll lock the front door and you'll celebrate along with Josefina and her girls. Yes?'

'Yes, *mamacita.* And tonight when I arrive I want to see you wearing these. They belonged to my grandmother and we both know how she felt about you....'

'Hated the very sight of me.'

'And you can't blame her. But look, *mamacita,* she loved me. And I know that if she were alive tonight, she would be here thanking you herself. But as she cannot be here, I want you to have these which belonged to her,' he opened the lid of the velvet box to display the corruscating fire of the opals and placed the box in her lap.

'For me? These?'

'Yes, Josefina, for you.'

'I should refuse them, Miguelito. They are far too valuable and far too grand for me. But I am an avaricious old woman, Miguelito, and in all my life I have never had a gift like this. I've never had any sort of a gift, Miguelito. People never gave Josefina anything; she had to fight for all she ever got. So, I shall keep them, Miguelito. I shall keep them because they are beautiful and costly but the main reason I shall treasure them is because they come from you.' She lifted the tiara out of the box and placed it on her uncombed hair. 'The Queen of Spain could be no prouder than I am.'

He stepped up to her, straightened the little crown and bent and kissed her. 'But there is more, Josefina. You paid a lot of money for me. Your investment has suddenly vanished into thin air. I want to pay you back.'

'Por dios, chico, I didn't invest a cent in you. Enrique bought you, taking it out of one pocket and putting it into another. It was all his idea. Believe me, it was. I liked Enrique and I felt sorry for him. If he had had a chance, he would not have been a bad fellow but he was so full of hatred that he couldn't be good. I knew what he was going to do but I didn't know about his having Rodriguez falsify the books. He told me he had discovered the entry himself. I thought it was true; that you were really the son of a slave girl.'

'But the strange thing, *mamacita,* is that I am still the same person that I was when I was The Santiago and that I was when I was your slave Miguel. *Dios mio,* I must run. Juan has a bath waiting for me and half of Havana will be at my house tonight. Yes, all of Havana welcomes Miguel de Santiago back. There'll be champagne and toasts and embraces and well wishes for me tonight, *mamacita,* and then they'll go and I'll take Margerita home and kiss her goodnight and try to put into words all my love for her and perhaps we'll set the day when we'll be married and then....'

'And then, Miguelito, there'll be champagne and toasts and embraces and well wishes for you here in Josefina's house tonight when you return. And,' she paused for a moment, 'I do hope you and your *novia* set the date for your wedding tonight. It's better for you to be married and settle down. But,' she waggled her finger at him, 'before you settle down, remember, you are always welcome here.'

'I'll remember,' he opened the door to leave, 'but, methinks, *mamacita*, you're going to have a hard time finding a replacement for me.'

'*Por supuesto!*' she agreed, 'but I've already got a likely candidate. Not more than an hour ago there was a knock on my door. It was a young *mestizo*, all oily hair and *patillos* half way down his cheeks. He said he had heard that you were gone and offered himself for your place. *Verdad*, he's not you, Miguelito, but he'll do.'

'Then have him here tonight, *mamacita*. Let him perform before an expert and I will judge him. And now I must go. *Hasta luego, mamacita*. Until tonight.'

'Until tonight, Miguel. And let me tell you one thing. You have made Josefina very happy; happier than she has ever been before in her life.'

Chapter Thirty-four

MIGUEL BURST INTO the patio of the Casa de Santiago, prepared to run upstairs and take advantage of his long-awaited bath but it was again to be delayed. Antonio and Julio were standing beside the fountain talking with each other and when they saw Miguel they both advanced to meet him. Miguel flung his arms around both of them in a hearty *abrazo*, his lips near Julio's ear. 'Did you?' he whispered, and Julio nodded his head so imperceptibly that Antonio did not notice. Miguel led them across the patio, under the colonnade and into the large drawing room, noting the still damp spot on the rug where the wine stain had just been removed. He motioned to them to sit down and stared at first one and then the other.

'*Amigos mios*, for truly you have proved your friendship to me. When every hand in Havana was raised against me, you two stood by me. How can I repay you? What can I do for you to show you the depth of my friendship?'

'Just having you back here again is enough,' Julio said. 'What more could I ask for?'

'And as for me, you owe me nothing, Miguel,' Antonio spoke. 'Only let me be with you and Margerita always, that's all I ask. I have but one sorrow and that is Fidel. I've missed him but I'm proud of him. I know what happened to him. Tomas told me. He was a man, our little Fidel, after all. Now that he has gone I must take his place and serve you both doubly well.'

'Will you both excuse me for just one moment?' Miguel snapped his fingers as though he had suddenly remembered something. 'I'll be right back. I left something in the dining room.'

'I think it was the kitchen, Miguel. Yes, I'm sure it was the kitchen.' Julio emphasized the last word, 'and if Antonio will excuse me too, I'll go with you, Miguel.'

Cautioning Antonio to wait for them, they went out and closed the door behind them. Antonio sat where he was, fingering the upholstery which, so many lifetimes ago, he had ordered for the drawing room chairs. He too was happy to be back in the Casa de Santiago although he had missed Fidel's welcome which he had looked forward to all the time he had been away. His first question to old Tomas, the first person he had met in the house, had brought the news of Fidel's death in his attempted assassination of Enrique. Well, so be it! Fidel had tried. Antonio fingered the soft bit of leather in his pocket.

He heard the click of the latch on the drawing room doors and looked up to see the big double doors slowly open. For a moment a ray of sunshine, creeping between the pillars of the portico gilded the figure standing there, turning the hair and skin to gold.

'Antonio!' there was no mistaking the voice. It was Fidel.

Antonio felt his knees turn to water. He had to support himself on the arms of the chair in order to stand up and then, his strength returning, he ran across the room meeting Fidel half way. For a long moment they stood, clasping each other tightly and then Antonio pushed Fidel away at arms' length so he could look at him.

'But you are real, Fidel. This is no ghost but warm flesh and blood.'

'Even warmer than you imagine, Antonio.'

'But Tomas told me . . . he said . . . he had seen you . . .

Juan and Enrique were carrying you out the back door . . . a lifeless corpse. He said Juan and Enrique had dumped you like a bag of meal at Josefina's back door.'

'Yet doors have a way of opening,' Miguel cried out as he and Julio came back. 'Yes, I opened the door and found Fidel lying there. His face was purple and his tongue was hanging out. I carried him in and laid him on the bed, holding him to me in my sorrow. My head was on his chest and I heard a heartbeat. It was faint to be sure. I put a pillow under his head, dribbled a few drops of water down his throat and with my lips against his I forced my breath into his lungs. Soon he started to breath, haltingly at first and then a little stronger. Then, forgetting I was a slave and that I might be found and dragged back, I ran out the door.

'I knew if I was seen running through the streets, people would think I was trying to escape. I prayed. *Dios mio*, how I prayed, especially to my namesake, Michael the Archangel. The good St Michael must have gone before me, sweeping everyone from the street: I reached Julio's home, routed him from his siesta and brought him back with me. Fidel was still breathing but Julio got him into the carriage and took him away, hiding him in his home so that Enrique would not find him. Enrique never knew that he lived. It is to Julio and his sainted mother that you owe Fidel, Antonio. They nursed him back to health.'

'How I wish I'd killed the bastard,' Fidel relinquished Antonio's hand and raised a clenched fist. 'I slipped or I'd had the knife in his heart.'

Antonio walked over to one of the small tables in the room. For a second he fumbled in his pocket. From it he withdrew an empty sheath of leather. It hung limp in his hands before he threw it down onto the table.

'One blade is as good as another, Fidel. Where yours missed, mine found its mark.' He reached in his pocket again and brought out the ring with the Santiago crest and laid it beside the little leather scabbard. The two articles reflected the shine on the table – the ring brilliantly, the leather but dully. 'Here,' Antonio passed the ring to Miguel, 'and here' he passed the limp leather to Fidel. 'Let us never mention the matter again.'

Margerita and Miguel stood at the head of the long staircase leading from the second floor of the Casa de Santiago to the patio. All the Santiago male servants, in liveries of violet and silver, lined the staircase, each with a silver candelabrum with a dozen wax candles. Somewhere behind the shrubbery an orchestra of violins and trumpets swept into the triumphal strains of 'La Virgen de la Macarena' the proverbial song that always escorts the *toreros* into the bull ring. Slowly, step by step they descended the stairs, Margerita, her face radiant, her white mantilla caught back with red carnations and her dress embroidered with them. The Santiago rubies glowed on her neck, in her ears and on her wrists like liquid fire. And Miguel, he who had so recently emptied the slop buckets of Josefina's house, was equally resplendent in scarlet and gold. (Evidently Enrique had not liked the colour for the suit still hung in Miguel's wardrobe.)

At the foot of the stairs, they stopped to greet the Governor and the Minister of Justice and then, with Margerita's hand on his arm, Miguel led her around introducing her to all of Havana, for not a single person had missed the opportunity to be present. Everything worked out exactly as he had anticipated. There was not a single person present who had felt there was a bit of truth in Enrique's accusations. *'Que lastima!'* 'What a pity!' 'Never believed a word of it.' 'Oh, Miguel, we did so want to help you but there wasn't a single thing we could do.'

And, of course, he accepted all their protestations and their congratulations and their good wishes. To each one he had a gracious 'good evening' and a sincere 'thank you'. When he and Margerita had completed the circle, he stopped before a high backed chair and seated her in it, standing beside it himself, and motioning to Fidel and Antonio to come and stand beside him. He held up one hand for silence.

'My good friends,' he bowed in all directions, 'you have

all heard much of the Santiago affair. Most of you were at the church this morning and most of you were at His Excellency's *tertulia* the night it all started. But none of you may know the actual facts of the case. So, if His Excellency and the good don Francisco are willing, I am going to have them give you an official version that you may all understand exactly what happened. And then, my friends, having understood, may I beg of you to forget the Santiago scandal?'

The Governor and don Francisco were more than anxious to accept the centre of the stage and together, one interrupting the other, they told the complete story of Enrique, of Rodriguez, of Margerita and of Antonio. When they had finished, there was no doubt in anyone's mind; there was actually nothing to talk about because it had all been said and not a single person could add anything to it or whisper another juicy titbit behind her fan or his cupped fingers. The Santiago affair was ended. Many of them had seen it start; many of them had seen its conclusion; and now all of them knew the why's and the wherefore's. The only thing many of them did not know was what had happened to Miguel in Josefina's house although a few of them, like the young Conde de Caradonga and the old Señora Gutherez, knew about that too but their lips were sealed; it was something they would never tell.

And now, having heard the story and sipped the champagne and nibbled at the little cakes, they were ready to leave and they bowed low over Margerita's hand and then shook Miguel's. Not a few of them shook Antonio's and Fidel's hands too. After all, they were free men and not too very dark. And, of course, they were sponsored by The Santiago. Finally they were all gone, even Julio had departed with his *novia* and Antonio and Fidel were nowhere to be seen. The candles had guttered in the breeze and some of them had gone out.

Miguel's lips touched Margerita's – hungry lips that could not be satisfied. They wandered from her lips to the ruby encrusted earlobes, then slowly down her neck, close to the spicy carnations, to her throat and then lower still. His tongue discovered the thin gold chain, hidden under the heavy necklace and his lips and teeth closed around it, slowly pulling at it until from the lace edged bodice of her dress, there escaped the little miniature of himself. It was warm from her flesh and he kissed it.

'When, Margerita, when?'

'My whole body says tonight, Miguel, it has ached for you so long but somewhere in the back of my mind there is a little voice that says "tomorrow". Yes, Miguel, tomorrow. I do not need a dress of gold embroidered with pomegranates. We do not require the bishop in his mitre nor the cathedral. Tomorrow we shall drive out to Estrellita. The little priest there shall say the words that will unite us. Fidel and Antonio will be our witnesses. And then, Miguel, then . . .'

''Tis better so, beloved, if I can last that long,' he agreed. 'I'm sorry all this had to happen, my dear. It has been a difficult time for you.'

'Now that it is over, I do not regret it. We are both the better for it. You are a bigger man than the Miguel de Santiago I first knew and I, my darling, know the meaning of love. I know another thing: as long as you live you will never sell nor buy a man again.'

'Never,' he admitted.

'And look!' she pointed to one remaining candle whose flame burned straight and tall. 'I have never forgotten the candle at La Estrellita. In those long days aboard ship; in that frantic search in New Orleans; during the voyage back, I had only to close my eyes and see that one candle burning at Estrellita and here it is still burning for us, Miguel.'

'And so it will always burn, my love. Here,' he opened the buttons of his shirt and slipped her hand inside that she might feel his heart pounding. It felt warm against his burning flesh and her fingers, caressing his nipple, plucked at it, 'and here,' his hand slid down inside her bodice to discover the pounding of her heart. 'Oh, my love, if I did not love you so much, I would plead with you for tonight. But there will be tomorrow.'

'And all tomorrow's tomorrows, Miguel.'

Kyle Onstott & Lance Horner

Three titles in the popular Falconhurst series

Mandingo 80p

Mandingo blood – the finest slave strain you could buy. The Maxwells of Falconhurst treasured it, bet on it, bred from it . . . and in the end it wrecked them; tore the plantation apart, with death and unforgettable dishonour. A shattering novel of slavery as it really was in the Old South.

Drum 80p

A sweeping novel, ranging from the jungles of Africa to high life in New Orleans and the slave-breeding plantations of Falconhurst. An electrifying story that unmasks the emotional conflicts of black-white relationships.

Master of Falconhurst 95p

The Civil War strikes the rich Alabama plantation where slaves are stripped bare in the market place, and sold like fertile cattle. This is the exciting story of Drummage, the proud and powerful ex-slave who becomes master of Falconhurst – and of the selfish, sensual woman who rules it.